For:

A thought –

"Make your TOMORROWS better than the best of your YESTERDAYS – the guarantee is a perfect TODAY."

Peter Rumens 2014

…But like there's no tomorrow

A Portrayal of Love, Compassion, Betrayal and Erotic Desire

Peter Rumens

Matador
9 Priory Business Park
Kibworth Beauchamp
Leicestershire LE8 0RX, UK
Tel: (+44) 116 279 2299
Fax: (+44) 116 279 2277
Email: books@troubador.co.uk
Web: www.troubador.co.uk/matador

ISBN 978 1783065 073

British Library Cataloguing in Publication Data.
A catalogue record for this book is available from the British Library.

Typeset in Garamond by Troubador Publishing Ltd
Printed and bound in the UK by TJ International, Padstow, Cornwall

Matador is an imprint of Troubador Publishing Ltd

Dedicated to Scampi and to those who overcome adversity in the name of love.

Preface

To love, and to be loved, is a feeling like no other.

But what is love…? And at what point does it become forbidden love? Perhaps, all too often, emotion and desire override all other considerations and sensibilities; but who of us has the right to be judgemental? Sadly, and all too easily, the emotions of love or respect can turn to disappointment and even hatred, bringing with them a lust for revenge. There is little that is more desirable than commitment between a man and a woman, but little sadder than total commitment that is destined to fight its way to a conclusion. Along the way, if the bubble of self-delusion is pricked, a broken heart is inevitable.

Chapter 1

It was a gloomy day in Nottingham.

Margaret was busy boxing items for the charity shop when the telephone rang.

¨Hi Mags, it's Cliff, how are you? It must be difficult coming to terms with—¨

Margaret interrupted, not wanting to continue with the nature of Cliff's conversation.

¨I'm O.K. I'm keeping busy with packing and the final arrangements before the move to Spain.¨

¨We must get together before you leave,¨ Cliff continued, but then cut straight to the purpose of his call. ¨Mags, any chance that Sally could sit for us on Saturday?¨

¨She's not here at the moment, but I'm sure it will be O.K. It will help to take her mind off things. I'll get her to ring you when she comes home.¨

¨That's great, thanks Mags, speak later, bye.¨

Cliff operated his own successful company, supplying specialist-heating systems to commerce and industry. A large contract had been signed that week and Cliff had arranged to celebrate with his wife and friends. Sally had always welcomed child-minding for them. She liked his wife, Jenny, and Cliff was over-generous in payment.

That Saturday she was collected by Cliff and arrived at his house, carrying a range of reading matter to supplement an evening in front of the television.

Sally was a rather quiet and very pretty fourteen-year-old, on the cusp between teenage and womanhood. Since her childhood, people had frequently remarked on her dazzling eyes and beautiful smile.

1

"The children are already settled and fast asleep," assured Jenny. "They'll not be any trouble, but you have our mobile number if you need to contact us. We should be home soon after midnight."

*

It was three years later when Ben first met Margaret and her family in Spain. Originally from South Wales, Ben was a thirty-six year-old British ex-pat, who had decided upon a change of lifestyle, following financial success developing property in and around Leicester. Though not a builder, he did have a natural management skill, which brought together the right people to achieve the end result. He had never married, but for three years had lived as a couple with his secretary. It was a relationship based on convenient lust, more than on love and respect. Parenthood was the one thing that could have cemented a closer bond between them, but sadly she had suffered two horrendous pregnancies, which had ended in termination. Her prognosis was that child-bearing would continue to be a problem and she struggled in coming to terms with the idea of never enjoying motherhood.

In a strange moment of responsibility, guilt, and self-sacrifice, Ben paid privately to undergo a vasectomy. However, it was perhaps inevitable that feelings of disappointment, and a basic lack of mutually sincere love, led to them drifting apart and finally ending the relationship.

Though without a partner, or an immediate desire for fatherhood, Ben soon felt that he had given up his manhood needlessly. Over a period of six months and two attempted reversal operations, masturbating into a plastic bottle confirmed that the second operation to rejoin tubes had been successful only briefly. Ben accepted that his penis was now "firing blanks" and settled into the enjoyment of unprotected sex whenever the opportunity arose. He sometimes pondered that justice may one day demand that he would pay the penalty for his unbridled and loveless passion.

Now in Spain, he had been an ex-pat for three years.

Though a changed man from his earlier years, he did enjoy the occasional sexual encounter and hadn't taken the idea of a more celibate lifestyle too seriously. Generally speaking, he was unattached and had avoided serious relationships. Furthermore, most unmarried women would be looking for a man that could provide them with the joy of motherhood. The bulk of his affection was lavished upon his adopted stray cat, Scampi, who, at considerable expense, had emigrated with him.

If reincarnation were possible, Ben would want to return to this world as Scampi.

He loved that cat with all his heart and spoiled him rotten. His furry friend enjoyed endless stroking and a diet of chicken livers, gambas, and boiled fish. Scampi developed a taste for anything expensive; no tinned shit for this boy. But Ben had failed to wean him off his craving for houseflies and pigeons; a throwback to his earlier feral days. A hunter by nature, and certainly never driven by hunger, Scampi had also taken to Spanish cuisine and relished the occasional lizard or gecko. His favourite treat was finely grated parmesan cheese.

In adulthood, Ben had always been a fairly snappy dresser; his slim build wore tailored clothes well. Having been a keen sportsman since childhood, his active lifestyle had left him with a six-foot frame that was strong; athletic and toned rather than over-muscular. Though not a vain man he did fear hair loss and was blessed with a full head of dark brown hair, without the slightest touch of grey. Overall he was quite a handsome man, but without being a "pretty boy". Having worked in various regions of the U.K. from his early twenties, his rich voice had been left with only a trace of the Welsh accent. He was free of tattoos and wore a conservatively thin wristwatch. He didn't crave gold chains, bracelets or sovereign rings, but in Spain's sunny clime did succumb to boyish desire, when his eye was caught by a pre-owned but gleaming red Ferrari, finished with pale cream interior.

He had abandoned the U.K. drinking culture and now confined his consumption of alcohol to occasional binge drinking. Such unhealthy sessions often ended with him talking bollocks in the back of a taxi, getting ripped off by the driver, searching for his bed, and gently slipping into a ten-hour coma. It would take a full two days for his liver to recover from such excesses.

Ben's financial success in the U.K. had been considerable, but not

3

driven by the mindless desire for continued acquisition of wealth; his decision to start a new life in the sunshine came with mixed blessings. He had sold one of his properties in order to finance his move to Spain, but left the bulk of his business in the hands of a management company. It was a mistake. At thirty-six years of age, he was far too young to be indolent and had begun to take the lifestyle for granted. He loved the climate, but was tiring of occasional boredom and some of the ex-pat Brits who were acquaintances from his local bar.

Most were good company, but others had enjoyed even greater financial success than him and enjoyed to gloat accordingly. The less fortunate were envious of Ben's financial status and would grill him on such things as the cost of his house, insisting that they, and only they, had managed to buy the bargain of the century. Some would demand information on all manner of unimportant things. What did his curtains cost? How much had he spent on his garden? What size was his swimming pool? – And not least of all, the age of his car. One acquaintance would claim that his twin turbo, four-wheel drive lump of shit regularly returned a zillion miles to the gallon. Sad bastard!

He was fortunate that even though his command of the Spanish lingo was less than perfect, he had also developed a large circle of genuine Spanish friends. He had never had a problem with self-deprecation, and with tears of laughter on their cheeks, his friends would revel in the humour of his efforts to communicate in the native language. The histrionics involved on the day that he attempted to buy a *two-way* lighting switch from a local store were a joy to behold.

He had become a world-class champion of charades!

Spaniards are good-natured people who often laugh at comedy that British people consider rather puerile. When, with stories risqué and clean, he introduced them to the unique British sense of humour, it was for them something of a revelation. His stories were sometimes not fully understood but always warmly appreciated.

Then Margaret came into his life.

Their first meeting was clumsy in the purest possible sense. It was a beautiful summer evening and, like so often before, he had taken a walk at the seafront. It was time for a coffee. As he walked onto the restaurant terrace, his thigh brushed against a table, it wobbled, his arm reached out and, despite his almost successful attempt to avoid disaster, a bottle of cola did a similar wobble, fell sideways and spilled the contents into the lap of the only occupant of that table – HELLO MARGARET!

His embarrassment was extreme. The apologies rushed from his mouth in gobbledygook. She seemed largely unfazed by the incident, assuring him that accidents will happen. A helpful waiter quickly arrived with mop, bucket, and paper towels. His victim made off to the ladies to clean up as best she could, and his banal attempt at recompense was to order a replacement cola and a coffee for himself. When the drinks had arrived and the unbelievably gracious lady reappeared with an oval stain of pale brown from waist to knees, he found that he had joined her at the table uninvited. Her misfortune could not have been worse. The dress, though not expensive, was a white shift. Why could it not have been cola-coloured or at least black? Ben spent the next couple of minutes searching for more and more words of apology, with her equally finding more words of reassurance that he was not a complete twat.

"You're not in any rush, are you?" he asked.

"No, I'm waiting for the children," she replied.

With that, he excused himself, legged it to an up-market souvenir shop, and returned with an over-expensive display of silk flowers and a beachwear modesty wrap to camouflage the offending stain.

On his return to her table she was very embarrassed to accept his offering, but even more embarrassed by the spontaneous round of applause that his gesture generated. He was confident that the flowers had cost more than her dress, but it was a small price to pay.

Several ladies invited him to join them, to spill more drinks.

Ben and Margaret introduced themselves and their future friendship was born. Margaret, he guessed, was in her early forties, fair skinned, a good figure though slightly overweight, but certainly not unattractive. Her greatest asset was her face; bright eyes, a broad smile, and above all, a face full of kindness. Soon into their conversation, the waiter returned to check their drinks and he chatted briefly with Margaret. It became apparent that she was completely fluent with the language. Ben remarked on her command of Spanish, which led to her opening up to a complete stranger, the desperately sad tale of how she and her family had come to live in Spain three years earlier.

Her husband, Miguel, was a Spanish national working in a Nottingham hotel when they first met; hence the reason behind her fluency. They fell in love, eventually married, bought a modest house, and produced boy and girl twins. They enjoyed a happy, but not over-comfortable life. Miguel had long yearned to return to Spain and had managed to land the position of managing a decent three-star hotel on the coast. The appointment didn't come with family accommodation and it was with some difficulty that he persuaded his wife that selling up was a good move. It was an even harder sell convincing his children. The almost totally fluent Michael and Sally, he assured them, would have no problems making new friends, with the promise that they could return to the U.K. if things didn't work out.

Regardless, he insisted, close families should stick together.

Ben had been given a brief summary of Margaret's background and she continued.

"We had no difficulty in finding a buyer for our house; our relatives here in Spain helped to arrange a small mortgage for a three-bedroom apartment and a ten per cent deposit was borrowed and paid to the vendor's solicitor. Everything was on track." Margaret paused, her countenance visibly changed; she swallowed hard and tears began to well in her eyes as she murmured the words, "and then tragedy struck."

Ben became very uncomfortable and suggested that they should perhaps change the subject. Twenty minutes earlier he had drenched the woman in cola and here he was, delving into a stranger's personal life.

She protested that it sometimes helps to talk about things that hurt.

He wasn't ready for what came next.

"Miguel went to bed early one night nursing a headache… Two hours later I found him dead. He had no history of medical problems, but without warning, a massive cerebral haemorrhage had taken his life in an instant."

Cruel fate had robbed Margaret and her children of husband and father, and left their lives in turmoil.

How do you handle such sudden trauma? thought Ben.

As the tears welled in her eyes, he insisted that they should talk no more at that stage. It was fortunate that a few tables had vacated; they were in a relatively secluded area of the terrace, away from flapping ears and inquisitive eyes.

They were rescued by the arrival of her children. The boy, Michael, had been named after his father and the girl, Sally, for no other reason than Margaret loved the name.

"What's wrong, Mum?" enquired a concerned daughter, noticing that her mother had paper tissue to her eyes.

With a bit of quick thinking on Ben's part, he applied a paper napkin to his face and explained that a sudden gust of wind had blown dust into their eyes. Sally didn't pick up that it was a still evening, without so much as a gentle breeze.

"Whose are these?" demanded Michael pointing to the silk flowers.

Margaret quickly composed herself and was immediately into her maternal role. She introduced Ben and related the story of the wobbly table. Without the experience in life to appreciate a tale of chivalry, they thought the whole episode was absolutely hilarious and their young laughter rang out throughout the terrace.

Ben and Margaret found themselves belly laughing along with them.

The twins had been kicking a ball around at the beach and were now ravenous. Ben folded beer coasters and carefully positioned them beneath the offending table leg, securing stability for the banquet to come. Over the next three hours they consumed burgers, pizza, chips, sorbet, and copious amounts of cola.

"In *non-wobble glasses,*" Ben insisted.

The time was spent getting to know each other.

At close on eighteen and dressed in a summer top with a short matching skirt over her bikini, Sally was a virtual woman – five feet five inches of perfectly formed teenager. Spain is not short of beautiful young women, but the blend of British and Mediterranean bloodstock had produced something really special. What a face! – Fine-featured, flawless bronzed skin, perfect white teeth, and sparkling blue-grey eyes, framed by long, silky, dark hair. *A photographer's dream come true,* thought Ben. Despite her earlier laughter, she seemed slightly unsure of herself, a little withdrawn, and certainly not over-conscious of her young beauty.

He recalled that from time to time, he and his working-class contemporaries shamelessly submitted to a visiting school nurse, who voraciously searched for head lice. *What a bunch of poor little shits we were!* he thought. Sally's early schooldays must have been diametrically opposite to his. To draw her into conversation, Ben enquired about her future. She was very sure of her ambition in life. She loved animals and had considered training as a vet, but had abandoned the thought in favour of her adoration of young children. With A-level examinations behind her, she would soon begin training, to teach at primary and junior-school level. Sally was delighted when Ben's words praised her commitment.

¨I believe that the most important teachers in the education system are those who rise to the challenge of teaching children at the first and basic level. A child learns more in its first ten years than it will learn during the rest of its life. Without that solid grounding, a teacher fails not only the child, but also the teachers who are then expected to pick up the pieces in later education.¨

Sally flushed and swelled with pride.

¨I couldn't agree with you more,¨ added her mother.

In the absence of any deep commitment to lovers from his past, Ben lacked a strong desire for fatherhood, but he too had grown to love animals. He talked to the group about Scampi, confessing that when his beautiful black tomcat had died on the vet's table, he openly wept like a baby. Strangely, he had never been over-moved by the death of people; unless children. His apparent lack of compassion extended even to family members. Though a sensitive man, he viewed the issue of mortality as the inevitable part of life. Since Scampi's departure, and not out of choice, he had become hotelier to abandoned or feral cats. Sometimes they would do an overnight stay, sometimes not. But they were always there when the "restaurant" opened. Perhaps Sally would one day meet the six that he currently fed on a daily basis.

Twin brother Michael had drawn the short straw. He was a little taller than his sister and a handsome lad, but resembled one of the thousands of British tourists jamming the seafront – baggy shorts, football shirt, a peaked cap shading his slightly freckled nose, and his teeth fitted with a corrective brace. There was little evidence of the Mediterranean blood in *his* veins. The boy could have sprung from different loins; but what a lovely, lovely, young man. He was full of self-confidence, full of life, and chopsy in a pleasantly roguish manner. Michael proceeded whenever possible to dominate conversation and Ben mused that the lad would either be hugely successful in his chosen career – or do time! Michael had his eyes set on a more lucrative career and had decided to study I.T. and Sports Science, though keeping his options open to teach at a later stage. Both he and his sister would attend the same university. It came as no surprise to Ben, that in a perfect world, the lad would choose to be a professional footballer. Michael loved and talked at length about the "beautiful game".

Educated in a South Wales Grammar School and indoctrinated with the game of rugby, Ben was unable to talk with any authority on football, but he and Michael did share a love of cars and motorbikes – it's a man thing. Ben produced from his wallet a picture of the bike that he had shipped to Spain; a blue and white Suzuki GSXR 750. A machine that was absolute shit off a shovel, and another "toys for boys" moment. Michael's eyes widened and a lump of burger fell from his mouth as his jaw dropped.

"My dream bike!" he yelled.

He could *not* believe that Ben had sold that beautiful possession. He refused to accept the explained reasoning that Spanish drivers are amongst the least considerate of all other road users; often oblivious to the presence of others and annoyingly, drivers who never use indicators. Ben stressed at length the vulnerability of bikers; Spanish traffic regulations demand a strange and different knowledge of priority at roundabouts. Another reason, he continued, was that though quite a fearless rider, he never felt fully protected unless wearing full leathers, helmet, and gloves.

"In the Spanish climate," he explained, "that's akin to riding in a sauna."

Michael was unconvinced.

All three were amused by Ben's final piece of reasoning.

"I was riding through town, protected in full biking gear and diligently observing the rules of the road. Amidst the screeching whine of a 50cc scooter, a local urchin overtook me at breakneck speed. He playfully waggled a foot as he swerved into my path. The cocky little sod was dressed in no more than a pair of swimming trunks and flip-flops. As if to twist a knife in the wound, the little bugger was riding *side-saddle*. It was time to sell the bike! It was time to grow up a little."

As if not to be left out of the conversation, Sally politely asked what car Ben owned.

"An ageing Audi A4," he replied.

Not a lie, thought Ben. *The Audi was his runabout car. The Ferrari was not for day-to-day use.* Not surprisingly, she was unimpressed or not really interested, but Ben had avoided the situation of Michael going into a state of life-threatening convulsions of delight and envy. More importantly, he would have felt pretentious had he revealed ownership of an Italian stallion.

"So, Michael, where is your girlfriend tonight?" Ben asked.

"I'm working on it. There are a couple I fancy at the moment," he replied.

"Career first!" added his mother.

"And you, Sally?" Ben continued.

"I'm not interested in men," she replied with some authority.

Time flew by as Ben found himself entertaining the family with anecdotal stories from his past. What started as a disaster had developed into a thoroughly enjoyable evening. All too soon it was time to go. During an earlier visit to the toilets Ben had grabbed the opportunity of paying the bill in full. Margaret was embarrassed, but accepted his generosity graciously. He didn't want to be pushy, but he had enjoyed their company and hoped that they would all meet again in the future.

The family apartment was a short walk inland from the sea. They strolled leisurely past the souvenir shops along the seafront, dismissing hawkers and talking about nothing in particular.

Onlookers would have perceived them as a family unit.

Be it pretentious or not, Ben decided that he would pull a stunt on the kids.

"It has been lovely meeting you all," he said, moving to open the door of a parked Porsche.

"Is this yours?" Michael yelled.

"No… Sorry," Ben admitted. "My idea of a joke."

Michael looked disappointed and somewhat cheated.

They had walked a further fifty yards when Ben hit the remote. With a beep and flashing of lights the sensual prancing horse sprang into life.

"You are *joking,*" Michael said quietly.

"Really?" gasped a wide-eyed Sally.

"Go on then, jump in," was the only invitation they needed.

They fought over who should take the driving seat – Michael won.

"Beautiful car," observed Margaret. "You have just made friends for life."

With interested diners looking up from their consumption of steak and kidney pies, the stunt was far more pretentious than Ben had intended.

Whilst the youngsters enjoyed their newfound status, Ben and Margaret offered final apologies and reassurances; Ben for having spoilt her dress and she for having disclosed a stressful episode in her life.

Fondling the shiny knobs and dials was now no longer enough for Michael and with typical forthrightness, he was out of the car, tapping Ben's chest and requesting a spin. This was Ben's opportunity to ensure that they all met up again. He went straight in.

"Well, if it's O.K. with your mum, we could meet up and I could give you a blast next Saturday."

Looking at her son with the warm expression of love that only a devoted mother has, she couldn't deny his pleading eyes. He yelled and punched the air when she agreed and rushed off to tell his sister of his achievement. They arranged details of the next meeting and said their farewells – an awkward two-cheek continental kiss from Margaret, the same from Sally, and a high-five from Michael.

Ben blasted the V12 engine and Michael waved excitedly from the kerbside.

Chapter 2

Ben spent the following week in much the same way as any other week – he fed the cats, knocked several buckets of balls at the golf range, talked politics with friends at the local bar, flirted with a waitress or two, and swam a little in the pool. He had taken to maintaining the pool himself (not exactly rocket science) and did a little gardening in his large, rather unkempt plot. Reliable gardeners who aren't lazy or thieves he found to be a rarity. On Wednesday, he avoided the usual temptation, when his Argentinean lady cleaned, washed, and ironed for him.

She was a pretty lady and, he thought, game for a casual shag or two; but her husband was built like the proverbial brick shit-house. More alarmingly, he had fairly serious concerns about the early onset of a disinterest in sex and a flagging libido. His ego dismissed the idea of seeking a medical opinion or dabbling with pills.

He found himself looking forward to Saturday and spent most of that morning polishing the Ferrari. Michael would not have wanted a single speck of dust! He booked a table for 10.00 pm at one of the better restaurants, with private parking in the adjoining terrace – the lad would love that!

At 8.00 pm Ben pulled up at the arranged meeting point. The girls had over-spruced themselves up for the occasion, though Michael, it was explained, would not move from the apartment without the obligatory shorts and football shirt. That was no problem for Ben. Margaret was a different woman; she had obviously taken a trip to the hairdresser and was wearing a little make-up. Ben had done her an injustice in his first appraisal of her appearance. Her attention to grooming had turned her into a *very* attractive woman.

As for Sally, fresh from the shower and with no need for cosmetic enhancement, her beauty could only be described as stunning.

"First things first," Ben said. "As promised, Michael, jump in."

He was in the passenger seat like a jackrabbit. His face beamed as they left his mother and sister sitting on the sea wall.

His enthusiastic exaltations of delight were a huge reward for Ben, as they cruised the length of the resort.

"How fast will it go?" he asked.

Without replying, Ben lifted his sunglasses, smiled at Michael and winked. He did a quick detour to the coastal dual carriageway and opened it up. Michael couldn't contain himself.

"Fuucking hell!" he screamed, almost wetting himself with excitement. Ben scolded him.

"Oi... language!"

Above the roar of the engine Michael came back with a sheepish apology.

Ben tapped Michael's thigh and smiled. Michael smiled back. It was a full thirty minutes before they got back to the girls. Ben apologised to Margaret that they had been so long, blaming Michael for their lack of consideration.

"My turn, my turn!" insisted Sally.

He shrugged submissive shoulders at Margaret and rescued Sally.

"O.K. just a quick pose up and down the seafront."

Sally settled in and he scolded himself for admiring her perfectly shaped breasts parted by the seat harness. They drove off, leaving her brother jumping on the spot, re-living the experience with his mother. Sally's enthusiasm equalled that of her brother, but the performance of the machine was of no interest. She was just girlishly happy to be paraded in a car that most people could only dream of owning. Fifteen minutes later saw them all re-united.

"Now it's Mum's turn," Ben announced. "Here is the plan. I have booked a table for us for 10.00 pm. I will take Mum there now and leave the car at the restaurant terrace. Mum and I will go for a walk and we'll all meet up there at 9.45."

The children confirmed that they knew the whereabouts of the restaurant and nobody seemed to mind that Ben had taken control of the evening's agenda. He pressed a twenty-euro note into Sally's hand, pointing out the Crazy Golf and an amusement arcade that they might enjoy.

"No, Ben, you mustn't," protested Margaret.

He put his finger to his lips, indicating playfully that she shouldn't interfere. He called Michael to his side.

"Here's a spare set of car keys. If you are at the restaurant before us, you can wait in the car if you prefer. Guard them with your life, do *not* put them in the ignition, and do *not* touch the handbrake. If you do I will be in trouble with the police."

Christmas had come early for Michael.

"I promise," he confirmed.

Ben ruffled his spiked hair and off they went. Their mother watched as they ran off down the promenade.

"Nice kids," said Ben.

Margaret readily agreed. She lowered herself into the car with far less athleticism than her children. Passers-by perhaps thought that he was selling joyrides; his third passenger in less than an hour.

"You are very kind and too generous – you are spoiling my kids."

Ben explained that he had been brought up with generosity. His family had been born with spoons of base metal in their mouths, but consideration shown to others was boundless and instilled from an early age. Ben's aunts would go hungry, rather than be unable to buy a birthday gift for a nephew.

As a child, and much to his annoyance, it wasn't unusual for Ben to lose a favourite toy, or a comic collection, to some little shite that his mother perceived as less fortunate. But over the years, Ben had learned to appreciate the deep satisfaction that giving can bring. He had also come to treat with contempt those who were ultra-mean.

"All too often," he would frequently say, "those who can most afford to give are those who are the meanest of spirit."

He dropped the car at the restaurant, pointed to his watch, and raised ten digits towards the staff. A nearby waiter acknowledged his understanding, smiled, and waved as they strolled off in the direction of the harbour. Ben continued to give her a potted history of his life, leaving out the naughty boy bits. Their friendship was growing, but they were not yet that close! She, in turn, wrapped up her life in a few short sequences.

From a professional family, she had taught English Grammar and Literature at secondary-school level, taken temporary leave after the birth of the twins, but did occasional sessions as a relief teacher. That explained her bilingual children's excellent diction, with no perceivable regional accent. Margaret's parents had overcome their initial horror that she was to marry a humble hotel worker. Miguel had charmed them into submission and provided them with two lovely grandchildren.

"You would have liked Miguel," she said wistfully. "He was a lovely man and a wonderful father. Sally was always a mummy's girl and seems to have handled things better than Michael... at times the poor boy misses him so badly."

Now in Spain, she had been fortunate in securing a teaching post at a privately operated school for English students.

Without the financial means for private education, Michael and Sally attended Spanish state school. That presented no problem, as their father had taught the family well. Both were all but totally fluent. They had recently achieved excellent grades in A-level subjects and were set up to further their careers. Margaret supplemented her income with private English-learning classes for Spanish nationals and occasional translation services for the police and local businesses. With the financial expense of two students, things were not easy, but she felt that she could adequately service the mortgage and provide a secure future for her kids. By now they were walking along the breakwater. Most people were walking along the seafront. They were all but alone. Ben queried her decision to move to Spain after Miguel's death. She continued.

"If I had backed off from the purchase I would have lost the ten per cent deposit that had been paid, everything was in place, and at the time it just seemed the right thing to do... There *were* other issues, and it was time to start a new life."

She paused and her facial expression turned to anger. Ben had a sense of foreboding and invited her to continue some other time. To no avail – the woman needed a friend and wanted to talk.

Her next revelation was a kick in the guts.

Back in Nottingham, three years earlier, Cliff and his wife, Jenny, had returned from their foursome evening out. Not a heavy drinker and respectful of the breathalyser, Jenny had sipped on only two glasses of wine throughout the night. She assumed the responsibility of driving and had dropped off the other couple safely to their home. Affected by alcohol, men often display unnecessary bravado and, despite being over the legal limit, Cliff insisted on driving Sally home. Ben wasn't made privy to the full sordid details, but as he drove, Cliff had taken the opportunity of sympathetically stroking Sally's thigh, whilst consoling her on her father's death. He pulled into a lay-by and forced himself upon her. There wasn't a vestige of sympathy in the man's mind. He quite simply wanted to fuck her. He succeeded, and stole the girl's virginity in the process. He urged Sally to say nothing; her mother was handling more than enough problems. With her husband's premature death, she wouldn't want to deal with additional stress in her life. In a daze of distress and without thinking, Sally accepted the fifty-pound note that he pressed into her hand. Drink or no drink – what a bastard!

He probably spent that night praying that his actions wouldn't come back to bite him in the arse, perhaps inventing a safety net and fabricating tales of consensual sex. Forget it, Cliff! She was fourteen years of age.

Mum was waiting up for her. Sally excused herself, saying that she was tired. There is nothing keener than a mother's instinct – she knew that all was not well. Margaret's worst fears were realised when she found Sally sat astride a bidet, sobbing quietly and scrubbing furiously at her private bits. A fifty-pound note lay screwed up on the floor.

Apart from brief pauses and the appearance of tears beginning to well, Margaret had remained remarkably composed as she related the terrible story.

"Cliff was so helpful after Miguel's death, with funeral arrangements and things."

She paused, then lost her composure, and screamed, "But it didn't give him the right to have sex with my lovely daughter!"

With that she fell into Ben's arms, wailing uncontrollably. He held her tight, she wept, and Ben forced back his tears of sympathy. He spoke the only words of consolation that he could find.

"Let it out, girl… have a good cry."

They stayed locked in that embrace for some time. When she finally released herself from his arms, she almost chuckled.

"I can't believe this. It's only our second meet, on both occasions I have burst into tears, and now told you a dark family secret."

Ben squeezed her hand and reassured her.

"Don't worry. Whatever you may tell me goes no further."

Time had passed quickly and they should have been moving on. They quickened the pace as they hurried towards their rendezvous with the children. Ben glanced at his watch and decided that there was enough time to grab a drink at a bar en route. Without consulting Margaret, he ordered two coffees and large brandies. She excused herself and disappeared to the ladies' room to repair her now slightly swollen face. What little make-up she had been wearing was now on his chest. She returned with little or no sign of the trauma that she had been through.

"Revenge," she said, pointing to his shirt. "Oh, and by the way, no problem with shifting the cola stain."

It was remiss of Ben not to have enquired.

He, in turn, disappeared and with tap water and handkerchief successfully removed all traces of her tears. When he rejoined her, Margaret had finished her lukewarm coffee and was sipping gently at her brandy. He could tell that she was no drinker of strong spirits. With a ten-minute walk to the restaurant ahead of them, it really was now time to shift themselves. Ben's coffee and brandy disappeared in a flash. She smiled and pushed her glass across the table, but he declined a second gulp of strong alcohol. Five minutes into their brisk walk he stopped in his tracks.

"Don't worry," she said. "I paid for the drinks."

Suddenly this woman was reading his mind!

They needn't have worried about being a little late. Predictably, the kids were posing in the car, and despite his promises, Michael had gained access to the sound system and was blasting out one of Ben's several Queen albums. Sally spotted them, jumped out, and came rushing over.

"Mum! You should have seen their faces when we got into the car."

17

Her youthful face was alight, with sparkling eyes and a smile that could illuminate the world. What a lovely girl!

They were shown to their table and Michael reluctantly joined them.

Back in the company of her children, Margaret soon perked up, and what followed was an evening of absolute joy. Ben cracked some non-risqué jokes and related more stories from his vast library of amusing incidents. They all laughed, and laughed, and laughed some more.

Sally was more relaxed than during their first meeting and would occasionally take a subdued centre stage. As she spoke, she would gesture with delicate hands and perfectly manicured fingernails.

It was impossible for Ben not to reflect upon her unfortunate past.

Gorgeous or not, how could that low-life have stooped low enough to abuse her virginal body?

As the family talked, Ben's mind wandered.

It has been said, tongue in cheek, that the only difference between a rapist and the rest of us is self-control and fear of the consequences.

It's normal that older men admire the beauty of a developing teenager; it's the man thing. *Show me a man that disputes that*, he thought, *and I will show you a liar*. Thankfully, the desire to *abuse* a fourteen year old is not the normal man thing.

Ben was brought back into the spirit of the evening with Michael insisting that he share a few of *his* jokes. Ben chose to assume that the lad was completely unaware of his sister's traumatic past. If true, it should stay that way! He wondered about the outcome of it all.

Was Cliff in prison, justice being done at the hands of other prisoners? Probably not – abusers would be segregated for their own safety.

No doubt Margaret would one day finish the sorry saga, with or without tears.

During dinner, with guidance from Ben, it was agreed that British ex-pats had wrongly adopted the continental kiss as the norm, when greeting or parting.

"It's courteous that we should observe the culture when amongst our Spanish friends, but surely not amongst ourselves," insisted Ben.

Though friendly, Ben had always felt that the kiss, lightly planted on both cheeks or in fresh air, was over-formal and lacked a degree of sincerity. Currently lacking a girlfriend, Michael's input was that we shouldn't kiss at all. He had yet to suffer the pangs of first deep love.

Despite brief moments of pensiveness, Margaret and Ben had given the children a bellyful of good food and a really enjoyable night out. It was close on 2.00 am when Margaret decided that it was time to call it a day. Ben motioned for the bill and clasped Margaret's hand as it reached towards her purse.

"Don't even think about it. You are my guests, and besides, I've had a sizeable win on the lottery this week."

"How much?" demanded Michael.

They laughed at his reply.

"Four euros, twenty-five cents."

Somehow Michael had become treasurer of Ben's earlier generosity and the quip prompted him to produce five euros and some bits from his pocket.

"Sorry, I forgot. That's your change."

"Tell you what," said Ben. "I'll buy some more lottery tickets with this and we'll share the winnings."

He insisted that he should walk them partway to their home and collect the car later. As they ambled, Michael enthused endlessly about how he was going to spend his share of millions. It was time to part and Ben wondered if they had remembered the conversation about the continental kiss. Margaret duly gave him a continental kiss.

"You forgot!" he scolded.

Her palm rubbed a kiss from one of his cheeks; she laughed and gave him a warm hug. He hugged her back, her ample soft breasts against him for the second time that night.

The hug from Sally was brief but sincere. By contrast, her developing breasts had the consistency of tennis balls, and he later felt shame over his regret that it hadn't been a longer embrace. For obvious reasons he harboured a huge sympathy towards her and sensed the seeds of a mutual affection based on trust. A trust, he vowed, that he would never betray.

Michael whacked him with his high-five and forever upfront, blurted, "What are we doing next weekend?"

Before his mother could reprimand him for his cheek, Ben gave him the response he wanted.

"Well, if you are all free, I have a plan in mind. I will ring your mum and make some arrangements."

They exchanged telephone numbers, waved their goodbyes, and set off in opposite directions.

There *was* no plan, but he would come up with something. He enjoyed being with the family and wanted contact to continue.

The restaurant was still buzzing when he returned.

Spanish traffic police are merciless and he had resisted alcohol for most of the evening, but with Margaret's revelations that night, he needed a drink!

Over coffee and a large brandy, he reflected on the poignancy of Sally's troubled past, for he too had experienced sex with an under-aged girl. At the time, he had genuinely believed her to be at least seventeen, and perhaps older. It was, and would always be, the most bizarre sexual encounter of his life. Back in Wales, and in his early twenties, he and a group of friends had met up for a drink. They decided to move on to another pub. Try as he may, he couldn't remember the exact circumstances under which one friend, a man in his early thirties, had asked him to collect his babysitter and deliver her to her home.

The relief minder, daughter of a neighbour, would take over. Both sitters were watching television when he arrived. As he left with minder number one, he caught the eye of the relief minder. He recognised that signal of availability. He stopped at the car. Those were days of which Ben was not proud, but always one to grasp at an opportunity, pretended that he had left his car keys inside the house. He rang the bell and the door closed behind them.

Her eyes had invited his return and she knew why he was there. They moved swiftly to the living room, embraced, and almost falling to the floor, she helped him to remove the knickers from around her ankles. The union was immediate and urgent. He selfishly satisfied his lust, with no thought given to *her* needs. The whole encounter lasted no more than sixty seconds.

With minder number one waiting in the cold outside, there had been no time for foreplay and now, they both knew, no time for the niceties of pillow talk. She wiped a tear from her cheek, he wrapped his dick in his handkerchief, and left.

Some weeks later his car pulled in through the gated entrance of a farmer's field. He was on a mission. He was there to shag her sister; a tiny little girl with tits no bigger than thimbles, but whom he knew from previous conversation to be nineteen. She was a sexy little bitch who, despite the broad daylight, insisted on removing every stitch of clothing before getting down to business. She was very easily satisfied; it was a pleasant little fuck, though a tad clinical. As she re-dressed, she casually spoke words that Ben would have preferred not to hear.

"By the way, you haven't been fucking my sister, have you?"

There had obviously been some sisterly chatter.

Ben denied such nonsense.

"That's O.K. then, because she's only thirteen, you know!" her sister announced.

His heart sank. Quite why she felt the need to champion her sister's welfare defeated Ben, because she then revealed that the very man who had asked him to do the babysitter run had taken the girl's virginity when she was just eleven years of age. Her parents knew of the ongoing criminal relationship, but chose to do nothing about it.

What were they all thinking of? thought Ben.

Ironically, it was *she*, the source information of this family tragedy, his little fuck in a farmer's field, who could have passed for thirteen or fourteen. He had a vivid flashback.

The tear on the face of that nameless girl suddenly had meaning.

After he had done nothing more than use her body, she probably contemplated that her only worth in life was to get laid. His mind raced with questions. Had her neighbour destroyed her future? To what extent did *his* brief encounter scar her life? What excuse for parents did she have? Had he been set up? He preferred not to dwell on what other family secrets there were to be told.

After that day, he avoided contact with the family at all costs.

His mind wandered back to Sally. He identified uncomfortably with the trauma that she had suffered as a young teenager. When they parted earlier, she was lively and vibrant, but were there scars beneath the

21

surface? He probably would never know. He signalled for the bill.

"On the house," said the boss.

Ben had spent heavily and left a handsome tip earlier. They shook hands; Ben thanked him, and left.

He pulled onto the drive and six cats rushed from all directions. He had forgotten to feed them and the poor little buggers were starving. He fed and watered them, poured himself a final brandy, and had a sleepless night.

With the arrival of late morning, Ben woke up with an almost paternal concern for Sally. He brewed tea to calm his slight hangover.

The telephone rang. It was Margaret.

"Thank you for a lovely evening, and I'm sorry that I burst into tears again."

Ben stopped her.

"I fully understand, and I'm glad that you've rung because I would like to meet for a chat without the children being around."

"There's nothing wrong, is there?" she questioned with concern in her voice.

Ben reassured her.

"No, no – just a chat."

Chapter 3

They met that afternoon in the bar where they had cleaned themselves up the night before. He had thought of a plan for the following weekend, but more importantly, there were pieces missing from the story, which he felt he had to know. If possible, he wanted to help the family.

How many years did Cliff get? What effect did the episode have on Jenny and her family? Had Sally needed the services of a counsellor here in Spain? With Margaret for support, Ben suspected not, etc. etc.

At that time of the day most people were on the beach, so they had the place much to themselves. He ordered coffee and they settled in a shaded section of the terrace. She had read his mind again.

"I have told you so much, I think you should hear the full story."

The worst had been revealed and she was now at ease and quite calm.

"After I had found Sally in the bathroom, my first instinct was to contact the police, but she begged me not to. Life was bad enough having lost her father, and she did *not* want to handle the trauma of a court case and the notoriety of being the victim of a rapist. I cuddled her for hours and we talked through the options. Rightly or wrongly, I finally came to the conclusion that even though still a child, her wishes should come first. We agreed that we should move to Spain, just as Miguel had wanted, become anonymous, and to move on as best we could."

"So the bastard got away with it!" Ben gasped.

"Not quite," she continued. "I knew that I couldn't live with that. Quite apart from anything else, another young minder could be his next victim. Had Miguel been alive, he would have killed him. Something had to be done. Maybe not full justice, but a price had to be paid… It would be a week before the removal van would be at our door. That gave me ample time to devise something. The following day I went to my computer and began to type."

She reached into her bag and handed Ben a copy of the letter that she had given to Jenny the morning of their departure to the airport. The unsealed letter for both Cliff´s and Jenny´s eyes had contained also the creased fifty-pound note. Margaret had put a lot of thought into what she should do and into her parting message. Ben read and absorbed the content.

Cliff,

I feel so sad for Jenny and your children. They have a rapist for a husband and father. Because, until now, there has been no kickback, you are probably feeling comfortable that you got away with it. To a point you have, but Jenny is a loving mother and will understand why Sally is desperate not to be part of police proceedings against you. If only you had one fraction of your wife's compassion.

Despite this coming on top of our other problems, we will do our best to move on and make a new life. But know this –

1. Fifty pounds wouldn't buy you an hour with a decent whore. It certainly doesn't buy you the right to have sex with my virginal under-age daughter.

2. My daughter's underwear (complete with proof of purchase), together with a copy of this letter, is anonymously stored in police custody. Her underwear is defiled with your DNA. If, later in life, Sally or I regret not taking more drastic action or should there ever be need for evidence against you in other under-age or violent sexual activity, I will not hesitate to involve the police.

3. My family needs to put the past behind them. Our lips are sealed. But if you or Jenny ever discuss the issue with others, I will not hesitate to destroy you, and your family if necessary. Regardless of what lies ahead for you, I suspect that Jenny will never want her children to know that their father is a rapist. I am sure that you will be full of denial, with a story of Sally being a willing partner. You would be wasting your breath. Jenny knows Sally well – for Christ's sake, she has never even had a boyfriend!

She has to live with what you did to her.

Now you live with the Sword of Damocles – and may you one day rot in hell.

Margaret

Ben's reaction was immediate and instinctive.

"Wow… I think you handled it perfectly."

Margaret had decided that Sally should have sight of the letter after they had completed the move to Spain. It would be a form of consolation for her, and confirmation that her mother would always be there to support her. Margaret continued.

"I was surprised that Sally was horrified that I had written the letter. She is such a kind girl and was worried about the effect it would have on Jenny's marriage and family. I insisted that it was right that Cliff should be punished regardless. Of course, I went to the chemist and made sure that Sally didn't become pregnant. That would have been devastating."

As Margaret spoke, Ben pondered on Sally's adult, forgiving, and selfless attitude. He easily identified with Margaret´s need for justice, but like Sally, he began to dwell on the unjust suffering for innocent people not connected with the crime. He concluded that Margaret's actions had not been entirely vengeful, but simply based on there being nothing more potent than a mother's love. Or was he wrong?

Did Margaret deliberately set out to destroy his marriage, at the expense of his wife and children?

"Margaret," said Ben. "Sally is more than kind. She's a very special kind of person and I can see where she was coming from. And yes, it is a shame that Miguel wasn't around. If I were her father, your letter wouldn't have been necessary." He continued. "I think that it was a *young* feminist Germaine Greer who wrote that the 'C' word should be used as liberally as one felt necessary. To her credit, in an article many years later, she retracted her opinion. She then wrote that it should be used only when expressing complete and utter contempt for someone. I think that we can agree that Cliff is a cunt with a capital C."

Margaret was shocked by Ben's unashamed use of the expletive, but nodded agreement.

At the risk of it becoming a lecture, he had to spill out what had been wandering through his mind.

"Margaret, how many people know about the Sally problem?"

He was relieved at her answer.

"Only you, me, and of course, Jenny and her husband. I decided not to tell my parents."

Ben continued.

"Good, you have my word that it's a secret that I will take to the grave. I think your letter has silenced Cliff and Jenny for life, but promise me, and promise yourself, that you will never tell another soul. I am flattered that you trusted me when you needed a shoulder. That shoulder will always be there for you, but it could have been a huge mistake on your part. It is so important that even close family members should be kept in the dark. Michael must never be told. Sally must never know that I know. Sally must never tell all to her bestest, bestest friend. Friends drift apart, even become enemies, and loyalties can disappear. People can be absolute shits, happy to wallow in the misfortune of others, and even revel in tainting the reputation of the victim."

Ben droned on, insulting her intelligence that she hadn't thought of every angle. Margaret reached across and touched his hand.

"I think I've got it covered, but thank you anyway. You are a kind man."

If nothing else, she could now be comfortable with *his* position in the sorry saga. She finished the story.

"The last I heard was from my mother. Cliff and Jenny are now separated."

She quickly removed her hand from Ben's.

The timing of Michael's arrival was less than perfect. His mother would not have wanted him to witness that moment of intimacy. He was out and about with his Spanish pal on their bikes, when he spotted them. Though good friends, he and Sally were obviously not inseparable. She was on the beach with girlfriends. She was possibly flirting, but probably rejecting the attentions of young studs that wanted more than masturbation in their lives. For the girls, the pleasure of the middle finger, for most, would suffice at this stage in their lives.

In the context of the Sally issue, it's worth contemplating, Ben thought, *that in Spain, consensual sex is legal at thirteen years of age! Is it likely that pressure from other European countries will one day drag Spain into the twenty-first century?*

Michael was surprised but pleased to see Ben.

"What are you doing here?" he demanded in his usual abrupt but pleasant manner.

"I have just been discussing some ideas for next weekend."

"Tell me, tell me," he enthused.

Ben continued.

"Well, from Friday onwards in my town, we have the three-day annual celebration of San Juan. Lots of street music, dancing, fairground, etc. If your mum agrees you could all stay at my place for the whole weekend."

His face lit up. His pal looked a bit pissed off. Here was Ben, for somewhat selfish reasons, taking control again. He was beginning to see these people as family.

Margaret firmly took the reins.

"Michael, we shall talk about it later!"

The idea had been planted. There was no way that it wasn't going to happen.

He ordered more coffee, water for Margaret, and a couple of cokes for the boys. He remarked that Michael's bike was a bit knocked about and on the small side for his stature.

"I'm hoping for a new mountain bike for Christmas," Michael disclosed with a smile, directing the statement towards his mother.

They refused to believe, but laughed at the description of Ben's first pushbike.

"It was far too big for me. I scavenged it from the local rubbish tip. It was an adult-size frame and two wheels, with pedals but no chain… no brakes, no saddle, no bell, no lights, no mudguards, and wait for it… no tyres! With metal sparking on tarmac, my approach could be heard from 200 yards. It lacked all of the basics, but it did, however, come equipped with a shopping basket."

The boys thought that the story was hilarious. Margaret suspected exaggeration. Ben wished that it had been.

"When you are a child and poor, and your pals are equally underprivileged, image doesn't enter the equation," Ben concluded.

"So, how come you are now so rich?" shouted Michael.

Margaret sighed exasperation. They eagerly waited for his answer.

"Easy... I robbed a bank!"

Everyone laughed. They were always ready for a laugh and now, it seemed, always comfortable in each other's company. Before leaving, Michael asked his mother for snacks money. Margaret refused, saying that the family would eat together later at home. Ben sensed that her refusal was based on having a finite expendable income. He would want to help the family if possible. He surreptitiously pressed a ten-euro note into Michael's hand before they parted.

"Aw, Ben, thank you," whispered an embarrassed Michael. "It wasn't a hint, you know."

Chapter 4

On Friday afternoon, he answered a telephone call from Cardiff. Not good news. Long before his time, a close friend, and fellow golf club member from his past, had died suddenly. He should attend the funeral. He scribbled down the arrangements, but would think about it later.

Ben punched Margaret's address into the sat-nav of the Audi and set off to collect them for the weekend. He pressed the bell marked Perez and Sally came to the door of the foyer. She gave him a little hug and invited him in. He admired her beautiful, slim, suntanned legs as he followed her up a single flight of stairs to their first-floor apartment. They all greeted each other enthusiastically. Margaret was busy putting last-minute items into overnight bags. The apartment was not lavish, but spotlessly clean. It had the sort of fresh cleanliness that only a woman can apply to a home. The kids were keen to leave.

Soon onto the motorway, it was a mere thirty minutes to when he pulled onto his drive. From the street, his home looked like a humble, single-storey bungalow, but it concealed a good-sized, four-bedroom hillside villa built on three levels. His guests jumped out of the car, the cats scattered, he unloaded their bags and invited them through to the lounge area. He unlocked the patio doors and Michael rushed out to the large balcony. Sally was busy attempting to gain acceptance by the cats.

"Wow... Sally, come and look at this!" urged Michael.

Below was what would be their playground for the next few days.

For them, the major attraction would be the large swimming pool with a range of pool toys.

Ben showed them to their rooms.

Margaret and he would take the two bedrooms with en-suite

facilities. It would have been an insult to their friendship to contemplate that he would get to share a bed with her that weekend. The children would have separate bedrooms, but share a family bathroom. Michael's room was quite sparse, but Sally's bedroom had quite a girly feel, with a liberal scattering of soft toys, which Ben had won in raffles at various animal charity events. For other items, he had paid stupid prices at animal welfare fund-raising auctions. Sally could share her mother's bathroom if she preferred. He left them to unpack. Michael raced around like a blue-arsed fly searching for his swimming trunks. Ben unlocked access doors to the gardens and pool below, returned to the balcony above and poured a glass of fresh orange juice. Within minutes, he was enjoying the laughter of two teenagers splashing about in the pool.

Margaret joined him on the balcony and welcomed the offer of orange juice. They sat in the shade of the pergola and chatted. Without a hint of envy in her voice, she commented on his lovely house and how lucky he was to have uninterrupted views of the mountains across the valley. By Spanish villa standards, he hadn't deemed his house to be over-special, but compared to her modest apartment, it must have seemed palatial. His mother was summoned to watch from the balcony as Michael performed somersaults from the poolside onto a floating Li-lo.

"Be careful," she warned.

Like mother hen, she dutifully watched over them, their interests' paramount at all times. Ben admired her firm buttocks as she occasionally leaned over the balcony to improve her view. He wondered if she would ever want to move on and re-marry. *She was too young*, he thought, *to spend the rest of her life in mourning for Miguel.*

At that stage, he had no thoughts of a romantic relationship.

The golden rule should be observed – friends and family don't fuck.

Ben retired to the kitchen to make a pot of tea. For as long as he could remember he had always consumed several large mugs of it each day – it's a Welsh thing. His mother's teapot had cooled only during the hours of sleep.

He placed a tray of tea for two and biscuits on the table and joined Margaret at the balustrade. He shouted down to the children below.

"In the summer kitchen, you will find a fridge-freezer full of soft drinks, ice cream, and other nice things. But don't spoil your appetites; we'll go out for a meal tonight. Who likes Chinese?"

"Love it!" they shouted in unison.

Michael was out of the blocks like an Olympic sprinter to raid the goodies; Sally wasn't far behind him. Margaret joined Ben for tea.

"Ben," Margaret began. "We really must talk about money—"

Ben interrupted and cut off her conversation.

"Listen to me, Margaret. I know little of your financial situation, but I'm sure that teenagers in full-time education are a huge drain on resources. More importantly, and without being trite, I am financially very comfortable. I enjoy having you and your family around. If at any time when you are in my company I see you reach for your purse, you will get a very firm rap on the wrist."

She shook her head gently in disbelief, but said nothing. She leaned across and kissed Ben gently, but briefly, on the lips. It had been some time since he had felt such a kiss. The kiss of desire, yes, lust, yes, but not a kiss with the warmth of affection. He leaned forward and returned her kiss with equal affection. He suspected that her children must never witness physical intimacy between them. They would possibly misconstrue it as an affront to their father's memory. Shouting from below demanded their presence poolside.

Ben slipped into a pair of fitted trunks and with a backward somersault joined Michael in the pool. Sally, dressed in a tiny lemon-coloured bikini, was busy on her mobile. It was impossible not to marvel at her perfection. Margaret caught his eyes paying attention to her curves. He lightened the moment.

"Margaret, your daughter is perfect. Don't ever allow her to have a tattoo. If she changes her mind about teaching, she can always be a model or an actress."

"Absolutely not!" retorted Sally.

She was flattered nevertheless. She was going through that period of rapid development, but, it seemed, still not completely aware of the effect she could have on man or boy. She sat with her mother in the shade of a parasol, relating that she had tweeted her friends to describe the villa and the group of adorable cats. Young people text each other every ten minutes, if only to say "nothing else has happened yet!"

In the pool, Ben threw a beach ball back and forth with Michael.

He pondered on what a ridiculous word "tweeted" is. Surely, the past tense should be "twatted". His mind played with the tenses – *sit/sat, shit/shat, tweet/twat*. He smiled at his own humour, but decided best not to share the joke with the kids. Perhaps with Margaret at some other time – or perhaps not!

Sally screamed with delight as one of the cats arrived on the scene.

Ben left the pool to encourage acceptance of the human intruders onto its territory. Perhaps cats have a sixth sense. A normally quite timid feline readily enjoyed Sally's attentions. Michael showed little interest, having decided that it was time to attempt diving from poolside through a large rubber ring. Ben pulled up a sun-bed, sat in the heat drying off, and told the story to mother and daughter of how he came to adopt his favourite cat, Scampi.

"After various career moves, I had ended up living in Leicestershire. One beautiful summer day I had finished mowing the lawn and was snoozing on a sofa in the sunny conservatory. I was suddenly aware that I was being watched... Sitting on its haunches, in the doorway, was a miserable bag of bones. It looked close to death, with a huge weeping sore along its side. I had never craved the company of a cat and, for my sins, promptly chased him off. I laid back and snoozed a little more... When I awoke, he was back, with such sadness in his eyes. I couldn't turn my back on that poor creature. I lay on my side, propped my head on my hand and invited him a little closer. With two nervous approaches, he was at the sofa looking up at me. I tapped the edge and he jumped up to be alongside me. For a while he simply sat and looked at me... He then settled and lay down. Gradually, he moved closer to spread his fragile little body close to my bare chest. He pressed his underside close to me."

Tears were already welling in Ben's and the girls´ eyes, but what came next destroyed them.

"Using his haunches and his shoulder, he edged his way further upwards, placed his head on my shoulder, and went fast asleep... I looked down at the desperate animal, with puss oozing from its open sore, and knew then that only death would part us."

Margaret sniffed back her mucous and Sally's lips trembled as torrents of tears flowed down her lovely face. They laughed at their loss of self-control.

"Let me show you something," said Ben to Sally.

He took her by the hand and led her to a nearby flowerbed. He showed her Scampi's shrine – an area of dark gravel, circled by white stones. The centrepiece was a plinth upon which sat a porcelain figure of a black cat not unlike Scampi.

"Aw... Ben, that's lovely," she whimpered.

She had taken Ben's upper arm in her hands and placed her head lightly on his shoulder. Despite his paternal feelings, he instinctively enjoyed the presence of her firm breast nestled against his bicep.

Having missed out on the proceedings, Michael was getting a potted version of events from Margaret. Ben and Sally returned to the fold.

"Mum has been telling me about Scampi," said Michael.

"Yes – he was special and very clever. Do you know, he used to bury his poo in the garden?"

"That's not clever, all cats do that," insisted Michael.

"Using a shovel?" quipped Ben.

The group laughed at his silly humour and he wrapped up the story.

"Now you understand why I wept like a baby when Scampi left me."

The account cemented an ongoing closeness with Sally.

"What time are we going to the fair?" asked Michael.

In the past, when family with children had visited, Ben knew from experience that two consecutive nights at the Feria were too much.

They would be exhausted on Sunday!

At first, Michael was disappointed with Ben's reply.

"Fairground tomorrow night. Like it or lump it, tonight it's Chinese and tenpin bowling."

The teenage twins had never been to a tenpin alley and became quite excited by the prospect. The rest of the afternoon was spent just messing about and chatting, punctuated with trips to the kitchen for nibbles and soft drinks. Margaret promised that she would get into the pool the next day. The group had reached a level of comfort where sometimes just sitting was enough. Embarrassing silences were not an issue – and anyway, people who talk continuously, rarely have anything to offer worthy of attention.

Early evening, showered and scrubbed up, all were now hungry as Ben pulled up outside his favourite Chinese restaurant in town. He had been eating there at least weekly since his move to Spain, and the little bandy owners had got to know him very well.

He was greeted enthusiastically by Li, who took the entourage to be yet another group of family or friends from the U.K. He couldn't be bothered to explain otherwise and allowed her to make up her own mind on the connections. His guests were unsure about choices, so he made a few recommendations. They waited eagerly around their large round table, pouring soy sauce onto prawn crackers to stave off their hunger. Anything but conceited, and ever ready to acknowledge the quality of others, Sally drew her mother's attention to Li's daughter.

"Mum, isn't she absolutely beautiful!"

The young girl, whose name Ben couldn't recall, was sitting to one side, putting together a jigsaw. On previous visits, he too had recognised the striking beauty of her face. With eyes wider than the typical ethnic features, she had the face of a porcelain doll – almost too perfect to be real. She sensed that she was being admired, looked up briefly, and smiled. The feast arrived. Ben had over-ordered, but they did their best to do justice to a table heaving with spare ribs, Peking duck, prawn tai-pan, sweet and sour chicken, crispy beef, rice, noodles, and more. Dessert was out of the question. As usual, and without request, the leftovers were bagged and delivered to the table. Ben had enjoyed the previous day's restaurant food on many past occasions. He joked that if it ever came to it, he could probably survive living out of skips. Li insisted that they have drinks on the house before they left. Michael was itching to get at the bowling balls. Ben paid up and they left with beaming farewells from Li and her family, including her chef husband, who had been summoned from his steaming kitchen.

A half-hour drive brought them to the intensity of noise that's unique to a bowling alley – excited voices, the explosion of pins being

34

scattered, and arcade machines screaming out a cacophony of electronic warbles and screeches. Fully kitted out, feet in plastic bags inside red and white shoes, the kids were visibly excited. Michael decided that it would be young people versus the wrinklies – cheeky little bugger!

With names punched into the electronic scoreboard, this was going to be war! For a first-timer, sporty Michael, with his aggressive, almost thug-like approach, pulled off some impressive scores. Sally, struggling to even lift a ball with her delicate fingers, sent them down the alley quite slowly, but scored a couple of fluke strikes. Ben, with greater experience, was bowling with some panache. Margaret was fucking useless!

The final four rolls of the match arrived and the scores were very close. Ben sensed that Michael wouldn't be able to handle anything other than victory. At the wrong time, Margaret rolled her only eight of the night. Final bowl was down to Ben. He consulted the scoreboard. Anything more than five would give the trophy to the wrinklies. There was huge tension in the air. On the run-up Ben feigned a slight stumble and rolled a zero. The lad was ecstatic. He ran in circles, gloating, and punching the air with both fists. He now had a taste for glory and begged for a re-match. Ben allowed Margaret to go to the desk to pay for another session. Sally moved to Ben's side and put her mouth to his ear. He slipped his hand around her tiny waist.

"You missed deliberately," she whispered.

He turned his head to face her, winked, pursed his mouth, and blew her an air kiss. Their faces close together, he so wanted to plant that kiss on her full, beautifully contoured lips. Had his face revealed his inner thoughts? He scolded himself for even contemplating the thought. She smiled back at him.

Perhaps the most famous rear end in the world is that of Kylie Minogue. During session two, Ben decided that Kylie had serious competition. He watched as Sally bowled – he wasn't observing her lack of technique. He did nothing to control his admiration of her high-slung, rock-hard buttocks, supported by slender, perfectly contoured legs. Her beauty hadn't gone unnoticed by other red-blooded males. Perhaps it was his lack of attention to the game, but it was a walkover for the youngsters. Having annihilated the opposition, Michael was delighted to accept ten euros to feed the arcade machines. Sally accepted the same, but with some reluctance and embarrassment.

It was decided that Ben and Margaret would go for a coffee in the quieter surroundings of the large adjoining foyer and meet up with them later.

Ben arrived at their table with two coffees – mostly in the cups, but some in the saucers.

"She's beautiful, isn't she," said Margaret.

Ben knew to whom she was referring.

"Who, Sally?" he questioned.

"Yes," she continued. "Wherever we are, I see that men of all ages can't take their eyes off her."

Ben smiled and raised a hand.

"Also guilty, does it bother you?"

"It frightens me a little," she confessed.

Ben explained as best he could.

"I can understand your concern, but you must understand, Margaret, that it's nothing more than a man thing and not automatically something to fear... It's an instinct, over which men have no control. In the future, Sally's beauty may well be her greatest asset. Yes, she is physically very beautiful, but I think also beautiful at heart."

He explained a little more.

"The bestselling tabloid in the U.K. rightly vilifies paedophiles and child abusers, *but* the same newspaper's page three, every day, features topless young women in provocative poses. Before it became politically unacceptable, these young women would often be posed in school uniforms or, should I say, posed in part of a school uniform – perhaps a tiny gymslip off their shoulders, straw boater, breasts and knickers everywhere, and even pigtails, with school tie parting the cleavage... Absolute hypocrisy! Margaret... It's soft pornography aimed at middle-age men. Sixteen-year-old boys do not buy tabloids!"

Margaret shook her head and looked slightly disgusted. Ben continued.

"We men are nothing more than an extension of the animal kingdom. The rear end of a female monkey is massively more rounded than that of the male – it's that man thing again. Our eyes are attracted to rounded things – swollen breasts, and bums accentuated by a slimmer waistline than the male. But don't worry... Sally, I'm sure, is a sensible girl and though it's natural for you to be protective, she and her girlfriends know what it's all about. They are probably more streetwise than you imagine. Sally's unfortunate past has at least equipped her to err on the side of caution. Despite your fears, there isn't a rapist on every street corner."

Perhaps with Cliff in mind, the obvious had been bothering Margaret.

"Ben," she said quietly. "I can see that Sally likes you so much... *you* would never hurt her, would you?"

Ben shook his head slowly, in disbelief that she would need to ask. "Of course not... you have my word."

His reassurance was genuine and sincere. Margaret smiled.

The children joined them penniless. It doesn't take long for arcade machines to gobble up twenty euros.

"Can I have a coke?" Michael asked.

He was surprised at Ben's firm reply.

"No. We are going to my favourite ice cream parlour to round off the night. You will never taste better ice cream in the whole of your life."

"Even better," they all agreed.

Back in his hometown, they were wide-eyed at the vast number of choices of homemade ice cream in the freezer cabinet before them.

Decisions, decisions... but it wasn't long before all four were sitting outside in the warm evening air, spooning into each other's tubs, eager to taste all four flavours available. During this time, several young Spanish couples in their twenties, or groups of young ladies passing by, would rush over to greet Ben with continental kisses and warm hugs.

Did Ben imagine it, or did Sally slightly resent the intimacy of these female interlopers?

"You are very popular with young people," observed Margaret.

"I met a lot of them, and their parents, at dance classes. I sometimes socialise with the parents, but I mostly enjoy the company of younger people. They are such good fun. Maybe I'll grow up one day. Now that's a thought – tomorrow, Michael, I will teach you Salsa, Tango, and Sevillana."

"You must be joking," came his swift reply.

Sally jumped in.

"You can teach me!"

"And me!" added Margaret.

It was now late, big day tomorrow, and all concerned were ready for their beds. Back at home, Sally insisted on helping to feed the cats.

Wearing pyjama shorts, Michael appeared from his bedroom below to say goodnight, kissed his mum, gave Ben his high-five, but resisted giving him a hug. Sally, for the first time, put her arms around Ben's body, squeezed him gently, and nestled her head to his chest.

"Thank you," she said warmly.

He smiled, placed his hands on her tiny waist, but didn't return the embrace. Sally hugged her mum and, with a kiss, she too was gone.

The two wrinklies were feeling the after-effects of tenpin bowling.

"Margaret," said Ben. "In the mornings I'm not the liveliest of animals. If I am still rotting in my bed, can I ask you to take charge and feed the rascals?"

"Of course, no problem," answered Margaret. "After all, they are *my* rascals."

Ben showed her the whereabouts of everything she would need.

Margaret walked to him and, with arms around his waist, hugged the full length of her body against his. Those few seconds of contact, for both of them, were full of affection, but not sexual.

"Thank you, Ben," she said quietly. "Goodnight."

She kissed him lightly on his cheek and went to her bedroom.

Ben locked up and went to his bed. He reflected for a while what a good day had been had by all, but soon was deep in sleep.

He slept late and, turning in his bed, was conscious that joints ached from the previous night's bowling. There was already laughter from around the pool, but he wasn't ready for it and dozed some more. He forced himself into the shower, cleaned his teeth, and shaved.

He was feeling better already. Margaret had heard bedroom activity and was already up and about, catering to her children's needs.

Minutes after slumping into a chair on the balcony, Ben was presented with toast and a pot of tea.

"Bless you," he said gratefully. "Do your joints feel like my joints?"

"Oh yes," Margaret chuckled.

She joined him for tea. She and the children had already had a breakfast of cereals with fruit, yoghurt, and fresh orange juice.

He declined her offer of preparing something for him – he had never been much of a breakfast man. After a second cup, he was ready to face the onslaught of inexhaustible youth. He walked to the balustrade and shouted to them scampering about below.

"Good morning!"

"Hiya Ben, come on down," yelled Michael.

"Ben, I think you mean good *afternoon*," added Sally.

Was it really that late? Yes, it was. He and Margaret watched them at play for a while. They admired their young energy, forgetting that they too had been just as active when teenagers. He noted that when diving into the deep end, Michael, in mid-air flight, had all the grace of a pellet-ridden pheasant. With limbs flailing, his ankles all but knocked his shoulders as he entered the water. The boy was made of elastic.

He would teach this boy to dive before the weekend was out.

"Come on girl, into that swimsuit," demanded Ben.

He was first at the poolside. Michael was just happy to be a tearabout, devising all manner of crazy things to do with plastic inflatables.

Sally, all of four minutes his senior, and more refined and ladylike, would occasionally bore of his wildness. At times, she would retire to her mobile, no doubt updating her friends on the latest.

Perhaps prompted by the conversation the previous evening, Margaret had found a modesty wrap for Sally's lower half when not in the pool. *Spoilsport!* – but perhaps just as well. Margaret's faith in him would have been shattered had he developed a lazy lob or even, God forbid, a stonker!

Her arrival heralded a new woman. She was somewhat self-conscious at revealing so much of her body in one hit. The man thing was able to appraise in a few nanoseconds. Very good skin, lightly tanned, a very slight sag in her buttocks, no sign of cellulite, a good bulge to her Venus mound, and soft, ample breasts.

Two sucklings, simultaneously swinging from her tits, hadn't done too much damage. Ben could half imagine having sex with her, but repeated to himself the golden rule – F.A.F.D.F. Michael grabbed his mother and promptly pushed her into the deep end. Any thought of preserving her hairstyle was the last thing on his mind. Bloody kids! She adored her children and took it in her stride. Soon all four were in the water, generally splashing about, and then racing each other over various distances. That developed into mixed-style relay races over three lengths, but the hilarity came during a race of two lengths in doggy-paddle stroke. Strange that, as children, it's how we all learned to swim – but it's the quickest way of going nowhere. The exercise soon brought relief to stiff limbs, but Ben and Margaret welcomed the excuse of fetching drinks. It was hard work keeping abreast of the kids' boundless energy. Sally had huge affection for her brother, but as the day progressed she preferred to spend time with her mother and Ben in the shade of parasols. She was rapidly growing up and welcomed talk at a more adult level. She had become very comfortable with Ben and engaged him in conversation about her friends and her future career. She even sought opinion and advice. Margaret looked on, grateful for Ben's intelligent input, but wishing that Sally's talk of the future could have been with her father. Ben, she thought, was developing into a father figure, but he could never replace Miguel.

"Let's eat!" suggested Ben.

The girls prepared a mix of sandwiches, placing pickles and nibbles in dishes. Ben took charge of the microwave and re-heated the Chinese leftovers. With so many hands on deck, they were soon around a diverse mix of culinary culture, complete with soft drinks and the obligatory pot of tea. Ben jugged and melted a large tub of vanilla ice cream into a litre bottle of cava. His guests were not lovers of alcoholic drinks, but the ice cream mellowed the sharpness of the cava. A second jug was mixed and the way Michael was shifting it, he could end up pissed. After more chatter, mainly from the lad, the girls obligingly cleared and washed crockery. Now relaxed, the day's exertion and the heat were taking its toll. Margaret looked tired and welcomed Ben's announcement.

"Look, guys, it's going to be a very late night. It's not an order, do as you please, but I think we all could do with a rest. I'm going to bed for an hour."

"Good idea!" Margaret readily agreed.

Ben dropped the shutters to exclude the daylight, sprawled naked on his bed and was soon asleep.

The house was silent when he awoke. He had no idea of time.

Raising the shutter blinds, he was staggered to find that the sun wasn't far away from setting. His bedside clock told him 9.30 pm – surely not, he had slept for three hours. He showered to liven himself up, fearful that his guests thought him rude to have abandoned them. He threw on underpants and a lightweight summer dressing gown, went upstairs to the kitchen, and filled the kettle. He found Sally and Michael sitting on the main balcony, fully dressed and raring to go. Ben was relieved when told that Mum was still in bed – Sally, bless her, had forbidden her brother from waking her. Michael was chomping at the bit and convinced that the fair would be closed long before they got there.

His eyes widened in relief. Ben's movements had disturbed Margaret's sleep and the sound of her preparing for another night out filtered up from her bedroom below. Michael needed confirmation and rushed off down the stairs. Ben sat down opposite Sally. She looked like something that could only have descended from heaven. Her young, gentle face glowed with summer health and freshness. Ben couldn't recall seeing a girl more lovely.

He reached across and placed his hand gently on the back of hers.

"Are you O.K.?" he said quietly, giving her a gentle wink.

She replied not with words, but with a soft, warm smile and a gentle nod of the head. There was something in the moment that was so special. It was a moment that was special, but not sexual – a father/daughter moment. He returned to the kitchen and poured boiling water onto teabags.

"There's tea in the pot," he said to Margaret as they hurriedly passed on the stairs. "We are in big trouble with Michael!"

Ben re-emerged wearing shorts and a short-sleeved summer shirt.

"Good legs!" remarked Margaret, which prompted a look of surprise, if not disapproval on Sally's face. They admired the sunset for a little while, but gave in to Michael's insistence. Sally had already fed the cats.

Ben grabbed his camcorder and they were off.

They wandered through the multitude of stalls on the approach to the fairground. Ben and Michael were peckish and tucked into hand-held hot dogs, leaving the girls to haggle over the price of tacky Moroccan bracelets. Tomato ketchup dripped onto Michael's shirt and a considerable amount was spread across his chin. Mother hen would clean him up later. Ben's camera bag was slung at his waist, always at the ready to surreptitiously grab a bit of non-posed action.

At the fairground entrance, several Spanish horsemen were displaying their mounts. A truly superb sight, each male equestrian wearing various forms of full traditional dress – waistcoats, frilled shirts, boots, tassels, leather chaps bedecked in brass studs, and, of course, the unique headgear, the Cordoba. The most striking of them all was astride an enormous, perfectly groomed white stallion. Behind him, sat side-saddle, was a beautiful young woman, high comb and flower in her hair, and her Flamenco dress flowing down the flanks of the magnificent animal.

They were keen to pose for Ben's footage. Unfortunately, but much to Michael's delight, the animal decided to take a shit. What seemed like an endless flow of manure fell sixteen hands to the concrete below. Ben could edit that out – or maybe not. These events, always well organised, demanded a man in fluorescent vest soon shovelling the manure into a large plastic bag. Nothing should be wasted – it would be sold after the weekend either door-to-door or to the local garden centre.

They walked slowly through the crowds, past the dozens of casitas, taking in the melange of aromas – freshly popped popcorn, burgers, hot dogs, pizzas, candyfloss, barbequed chicken and pork, freshly cooked mini doughnuts. The choices seemed endless. Various styles of music hit them from all directions – Flamenco from one casita, disco from another. It blended with the myriad of electronic beeps and blasts from small roundabouts.

Nothing compares with the laughter and happy faces of very young children and Ben spent a little while filming their enjoyment on a merry-go-round. They circled, aloft a motorbike or tiny pony, or sat inside a fire engine, stagecoach, or locomotive, or simply within a fibreglass duck with a stupid smile on its face. Ben was spotted by a number of ex-pat friends, but with a wave, he ignored them and moved on. He was not prepared to fuel their speculative minds by way of introduction to his new family.

The atmosphere became more urgent as they approached the "big-boy" dodgems and white-knuckle rides. The music became more intense and ear-deafening. Ben bought a bunch of tickets and the kids clambered together into a dodgem car. Good footage was filmed as they risked whiplash without a care in the world. The Tannoy boomed out with instructions that they were *dodgem* cars and not *bumper* cars.

Even better footage was shot when they insisted on another session in separate cars. Ben's camcorder recorded still better footage when he persuaded Margaret to join him. She took control of the steering wheel, whilst he took on-board shots of the kids in their individual cars.

A gypsy-looking attendant wagged a warning finger at Michael who was attempting to destroy everything in his path. Michael, of course, ignored him. They moved on to the white-knuckle stuff.

The terrified screams could be heard well above the megawatts of music.

Ben had always believed that people who ride these monsters are either very brave or very stupid. Nothing that confronted him would convince him otherwise. Or is it that young people are less fearful than adults?

Michael *was* fearless and queued for every gut-wrenching motion there was on offer. Sally was more selective and shied away from the most terrifying rides. Ben's camera was ready at every opportunity.

The time came when he was persuaded to behave like a red-blooded man. With Michael and Sally, he took his seat on a high-flying Waltzer that, from ground level at least, didn't look too intimidating. Margaret categorically refused to be anything other than a spectator. She had made the right decision. Michael loved the ride but Sally clung to Ben's arm throughout, with head buried and eyes firmly shut. Rejoining Margaret,

Ben claimed that it hadn't been *that* terrifying, hoping that the slight tremble in his legs wouldn't be noticed.

The girls hadn't eaten and Ben insisted that they should be fed and watered. Michael had a good appetite and raised no objections.

They settled for a slightly quieter terrace serving burgers and kebabs. Washed down with cokes and lemonade, they sat contentedly and satiated their hunger. Incredibly, time had flown by and it was now close on 3.00 am. The fair wouldn't close until 6.00 am, but the grounds were beginning to thin out and three of the group were flagging a little.

Ben had over-bought on dodgem tickets and sent the siblings across the way for a final ride or two. He and Margaret reflected on the difference between British and inland Spanish fairground celebrations. British fairgrounds have an underlying feeling of tension and threat, where trouble could erupt at any moment. Their Spanish counterparts were family occasions; well organised, well policed, medical facilities, no extreme drunkenness, and small children in buggies sleeping through the intense noise. Spanish couples wouldn´t understand the meaning of the word "babysitter". Worst possible scenario would be the occasional arrest of a pickpocket.

They joined the kids as they completed their final ride and set off on the half-hour walk to the car. Michael walked ahead, Margaret took Ben's arm, and Sally slipped her hand into his. Ben squeezed her hand affectionately. She squeezed back.

The walk took them past the ice cream parlour.

"Why not?" said Ben. "It's only 3.20."

It was 4.00 am when Ben opened his front door. The cats welcomed the re-opening of the "restaurant". Not a lot of time was spent saying their goodnights – they all were shattered.

Ben received a hug and a gentle kiss on the cheek from both Margaret and Sally.

"Hasta mañana, Ben," from Michael.

"Goodnight, Michael, see you tomorrow."

There would be no early risers the following day.

The group came together in the early afternoon of Sunday.

No one was overly hungry, but enjoyed a breakfast/lunch of fruit and cereals, fresh orange juice and, of course, the obligatory pots of tea.

Even Michael was quietly knackered, but would no doubt regain his normal self before the day was out.

"I've been thinking," started Ben. "I've been referring to you young people as children or kids, and, of course, you are not. You are young adults. I have decided that in future you will be... " the Crew."

They liked the idea.

"If you are captain," said Michael, "you need a second in command."

He was already looking for promotion through the ranks.

"In my absence, who controls the Crew?" questioned Ben.

"I do!" was the rapid response from Margaret.

It was agreed that their mum could have a probationary period in the position of "second in command". It was all childish banter, but the Crew enjoyed it. Sally changed the subject.

"Ben, I love that scatter cushion in my bedroom."

She was referring to a large, yellow, heart-shaped cushion, which Ben had won as a raffle prize. It featured a couple of cute little bears in an embrace beneath a parasol, with the words "Te quiero" (I love you).

"I'm going to the pool," interrupted Michael.

His interruption shifted Ben's attention to another matter, which needed to be addressed.

"Before you go, Michael, a friend of mine from Cardiff has recently died and I must fly over for his funeral. So before you ask what we are doing next weekend, I shall not be around."

Before Michael could come up with a cunning plan, involving his mum and the Crew attending a stranger's cremation, Margaret took over.

"I'm sorry to hear that – were you very close friends?"

"Not *very* close, but close enough to feel that I should pay my respects," replied Ben.

"As it happens," Margaret continued, "next weekend is Sally's and Michael's eighteenth birthday and we are committed to spending some time with the grandparents."

It suddenly dawned on Ben that he had become so absorbed with this family that he hadn't given a moment's thought to Miguel's family here in Spain. He must apologise to Margaret at the right time.

Michael went to the pool, whilst the others cleared up. Margaret began fussing around, cleaning sinks and wiping down surfaces unnecessarily. Ben took the cloth from her.

"That's what I pay Juanita for!"

The rest of the afternoon was largely a poolside, lazy day of recovery, though Michael seemed beyond destruction. The others sat in the shade, sometimes chatting, sometimes in silence – it didn't matter either way. Out of earshot of her brother, Sally spoke.

"Be-en," she began, in a pleading manner. "When you come back from Cardiff, we will have started college. Several of my girlfriends from school are also going on to teacher training. I would love to see the look on their faces. Would you collect me one day from college in the Ferrari?"

Ben glanced across to her mother. Margaret gave a delicate nod of approval. She trusted him implicitly and Ben would deny Sally nothing.

"Let me have your mobile number before you go; I'm sure that we can arrange something."

Sally beamed.

"Right, Michael," shouted Ben. "It's time that you learned to dive. You have the grace of a pregnant toad."

The girls watched as Ben knelt at the edge of the pool holding Michael's ankles together in a firm grasp.

"Now then – legs straight, arms straight above your head, lean forward from the waist, drop your head, and fall forward into the water. You must remember to keep your legs straight and ankles together throughout."

Michael picked it up very quickly and before long progressed to pushing off from legs slightly bent at the knee. He was pretty damned pleased with himself. Beginning to look like a professional!

"Teach me, teach me!" insisted Sally, rushing to Ben's side.

Ben held her ankles. The swell of her mound and firm buttocks were less than twelve inches from his face. He fought to avert his eyes, speaking to her, but looking up only at her face. Even then, he was looking from below her perfect breasts.

Michael's comments were less than gracious about his sister's efforts.

"Come on then, know-all, you teach her," said Ben.

He was grateful that her brother's criticism had interrupted his instinctive interest in Sally's body. It had let him off the hook and went off to fetch strawberries, ice cream, and soft drinks all round.

They postponed diving in favour of eating. With the arrival of late afternoon, Margaret decided that her family should return to their home.

"It's been a lovely weekend, Ben, but we really must be making a move," apologised Margaret.

"If you must," replied Ben. "But we haven't eaten much today and Sunday isn't Sunday without roast beef and Yorkshire pudding. Get the Crew together and we can stop off at a very good carvery restaurant that I know."

The Crew weren't keen to leave. A destroyed Li-lo, draped over a nearby balustrade like a discarded giant condom, was evidence of their enjoyment of the weekend. Ben reminded them of their mum's status as second in command.

Sally slipped a note of her mobile number into his hand.

While his guests packed, Ben took a shower, shaved, and splashed on some aftershave. For their farewell dinner, he donned a crisp white sports shirt, denim jeans, and deck shoes.

"You look very smart," observed Margaret.

As always, the carvery food was perfect and the best meal they had eaten together. It brought to a close a perfect weekend.

At the apartment block, Ben helped to unload their bags and amongst sincere expressions of gratitude, they said fond farewells. There were the usual warm but not over-familiar hugs.

Ben walked to his car but suddenly stopped.

"Oh, I almost forgot," he smiled.

He opened the boot and took out a large plastic supermarket shopping bag and handed it to Sally.

She pulled out the yellow scatter cushion featuring the two cute bears.

A tear welled and she threw her arms around his neck.

"Oh Ben, Ben. Te quiero, te quiero," she shouted.

"Igualmente," he replied. "Feliz cumpleaños."

(I love you too) .... (Happy Birthday)

Pinned to the cushion was a sealed envelope containing a crisp fifty-euro note. Ben passed a similar envelope to Michael.

The family waved as Ben drove off.

At home, he fed the cats yet again and poured himself a brandy.

He pondered on what a tiring but enjoyable weekend it had been.

What a lovely family group; each one of them special for different reasons. An uncomfortable thought entered his head – should he not have attached that envelope to the cushion? Would the money raise connotations in the mind of Margaret? – Even worse, remind Sally of traumatic times?

Surely not – he wasn't a threat to Sally, and Margaret had his solemn promise that he would never hurt her daughter.

He put the thought out of his head and went to bed.

Chapter 5

Ben awoke feeling remarkably fresh. After a shower, he went online to organise a return flight to Cardiff, compact car hire, and budget accommodation. His under-privileged early years had made it impossible for him to contemplate using expensive hotels and spending hundreds of pounds simply to crash out. The telephone rang. It was a mobile number that he didn't recognise and anticipated an insistent salesgirl urging him to change internet providers.

He picked up anyway.

"Te quiero, te quiero!" It was Sally.

"Hello sweetheart," Ben responded.

He was surprised, though pleased that she had called.

"Ben, it was *so* kind of you to give me the cushion. I will treasure it always. It's on my bed and looks great! But Ben, the money wasn't necessary; te quiero was more than enough."

She had ignored the instructions: "*Not to be opened before your birthday.*"

Ben was relieved that the contents hadn't re-kindled bad memories.

"It's not a lot," said Ben. "Buy yourself something nice."

Sally continued.

"You won't forget to ring me when you are back from Wales, will you?"

Ben reassured her.

"Of course not. I look forward to seeing you again and surprising your girlfriends. Bye for now. Te quiero."

"Bye-bye Ben, and thank you again," replied Sally. "Te quiero."

Michael made a similar call later in the day, thanking Ben for his generosity. Ben felt close to the Crew, who were of an age when they could now be taking driving lessons. As a birthday gift he would have happily financed the cost, but knew that Margaret would have objected strongly to an over-generous gesture.

Ben went back to organising his trip, having confirmed that his neighbour was available to feed the cats for a few days. He calculated that it would be possible to fly the same day as the funeral and still have plenty of time to get to the church.

As he boarded his budget airline flight, he commented to a fellow traveller that he returned to his homeland only for weddings and funerals. He wondered how many would make the trip to Spain when it came to his turn to be led off by the Grim Reaper.

His infrequent trips to the U.K. rarely went smoothly and this one had started with a two-hour delay! He was travelling light with only hand luggage. *That will save some time at the other end,* he thought.

His mind wandered during an uneventful flight. His visits to family members and friends in the U.K. were rare. For obvious reasons of climate, they preferred to visit *him*. For selfish reasons, he felt that any future visits by them would strangely constitute an intrusion into life with his adopted new family group.

He observed that one of the Polish cabin crew had a nice rear end – not like Sally's, but nice nevertheless. He planned that when buying a snack and coffee, he would explain that the delayed departure had caused the serious predicament of arriving late for a funeral. She was very helpful and promised to get him off the plane ahead of all other passengers.

So far, so good, but his trips were never without incident.

This one would be no exception.

True to her word, on landing, she announced that a passenger was running late for a family funeral.

"Please remain seated," she demanded.

Most of them obeyed.

Ben grabbed his bag from the overhead locker and made his way forward.

"Thank you," he said. "I love you."

She smiled at the incorrigible flirt. The plane came to a standstill.

"Nice landing, Biggles!" he shouted through the open door of the flight deck.

"We get it right occasionally," came the reply.

From tarmac to exit, Cardiff airport is something of an exhausting assault course. Ben looked at his watch and started running. He was panting heavily as he cornered like Road Runner into Passport Control.

All other passengers were a good five hundred yards behind him. Avoiding the barriers, he made his way down a side aisle.

"Use the crowd control barriers, sir!" a voice boomed out.

Ben stopped and turned to face an enormous woman planted in the corner of the hallway. She stood dressed in security uniform, arms folded, and legs apart.

Oh fuck! – Here we go, he thought.

"What crowd?" he enquired, looking around mockingly.

"You *must* use the designated channels, sir."

"Give me a break, I'm late for a funeral," protested Ben.

She would not be budged.

"Sir… you are going nowhere until you have passed through the crowd control channels."

How ridiculous this officious woman was being.

Under different circumstances, Ben would have taken up the challenge and fought against the mindless bureaucracy, but a further glance at his watch gave him no option but to comply. He raced through the channels of the pen like a demented sheep, but stopped mid-way to confront his adversary.

"Am I doing it properly?" he enquired.

She replied only with a look – a look more powerful than a cosmic ray – a look capable of melting tungsten steel.

He arrived at the Passport Control desks to find them un-manned.

The situation had become farcical.

He confronted her yet again.

"I will give it five seconds. After that, I'm going through those doors."

She smiled. The time elapsed and he strode purposefully to the exit doors – to find them locked. She smirked. A Passport Control officer arrived and saved the day.

"Get a fucking life," he murmured to himself, as he rushed through the baggage hall. He wondered if the bitch might have phoned ahead to Customs to have him further delayed.

The Customs officer at the green channel and Ben had history. That very officer had crossed swords with Ben in the past. That's another story, but can be summarised by Ben's Crown Court victory over Her Majesty's legal representatives´ attempt by entrapment, to give him the criminal record of smuggling. The judge found in his favour and Ben´s only regret was that he hadn't involved the media at that time to expose a serious misuse of power. It had been some years since their confrontation, but they recognised each other. Time wasn't on Ben's side and, to his relief, the officer thought better of challenging his old adversary.

Hire car collected, checked in to his motel, a quick change, and a five-mile drive found Ben at the church. He had missed the funeral service, but slipped into, and mingled with the huge turnout now in the church grounds.

He made his way to the weeping widow of his friend, who thanked him sincerely for travelling all the way from Spain. He expressed his condolences, took her gently in his arms, and patted her shoulder. She had no way of knowing that he had just that moment arrived.

Family and very close friends clambered into sleek limousines and set off for the crematorium. The rest of the gathering made their way to the golf club house to feed at the expense of the widow.

As is normal, the atmosphere was respectful in the presence of the principal mourners, but after their early departure, it became a more light-hearted affair.

"So what's life like in Spain?" people would ask.

Ben tired of repeating the same patter to each of his past friends and wished that he could call a meeting to put it to bed once and for all. The attendance thinned out over a couple of hours and predictably the day degenerated into a piss-up. Come midnight, Ben was with a group of his more earthy pals. All were the worse for wear, sharing dirty humour, having forgotten why they were there. One of them entertained the group with his often-performed feat of getting his head into a condom. Many had tried, but he was the only one who could then exhale breath into the rubber to the point at which it burst.

Definitely not to be tried at home. There is a special technique, which avoids asphyxiation and permanent damage to eyesight; and there *are* better uses for a latex tube.

All were eventually gagging for a curry. Taxis were called and the steward was relieved to lock the doors behind them.

At around 2.00 a.m. and after more drinking at the Taj Mahal, Ben was beginning to wonder if he could keep his prawn dansak down. He had once witnessed a drunk disgorge the contents of his gut over a restaurant table and did *not* want to be part of such spectacle. He mumbled his apologies, paid up his contribution to the meal, and zigzagged to the taxi rank opposite. When the cab arrived at his motel, he was relieved that the upholstery was unspoilt. He paid up with tip.

The taxi left, he deposited his dansak into a flowerbed, and mumbled a farewell to the night porter.

"Good night?" enquired the porter, as Ben stumbled up the stairs.

He didn't reply, found his room, had one final wretch into the sink, and went comatose.

He awoke feeling like shit! He had slept through breakfast and lunchtime. A shower and cleaning his teeth did little to help. It was mid-afternoon when Reception telephoned a taxi company. He waited outside in the fresh air, watching as a hotel worker hosed curried vomit from the leaves of a rose bush.

That was a waste of money. He smiled to himself.

Reunited with his hire car, he must now eat. It was the only thing that could resurrect him from that terrible feeling of impending physical implosion. He found the nearest transport café and only just failed to finish off a second full English breakfast.

He would be flying home the next day and had promised himself that he would do a little shopping. Inland from the coast of Spain, he had found it virtually impossible to buy two of his favourite foods – Marmite and corned beef. He drove to a supermarket and loaded up. With food inside him he now felt tired but almost human. He could relax for the rest of the day. He dismissed the idea of looking up a few contacts. Instead, he walked for a while around Cardiff Bay before returning to his motel.

He spent the early evening in the bar adjoining the motel. He was tired and didn't take up the opportunity of engaging in conversation with guys at the bar – they would only have wanted to know what life was like in Spain. Ben had had enough of that! He was happy to sit in a corner, observing people and their personalities. He'd had a good time with old mates, but after just a short time away, he was feeling strangely homesick.

He went to his room early, and squeezed his Marmite and corned beef into the less than adequate space of his hand luggage, accepting that there was no option but to travel wearing a suit the next day.

At the airport, Ben had checked in, his bag was neither overweight nor oversize, and he had his boarding card. Nothing could possibly go wrong this time – or could it?!

The X-ray machine spotted something worthy of investigation. Ben was invited to step to a side area, whilst the contents of his bag were examined. He was beckoned by a young security lady.

"Sorry, sir, but you can't take this Marmite in your hand luggage."

"Why not?" enquired Ben in astonishment.

"Because it's a liquid, sir."

Ben had seen shit that morning that was more liquid than Marmite, but he kept his cool. He was, however, beginning to feel somewhat persecuted by the staff at this airport.

"Forgive me," said Ben, "but Marmite could hardly be described as a liquid. It is closer to the consistency of plastic explosive – on that I would agree with you. But it is *nothing* like a liquid."

Ben knew that he would lose the battle, but continued anyway. His offer of eating a spoonful from each of his six large jars cut no ice. "Sorry, sir, the regulations say that Marmite is a liquid."

She suddenly developed what Ben thought was a nervous tick. Her head began sudden small backward movements and her eyes jerked upwards. He then realised what was going on.

He looked over her shoulder, to be confronted by the officious interest of another small but dominant security lady. She had become very interested in the proceedings. Had the very mention of plastic explosive set off a full-scale terrorist alert?

Repacking his bag, she leaned forward and quietly whispered, "That's my supervisor, sir... and if you're not careful, you won't be taking your ten tins of corned beef either."

Bless her – she was trying to be helpful.

Ben smiled and moved on to the departure lounge... without his Marmite.

During the flight back to Malaga, Ben pictured scheming bastards tucking into his delicious spread on toast. Should he have excused himself to the toilets, reappeared with six squares of toilet paper and stuffed one into each jar? Would that have been malicious? – No, just his sense of humour.

On the positive side, the Crew were going to love his stories of crowd control, Marmite and corned beef.

Ben smiled as he pondered – we are surrounded by humour.

Chapter 6

On his driveway, only one of the cats rolled over to have his belly tickled. On a later headcount, six had become seven. More money for the vet; she needed to be spayed. The addition to the family was a well-cared for and pretty tri-colour female kitten. He was coming to believe that unwanted pets were being dumped over his gate. He had learned not to expect the devotion that is built into the nature of a dog. None of his cats returned affection that matched Scampi's devotion, but he loved his feline friends regardless. Ben had considered adopting a dog from the local animal rescue centre, but decided that it would be too much of a responsibility. Besides, the cats would tear it to shreds.

As a young man, he had never yearned for the company of "man's best friend". *His* best friend had been kennelled in his underpants.

He unpacked, undressed from his suit, and took a shower. Was it inconsiderate to leave for Juanita the curried skid mark in his underpants? Yes – but he would leave it anyway.

He rested awhile, but was soon at his computer, working on an edit of the fairground footage. Some years earlier he had taken an avid interest in videography. Over time, he had acquired semi-professional cameras and editing software. On first viewing, he was pleased with the quality and quantity of footage that he had grabbed with his consumer-level camcorder. After tweaking, re-tweaking, and adding background music, it was eight hours before he was content with the end result. He burned a couple of copy DVDs for the Crew.

He poured baked beans over toast, spread with the last of his Marmite.

"Bastards," he muttered.

He was tired and soon in his bed.

It was Wednesday when Margaret telephoned.

"Hello Ben, how did the funeral go?"

"It was more like a party," he replied, "but in Wales at least, that's normal. How was the Crew's birthday?"

"I think Sally enjoyed it, but Michael moaned that he would be having more fun if they were with Ben."

"Never mind, if you are free we can get together at the weekend."

"That would be good," Margaret said with some enthusiasm.

Sally came on the phone.

"Hi Ben, you haven't forgotten?"

"Of course not. I'll get a pad and scribble down instructions on where to collect you."

Arrangements were made for Friday and the Ferrari would be gleaming. That organised, Ben and Margaret set a time for them all to meet on Saturday night.

Sally would be devastated if her little bit of theatre went wrong, so Ben did a recce of the meeting point well before the group would be there. Out of sight, he sipped at a soft drink in a bar around the corner from the teaching faculty. When not involved in after-college activities, Sally and Michael took advantage of shared transport, arranged by several of the mothers. Today, she would have special transport. He spotted Sally with her group of nubile young student teachers. Once beyond college confines, most were flaunting recommended guidelines, with skirt waistbands rolled several times to reveal legs of varying appeal. Sally chose to preserve her modesty, but Ben knew her legs to be second to none. With a blast of the twin horns and a scream of the V12 engine, he roared to where they had gathered. He parked in the middle of the road.

Everyone, including parents doing the college runs, turned to observe. It was exactly what Sally had hoped for. Ben jumped out and opened the passenger door. She ran across, put her hand around his head, and pulled it to a firm kiss on the lips. Ben was stunned.

Busy waving back to her friends, she fell into her seat with legs straddled wide apart. She revealed her crotch, her fanny hidden from view only by a few microns of brilliant white cotton polyester. Ben couldn't avert his eyes – it's that man thing. Her labia were probably slightly parted.

As she fastened her harness, he noted that a middle button of her blouse had become unfastened, revealing her firm developing breasts nestled in an equally white mini-bra. Briefly ignoring his paternal feelings for the young woman, God, how he wished that he were fifteen years younger. They roared off, amidst looks of disapproval from parents, astonished looks from her girlfriends, and envious looks from a large group of young men. Wherever Michael was, he would have to settle for the humble college-run vehicle or find his own way home.

"That kiss was a bit passionate," said Ben.

"Of course," replied Sally. "Unlike most of my friends, I'm not forever talking about men – I have a bit of a reputation for being frigid; maybe even a lesbian – so I told the girls I was being collected by my new boyfriend."

She screeched with laughter, throwing her knees in the air.

Little bugger, thought Ben.

"Mum won't be home for a while; she has a private English lesson. Can we stop off for a coke or something?" begged Sally.

Ben readily agreed and drove to a café bar near to the family apartment.

"Tell me more about Scampi," Sally pleaded, her full lips sucking cola through a straw.

She didn't realise it, but almost her every movement had a certain sensuality.

Ben was always happy to talk about his special friend.

"Well… in many ways it was more like a man/dog relationship. He would spend a lot of time following me around. I talked to him constantly and he would look up at my eyes as if he understood every word I spoke. He would sit with me and watch as I did little jobs around the house. Perhaps changing a fuse or replacing batteries in the remote; almost as though he was checking on my skills. Then we would play and then we would cuddle."

Sally seemed thoughtful and then spoke with the inspiration of adult maturity.

"Wouldn't things be wonderful, Ben, if we could love each other the way we love our pets?"

Ben was astounded by her compassion for mankind and felt the need to reply.

"At least, *you* will always be loved. Your mother adores you and one day you will have a husband who will worship the very ground—"

Sally interrupted and grinned.

"I don't want a husband, unless there's another Ben. Come on, I want to show you something."

With difficulty, Ben resisted another peek up her skirt as she fell back into the car seat.

Just a teenage crush, thought Ben, as they drove to the apartment. He took a package from the glove box and Sally excitedly pushed the two Feria DVDs into her briefcase.

Margaret had still not returned home.

"Come in here," Sally shouted from her bedroom.

Ben glanced at "Te quiero" on the bed and found her removing a hanger from her wardrobe.

"This is my birthday present from you," she beamed. "Do you like it?"

It was a short, white linen summer dress, embroidered and trimmed with delicate lace.

"It's beautiful," admired Ben.

Without a second thought, Sally was removing her clothes and she stood before him in her underwear. Was this girlish innocence or was she teasing?

Jesus Christ! If Margaret were to walk in now! His penis hardened a little. He was transfixed. As she slipped the dress over her head, he gazed upon the curves of her breasts and the swelling of her Venus mound. Her firm rounded buttocks moved invitingly as she wriggled into a garment that fitted her body perfectly. Ben's hands trembled a little as he complied with her request to zip her up at the rear.

"I love my dress. Thank you, Ben," said Sally quietly.

She turned and stepped towards him, placed her forearms around his neck, and pulled her body upwards to place her cheek next to his.

She was on tiptoes and the length of her body was pressed close to his. Their loins were in direct contact and his penis was hardening by the second. He was sure that Sally had pressed her mound closer. She *must* have felt, and welcomed the pressure of his swelling.

Ben had one of two choices – urgently fuck her or urgently leave.

He had crossed the line too many times in his life – he must *not* step over this one.

His face became flushed and latent desire was at fever pitch, but he leaned forward and lowered her onto the soles of her feet.

"I should go," said Ben.

"Why must you go?"

Ben answered with words he wished were not coming from his mouth.

"You are an incredibly beautiful young lady. We are together in your bedroom. I am fighting a battle with desire. I am twice your age *and* your mother would kill me!"

He hadn't misread Sally's intentions. She looked a little hurt.

"You are a very kind man, Ben. Too kind... but I understand."

She reached up and kissed him gently on the lips. It was the second time that their lips had met, but this touch of mouth on mouth was different. His head swam with emotion. He wanted to pull her body close to his and abandon all thoughts of morality. He fought against his instinctive desire.

"We are all meeting up tomorrow night," croaked Ben. "I should leave now – and I *haven't* seen your new dress."

"Perhaps for the best, Mum should be home soon" conceded Sally. "I'll watch the DVD."

Ben was thankful that he didn't pass Margaret or Michael on the stairs. He reached into his pants and rearranged his swollen tackle. The encounter had revealed something very important. It had been through a period of boredom – but there was nothing wrong with his libido!

What the fuck is happening here? he thought.

He returned to his balcony at home, to get his mind together.

Does a young woman fully understand the thinking of a man? Does she understand that on a beach, the sight of a topless woman provokes nothing more than mild interest? Does she realise that a stolen, forbidden glance up a woman's skirt provokes *intense* interest? Does she appreciate the difference between a woman in a bikini and a woman in underwear? Does she know of the male arousal involved, when in the presence of a woman wearing underwear, *in her bedroom*? Does she not know that it's a completely different ball game? Does she not know that man's most active sex organ... is his brain?

In her bedroom, Sally had tested the boundaries of his self-control to breaking point. He had so wanted to put aside his promise to Margaret. He so wanted to have taken her.

He was now a little unnerved. Without temptation, he was confident that his almost paternal love for Sally would always win the day.

Would desire win the day in similar circumstances? He must never again put himself in a situation where conscience and emotion would be at war.

Chapter 7

Ben spoke with Margaret the morning of Saturday to make final arrangements for that evening. She insisted that she and the Crew would eat at home and they could all meet up for drinks later. She knew that to meet for a meal would result in Ben picking up the check. She admired but was somewhat embarrassed by his generosity. He didn't press her on the matter.

He was looking forward to seeing Sally again, but with a mixture of emotions. He hadn't crossed the line, but was his toe just edging over it?

"Hi Crew," Ben shouted as he approached the bar terrace.

"Hi Ben, how are you?" they shouted back.

Sally was quickly on her feet and moving towards him.

"Do you like the dress that you bought for my birthday?"

"It's beautiful," he replied with widened eyes. "Give us a twirl."

She obliged and blushed with embarrassment.

He took her by both hands, squeezed them gently, and kissed her cheek. That was the first and, Ben hoped, the last time that he and Sally would have conspired to deceive Margaret.

"Hey Ben, loved the video! Especially the horse," shouted Michael.

"Hello Ben, you're looking very elegant," Margaret remarked as Ben kissed her cheek.

He settled with them at the table.

"I'm in trouble with my mum," said Sally, with an over-exaggerated, lowered bottom lip. "The mother of one of my girlfriends telephoned to tell tales about when you collected me yesterday."

Ben reassured Margaret.

"Don't be angry with Sally, it was only a bit of harmless fun. Besides, I'll bet that woman was more interested in sniffing around on how I fitted into the equation with *you*."

"Well, that's certainly true," conceded Margaret.

"Sorry, darling," she apologised to Sally.

She reached across, stroked Sally's hair, and was rewarded with a kiss. Margaret lived in mourning for her deceased husband, but at least was comforted by the love of her children. Ben had repaired the damage and Sally thanked him with her eyes. Ben responded with a wink and a smile.

"I've got an idea," enthused Michael. "Next week, you collect *me* from college. I will run up to you, throw my arms around you, and give you a long passionate smackeroo on the lips."

The group descended into tears of laughter, picturing the facial expressions of the assembled crowd. Michael was delighted and proud that he had been the source of such hilarity.

"Michael," said Ben, laughing and wiping tears from his face. "I'm always up for a laugh, but I draw the line at necking with an eighteen-year-old boy outside a university."

They fell about into continued laughter.

The waitress took the drinks order, wondering what on earth could have been so funny. Things settled and Margaret produced family photographs for Ben's admiration. It was the first image that he had seen of Miguel. He was a typically handsome Mediterranean male – not tall and with a fairly powerful build. He could understand why Margaret had fallen for him. Family photos were passed around the table, with running commentary from Margaret on locations, the children's ages at that time... et cetera, et cetera.

Ben glanced up from time to time to find Sally admiring him and taking minimal interest in the pictures. The twins´ young faces looked back at him from shiny photographic paper and, losing interest in the continuous, loving commentary on each snap shot, his thoughts drifted back to his own working-class childhood. At that time, it was commonplace that, in addition to the accepted corporal punishment meted out in schools, a child would regularly take a good beating from its parents. They were punishments that were rarely deserved and often no more than the release of pent-up frustration of disadvantaged parents. In later life he would become angry with "thugs", justifying their own cruelty, proudly boasting that *their* fathers had regularly taken a belt to them.

"And it didn't do *me* any harm," they would boast.

"Let others be the best judges of that," he would object.

He harboured a fervent belief that to strike a child is about the most cowardly thing that an adult can do; and an admission of failed parenting.

How strange, thought Ben, *that in most of the civilised world it is a criminal offence to strike an adult or kick a dog, yet socially acceptable to smack a child.*

He drifted back to the photographs of their happy smiles. There was no way that Michael and his sister could have been subjected to a background of cruelty. They could only have known devotion and kindness from their parents. Michael brought the now tedious viewing of five fat wallets to a close.

"Come on, Mum, Ben doesn't want to look at photos all night. Tell us about your trip to Wales."

Margaret looked hurt, as she herself never tired of living recollections of the past.

"O.K.," said Ben. "We'll come back to the pics later."

Ben's vocabulary wasn't immense, nor was his grammar perfect, but he did have a way with words that listeners found entertaining.

His grammar school education had provided him with good communication skills, but he thought it pretentious to use vocabulary that others wouldn't understand. He always endeavoured to tailor it to the age and the background of the company.

He told the story of the airport crowd control barriers. They loved it and marvelled at the security officer's intransigence. Michael wanted to know more details about Ben's run in with Her Majesty's Customs and Excise.

"A long story," said Ben. "I'll tell you some other time."

They enjoyed even more to hear the adventure involving his Marmite and corned beef.

More laughter, more drinks, toasted sandwiches, more photographs, and more general chatter. So soon into their short friendship, they had become so content when together. Sally took the floor, to talk of her enjoyment of life now that she was moving towards her ultimate goal. Her new dress highlighted her tanned skin. It was skin that had a shine to it. Ben re-imagined the skin of her torso, which he had viewed the previous day. He re-pictured her in underwear. With sensuous but without lecherous thoughts in his head, he began to fantasise on the beauty beneath the new garment that she so proudly wore.

And her face, her eyes, the full lips of her mouth!

Given the opportunity, he could watch that mouth talk for hours.

Down, Ben!

It was a beautiful evening with a warm breeze from the sea – so easily taken for granted when you have lived on the Costa del Sol.

Ben and the family walked the promenade. They bought ice creams and sat on the sea wall opposite a group of Peruvian players of pans pipes. What a tragedy that such skill had to be hawked at holiday resorts. Musicians were probably the only people that Ben envied.

What a gift, he had often thought, *to play a musical instrument, especially piano*. When he was a young working-class boy, only middle-class sissies took piano lessons and, in any event, the cost of such lessons would have been beyond his parents´ means. Furthermore, the skill in his *left* hand was limited to picking his nose. He bought a CD of their recordings and handed it to Margaret. She thanked him and he dropped the change into their begging bowl.

They walked on. The Crew stopped to inspect an array of wristwatches. The looky-looky man eagerly began to interfere, smelling a possible sale.

"Be patient," Ben scolded him.

Margaret pulled the face of not wanting Ben to spend on her children. Ben put his forefinger to his lips.

A fake Rolex had caught Michael's eye. It was the size of an alarm clock and heavier than his arm, but that was the one for him!

Sally was undecided.

"Which do you like, Mum?"

Sally was torn between identical bracelet watches – one in black, the other in white.

"Well, they are both nice," replied her mother.

"Which do you think, Ben?"

A positive reply came from Ben.

"The white one would be perfect with your dress."

She welcomed another taking control of her indecision.

"I think so too," she agreed.

Job done!

The street vendor began to talk price. Past dealings had taught Ben how to handle the transaction.

"This is what we pay – take it or leave it," he interrupted.

It was a generous offer and the vendor knew it. They shook hands. Sally reached into her small shoulder bag. Ben stopped her.

"But I still have birthday money," she protested.

Ben simply shook his head. She kissed his cheek.

"Gracias." .... "De nada."

"Thank you." .... "You're welcome."

Margaret asked herself if they were becoming over-familiar, but dismissed the thought. She trusted Ben and she mustn't put her daughter in a straightjacket.

If anything, she thought, *Sally should be encouraged to learn that not all men are a threat.*

For a perfect fit, thirty minutes was spent removing surplus links – in the case of Michael's Rolex, almost enough to make a separate bracelet.

The family deserve better times than their finances allow, thought Ben.

"Margaret, give me two euros," demanded Ben. "I'm feeling lucky."

He crossed to the lottery office and bought two tickets. He returned as the Moroccan completed final adjustments.

"We'll share the winnings," he promised Margaret.

"That would be nice," she sighed. "That would relieve some pressure."

Ben had accurately assessed that Margaret was probably struggling to cope with financial demands.

Now bedecked with designer wrist-wear, they moved on.

"I think you could have got them cheaper," said Michael.

"Yes, I know," said Ben. "But we are all entitled to earn a living."

He told them of the Rolex watch that he had bought from a street vendor in Casablanca. It cost twenty-five euros and came with a lifetime guarantee – any problems, he was assured, and the money would be refunded in full or the watch replaced.

Simply return it to "Mohammed, care of Morocco".

The slightly naive Michael didn't catch on to the joke and questioned, "Has mine got a guarantee?"

The girls laughed loudly at his expense.

He fell in, took the mockery on the chin, then strode ahead checking the time every thirty seconds or so. Ben and the girls took a leisurely pace. He noted Sally's gait and posture as she moved. It wasn't contrived. She had a natural catwalk movement of placing one foot almost directly in front of the other. Her body flowed with a grace that set her apart from most young women of her age.

For some reason, the more ungainly and delightfully naive Michael had always been the sibling that required more care than his sister. He had wandered off out of sight and Sally was despatched to retrieve him. As she hurried off down the promenade, Ben spoke.

"You have lovely children, Margaret."

"Yes, I know," she replied. "Though I don't know how. I was never highly sexed."

Was this her way of putting Ben down? Was she saying that he would never get to lie between her legs? It wouldn't have mattered to Ben had she come straight out with the words. From their first meeting, he hadn't *really* considered her to be anything other than a friend.

A large group had gathered and were looking over the sea wall. Margaret was curious and joined them. A couple of Rastafarian, pot-smoking guys were putting the finishing touches to an elaborate sand sculpture.

She waved Ben over, took him by the upper arm with both hands and led him to the wall. Ben had to agree that he had never seen sand sculpturing quite as skilled. They watched them at work for a while.

"Look what I've found," shouted Michael.

He and Sally had returned with their grandparents.

Their grandmother's eyes were firmly fixed on the hands that were still around Ben's upper arm. Margaret quickly broke away from physical contact. It was a needless gesture of embarrassment and guilt. Ben couldn't follow the uncomfortable Spanish conversation that followed between Margaret and her mother-in-law, but he knew that there was at the very least, a strong element of confrontation.

The adoration of a Spanish mother for a son is something quite obsessive and this mother had witnessed what she perceived to be an insult to Miguel's memory. Sally listened from the wings, understanding all that was being spoken. Michael held his grandfather's attention, showing him the various dials on his new watch. Sally, as if in support of Ben, moved to his side and linked her arm through his. Her mother gave her a fierce look of disapproval. Sally raised her eyebrows, but conceded and stepped away. The in-laws left without introductions or eye contact with Ben.

Margaret was visibly upset.

"I didn't have to be fluent to know what was going on there," said Ben. "Margaret, you can take a lover or you can take a new husband. You certainly don't need the permission of Miguel's mother to have a friend."

She came back with authority that he had never witnessed in her.

"Leave it, Ben. You don't understand!"

Ben was stunned into silence.

Michael was bemused by what was happening. Sally attempted to speak. Margaret cut her short.

"Sally, not a word! We have to go. Come on, I will ring you in the week, Ben."

With that, she walked off. No kisses, no hugs – simply gone! Her children had no option but to follow. Sally hurried back briefly, with a tear in her eye.

"I'm sorry, Ben, that was so rude of Mum."

"Don't worry about it," said Ben reassuringly. "I'm not offended. Mum will calm down."

She scurried away, to have, Ben thought, a rare confrontation with her mother. She was no longer a child.

He crossed the road to a bar and ordered coffee and a liqueur.

Fucking hell! Ben *was* offended – one moment they were having a good time together and now he was a liability to the family. The grandparents passed by in the opposite direction, but he avoided eye contact. When they had passed, he realised that it would have been beneficial had they seen him there alone; at least, confirmation that he wasn't screwing their deceased son's widow.

He was driving and, though he felt a degree of anger, he must *not* get involved in a drinking session. As he left the bar, Sally appeared from around the corner, quite obviously looking for him. She rattled off apology after apology.

"I'm sorry, Ben, you don't deserve to be treated like that. I've had a row with Mum and I stormed out."

It was almost fully dark.

"Come on. I'll walk you home," said Ben.

He slipped his hand around her tiny waist and she clung to his arm with both hands. In a quiet side street, they stopped just short of the apartment. She kissed him goodnight. This kiss was different. Her eyes were closed and her lips were slightly parted as they settled gently onto his. Through his thin shirt and even her linen dress, he could feel that her nipples were heavily aroused. Ben could hold back no longer. They locked into an urgent embrace, their mouths passionately working one against the other. Ben felt that he had fallen over a cliff. His head was spinning with emotion. He took her solid buttocks in his hands and lifted her upwards. He pulled her fanny hard against his swelling beast.

She groaned and responded with a gyration of her hips.

The line had been crossed. Now, it was not if… but when.

Ben gasped.

"Your mum could come around that corner at any time. She will be worried about you. Go now, but ring me when you can."

They kissed once more, genitals pressed hard against each other's. He took her breasts in his hands and squeezed erect nipples before she left. Sally responded with pressure from her loins. Ben stood in the shadows, watching as Sally sat on a bench outside the block, regaining her composure before going inside.

Her mother appeared, placed an arm around her daughter's shoulder, and led her to safety. It was a full twenty minutes before Ben could re-emerge from the side street. It felt that two-thirds of his blood supply had been pumped to his penis. The helmet refused to withdraw to a position below the waistband of his underpants.

He lay in his bed that night, mulling over the developments of the day. Would he regret meeting this family? Had he really made life that uncomfortable for Margaret? Would Sally make that phone call? Was he in over his head? Should he jump back over the line before it was too late? Questions… Questions.

A day earlier, his self-control had won the day, but now he had to face the most challenging realisation of all. He not only wanted Sally… He had been refusing to admit that his compassion for the girl had rapidly developed into love and desire. The physical and emotional turmoil of being in love was unmistakable. Ben queried his feelings.

"Do I love Sally? – Or am I *in love* with Sally? Surely my past has taught me the difference. Grow up, Ben – I'm just about old enough to be her father!"

He did *not* sleep well that night.

Chapter 8

Sunday morning started with apologies – with so much on his mind, he had gone to his bed without feeding the cats. After a restless night, he had risen late. As he showered, he wondered if he would get that call from Sally; and if he did, should he not pick up? It was another warm day. He threw on a lightweight dressing gown.

The doorbell rang. Bollocks!

"It's Sunday morning, so it's either Jehovah Witnesses or somebody selling something that I don't want," complained Ben to himself.

Ah well, he thought, *if it's Born Again Christians, I'm an atheist… if that doesn't work, I'll flash the genitals… If it's someone selling, it will have to be a polite fuck off.*

He opened his front door. His heart leapt. Standing outside his wrought-iron gates, a little breathless, was Sally.

He pressed the remote lock release and she ran up the pathway. He closed the door behind her and they passionately kissed and embraced. His head was spinning again. His tackle was immediately aroused, but this was not the moment to make love. He sensed that she was upset.

"Come through," Ben said quietly. "What's the problem?"

They stood facing each other, holding hands.

Sally replied through her sobbing.

"We have all been fighting this morning. Mum says that we mustn't meet with you so often, because it's disloyal to my father. The stupid woman wants to spend the rest of her life in mourning!"

She cried onto Ben's chest.

"Michael's gone off in a huff to play football and I've come to you."

Ben comforted her.

"Don't worry, everything will be O.K. Come and sit down, dry your eyes and I'll get you a drink."

He fetched cold apple juice from his fridge.

"Your mum will be speaking to me and I'll see if something can be sorted out," Ben comforted. "It isn't only that she misses her husband. She is very wound up... I believe that she is also under financial pressure, but I can help with that."

"Ben, you are very kind," sobbed Sally, "and yes, I know that things aren't easy for her, doing her best to provide us with a decent education. I feel guilty about that, but it isn't *your* responsibility to help. Anyway, Mum would be too proud to accept and she would probably think that you wanted to take over as a father figure."

"Leave it with me," said Ben.

Sally seated herself in an armchair. Ben sat opposite on a sofa, reaching across the coffee table to hold her hands.

"Ben," Sally whimpered. "If Mum insists with her attitude, can *we* still see each other?"

She looked at him with eyes that would melt the heart of Satan. Ben loved this young woman and would want nothing less.

"Of course," came his whispered reply.

Sally got to her feet and moved to him. Her short skirt flared outwards, as she settled astride his thighs. They held each other close. Their hearts beat rapidly. In tune with Sally's distress, Ben's penis had chosen to sleep, but now with crotches just inches apart, it wouldn't be long before it rose from slumber. They embraced tenderly. He moved her flowing dark hair from her shoulder and planted gentle kisses on the nape of her neck. It was only a few weeks since he had first admired the stunning beauty of this young woman and now she was in his arms, submitting to his adult adoration.

Ben was naked beneath his dressing gown. He trapped his erect penis beneath his legs. He could feel his pre-entry juice seeping onto the underside of his thigh. He began to tremble with desire. Sally removed her head from his shoulder and sat erect. She spoke quietly.

"Ben... will you make love to me?"

Those words... those wonderful words. Ben had no need to answer.

She unbuttoned and removed her cotton top. Her breasts heaved a little inside her bra, wanting to escape the restriction. Ben reached to the back and unfastened it. He slowly dropped the straps from her shoulders. He didn't want to reveal that rounded flesh in anything other than slow motion. He allowed the fabric to fall away slowly. Her breasts wobbled a little, but didn't drop one fraction. They were full, firm, and a little over-large for her delicate frame. Ben gasped.

"Oh Sally… you are beautiful."

He cupped them and gently squeezed their firmness in his hands. He could wait no longer. He devoured her left breast into his mouth. Sally groaned and threw her head backwards as the blood rushed to her nipples. Ben worked his tongue feverishly from one to the other. The responsive pink delicacies grew larger and harder. Her begging loins gyrated. His enormous beast was screaming – fuck her!… Fuck her! Ben held back – he wanted each moment to last forever. He moved his hand slowly downwards to between her legs. He caressed the crotch of her panties and settled her swollen flesh in his palm. Her knickers were a little moist. He squeezed. She groaned a little louder. She spoke quietly.

"Oh Ben… Te quiero."

His hands moved to the elastic waistband. His left entered and clutched at her buttocks. From the front, his right hand approached the object of his erection's desire. Her vulva was open, inviting penetration. Her labia were swollen. She was wet – very wet. Ben's hand was at last in contact with the most intimate part of a woman whose beauty he had kept at arm's length. His middle finger slid into her body and she submitted to blissful rapture, as he rubbed her G-spot with a beckoning motion. A finger of his left hand pressed gently on her little bum hole. Sally moaned and moaned her pleasure. Her pubescent body soaked up the joy of adult love. Ben withdrew his finger slightly, to seek out her clitoris. It wasn't difficult – it felt the size of her nipple and was rock hard. Sally let out a muffled screech as his finger found the magic button. Just a few seconds of contact was all she could take.

"Stop, Ben, I want you so badly, but please stop… I'm coming, I'm coming. Not yet, not yet… I want it to last a long time."

She stood and removed all that she wore. She settled again, now totally naked, astride his thighs. They cuddled and kissed whilst Sally's libido settled. Ben's libido was anything but settled. He could barely take in the beauty of this creature and his beast would *not* be denied. It was like a dragster on the start line. It was time to release its power. He parted his legs a little and it sprang upwards like a furious guard dog. It slapped into the cleavage of Sally's buttocks and but for Ben's control would have been content to unload there. It took Sally by surprise. She looked down and mouthed just one word… "Wow!" She removed Ben's dressing gown from his shoulders and kissed his neck.

He moved Sally forward towards his knees, to give the big boy some space. It raised its head into full view. Sally was in awe. She took it in her delicate hand and fondled and stroked its considerable length. Ben took it from her and spread her legs wider. He massaged her vulva with the throbbing helmet and her labia willingly parted, giving access to the lubricated entrance of her vagina. Ben now felt the warmth and the soft but gripping texture sliding slowly down the length of his dick. Not yet into full penetration, Ben's gentle growls of ecstasy were interrupted.

"Sorry, Ben, please wait a moment… I'm coming again… Sorry."

Every nerve cell in his body was demanding an orgasm, but he managed to hold off.

Sally planted her feet firmly on the floor, raised her buttocks, and released Ben's throbbing beast into fresh air. She took control. A little at a time, she lowered her vagina onto the full length. Ben leaned back a little to watch his entry. She was tight but well wetted. The erection slid to full entry. She squealed when it was fully home. To Ben, it felt that he had impaled her. They groaned, stayed motionless, and whispered their love for each other. Those moments of dizzy emotion had been too long coming, but at last their bodies and minds confirmed mutual adoration. Ben´s compassion for Sally was unshakable, but any paternal feelings that he had felt in the past disappeared at that moment. With hands on Ben's shoulders, Sally looked down at the glorious union of her vagina with his body. Her clitoris and his helmet were craving satisfaction. Ben took her by the waist and lifted her until his helmet was at her labia. She slid on her juices, the full length and back again – in and out, in and out. Her clitoris quivered with every stroke. Her legs trembled.

"Slowly, Ben, slowly… Ooh, that's wonderful."

Ben was almost at the point of submission to the orgasm. He knew that he would *not* be able to pause again. Perhaps Sally also knew. She quickened her pace and then a little quicker. Her breasts jiggled up and down, in time with her movement.

"What a feeling… I'm coming, I'm coming… Ooh, Ben… I'm coming!"

She thrust down onto the full length; Ben took her tits in his hands, nipples between fingers and thumbs. She screamed throughout her climax, rocking her mound back and forth on the base of the animal inside her. Her excitement prompted Ben's eruption. The nerve endings in his helmet were on fire. The climax just went on, and on, and on. He grunted shamelessly, as he felt his juices, first, squirt and then pour into her cavity.

Just as the reflex action of a dismembered bee's abdomen continues to deliver its sting, so it felt that his testicles contained an endless supply of fluid. It was the orgasm of his life. He felt that he would never need another.

They panted.

"Oh Ben." ………… "Oh Sally."

They sat breathless in that position for some time, Ben's penis wallowing in liquids of love, settled in the depths of Sally's vagina. They looked into each other's eyes. They could find only the words, "Te quiero." ………… "Te quiero."

The beast remained large and was slow to soften. Ben got to his feet with hands beneath Sally's buttocks. She threw her legs around him and gripped tightly. In that locked position, he carried her to his bathroom.

He knelt at the bidet, but still she clung firmly to his body, her vagina refusing to release the source of her pleasure. Whilst warm water filled the bowl, Ben stood and lifted her from his penis. A little of their love liquids fell to the marble floor. Sally giggled. They were totally at ease with the intimacy of each other's nudity.

Ben sat his spunk-filled lady astride the bidet. He knelt beside her and, with an arm around her waist, gently washed between her legs. For

Sally, it was as much sensual as it was relaxing. He moved to a position behind her and planted kisses on her shoulders and back. She murmured contentment as he continued to wash her. He sponged warm water onto her breasts. It ran over her bronzed skin, down through her delicate pubic hair, into the bowl below.

"I wanted you to make love to me in my bedroom," Sally sighed.

"I know... believe me, it was difficult to resist."

Sally continued.

"You are such a kind person, Ben. When did you first want to make love with me?"

He hesitated.

"Probably from the moment I first saw you."

Sally smiled contentment, then got to her feet, drying herself before a kneeling Ben, his face just inches from her intimacy. He looked at her swollen labia and then her face.

He continued.

"You remember when I was teaching you to dive?"

She nodded.

"This is what I wanted to do to you."

He took her by the hips and turned her to face him. He parted her legs, took her buttocks in his hands, and pulled her vulva firmly onto his face. He rammed his tongue into her vagina and it waggled feverishly, seeking the clitoris. Sally gasped. Her fingers parted her labia, urgently wanting the eager appendage to strike home. Then with one hand on his shoulder, the other behind his head, she gyrated her hips gently to receive the attention. Her clitoris had barely calmed down, but she found herself aroused again. Ben wanted to look at her. Her fabulous body must hold no secrets from him. He stopped and moved her swiftly to the bed. Now on her back, her legs wide apart, he planted her heels to each side. He gazed for a moment at her adult loins, transposed, it seemed, onto the body of a delicate teenager. A combination of his saliva and her opaque juice welled in her pinkness. He went down and the tongue found its target immediately. His lips grasped her swollen clitoris and sucked, and sucked. Sally took Ben's head in her hands and pressed it to loins that worked gently in a circular motion.

She would *not* ask him to pause this time. Her lips pursed, as she felt the onset of a second wonderful moment that day. Head lifted to watch Ben's animal enjoyment, she yelped loudly through her orgasm. The beast had grown large beneath his belly. Ben knew that there wasn't another climax in him that day – Sally's vagina had drained him of every vestige of an orgasm. Nevertheless, he wanted to be inside her again. With her pelvic muscles totally relaxed, and reproductive organs craving procreation, Sally gladly welcomed its penetrating thrust. Ben kissed vaginal fluid and saliva onto her lips.

"Te quiero."........"Te quiero," they gasped.

Desire had become a declaration of love.

They rolled onto their sides and held onto each other tightly. Sally's closed legs ensured that the penis was firmly grasped within her body. Calm eventually set in and they could welcome sleep, but both knew that it was out of the question. They relaxed for a while.

Sally spoke first.

"Ben... I think that since we first met, I have been falling in love with you. I spend hours every day just thinking of you. I want you to love me, but there are things I must tell you. Things that you have to know... You and Mum are quite close... has she spoken to you about my past?"

His heart skipped a beat. He knew what she was getting at, but asked with feigned innocence, "What do you mean?"

"Has she told you about when I was babysitting?"

He couldn't lie to her and wouldn't pursue the pretence.

"Yes, Sally, I do know. Your mother didn't mean to tell me, but she was upset about your father's death, one thing led to another, she needed a shoulder, and told me the whole tragic story."

Ben left it at that. All was quiet for a while. Sally spoke again.

"Ben... there is something else you must know."

His mind raced. *Is she going to confess that it was consensual sex or that she had enjoyed every moment of being raped?*

Sally paused, swallowed hard, and began to weep.

"He wasn't the first," she murmured.

Her words hit Ben like a hammer and he intuitively sensed the worst.

"Your father," he said quietly.

Sally's silence confirmed the worst. She had at last taken someone into her confidence and sobbed heavily into Ben's chest. He held her close.

"Why me, Ben? Why me? What's wrong with me? I'm not a bad person, Ben… I was only thirteen. Before today, rape is the only sex that I've ever known."

Ben wept with her and comforted her. He whispered into her ear.

"Sshh now, sshh now… Sally, Sally, Sally. Listen to me, there are some very bad people in this world and you have been the victim of two of them, but there is nothing wrong with *you*… I have never known a person more special. It's been hard for you… I see now that you've kept this to yourself to protect your mother's feelings. She loves you dearly, but it's so sad that she has no idea of just how you have suffered all this time. She has no idea of how kind and special you really are."

Sally spoke urgently.

"You will never tell her, will you?"

"Of course not," Ben assured her.

Sally calmed herself.

"Ben… Our love today was wonderful. I had no idea that sex could be so loving. Does my past make a difference? Does it make me dirty? Please tell me that you love me. Tell me that you'll always love me."

The bedside telephone rang. "Margaret" came up on the screen. He didn't pick up.

"It's your mother. You get dressed and I'll call her back."

Sally went to the lounge to retrieve her clothing.

Ben cleared his throat.

"Hello Margaret, I was in the garden. Just failed to get to the phone in time."

A worried mother enquired, "Has Sally been in touch with you? She went off in a hissy after rowing about you this morning. So I'll come clean, Ben, and tell you what I have decided."

She continued without giving Ben the opportunity of denying any contact with her daughter.

78

"It's not just the grandparents, Ben, it's *me*. I loved Miguel so much that I feel guilty when we have so much fun in your company. I know that sounds stupid and I know the children love to be with you, but you could never replace their father. I feel that we should have some space. Please don't be offended, you are a good friend and I don't want to lose touch, but give things a little time and I will be in touch when I've thought things through."

Being a surrogate father to Sally was the last thing on Ben's mind. Margaret was being ridiculous and selfish. Sally had returned to the doorway listening to one half of the conversation.

Ben measured his words carefully.

"Look, Margaret… I have no wish to replace Miguel. I love the company of Michael and Sally, but I have to respect your opinion. It's your life and I know that you want what's best for your children, but give a thought to this. What would Miguel expect of you? And don't worry about Sally; I'm sure she will return home soon. Speak to me when you are ready. Bye-bye for now."

Ben thought the words, but couldn't say them. *Other than Margaret and his parents, who gives a fuck what Miguel would expect or want?*

A close friendship had developed between him and Margaret and he would never want to be unkind to her, but he now realised that she was guilty of indulgence in self-pity. Yes, she was dealing with the early loss of her husband, but it was poor *Sally* who was dealing with the rape and the memories of full sexual abuse by her father. Ben's analysis was final. *I'm sorry, Margaret, but your daughter needs me more than you do.*

Ben turned to Sally and shrugged his shoulders.

"It doesn't matter now," she smiled. "This is the happiest day of my life."

Ben took her in his arms and spoke lovingly.

"I didn't answer your question… Yes, your past does make a difference. It confirms just how considerate and special you really are. It increases my love for you even more. And yes, no matter what, I will always love you, with heart and soul. I don't know what the future holds for us. It will not be easy, but for now, we will see each other as often as possible."

Sally held Ben tightly and wept tears of happiness.

"Ben... I've never been in love before. My body tingles from head to toe. It feels wonderful."

With the intensity of the day, Ben hadn't given a thought as to how Sally had arrived at his door. She had taken the coastal train and then jumped on a bus to the bottom of his road. He would drive her home to her resort, but not to her door. He used the time stressing to Sally that, for now, their love must be a secret love. She must never tell even her best friend. Her friend would tell her mother, her mother would tell Margaret. Game over.

In law, Sally was no longer a minor and no longer under the control of her mother, but Margaret would be horrified by the thought of them being an entity, even though it was based on love equally strong as her misplaced adoration of Miguel. Despite Spain's liberal approach to consensual sex, society in general would frown upon an older man having sex with an eighteen year old. Unless you are a global celebrity, the public's judgement of acceptability is all too often based upon an age difference – the wider the gap, the greater the perversion. Why should an ageing actor, industrialist or newspaper magnate be immune to the same prejudice and intolerance?

He pulled into a quiet side street. She made to embrace him, but he stopped her.

"Secrecy," said Ben.

Sally smiled and replied.

"I'll ring you soon, Ben... I love you. And I need you. I want to tell the world, but for now, I can't give my mother any more hurt than she is already suffering. I pray that one day she will move on from her grief, without the need to know what a horrible man he was."

He looked into the lovely eyes of a young woman that had unburdened herself of a tragic past.

"I love you, Sally... and I'll always be there for you," whispered Ben. It was the first time that they had substituted "Te quiero" with the English translation of "I love you".

It had an air of finality to it; an air of total commitment.

She gave him a little girlish wave as she skipped around the corner out of sight. Ben sighed. What a wonderful day. He hadn't wanted it to end, but for the first time, he was uncomfortable with their relationship. Because their love couldn't be declared, he and Sally were to be fully immersed into an existence of deceit and duplicity.

He needed to go home to his cats and ponder on where the fuck it was all going.

Chapter 9

Ben mulled over and over the situation that he found himself in. His and Sally's love at an emotional level was intense. Their love at a physical level was equally intense. Had Sally's apparent skill and appreciation of adult sexual activity been gleaned from talk with girlfriends? From adult movies downloaded from the net? Was it instinctive? Or was it from her father? How often had he abused her? Did she come to enjoy being abused by him? – Surely not. He refused to dwell on her father's role – that turned his stomach. He promised himself that he would never interrogate Sally on those matters.

He hoped that her sexual enthusiasm had been generated from natural development – usage of the finger of fantasy – the middle finger of fantasy. The wanderings of his mind were irrelevant – middle-aged idiot or not, she could do no wrong and he was desperately in love. He loved her like he had never loved before. He realised that he had never truly known the meaning of love for a woman.

He became gloomy. Could it be that Sally's euphoria was based only on Ben perhaps being the first adult male to have shown her true kindness? He felt fully committed and the prospect of one day losing her terrified him. His mind drifted to the other people involved.

Michael, though immature, would probably think their love to be quite cool and trendy. Margaret and the Spanish grandparents would be horrified. They were unaware of the full extent of Sally's past trauma and were entrenched in their own self-absorbed issues. They had placed Miguel on an unshakable pedestal. Ben recalled Margaret's words.

¨I was never highly sexed.¨

Had that been a problem that led Miguel to seek sexual satisfaction elsewhere? Even if true, you go off and fuck anyone – but not your daughter!

Part of Ben wondered if Sally should shatter their illusions, but even with the full picture, they wouldn't condone the relationship. Besides, he knew now that Sally could never be that unkind to her mother. In effect, she had declared that she would always sacrifice her own feelings to protect her. Now at least, she had unburdened her shame and the tragedy of it all. Ben asked himself how he would feel if he had a young daughter that declared love for a much older man. He chose to move on from that thought.

He pondered the future. They could continue with a deceitful, clandestine relationship, with the ever-present risk of exposure. The alternative was a declaration of their love, bringing with it a kind of emotional relief – but a declaration that was going in what direction? It would come with a mountain of problems.

What about Sally's relationship with her mother? What about her reputation at the faculty of teaching – her lecturers and her fellow students? What about her education? Would she become less enthusiastic? What about the social implications and the prejudice that she would have to confront? Would they be able to handle it? Where would it all end? – Did they have a long-term future together or was it nothing more than an intense sexual adventure?

Sally didn't know it, but Ben could never father a child with her. That raised another question. They had enjoyed unprotected sex that day. Protection was never mentioned. Was she using the pill in preparation for her first adult sexual experience?

Ben's mind swam with confusion, but he realised that a declaration would possibly lead to an early destruction of their love – he wasn't ready for that.

He saw before him a life of utter joy or, he dreaded, an ending full of misery and heartache.

His telephone rang late that night. It was Sally from beneath her bed sheets.

"I love you, Ben… Goodnight."

Ben replied softly.

"I love you too, precious… Goodnight."

It was then that Ben knew the immediate future. Even if he could put his own feelings aside, he could not, and *would* not, abandon her. There had been too much unhappiness in this young woman's life. As things stood, he was the main source of emotional support in her life. She needed the love and respect of an adult male who loved her beyond a desire for carnal lust. It *is* true that when he had enjoyed her body, his head span and he was carried off into a world of animal desire. How could he not have been? What right had a man of his age to be with this lovely creature? But there was nothing sinister about it – nothing dirty, nothing malevolent. He had relaxed afterwards and bathed in a sea of adoration for Sally the person – not Sally the body. He prayed that she felt the same emotions to an equal degree.

Whatever the future, he knew with certainty that he loved her.

God, how he loved her.

Chapter 10

Ben hardly slept, and thought of her throughout the night and the following morning.

During her lunch break Sally telephoned.

¨Hola Cariño, hello darling – Mum is out early evening, giving a private English lesson, and Michael is going straight off to football – I'll not have too long, but can you meet me after college today?¨

Ben welcomed the opportunity. He had decided that he must tackle a few issues. They arranged to meet near the apartment after Sally had been dropped off by an obliging college-run mother.

The butterflies in his stomach fluttered as Sally rounded the corner. The final session of her day had been one of sport. She still wore the netball uniform of a short gymslip. Sally hurried along, jumped in beside him, and kissed his cheek.

¨I love you,¨ she whispered.

¨I love you too,¨ Ben whispered back.

Ben drove off in search of a location more private – it wasn't long before they were in open countryside. As he drove, he began to offload some of the things that were going through his mind. He reeled them off.

At all times, they must observe total discretion. They must never show their affection in public. Affection in the company of her mother was a complete non-starter; her mother's intuition would very quickly sniff something out. What sort of deal did she have with her mobile phone provider? – Could her mother pick up on frequent calls to Ben? That wasn't a problem; the deal was Pay as you Go without monthly statements. Ben reached for fifty euros from the centre console and pushed it into Sally's bag – she must top up her account. Sally assured Ben that she had anticipated all that Ben was saying.

Like all that indulge in affairs, they were rapidly gaining the required skills of deceit and duplicity.

It was important to them that they weren't cheating on wives or partners. They were deceiving, but not cheating on Margaret. Ben convinced himself that their relationship wasn't hurting Sally. He was simply loving her – like she had never been loved before. They were cheating only on public opinion and the intransigence of society's values. Ben pulled into a large lay-by surrounded on three sides by forestry.

He turned to face Sally, took her hands in his, and looked her in the eyes.

"Sally, this is very important… I have spent all day thinking of you. *You* have probably been daydreaming in college. You know that I love you and always will, but you are in a vital period of training. It's important that you can show that our love never held you back. You must promise that you will not allow *us* to affect your future career."

"I promise," she said quietly.

Ben kissed her gently on the lips but continued.

"Sally, are you on the pill?"

Shaking her head, she blurted enthusiastically.

"Of course not – but it doesn't matter if I get pregnant. Then we will have to tell all and we can get married!"

Sally was much more mature than most girls of her age, but was that statement a romantic whim or was she confirming her total love for Ben? – At least for now. Ben told her of his past and how he came to have a vasectomy. She looked more than a little sad and disappointed, but delighted to hear Ben's reassurance that his past relationship was nothing compared to the love that they now shared.

Her face brightened and she smiled.

"Never mind… I will be working with children every day and *we* can keep lots of animals."

They embraced, kissed lovingly and then passionately. She wanted to relieve Ben of his concern. She released the shoulder fastenings of her gymslip to expose firm breasts enclosed in a sports bra. She placed his hand onto the cotton-lycra to caress her. She had over-sensitive nipples and murmured approval as Ben's finger and thumb massaged the swellings. His tongue gently licked the lips of her open mouth. Sally had known sex only in its perverted or violent form. She wasn't embarrassed to crave the delight of an intense orgasm, delivered with love.

"I want to make love with you," she whispered.

Ben's penis was already rock hard. The side windows of his Audi were heavily tinted. He looked around. The entry to forestry was blocked by heavy scrub. The car was a mere twenty yards from the road. There was little passing traffic, but a public road nonetheless. Sally followed Ben's instructions. They got out of the car. He opened the rear door and positioned her. Knelt on the rear seat, the roundness of her buttocks protruded from the car bodywork. He rummaged through the glove box and placed an open map on the car roof. Passing motorists would think that he was planning a route. He unzipped the top section of her gymslip and pushed the bra-strap towards her shoulders, releasing her lovely breasts from restriction. They fell and wobbled into fresh air. He lifted the tiny skirt and slowly placed it over her back. Her spine was arched downwards. An almost independent rear end swept up from her small waist. There it was again – the crotch of her knickers, bursting with swollen flesh, desperate for penetration. Ben had a flashback to when they had been bowling. He had reassured Margaret about the harmless man thing, catered to by soft pornography. If she could see them now! – Her daughter on her knees, her breasts hanging from her chest into the folds of a gymslip that could easily be associated with a schoolgirl.

But this is different, thought Ben. *This is love and this wondrous view is for my eyes only. Others must settle for wanking into page three of a tabloid newspaper.*

There was no time to waste. All must be revealed. He peeled her pants from rounded buttocks and very slowly to her knees. What a vision. First, her little bum hole and then her glorious quim.

A little of Sally's juice was already at her vulva. She was wet and fully prepared. With his thumbs, Ben parted her blood-gorged labia to reveal the pink and, with the waistband of his shorts hooked beneath his scrotum, the beast began its sensuous entry into her gripping vagina.

Sally groaned with every additional inch that her body welcomed. With a final thrust, the erection was soon fully encased to its base.

"Oh Ben... I love you. Please don't move," Sally sighed.

He wanted to shag her furiously but did as requested. He stood his ground, whilst Sally rocked backwards and forwards, grinding herself along the length of the hot, stationary dildo. Ben could feel the contact of her enlarged clitoris. He took her breasts in his hands and caressed them lovingly. Her fervour increased in tune with her vocal whimpers.

"Touch me," she pleaded.

Ben knew what she wanted. His right hand swiftly deserted her breast and in an instant his middle finger was at her entrance, rubbing her magic button. His left hand moved from nipple to nipple. Sally reached between her legs and rolled Ben's testicles in her hand. Her climax was almost instant. She howled pleasure.

"Fuck me, Ben... fuck me... fuck me hard!"

He was motionless no longer. He took her by the hips and pulled her firmly onto his beast. The animal thrust angrily, her buttocks slapping loudly against his pelvis. They shagged, and shagged and shagged. His orgasm was explosive. He filled her with an ocean of infertile fluid. His prostate gland was working overtime to produce the stuff.

They panted breathlessly after their combined efforts. Ben leaned back a little to look at her vagina, stretched tightly, but comfortably around his manly circumference. He knew from experience that girth, and not length, is more important to a woman. Some years earlier, he had woken up "piss-proud" one night and, boyishly, had taken the trouble to go to a tape measure. It stood proudly at seven inches long, with a circumference at the base of six and a half inches. From that night onwards, he had jokingly referred to it as "the beast". He was confident that he was sufficiently well hung. Even though the amazing vagina, when aroused, can increase in length by one to two hundred percent, he was in awe that Sally's delicate frame had hungrily consumed all that Ben could deliver. Their position of full penetration was a beautifully intimate sight. They dismissed the inevitable urgency to redress and rested; their genitals firmly locked.

"Sorry about what I said, Ben," apologised Sally. "I got carried away."

"It's not wrong to say what you feel," Ben breathed heavily.

Sally sought reassurance.

"Ben… is it rude or dirty of me to enjoy our love so much? Having you inside me, my body takes over. It just seems to be so natural."

"It *is* natural. It's wonderful that we enjoy each other the way we do. Use whichever words come to your mind. It's not dirty. We are talking desire and love… Desire isn't dirty and love *certainly* isn't."

Ben wanted to leave the beast in soak, until its lust had been fully satiated, but time didn't allow.

Sally sighed.

"I would like to stay like this for hours, but I must go soon."

"Just a moment," said Ben.

He always carried a roll of kitchen towel for cleaning the windscreen. He reached across and took it from the side pocket of the door. He tore off a couple of squares, folded them, withdrew his still enlarged penis from his lovely lady, and applied them to her vulva. Sally's hand reached between her legs to hold the paper in position. Ben tore off another large square, mummified his beast, and put it back into its enclosure. He completed the operation by placing a further folded square into the crotch of Sally's panties – instant panty liner. He took the towel from Sally's hand, before pulling her knickers up over her buttocks. He pulled them down again briefly and fondly kissed her buttocks, before returning her to fully dressed, with skirt placed back in position. From the start of their love for each other, they were at ease with visual and physical intimacy. It was an intimacy, greater than that enjoyed by many close married couples.

"I love you so much, Ben, it almost hurts. If only we had more time."

It had been a brief but fabulous coming together of their bodies and their souls, but the worst part of any clandestine meeting is that it must end when you least want it to.

They couldn't resist a kiss that was over-long when Ben dropped her back at the resort. Sally's parting words were spoken as though talking down to an unhappy child.

"Don't worry, Ben. If you love me as much as I love you, everything will turn out fine."

Ben responded with utter sincerity.

"I love you that much… and more."

He drove back to his home feeling elated about the depth of their feelings, but depressed that it wasn't possible to wake up the following day a much younger man. He took comfort in the thought that with Sally's sad past, a *young* man would probably perceive her as tainted. Without the experience of life in the raw, he would be delighted to use her body, but not look further beyond. Even worse, it could be almost guaranteed that an immature man would move on and her dark secrets would be shared with equally immature friends. Ben fully understood her attraction towards an older man that she could trust.

His furry friends were waiting for him. Some wanted a little love and all wanted food. In the bathroom, Ben peeled the firmly stuck kitchen towel from his relaxed penis. He put it to his nose and inhaled deeply. That unique smell of a woman – that smell that every man remembers from the first time he fingered a girl. He loved the intimate smell of his beautiful lover. Ben couldn't bring himself to flush it away and instead placed it on his bedside table. He waited expectantly that night for a call from beneath the bed sheets. Sally didn't disappoint.

Though now dry, the kitchen towel still held the faint aroma of Sally's loins. Ben fell asleep with the paper to his face.

Chapter 11

The weekend passed slowly. Whenever she was able, Sally snatched moments in mobile phone conversations with Ben. They made efforts to exchange light-hearted small talk, but there was little they could say, except to whisper sentiments of love. They missed each other desperately – so happy when together and so miserable when apart. Ben found each day almost unbearable, without the sight of his beautiful young woman. Despite Sally's promise, it was inevitable that if she were suffering the same pangs of unrequited love, her concentration in studies would fall apart.

He contemplated throwing caution to the wind, accepting that he was love-struck and facing the ramifications of a declaration to Margaret. He quickly dismissed the idea. Sally was far from being ready to face her mother's disapproval and he would risk losing her. But something had to be done. They couldn't go on like this. Their love couldn't survive on occasional phone calls, without knowing when they could next meet. He was now spending too much time in bars; mulling over this and brooding over that. The highlight of any day was the regular call from Sally's bed. How he wished that he could be in that bed with her, soaking up her love and returning it twofold.

It was a mid-week call from Margaret that came to the rescue.

"Hello Ben, how are you?"

They exchanged pleasantries.

"Michael is giving me a hard time, always going on about meeting up with you again. Sally seems to have accepted how I feel, but he won't let it go."

Ben interrupted her.

"Look, Margaret, I have no desire to become some sort of surrogate father to the Crew, but I do enjoy their company. I hope that one day you can move on from your loss, but in the meantime, no harm is done if they want to spend a day with me occasionally."

"No, I suppose not," she agreed.

Ben continued before she could have second thoughts.

"Tell Michael that I'll collect him at around midday on Saturday. Oh, and Sally can come as well if she wants to and, of course, you too if you wish."

Deceit, deceit, and more deceit – but that's how it had to be.

"O.K., that's kind of you, thank you, Ben. I'll tell them."

Ben replaced the receiver, hoping that Margaret would stay at home and that he and Sally would be able to snatch a few moments away from Michael. He had only his and Sally's interests at heart, but if her brother reaped some benefit, then fine. Michael was, after all, his lifeline.

The call came from under the bed sheets that night.

"Wonderful. See you Saturday… I love you."

The week couldn't pass quickly enough. Just to be in each other's company would be a small but frustrating compensation.

*

Ben arrived at the apartment block a little before twelve. He made a call from his mobile.

"Hi Margaret, I'm outside now. Send the Crew down, but you stay inside. I will come up; I would like a quick word."

Ben was waiting outside the main doors as the Crew appeared. He accepted a light kiss on the cheek from Sally without body contact and a playful punch of clenched fists with Michael. Ben feigned disappointment that Margaret wouldn't be joining them.

"Wait for me in the car," instructed Ben. "I'll just say hello to Mum."

The apartment door was open for Ben's entry.

"Hello Margaret," he smiled. "Sorry to be so mysterious, but I have some news that you may not want Michael and Sally to know about. Come and sit down."

They sat at opposite sides of the dining table. Margaret's expression was quizzical and a little concerned. Ben continued.

"You remember that I said I was feeling lucky?"

He passed across a photograph of a lottery ticket, followed by a cheque for €43,340 and waited for a reaction. Margaret's jaw dropped and her eyes widened.

"We won?" she gasped.

"Not the jackpot, I'm afraid, but runners up will do for now," beamed Ben. "I could have told you when I checked the ticket, but I couldn't believe it myself. I thought it best to first see the money in the bank."

"Oh Ben," sighed Margaret. "With the children in full-time education, it couldn't have happened at a better time... I can't believe it!"

"If you really can't believe," assured Ben, "check the winner's list on television. I promise that you'll find the numbers there and a figure of €86,680."

They rose from the table; Margaret threw her arms around Ben and wept tears of happiness and relief into Ben's chest.

"Are you coming, Ben?" demanded Michael, as he burst into their presence.

Margaret rapidly broke away from the embrace, always conscious of perceived disloyalty to her deceased husband.

"Where are we going, Ben?" asked an embarrassed Michael.

"Surprise," replied Ben with eyes wide open. "But bring your football."

In seconds, Michael reappeared with a World Cup souvenir ball from his bedroom and they left Margaret to gather her thoughts.

Ben drove to an adjacent resort and parked up outside the rowing lake.

"Great," yelled Michael. "I've used a kayak, but never been rowing."

The boats were quite small and he insisted that he have a boat of his own. His useless sister could be a passenger with Ben.

The lovers were not going to argue with that. Ben had said nothing, but he had been a member of a rowing club when in his twenties. The sport had given him strong arms and shoulders. Sally sat in the stern of the boat and they laughed as Ben rowed from the jetty like a professional oarsman, leaving Michael floundering about, catching crabs, and yelling, "Wait for me!" He could come to no harm; the water was no more than three feet deep.

Ben rowed at some speed to the far end of the large lake. As he rowed, the love-struck couple mouthed the words of love to each other. Ben moored in a secluded spot. He sat and took in her beauty.

"You are so, so beautiful," he whispered.

"I've missed you so much," Sally replied.

Ben wanted to kiss her, but knew that was out of the question. She was wearing a knee-length skirt, but for Ben's benefit had pulled it well up her lovely slim thighs. She parted her legs to arouse him. He had full view of her mound.

"Has *she* missed me?" asked Ben.

"Oh, so, so much. She thinks of you all the time," Sally said quietly.

Ben removed the deck shoe from his right foot. He stretched out his leg, his toes made contact, and Sally let out a long sigh as they worked at massaging her quim through the fabric of her knickers. Sally looked around to check for prying eyes. All was clear. Her hands went down to her loins, she pulled aside the fabric, and with fingers each side, stretched her labia wide, exposing for Ben the soft pink inside. Ben gasped in delight. He felt that he would faint. His bloodstream pumped his prick to bursting point and it swelled massively in his tracksuit slacks. Sally took his foot and positioned it for the big toe to work rhythmically against her clitoris. She looked down at her fanny, held wide open by her fingers. She groaned quietly.

"Where's Michael?" she murmured cautiously.

Jesus! Ben had become totally immersed and had taken his eye off the ball. Michael had somehow persuaded the attendant to swap his rowing boat for a canoe. He was making headway rapidly towards them. Sally could hear his enthusiastic shouts approaching.

"We have to stop," Ben apologised.

"I can't stop, please don't stop," Sally pleaded.

"We must," Ben insisted.

He took control and reluctantly withdrew his toe from her soft flesh.

Michael arrived as Sally regained her composure. She was still flushed and not satiated, but her brother noticed nothing untoward.

"What happened to your shoe?" asked the young nuisance.

"Oh, I caught it on the footboard," Ben replied, thinking quickly.

Had Michael looked further up his leg, he would have asked, "What's happened to your knob?" It was close to splitting seams. It was fucking enormous.

Sally and Ben worked hard at rejoining Michael's involvement in the fun of the occasion. It was difficult; there was only one thing on their minds. Michael paddled on ahead towards the jetty. Ben lagged behind. Sally reached across and touched his swollen penis.

"Ben, we have to do it."

"I know," he replied. "I'll think of something."

The attendant called time through the Tannoy. They left the boats, with Ben, hand in pocket, holding the beast under control.

Michael was despatched to the car to fetch his football. There was time only for a brief passionate kiss behind a wall, but no opportunity for sexual relief. They moved on to the adjacent parkland for a kick about. Michael dribbled the ball ahead. Sally and Ben touched hands when they could. It has been said that the best sex is either an urgent thirty seconds in a lift or four hours between satin sheets. Ben saw an opportunity and grasped it.

"Pass the ball, Michael," shouted Ben.

Ben took it in his hands and pumped it a good one hundred yards down a large grassed recreation area. Michael took the bait and chased after it at speed. Ben took Sally by the hand and pulled her quickly into an area of hedgerow and shrubs. His hands swept up her thighs and pulled her panties to her ankles. She stepped out of them, to be stuffed into his pocket. Quickly his slacks and underpants were below his buttocks. His animal towered at an angle of seventy degrees. He bent his knees and from below her buttocks, lifted Sally to his waist. She threw her legs around him in a tight grasp. Reaching down, she took Ben's hot throbbing penis in her hand and positioned the helmet at the entrance to her vagina. Legs straddled, it was wide open and already well juiced from earlier arousal. It had been days since their last sexual embrace and excitement was at fever level. She lowered herself on, and Ben thrust eagerly to full penetration. Their genitals went into a fevered attack mode, as though their very lives depended on it. Her arms around his neck, Ben with one arm around her waist, his other hand beneath her bum, the naughtiness of this fuck was intense beyond belief. Clitoris and helmet were screaming with pleasure.

"Come quickly and quietly," Ben whispered.

Through gaps in leaves, he checked on Michael's movements, still one hundred yards away, looking around and wondering what had happened to them.

Ben kept Sally informed.

"He's starting to wander back, so come whenever you can."

He pressed his middle finger gently to her bum hole. It triggered her orgasm. In turn, it triggered his. They muffled their voices as they erupted together in a crescendo of animal sex and emotional adoration. He watched the gradual approach of Michael as spunk pumped into the vagina of his sister. They wanted to stay locked, but that wasn't possible. He lifted Sally from his waist. The beast didn't want to be parted from its prey, but conceded with a gratuitous slurp. Ben handed over Sally's panties. She swiftly took a liner from her shoulder bag and adeptly positioned it in the crotch. Ben chose not to wipe himself with his handkerchief. His wish was to stay in the stickiness of their juices. There was just enough time for a brief but loving kiss, before surprising Michael.

They jumped out of separate bushes, with several loud "Boos!" He was quite startled, but took it in fun, after calling Sally a few choice names. Little did he know that in the few minutes that it had taken to retrieve a football, his sister had been fucked into a state of frenzy.

Your day will come, Michael, thought Ben, *and Margaret, there is more woman in your little daughter than you could begin to imagine… she certainly doesn't share your low sex drive.*

Sally and Ben could begin to relax and if necessary devote the rest of the day to Michael's interests. With sexual urges satiated, they would want nothing more than togetherness. The three kicked the ball about for a while. Sally kicked it away deliberately, for her brother to fetch.

"That was wonderful," she said.

Ben replied with a smile and a wink.

"We'll do it again sometime."

Sally sought further reassurance.

"Ben, how much do you love me?"

Ben thought for a moment.

"Sally, I have a confession to make."

She looked concerned.

"I can't imagine a life without you."

Sally smiled and mouthed those oh so familiar words. Ben responded with a blown kiss.

"Right, Michael – what now? Any ideas?"

The lad didn't hesitate.

"Tenpin bowling!"

"O.K.," agreed Ben. "But let's first feed the feral cats at Torremolinos beach."

He always carried cat food in the boot of his car. The furry things that greeted them were not short of cat-loving friends, but they always welcomed Ben's arrival because he usually provided tinned wet food in addition to dry pellets.

He observed the joy in Sally's face, as cats and kittens came to the bowls for meat and fish treats. She welcomed and involved small children that were drawn to the gathering. Her love of children was obvious and they were drawn to her natural affection. Ben dwelled for a moment on their inability to produce a child together. The expression of her lovely face was child-like and yet maternal in the company of the young children around her. It was a face totally different to that of the mature woman, who not long before had urgently mounted herself upon a muscle gorged with blood. She was part teenager, but mostly woman.

Ben was surprised that Michael too was somewhat enthralled by the cats, but was heavy-handed in wanting to handle them before they were ready for human contact. He became impatient.

"Come on, Ben, let's play footie on the beach."

Ben looked to Sally for approval.

"Go on, Ben, keep him happy. I'll stay with the cats for a while and watch from here."

With his insistence to meet with Ben, she knew how important Michael could be. Michael was being used, but it was vital that he should always want continued contact with Ben. If necessary, the lovers would stoop to any level in the interests of their love.

The boys kicked and headed the ball back and forth for some time. Ben looked towards the sea wall where Sally sat, happy to watch her men at play. A group of young men gathered to chat up Sally. Ben observed with interest; not concerned or jealous, but certainly curious. It seemed that she sent them packing fairly rapidly.

Mercifully, a young man of Michael's age joined them in play and after a short while Ben could excuse himself. He rejoined Sally on the sea wall.

"I see the boys can't leave you alone," he teased.

Sally's reply was delivered with some authority.

"They were Spanish. I had no problem getting rid of them. I was always getting chatted up at school and now in college. But I don't like Spanish boys… It's their dark brown eyes, they remind me of you know who."

It was a reminding statement of how deeply she had been hurt. Ben put his arm around her waist and pulled her close.

"Don't worry, you're safe now."

They sat for a while in silence. Passers-by would have taken them for father and daughter. That bothered neither of them. Ben spoke first.

"Not all young men are Spanish, you know."

Sally turned to him and raised her eyebrows.

"Don't tease, Ben, you know that I only want you."

How he hoped that it would always be the case. Sally's early life had been so badly damaged. She was vulnerable and needed constant reassurance. She spoke quietly.

"Ben… it's not just the sex, is it? You do love me for who I am?"

He desperately wanted to take her in his arms, but could speak only of his emotion.

"Sally, I will love you forever. For *who* you are… even if you break my heart, I will love you till the day I die."

98

She was reassured and placed her head on his shoulder.

She sighed.

"I will never break your heart, Ben."

She held Ben's hand and for a while they sat in silence again.

"Sally," enquired Ben. "Do you feel very bad about deceiving your mother?"

"Not really," she replied. "I'm grateful to her for all that she has done for me, but I'm no longer a child. I'm old enough to choose who I should love. Why do you ask?"

Ben's mind had been working overtime.

"Well, I think I should invent a lady-friend. You can understand why your mother is nervous about you being with older men. I think she would be relaxed about you being with me, if she thought I had a girlfriend."

"If only she knew," laughed Sally. "I think it's a brilliant idea."

"Hi guys!" Michael was back. "Can we go bowling now?"

"Let's have a cold drink first," suggested Sally.

They took a light snack and drinks at a nearby beach bar. Her mother had given her money for the day and Sally attempted to pick up the check, but Ben refused.

Chapter 12

At the bowling rink, Ben and Sally settled in one of the typical individual crescents of seating, whilst Michael busied himself entering the three names into the electronic scoreboard. He talked incessantly throughout and was keen to confirm his superiority of skills. He sent his first two bowls down the alley and was delighted with an opening score of nine. The lovebirds pretended enthusiastic involvement, but were interested only in being close to each other, touching hands and pressing leg against leg, whilst Michael was otherwise occupied. Michael was very fond of Ben, but not possessive. Any observed closeness between Ben and his sister would be perceived only as affection. In time, Michael would forego the use of his hand and, with hormones surging through his cortex, he too would enjoy the full extent of desire that his more developed sister felt on a regular basis. Her rapid sex amongst the shrubs had been glorious, but lacked the relaxed delirium that should follow. Her desire began to swell again.

Michael stepped up for the first of his second delivery of two bowls. After a furtive glance around, Sally threw her skirt backwards a little and sat firmly onto the back of Ben's hand. He turned his hand over and took her swollen mound into a combination of fingers and palm. Despite her panty liner, the crotch of her pants was slightly moist from their earlier lovemaking. Sally's joy was agonisingly interrupted by her presence demanded on the rink.

After a roll of just four of his twenty bowls and with the sudden development of backache, Ben asked Michael to bowl the remainder of his game. It was no surprise that Michael willingly obliged. Sally created a further delay whilst she visited the toilets.

"Come on, Sal," he urged as she returned. "It's your roll."

She delivered her next two bowls without any real commitment and from a very upright position. Her panties were now in her shoulder bag. Another glance around and she settled her demanding vagina onto the upturned fingers that were waiting to please her.

Four bowls later and above the clatter of pins scattering, Ben could hear her groan of frustration as she dismounted at the behest of her insistent brother. Whilst Sally bowled, Ben looked at the juices that glistened on his fingers. She returned her demanding loins to Ben's eager hand, but the constant interruptions of being called to bowl were becoming unbearable for her.

"Look," said Ben to Michael. "You are so far ahead of me and Sally, why don't you play the rest of the game on your own and try to get our scores nearer to yours?"

Sally added, "I don't mind, Michael, if that's what you would like to do."

Michael's eyes widened. This was turning into his perfect day. The day was also rapidly becoming perfect for his sister.

"Thank you, Ben, you really *do* love me, don't you?" whispered Sally.

Ben nodded. He could now devote around twenty minutes to nothing other than the pleasure of his young lover.

He manipulated his knuckles back and forth across her G-spot, being careful not to stimulate the clitoris too quickly. Keeping an eye on the scoreboard, he could time that for later. It was important that Sally should orgasm, but with maximum pleasure beforehand. If she wanted, she too could take control with gentle gyration of her loins.

With a careful and slight movement of Sally's skirt, Ben treated himself to a glimpse at the area of her buttocks' cleavage, working gently against his fingers. He thought that in the hedgerow earlier she had drained him of all sexual desire, but his penis was heaving in his pants again.

If only, for just a few minutes, they could be the only occupants of that building, he would throw her to hands and knees, mount her doggy style, and fuck her with fury. All other bowlers in the rink were absorbed in their own competitive enjoyment. They were oblivious to the level of ecstasy that a visit to the bowling rink could offer. Ben was careful to continue the deception, by shouting occasional congratulatory comment on Michael's successes. Even allowing for youthful naivety, Michael would have picked up on the status quo had he turned and found his sister and his friend in a state of delirium.

The scores were racking up. Ben withdrew his fingers slightly and moved his attention to the clitoris. Sally was now very wet. A few circular caresses were all that were needed to bring her to an intense climax. Her head went forward to her knees, her lovely bum quivered, and her muffled moans of delight were drowned out by the scattering of pins, the clanking of machinery, and the yells of enthusiastic, competitive banter. It was as though a crescendo of appreciation had been orchestrated to accompany her moment of nerve-tingling loss of control.

Ben slipped his handkerchief from left hand to right and pushed it firmly into her vagina. Sally sat up and noted that Michael was rolling the last few bowls.

She turned full face to Ben.

"Oh Ben."

"I know," said Ben.

Sally looked at Ben's penis, swollen in his slacks.

"I'm sorry," she said. "That was very selfish of me, and very naughty."

"It's the naughty ones that are exciting," Ben smiled.

Sally smiled back.

"That's true... it's not dirty, is it?"

Ben reassured her.

"No, precious, it's not dirty. It's called love."

Sally went off again to sort out her girly bits. Ben sat with elbows on knees, hands on face, feigning interest in Michael's achievements. Instead he was deep in the satisfaction of smelling the fingers that had been in Sally's wet cavity. She returned and with a smile handed Ben his wet handkerchief. It would be on his pillow later that night.

In the toilets, Ben smelt his fingers a final time before washing his hands. He arranged his tackle to a more comfortable and less obvious position and rejoined the Crew as Michael was bowling the last couple of bowls. Michael had tired, having bowled for all three, but proudly announced that he had managed to improve his sister's and Ben's scores significantly; but not enough to challenge his own outright supremacy.

"You're too good for us," Ben conceded, with a wink at Sally. "Come on, you must be hungry."

They made their way back to the home resort and decided on a pizza parlour. Ben over-ordered and couldn't finish his, but Michael's healthy appetite helped him out. Over colas and coffee they chatted happily. Michael talked mainly about college lecturers and his friends; those who he liked and those who were a pain. Sally chose not to talk about college. She preferred not to remind Ben that he was in love with a young woman half his age. She was contentedly quiet and a little pensive. Beneath the table she pressed her leg hard against Ben's.

"What are you doing tomorrow, Crew?" asked Ben casually.

"I've promised to help Mum tomorrow with washing and housework," replied Sally.

"Well," grinned Michael. "I usually play football with my pals on Sundays, but I could give it a miss if you want to take me to Puerto Banus to see the yachts and the cars."

Ben had engineered the conversation.

"Well, if it's O.K. with your mum, we could do Puerto Banus *next* weekend, but tomorrow I'm having a day out with my lady-friend."

Sally smiled knowingly.

"You've never told us that you have a girlfriend," said Michael.

"You've never been interested enough to ask," replied Ben with mock indignation.

"How long have you known her? What's she like?" asked Sally.

Ben continued the pretence.

"We've been together for about four months. She's very pretty, shortish, blonde hair – looks a bit like the young Britt Ekland, but even more beautiful."

Sally laughed.

"You could bring her along on some of our days out if you like," offered Michael.

"That's very kind of you," scoffed Ben. "She would be so pleased to have your blessing. But the truth is, she's not really a tenpin and football sort of person; she's more of a cocktail bar and fancy restaurant type. Bottom line, Michael, we'd have more fun without her."

"Why do you go out with her then?" demanded Michael.

Ben thought on his response.

"Well, because I'm a man and she's a woman."

Michael accepted the explanation without any need for a more detailed understanding of its depth.

Ben felt guilty that he was now involving Michael in the lies and deceit, but it also crossed his mind that Michael would be delighted if Ben exchanged "Britt Ekland" for his sister, Sally. If only!

"Let's go," said Ben. "If I get you home quite early, your mother may be more inclined to allow you to go to Puerto Banus next weekend – perhaps next Friday, as it's a national holiday."

Sally was quick to respond.

"Ben, it can't be Friday. The whole family is committed to going to Uncle Seb's fortieth birthday party at the grandparents' house."

"Boring!" groaned Michael.

"I know," agreed Sally. "We can't get out of it, but Saturday would be good, Ben."

It occurred to Ben how little he knew, or wanted to know, about their father's family in Spain. Uncle Seb, Sebastian, was Miguel's younger brother and, no doubt, another son held in awe by an obsessive mother.

They walked to the car; Ben and Sally hand in hand, Ben's arm occasionally around Michael's shoulder. On the journey to the apartment, Michael insisted on riding up front with Ben. It's that man thing – it mattered not. Ben and Sally looked into each other's eyes in the rear-view mirror.

Ben hoped that Margaret hadn't seen the warm hug that Michael gave him, before running off to the front doors. Any indication of surrogate fatherhood would be the kiss of death for them. He walked Sally to the doors and into the foyer. Michael had gone ahead. They grasped each other and locked into an urgent and passionate open-mouthed kiss.

"Goodbye for now, precious, I love you."

"I love you too, Ben."

Ben was almost at the car when Margaret shouted to him.

"Are you coming in for a coffee, Ben?"

Ben returned to her, but declined the offer.

"Thanks, Margaret, but I had better get going, the cats will be starving. We'll speak in the week."

Margaret smiled warmly.

"Thank you for the wonderful news today. I still can't believe it and thanks for getting them home early. I'll not be secretive. They are not ones to expect too much, so I *will* tell them about our lottery win. We'll speak soon."

Ben kissed her lightly on both cheeks and was soon, as promised, feeding his furry friends.

*

Back at the apartment, Margaret had given much thought to the issue of her children knowing of the lottery win. She had decided that news of the good fortune should be shared, but that it should be kept a family secret. For darker, self-indulgent reasons, she would be able to explain away the warm embrace that Michael had witnessed. Michael's initial shock at the news turned into manic celebration. His mother was quick to point out that a life-changing fortune hadn't been won and to expect nothing more than a modest treat. Sally simply sat shaking her head in disbelief. She joined her mother in congratulatory hugs, but instinctively knew that somehow Ben had conspired to help her mother through difficult times. She recalled that Ben had stated his wish to help, *before* they became lovers. She sat in awe of the kindness of her man.

*

At his home, Ben took a shower and cleaned his teeth. He placed his handkerchief on his pillow before returning to the lounge for coffee and brandy. What a wonderfully intense sexual day it had been for him

105

and Sally, but they were always robbed of those lengthy moments, to kiss and embrace with gentle emotion – those moments even more meaningful than the orgasmic climax. Those moments when you feel that you have fallen over a cliff – those moments when it hurts to be in love. Those moments would come. They must come.

Sally's whispered call came a couple of hours later.

"Hello my lovely man. I know your every thought. I don't know how you pulled it off, but there *was* no lottery win. You are so kind."

"I can't fool you, can I?" chuckled Ben.

"Thank you for a wonderful day, Ben, thank you for loving me and thank you for helping the family."

"Sally," urged Ben. "You must never feel obligation, in return for generosity."

"Oh Ben," pleaded Sally. "Please don't insult how I feel about you. Love has nothing to do with obligation."

"I'm sorry, precious," he apologised. "That was stupid of me. I know that you love me."

"Ben, I will love you forever. We'll speak soon. Goodnight my love."

"Goodnight Sally."

Sally was right – she knew how his mind worked and hadn't been fooled. Ben had bought a blank ticket and entered the winning numbers of the previous draw. The photograph that he had shown to Margaret conveniently didn't include the date of purchase. After another coffee and a little more brandy, Ben went to his bed and to his handkerchief.

He fell asleep pondering on how ridiculous it was to be besotted by a young student. He also wondered, could it be possible to be more desperately in love than he was? He thought not.

Chapter 13

Sunday morning found Sally helping her mother with a week's washing and ironing. She was careful to avoid Margaret having contact with her panties from the previous day – there were perhaps signs of overactive vaginal enjoyment.

"How much do you like Ben?" asked Margaret.

Sally flushed a little.

"I like him a lot. He's very kind and good fun."

"I've seen the way you look at him," said Margaret.

Sally stopped her.

"For heaven's sake, Mum, he's old enough to be my father."

Sally had misinterpreted.

"Oh I don't mean that way," said Margaret. "He *is* kind, and I'm so grateful that he pushed me into sharing a lottery ticket with him. A different man would have kept the full amount for himself, but you should know that I am not interested in Ben romantically, and he could never replace your father."

Margaret was kidding herself on more than one front.

Oh fuck, thought Sally. *Here she goes again. Will she never move on from her adulation of that pig of a father?*

"He's just good company, Mum. I certainly don't see him as a father figure."

Never was a truer word spoken. Sally continued.

"And Michael really loves to be with Ben, but he doesn't see him as a replacement father. He was devoted to Dad."

"And what about you, Sally?" asked her mother.

Sally swallowed hard.

"Well, I was always a mummy's girl, wasn't I? Oh, and by the way, did you know that Ben has a girlfriend?"

"Really?" responded a wide-eyed Margaret.

Sally continued with the deception.

"Yes, he surprised *us*. He's been with her for about four months. He told us yesterday, because Michael asked if he would take him to Puerto Banus today. Michael was disappointed that Ben is with his girlfriend today. But you mustn't worry, Mum, your son is more interested in cars and boats than he is in Ben."

Margaret was reassured by her daughter's words.

Sally set about organising.

"Ben has offered to take us all next Saturday, if it's O.K. with you, Mum. What do you think?"

"Yes, that would be nice – I'll speak to Ben later."

Margaret, no doubt, felt more relaxed that they would be in a location far less likely to be spotted by disapproving members of the Spanish family. Sally felt contented. Even with mother in tow, she would at least feel close to Ben.

Whilst Michael was away playing football with his pals, several hours were spent that day washing, ironing, and dusting. Despite her mother's blinkered outlook, Sally was happy to spend quality time with a mother that she loved. If only the woman could handle her daughter's love for the man of her choice. Later, on the pretext of needing a little fresh air, Sally telephoned Ben.

His line was engaged for some time, but eventually she got through to a very lonely man.

"Hello darling, I love you lots. Yesterday was heaven."

Ben was so happy to receive her call.

"Hello sweetheart. Well done – your mum has been on the phone and we've made arrangements for next Saturday."

"Brilliant," exclaimed Sally. "I'm only *really* happy when I'm with you."

They chatted for some time and she promised to ring, if her mum was involved with evening English classes during the week.

For her part, Sally was involved in various activities – tennis, netball, etc., but they recognised the risk of being caught out if Sally skipped any of them to be with Ben. A lapse in diligence must not be allowed to destroy their relationship.

The week passed slowly for both of them. Ben passed the time as best he could, looking forward only to the brief calls that Sally would make during her day; and of course, the nightly call from beneath the bed sheets. She hadn't missed one night since the declaration of their love. Sally kept her promise to Ben and dutifully concentrated on her study. That was mostly not too difficult, as occasional hands-on work experience within primary schools had begun. She adored being with young children. To their disappointment, Margaret had no after-school activity that week. They became desperate to see each other.

Friday arrived; just one more day before they could be together. It was another of those frequent saints' days, for which the region of Andalucía is famous – another excuse for overindulgence in the consumption of food and drink. For their grandmother, a devout Catholic, it was a huge celebration that she had managed to time the birth of her son Sebastian to a day of religious festivities dedicated to one of the major saints.

The party was in full swing when Margaret and the Crew arrived for the barbeque in their grandmother's garden. Sally and Michael had persuaded their mother to announce soon after their arrival that her children would be able to stay for only a couple of hours. Michael was involved in a soccer match and Sally was committed to play in a knock-out tennis tournament. In Michael's case it was true; he had taken his football kit with him. In Sally's case, she simply didn't want to spend countless hours amongst a crowd of noisy Spaniards, who would end up drinking too much. She confirmed the deception of her prior arrangement by having her tennis gear on board. Their grandparents' greeting was warm, but with less affection than had been shown to the two purebred boys of Uncle Seb and Aunt Rocio. Their grandmother's attitude towards Margaret had definitely cooled since that fateful day when she had been seen to demonstrate affection to a man other than Saint Miguel. For all the wrong reasons, it was a bridge that Margaret was anxious to repair. She was confident that, before the day was out, she could use the newly discovered information on Ben´s commitment to another woman to her advantage.

It developed into a gathering of more than family. With neighbours, it grew to around thirty people. It became very boisterous, with guests shouting over the loud Spanish Flamenco music.

Aunt Rocio was a very attractive native Spaniard, but a combination of not enough exercise and too much bread had left her carrying an amount of fat around her face, arms, and rear end that is typical of a mother who loses interest in her desirability. The birth of her fifteen, and fourteen-year-old boys may have contributed a little to her slight deterioration. Sally and Michael had little time for their cousins. They were very demanding of attention, plenty of which they received from doting grandparents. Sally didn't much like Uncle Seb, but largely because he reminded her of her father. In general, the Crew were ambivalent about how they fitted into the family. Even though from Spanish stock and now entrenched in the Spanish education system, they had spent most of their lives in the U.K. and considered themselves to be British.

The time dragged slowly for them. Michael made the first move.

"I have to go soon, Mum," he announced.

"Me too," added Sally.

She asked permission to change, went to a bedroom, and emerged as something more beautiful than anything that had ever graced Wimbledon.

"Hold on," said Uncle Seb. "I have to go for more beer. I'll drop you both off."

"That's kind of you," thanked Margaret.

They kissed their mother goodbye and left. Their departure was barely acknowledged by the crowd.

As usual, Michael grabbed the front seat.

"Uncle Seb, it will be best if you drop me off first, otherwise you will be going out of your way," suggested Sally.

"No, I'll drop Michael off first. Most of the off licences are closed today, but there is one open near the tennis courts."

Sally had no intention of going to the tennis courts, but she couldn't tell *him* that.

"Thanks, Uncle Seb – bye," said Michael as he slammed the car door.

"You can stay in the back," Sally was instructed.

Sally felt a little nervous, *but only because it's my father's brother*, she told herself. She had every reason to be nervous.

Sebastian knew the lie of the land well. He knew that throughout the day the whole local population would be throwing beer and wine down their necks. He drove to a deserted industrial estate.

Sally feared the worst.

"Where are you going? What are you doing?" she asked fearfully.

"It's O.K.," assured Uncle Seb. "It's just that you forgot to give me something."

He parked up and in a few strides he was alongside her in the back of the car. Sally had the face of a frightened deer.

"You forgot to give me my birthday kiss," murmured her uncle.

Suddenly his lips were searching for hers.

"No-oo, no-oo," she screamed, thrashing her head from side to side, avoiding the tongue that eagerly wanted to be inside her mouth. She pulled at his hair, but her delicate frame was no match for a man of his strength. He threw her sideways and onto her back. Grasping her wrists in one hand, he held them above her head. He sat across her and unfastened the buttons of her one-piece tennis dress. He parted the fabric to reveal her writhing body.

Sally wept and pleaded with him.

"Please, Uncle Seb. Please don't."

He ignored her and pushed her bra up over her hard breasts. His eyes widened like a wild animal as he savagely fondled her.

Sally struggled like a rabbit caught in a trap, as he spread her legs between his knees. She screamed and pleaded throughout, all to no avail. His hand tore the crotch of her panties to one side and he thrust his fingers into her vagina. He pumped his hand inwards and outwards in the hope that Sally would yield to desire.

"No-oo... no-oo... please don´t," she begged.

Her uncle was out of control. He moved to his zip, pulled out his penis and frantically sought to gain entry into Sally's body. As she writhed beneath him, she felt it brush against her thighs and then her vulva. He panted garlic-flavoured breath into her face.

"You filthy fucking pig," she screamed.

In desperation, she kicked out and her foot went through the side window of the car door.

Perhaps in realisation of a grave situation or the sound of an expensive repair to his Mercedes, her uncle ceased his attack. He dressed himself. He grovelled apologies. They were apologies that fell on deaf ears. When his false remorse was rejected, he resorted to threats.

"Say nothing. The family wouldn't believe you and even if they did, they would believe that you threw yourself at me."

"You bastard!" spat Sally.

She left his car sobbing uncontrollably. He threw her bag and racquet onto the concrete and left with tyres spinning.

Sally sobbed and wept as she buttoned her dress. She ran home to the apartment with her head bowed to avoid eye contact with curious onlookers. She felt dirty and that she wanted to die.

In her bedroom she sat on her bed and howled in distress.

"Why me? Why me?!"

She turned to the one man that she loved and trusted. Ben answered the phone.

Sally sobbed at the other end.

"Oh Ben… you said I was special… I'm not special."

Ben was instantly concerned.

"Sally, what's wrong? Tell me what's happened."

She could only weep. She was unable to speak.

"Where are you? – And where is your mother?"

Sally managed to convey that she was at home and that her mother would be at the grandparents' house for the rest of the day.

"I'm sorry, Ben… I'm so sorry… it wasn't my fault!"

Ben quietened her a little.

"Calm down, precious, calm down. Don't talk now, I'll be with you in thirty minutes."

He was there in twenty.

During the drive, his mind raced as to what had happened to upset Sally so much; and why wasn't her mother with her? He ran to the door of the apartment.

She fell into Ben's arms, still in a state of inconsolable distress. He held her tight and stroked her hair, but Ben could only allow Sally to speak in her own time. They sat on her bed, holding hands, as she gradually related the ordeal that she had suffered. The anger built in him.

Jesus Christ! he thought. *Eighteen years of age and she has just suffered sexual abuse for the third time.*

His reflex desire was to go to the grandmother's house and beat her uncle to a pulp. Attempted incestuous rape would carry a hefty prison sentence, but Ben knew that he couldn't make decisions for the family. He recalled Margaret's response to Sally's past rape, and for the time being acted on the alternative course of action.

"Wait here for a moment," he whispered to Sally.

Ben returned from the kitchen with several sheets of kitchen towel.

"Are you still wearing the same pants?" he asked.

Sally knew from her past misfortune what Ben was about. She removed her panties and placed them in the paper. Ben cringed at the damage that had been done to the leg elastic, when her uncle had ripped them to one side. He carefully folded the paper into a package to be placed in his freezer later that day. There would be more than enough DNA present should it be needed at a later date. Sally went to her bedside drawer and pulled on fresh knickers.

"O.K.," said Ben. "Now take me to that industrial estate."

Sally whimpered.

"Ben, honestly it wasn't my fault. I feel so dirty... do you still love me?"

Ben replied with tears in his eyes.

"Oh Sally. I know it wasn't your fault and it's a question that you never have to ask... I'll always love you, no matter what."

They held each other close for a while.

*

Ben pulled in to where her shit of an uncle had parked up. He took a few photographs with his mobile and gathered into his handkerchief broken glass from the door window; glass that could be matched to the Mercedes if necessary. He returned to the car and sat in the back seat.

"Come back here," he said quietly to Sally.

She sat to his right and curled up in a ball, seeking comfort. Ben put his arms around her and held her tight. He looked at her beautiful face, red eyed and puffed from constant crying – but beautiful nonetheless. She looked like a frightened, lost child. How could anyone bear to hurt her?

"I know it hurts," said Ben. "But tell me everything in more detail. Did he penetrate you?"

"Only with his fingers," she choked.

"I know it's a strange question, but which hand did he use?" asked Ben.

Sally paused for a moment.

"His right hand."

Ben trembled with anger as he interrogated Sally. He so wanted to kill that man. The questions continued.

"Where does he work and does he speak English?"

Sally looked concerned at what Ben might do, but answered anyway.

"He speaks very good English, because he has his own real estate agency and most of his clients are English-speaking. It's a small office called Casas a la Moda."

"I know it," said Ben. "It's one street in from the seafront."

Sally nodded. He continued.

"Most important of all, what do you want to happen now? Will you tell your mother?"

Sally looked at him helplessly.

"How can I?" she sobbed. "It would probably get out of control, I would get upset, and tell her about my father. That would destroy her and I don't know where things would go from there. Besides, at the moment she just seems to be obsessed with what the grandparents think of her... Ben, it's not fair! – Not when both of their sons are pigs!"

Sally broke into sobbing again. Ben cuddled her close, stroked her hair, and kissed her brow.

"It *isn't* fair," whispered Ben. "But I promise you that all will be well in the future."

"You promise, Ben?"

"I promise."

He silently vowed to himself that if he ever thought Sally to be at risk again, he would take her from the family home. If that involved removing Margaret's blinkers, then so be it. *There is only so much hurt that this girl can take.* Sally spoke.

"Ben, it may seem strange, but will you put your fingers inside me? I only ever want *your* fingers inside me."

Poor Sally – the horrific incident had resurrected all of her insecurities. She needed the reassurance of Ben's love. She needed to know that Ben would always love her, regardless of circumstances.

"I understand," said Ben.

She had done nothing to deserve the shit in her life and was in desperate need of his commitment to her.

He pulled her panties to her knees, Sally parted her legs, and Ben slipped two fingers into her warm vagina. She craved the feel of *loving* fingers inside her and moaned with delight as they caressed her clitoris. With his left hand, Ben released the buttons of her dress and took hold of her breasts; at first, the cups of her bra and then her flesh. His finger and thumb massaged her nipples, in rhythm with the middle finger of his right, gently rubbing her magic button.

He trembled with fury at the thought of her filthy uncle enjoying the touch of that very flesh; ignoring the pleadings of his niece. Sally mistook it for the trembling of desire.

"Do you want to make love, Ben?" she asked.

"Of course," said Ben, "but not today. I'll explain later, but for now you have a lovely come."

Sally didn't protest and, soon after, moaned as her body shuddered into a long and luxurious orgasm. It had been six days since she had felt the pleasure that Ben could deliver. She gasped as she wound down from the experience. She turned her head to place her lips on his.

She smiled gently.

"I feel better now. When you touch any part of my body, it always feels like love... I wish that we could make love every day."

Ben smiled and returned her kisses. He explained his refusal to make love. Despite the swelling in his pants, his overriding emotion was vitriolic anger towards her uncle.

She smiled again.

"Thank you, Ben. You are so special."

Ben helped to pull her pants back into position. He noticed a small cut on her ankle and the swelling of her wrists that would probably develop into bruises. He took photographs, before making a suggestion.

"If you are determined not to tell your mother and she sees bruising, you could perhaps tell her that you tripped when playing tennis."

Some years earlier, Ben had suffered similar wrist injuries when roller-skating.

They cuddled for a while, both deep in thought. Sally broke the silence.

"Ben, if I say nothing, there is one thing that bothers me."

He knew what was on her mind and stopped her.

"Sally... I know what you are thinking. Trust me. You have my word that your uncle will never lay a hand on you again."

She moved to speak. Ben placed his forefinger to her lips to silence her.

"Trust me."

"I trust you." She smiled.

They kissed gently.

"And now," announced Ben. "I am going to take you home, I want you to take a long hot bath, try to relax, and look forward to our day in Puerto Banus tomorrow."

Sally was calm and reassured. They travelled back in silence, content to place a hand on thigh or to hold hands. Ben walked Sally into the foyer of the apartment block. The events of the day had made him angry and non-caring of others' opinions. He took Sally in his arms and kissed her gently. She responded with a passionate open mouth. The tips of their tongues teased each other's.

He took her buttocks in his hands, lifted her, and pulled her mound hard onto his penis. He set her back on her soles. She looked up at him, her eyes softened with love.

"What would I do without you?" she said quietly.

"What would we do without each other?" replied Ben.

Sally giggled as Ben shooed her up the stairs. He blew her a kiss.

116

Ben embarked on a final mission before returning home. He pulled up outside Casas a la Moda to check the Saturday half-day closing time. After a couple of quick purchases at one of the beachfront souvenir shops, he was soon on the coastal motorway.

Chapter 14

Ben's first task on Saturday morning was to ring Margaret.

"Hello Margaret, something has come up – do you mind if I collect you all a little later? At two o'clock instead of one o'clock?"

"No, of course not," said Margaret. "Not a problem I hope."

Ben lied.

"No problem – a builder is coming to give me a quote for repairs to a garden wall, but he's running late."

"Fine, we'll see you at two then – bye."

Ben ate a little breakfast, but his gut was still churning with hatred and anger. At midday he threw his camcorder around his neck and set off. He parked his car well away from Casas a la Moda and walked the three hundred yards to the glass frontage. The interior was all but obscured by the dozens of property photographs displayed in the windows. Ben pretended interest in a range of villas, but was peering through the gaps. Fuck! – The slimy bastard was with clients. He was a stout man, balding at the temples, powerfully built, but barely taller than Sally.

He smiled large, yellow teeth and gesticulated theatrically to his potential purchasers. His friendly, over-animated demeanour hid the true nature of the disgusting animal within. The fury built in Ben as he pictured the man forcing himself upon Sally. But he must stay cool. He noted that the shops either side of the premises had closed for the day. *That's good,* he thought. The apartment above was empty and available for rental. *Even better,* he thought.

It was close on one o'clock when the clients moved to the door. Ben's heart furiously pumped adrenaline into his bloodstream, but he must show no sign of urgency. He fired up the camera and set it to record. Ben entered, to confront the situation that he had been planning. He pointed to an expensive villa displayed inside.

¨I see that you are about to close, but could you just pull out some printed details on that property?¨

¨Of course,¨ came the obliging reply.

The offender was about to become victim. Sebastian turned his back on Ben and moved to a large filing cabinet. Ben turned the sign in the door to "CLOSED" and quietly slid the lock. Whilst Sebastian rummaged through files, Ben positioned his video camera on a shelf and trained it towards the desk.

¨Ah, here we are,¨ Sebastian enthused.

He turned to face Ben.

¨Sit down,¨ said Ben calmly, motioning to a seat behind the desk.

Sebastian was surprised at Ben's tone and stood motionless. Ben reached for the first of his souvenir shop purchases. He revealed from his jacket pocket the butt of a fake handgun.

¨I don't have money on the premises,¨ Sebastian urged.

Ben replied calmly.

¨I will tell you just one more time… Sit down!¨

Sebastian obeyed. Ben continued.

¨You will listen to me in complete silence. You will say nothing without my permission. If you lie to me or give me any bullshit, I will kill you… I am Ben. I am a friend of Margaret and her family. To Sally, I am the nearest thing she has to a father figure.¨

The colour drained from the uncle's face to a jaundiced appearance.

¨Yesterday, you attempted to rape her and would have succeeded had she not kicked the glass out of your car door. Had you succeeded, you would now be dead. You boasted that the family wouldn't believe her if she said anything to her mother or informed the police. You are wrong to feel so secure – there is now, frozen in storage, the DNA on underwear necessary to send you to prison. Sexual abuse and attempted incestuous rape! For reasons that you don't need to know about, Sally has decided that she will not speak to the police or to her mother… But for you, the threat of that DNA and a promise of a prison sentence is nowhere near enough… Uncle Seb, you must be punished… Your fingers must be punished."

Ben pulled from inside his trouser leg, the second of his souvenir shop purchases – a short but heavy resin baseball bat.

Sally's uncle wept with fear and pissed his pants.

"Now you may speak," said Ben calmly.

"I'm sorry," Sebastian grovelled. "I didn't mean it to get out of control."

Ben stopped him and screamed, "I told you not to lie! You planned it. You planned it from the moment that girl got into your car!"

Sebastian continued to grovel.

"I'm sorry, Sally… I'm sorry."

He looked at Ben with fear in his eyes.

"Let me pay Sally some money in compensation," he pleaded.

He fumbled for a chequebook from his desk drawer and hurriedly put pen to paper. Ben spoke as trembling hands struggled to write.

"I haven't come here today to blackmail you. Sally doesn't want your money… She wanted your respect!"

"I know, I'm sorry," blubbered Seb. "But let me pay her anyway."

He handed over a cheque for twenty thousand euros. Ben put it in his inside pocket. He was delighted that the shit was grovelling for the camera – more evidence if ever needed.

Ben rested the bat on his shoulder and gave Sebastian instructions.

"Place your right hand flat on the desk."

He reluctantly obeyed and, sobbing throughout, pleaded with Ben. The uncle's fate had been planned and decided the previous day, but was sealed when he begged with the words.

"Please don't… please don't."

The very words that Sally had used.

The bat came crashing down from above Ben's shoulder. Sebastian didn't scream – he felt no pain. He was in shock – the intense pain would come later.

Ben moved to the heavy filing cabinet, tipped it, and sent it crashing to the floor. Ben pulled up a chair, sat opposite him, and watched him whimpering.

"O.K. Uncle Seb… you now have one of two choices. You can ring the police and ambulance and we will sit here together until they arrive. You can go to hospital and I will explain my part in all this to the police. I am prepared to face the consequences of my actions. After treatment, you can explain *your* part to the police, your wife, your children, and your parents. *You* can then face the consequences of *your* actions… The other option is that I leave before you call for an ambulance. You can explain that you were moving the filing cabinet, you tripped and stumbled to the floor, and it came crashing down onto your hand… It's your choice – you were attacked or you had an accident… What's it to be?"

"Accident," sobbed Sebastian.

Ben got to his feet and switched off the camera before speaking.

"If the cheque bounces, I will cut your penis off… And I suggest that you ring for that ambulance without delay. Your hand looks as though it's ready to explode."

Ben left and crossed to a bar, fifty yards up the street. He ordered a coffee, a very large brandy, and waited. Within minutes he could hear the distant sound of approaching sirens. Only medics arrived – no police. As the ambulance pulled away, he dwelled on the drama of it all. Sebastian's wedding ring had become oval from the impact. It would need to be cut from his finger. If his wife knew of the facts, she would never want it returned to his finger. Given the family history, she was fortunate to have given birth to boys and not girls.

Ben had always considered himself to be a kind man; certainly not a man with underlying violence in his character. He was a little unnerved by the premeditated level of revenge that the circumstances had provoked in him. He asked himself the question – *had Sally been fully raped, would he have been capable of murder?* The answer frightened him a little. He suffered no remorse for his actions and felt that a degree of justice had been achieved.

After more coffee, he made headway to collect Margaret and the Crew. He threw the baseball bat and fake handgun into the boot and set off, chewing gum to mask the smell of alcohol on his breath.

Chapter 15

He was a little late arriving at the apartment block. Sally appeared first. Her smile beamed as she welcomed him. She kissed him gently on the cheek. Michael swiftly followed and gave Ben a high-five and a fist bump. Margaret brought up the rear and offered her face for a continental kiss. The weather had turned chilly and all were equipped with topcoats.

"Sorry I'm late, but it won't take long to get there," apologised Ben.

"Did your builder turn up on time?" asked Margaret.

Ben had forgotten about the excuse of that morning, but quickly gathered his thoughts and answered immediately.

"Oh yes, no problem – he will have the quotation for me sometime next week."

They were all loaded up and about to move off, when Margaret's mobile rang. The conversation was in Spanish, but Ben's command was good enough to pick up the gist.

"Oh good heavens… that's terrible… how did it happen?"

Ben knew exactly the nature of the call.

Wow, he thought, *Margaret really did make some headway in repairing bridges yesterday.*

No doubt, Sebastian had done much that day to ingratiate himself to Margaret, fresh from having been astride her daughter with only incestuous abuse in his mind. It was unbelievable that a family member should telephone Margaret a mere thirty minutes after Sebastian's "accident". Her conversation ended a few minutes later.

"I'm sorry, Ben, but I don't think I should come with you. Sebastian has had a terrible accident."

For the benefit of all, she related what information she had.

122

"His car was broken into yesterday and now this… poor Sebastian!" Sally's eyes moved between her mother and Ben.

"I think perhaps I should visit him in hospital later on. Ben, if you don't mind, you take Michael and Sally for the day and I will visit Seb this evening."

Ben offered to drive her to the hospital. He was pleased that she declined. Margaret returned to the apartment and at least two of the occupants were content that she was not to be part of their day.

Ben drove away thinking how pathetic the scenario was. Here was a woman planning to make a sympathetic visit to her brother-in-law; a man who, less than twenty-four hours earlier, had pinned her daughter onto her back in an attempt to rape her.

Poor Sebastian indeed – *perhaps Margaret would like a necklace made from the fragments of glass in Ben's glove compartment!* He felt anger and frustration that Sally continued to protect her mother's delusions, at the expense of her own happiness.

Ben caught Sally's concerned face in the rear-view mirror.

She mouthed the words, "What have you done?"

Ben gave her a slow and deliberate wink.

A half-hour drive and Ben was parking up in Marbella. Much to Michael's frustration, Ben had decided that they would take the twenty minute walk along the seafront to Puerto Banus. Though viewed as an upmarket region, it´s well documented that like many other locations throughout the world, it has more than its fair share of poseurs and crooks. It wasn't a place that Ben was in any great hurry to visit. He could never quite understand why intelligent adult tourists on a two-week package holiday were drawn to gawp at other people's obscene wealth. Food, drink, clothing – you name it, it would be overpriced. He viewed it as a resort of designer sunglasses, sequins, and silicone tits. He could, however, understand why any *young* man like Michael would want to drool over expensive super cars cruising the resort.

They walked the coastal promenade. Michael went ahead, balancing on the sea wall like a high-wire circus performer. Ben and Sally strolled behind. Ben removed his topcoat and threw it over his shoulder. Sally opened her flared coat, took his elbow in both hands, and pressed against him as they walked. Ben loved the feel of her hard breasts pressed to his upper arm. He recalled his first dizzying experience of those swellings, when they stood together at Scampi's shrine. His penis swelled a little.

"What happened with my uncle?" enquired a concerned Sally.

"It's best that you don't know," said Ben.

They were quiet for a while, until Sally spoke again.

"Ben, I wish I were better with words… I don't know how to say just how I feel about you."

Ben looked into her beautiful eyes, he smiled and replied, "Simply *I love you* will do just fine."

She pressed her head to his shoulder and he inhaled the smell of freshly shampooed hair. Michael was becoming impatient and urged them to quicken their pace. They ignored him and strolled on in silence – conversation wasn't necessary.

Passers-by would take them to be family, which prompted Ben to speak.

"Sally, you *do* know that if people knew about us, they would dismiss you as a silly romantic young woman and brand me as a dirty old man?"

"I know that," she replied. "But *we* know that it's not like that. They can think what they like. It's what we think that matters."

"If only that were true," said Ben. "But I'm afraid that it's us versus society."

Sally frowned concern.

"You're not going to end things, are you?"

"Never," came his firm reply.

In time they rounded the corner onto the crowded Puerto Banus strip. Michael yelled delight and ran ahead. The protective Sally instinctively chased after him to warn her brother of the danger at the marina's edge. Ben didn't feel the need to run after them. He doubted that Michael was in any danger and smiled at the sight of a delicate Sally assuming responsibility for the safety of a strong young man. She had been protective of her sibling since early childhood and it was a habit not easily broken.

A young, attractive, Eastern European lady stepped from a doorway and spoke to Ben.

"Looking for action?" she offered.

Ben nodded towards the Crew.

"Not today. I'm stuck with the kids I'm afraid."

Sally had spotted the encounter. Ben arrived at her side.

"Who was that?" she enquired.

Her eyes widened when Ben mouthed the word, "Prostitute."

"Do you know that lady?" asked Michael.

Ben thought better of introducing him to a more adult world.

"No, she's lost her dog and asked me to keep an eye out for a white poodle."

Michael walked on, stopping to admire the yachts and motor launches of varying quality and value. He was oblivious to anything that others were doing or saying.

Sally was curious.

"What did she say, Ben?"

"Well… she told me the price of her various services, I said I didn't have enough money, but I would go back if I could borrow some euros from *you*."

Sally responded with a loud laugh and a playful whack around Ben's head. The issue of payment for sex led Ben to ask Sally a question.

"Sally, if I give you twenty thousand euros, will you be naughty with me?"

"Absolutely!" she laughed. "As naughty as you like!"

Ben produced from his wallet her uncle's cheque, made payable to S. Perez. Sally looked at it, speechless and said nothing. Ben quickly returned it to his wallet and explained.

"I wasn't expecting your uncle to attempt buying you off. I know that you don't want his money, but I accepted the cheque because if we ever need further evidence against him, it's an admission of his guilt. Besides, I think there's nothing wrong with you punishing him by enjoying his money… I would pay more than that for it not to have happened to you."

Sally's tears welled a little. Ben anticipated her response.

"I can't believe that anyone could love me so much."

Ben kissed her brow and continued.

"We must meet up ASAP and we will open a bank account... Come on, let's enjoy ourselves."

They strode out to join Michael.

"Which one do you want, Michael?"

"I can't make up my mind... All of them!" he yelled.

Nice young man, thought Ben. They strolled on, guessing what they considered to be the value of status symbols that rarely saw open water. Michael came up with ridiculously low figures.

"What about this one?" asked Ben, as they arrived at the deepest berth.

"Well, that's not really a motor launch," answered Michael. "That's more like a small cruise liner."

Ben corrected him.

"Wrong... that is the privately owned motor yacht of one man – the Sultan of Brunei."

As they walked its length, Michael, and even Sally, gasped at the beauty of the palatial, sea-going monster.

"So how much did that cost?" gulped Michael.

Ben shook his head and tutted.

"So much, that I couldn't hazard a guess."

"So what does he do for a living?" demanded Michael.

"I think he drills oil wells... Come on, Crew, let's have a laugh."

They approached the gangplank, where a member of the crew, in pristine white uniform and deck shoes, stood at sentry duty. He was probably a member of the security staff, but, stiff from boredom, was polishing brass fittings attached to ropes. Ben spoke with confidence.

"Permission to come aboard, Captain?"

The crewman turned to face Ben and lowered his sunglasses.

"Do you know who owns this vessel?" the crewman asked.

Ben kept a straight face.

"Yes, of course. Tell His Excellency that we'll not be a nuisance. We would just like to take a quick look around."

Sally turned and walked away, holding back the laughter that wanted to erupt from her lungs. Michael thought that it was a perfectly reasonable request and stood at Ben's side waiting for a response.

The astounded seaman's response was not in words. He threw his head backwards and puffed.

"I'll take that as a no then, shall I?" said Ben.

His question was answered with a slow nod. Ben would have preferred, "Fuck off, poor person."

They walked off down the quayside, Sally in stitches and Michael a little bemused. Michael wasn't stupid; he was simply pleasantly naive and not too streetwise. He appreciated the humour when Sally explained the cheekiness of what Ben had done.

"You *are* funny sometimes, Ben." Sally laughed as she hugged him.

"So where are all the cars?" demanded Michael.

Ben had taken visitors to Puerto Banus on several occasions, so could explain that during mid-afternoon the male poseurs were polishing their motors to a mirror finish and feathering off every last speck of dust. In time they would arrive, some with female companions. The ladies would have arranged every last strand of hair and bagged their silicone tits for the privilege of being driven around in circles, bored out of their minds. They would all come out to play later in the afternoon and throughout the evening. Ben suggested that in the meantime they should eat.

"After your lottery win, you can probably afford a Burger King," pleaded Michael.

Ben was happy to comply. He would give the Crew anything, but his background was to appreciate value for money. Globally, there was a limit on what the two big players could charge for a burger.

Walking down the strip, Michael spotted the young lady that had spoken to Ben earlier. Before he could be stopped, Michael shouted across the street and eagerly enquired, "Did you find your poodle?"

Her facial expression became a frown, which dissolved into one of contempt. Once again, Sally had to walk away, almost wetting herself with laughter. Ben stepped behind Michael and caught the whore's attention. He made a few gestures, which she eventually accepted as some form of apology.

"Come on, Michael, I'm hungry," demanded Ben.

They found Sally in a shop doorway, laughing uncontrollably.

"She's very pretty, isn't she?" said Michael.

"With my lottery win, should I treat him?" Ben asked Sally.

That sent Sally into further convulsions of laughter.

"I'm sorry, Michael," spluttered Sally, pulling herself together. "I'm not laughing at *you*. It's the situation... I'm going to have to explain."

They walked on. The delicate but more mature sister detailed the nature of the lady's work, and the funny side of "a lost poodle" dawned on Michael. Regardless, he seemed quite pleased to have encountered his first prostitute. It was one of those moments on which he could dine out, later in life.

They hadn't realised the extent of their hunger and ravaged through a second purchase of burgers, chips, and shakes. Michael went to the toilets. Sally spoke quietly and with deep feeling.

"Ben, isn't life strange... Yesterday was a terrible day; I wanted to die. But today, I feel so happy, I could burst into tears... It's as though yesterday didn't exist; you take away all the hurt."

As she spoke, she portrayed such adult beauty, but with the look of a vulnerable child.

"I thought you were no good with words," smiled Ben. "I *do* love you."

Michael returned.

"Anyway," he announced. "I still think she is very pretty."

He was maturing rapidly and perhaps those years of nightly cock in hand were coming to a close. His time was approaching when he could enjoy the smell of vagina on his fingers. Sally felt it important to speak seriously to her brother.

"Michael... we always have good fun with Ben. We have a laugh about the prostitute, silicone boobs and things, but you have to be careful about what you say to Mum. You know how old-fashioned she can be."

Michael understood. He would *not* jeopardise his time with Ben.

They walked slowly back to satiate Michael's need to drool over cars.

"So where's the strip?" asked Michael.

"This is it. You're standing on it," replied Ben.

Michael thought Ben was joking. They stood on a narrow one-way quayside strip of concrete, bordered by restaurants and designer brand shops on the one side, and moored boats on the other. The whole length was no more than two or three hundred yards.

"But they can't go very fast here," queried Michael.

"That's the advantage for poseurs," explained Ben. "With hundreds of tourists in the street, they have to travel at a snail's pace. That gives the onlookers a chance to admire, to envy, and to take pictures. They travel the strip, drive around the block, and do the same run... over, and over, and over again."

"That's O.K., I'll enjoy that," enthused Michael.

They sat at a table facing the road and Ben ordered coffee and cokes. The coffee, as usual, was lukewarm. Spanish waiters often choose not to understand, or to ignore, a request for *hot* coffee.

Michael's excitement grew with the revving of the first super car to arrive. Lamborghini was followed by Ferrari, by Mercedes, by Lotus, by McLaren, by Rollers, by outrageously Pimped Rides, etc. – different models and various colours – round, and round, and round the same block. Ben enthused for Michael's sake, but after an hour he and Sally were bored stiff.

"Let's go for a walk," suggested Sally.

"No way," objected Michael. "I want to watch the cars."

Ben settled the conflict.

"We'll do both," said Ben. "Come with me."

He paid up and they walked to the bottom of the strip, where the cars took a left, to head back to the start. Ben had come prepared. He sat Michael on a corner wall and handed him a pad and pen.

"Write down all the different makes of cars, the models, the colours if you want to, and how many lady passengers were yawning. Sally and I will go for a walk down the prom and we'll see you here a little later – agreed? Do *not* wander, do *not* get into trouble, and stay away from that prostitute."

Michael agreed to the plan but would have preferred Ben to have stayed with him.

Sally and Ben walked the promenade. They held hands, without need to speak of their mutual adoration. There weren't many strollers – they would be preparing to make their way to bars and restaurants, before perhaps hitting the club scene later. A few extroverts on roller blades were showing off their skills, but the area was free of huge activity. Ben saw an unoccupied bench, set back against a tall wall, and well back from the promenade.

He turned to Sally.

"Do you want to be naughty?"

"Yes please," she whispered.

"How much do you charge?" he teased.

"For you... for free," she smiled.

They walked to the bench. He sat down facing the sea. He positioned Sally to stand facing him. He unbuttoned the lower part of his topcoat, pulled down the zip of his jeans, reached in, and laid out his soft penis and his balls. Sally looked excited. He turned her to face the sea. His hands slid up her thighs to the waistband of her panties. He pulled them down to mid-thigh level. He glanced across to a newspaper that had been left on the bench. *This is becoming a union ordained by the gods,* he thought. Everything was falling into his lap. Now he wanted Sally's loins in his lap. Simply the act of preparing her body for sexual intercourse had sent the blood surging to his beast.

He lifted her topcoat and she lowered herself. His penis settled in the cleavage of her buttocks. He draped her coat over his legs, opened the newspaper, and placed it in Sally's hands. She began to understand the deception. Viewed from a distance; she was nothing more unusual than a woman sitting on her partner's lap, reading a newspaper. The beast needed only a little more arousal. In seconds it was at full extension. Ben took hold of one side of the newspaper. Sally's freed delicate hand went down to grasp the erection. She parted her legs slightly, lifted her buttocks, and placed the helmet in position. She worked it around her vulva and the knob immediately found its way past her lubricated labia. They groaned as it slid in one move to full penetration. They froze for ten seconds and sighed during those moments of the deepest union – it's only the sexual climax that rivals that moment. If it had to end there, they would both have enjoyed huge relief and satisfaction. It would not end there.

Sally closed her legs and his throbbing beast was held in a vice-like grip by her hot vagina. He pulled her knees around to his right. She sat sideways on his lap. She looked around before rocking her bum a little, back and forth. She set about fucking the side of his penis. She liked it. Ben handed over total control of the newspaper. He slipped his hand up Sally's sweater and blouse, pushed the fabric from her breasts, and fondled her warm flesh. Her nipples had swollen to huge and his fingers eagerly massaged them. He wanted her tits in his mouth, but that wasn't possible. He dropped a hand to her flat belly. Sally rotated her buttocks and his palm could feel his penis pushing against the wall of her abdomen. She gyrated slowly for several minutes.

He was *so* deep into the lovely creature. Sally moved to face the sea again and held the newspaper in front of her. The content of the print was of no importance, but the pretence made it possible to watch for intrusion into their lovemaking. Ben lifted her coat and skirt and took her solid buttocks in his hands. He leant back to watch as he pulled and pushed her wet loins backwards and forwards. Sally murmured low groans of delight.

"That's heavenly, Ben," she whispered. "That is so good."

At no time did the beast withdraw from the confines of her body by more than an inch, but it was distance enough to give Sally the friction she craved on her hard and swollen clitoris.

"I'm coming, Ben… I'm coming… I'm coming!"

Ben urged her on.

"You come, sweetheart. I'll wait… I want more time inside you."

She muffled her cries of delight as her body shuddered through an intense climax. The nerves in her clitoris were screaming for mercy. No mercy was offered. Her bum quivered and her nipples were at the point of explosion. She gasped, "Thank you, thank you… thank you."

"Oh shit," exclaimed Ben.

They had taken their eyes off the ball. Michael had spotted them and was approaching from the distance.

Ben spoke with urgency.

"Stay where you are, Sally. My dick is *not* leaving until my spunk is deep inside you."

He pulled Sally to a sideways position again and arranged her coat over his legs. She rocked gently again and encouraged him.

"Fuck me, Ben... fuck me."

Michael had broken into a jog and was almost upon them.

"Hello you two," he said loudly, as he plonked down alongside Ben.

Ben winced, gasped, and put his hand to his chest.

"What's wrong?" asked a concerned Michael.

Ben forced barely audible words from his mouth.

"It's O.K.... indigestion. Too many burgers."

Sally pretended concern, but knew what was happening. She could feel the spunk pumping into the depths of her fleshy tube. She was now so wet, the liquids could be running from her vagina. She rocked a tiny bit more.

"Me too," she winced, feigning indigestion.

She quivered slightly through a second orgasm – not intense, but worth the little bit of effort involved. Ben wound down and placed an arm around Michael's shoulder.

What a bizarre situation they were in. Without knowing it, and from a distance of no more than twelve inches, Michael had been alongside them and present during the fucking of his twin eighteen-year-old sister. He had been present at a moment of uncontrolled trembling, taking place beneath dishevelled clothing. He had been oblivious that, before his very eyes, he had shared the moment of his sister's vagina being flooded with spunk. He was unaware of the seven inches of hard throbbing flesh rammed into her female cavity. Had he breathed deeply, he could possibly have smelt their sex. Even more bizarrely, the three sat for the next half-hour as Michael talked at length about sports cars. With their genitals still joined in a stabbed embrace, Sally rocked a little whenever possible. It had been six days since their last coital embrace and Ben's erection refused to subside. It wallowed in a vagina that contained a sea of mixed love juices. The naughtiness of the event kept Ben and Sally fully charged up.

"Michael, do me a favour?" asked Ben. "Go down to that beach bar and pick up three ice creams. It will help my indigestion."

Ben handed him a ten-euro note and Michael willingly obliged.

With Michael out of earshot, Sally spoke.

"God, Ben, I feel so hot. It's because it's so naughty... fuck me again."

Sally's body had been blessed with the ability to enjoy multiple orgasms. Her demands would need to be fed with some urgency. Ben's sexual appetite had been fed, but he left the beast in place. He faced her towards the Mediterranean once more. Newspaper in position, his hand moved swiftly to her labia. He slid his middle finger inside to locate her clitoris. It had barely shrunk. He began with gentle circular motions. It enlarged quickly. He reversed the direction. He changed the stroke to in and out, then back to circular. Ben revelled in the moaned pleasure that Sally enjoyed. A few minutes had passed when Ben applied a little more pressure and quickened the pace. Sally gyrated her hips.

"That's it, Ben, that's it... rub my clit... I'm coming... I'm coming."

She wriggled and moaned, gasped, and dropped her head to her knees.

"I've come... I've come! ," she panted.... "Ben...I'm fucked!"

Ben laughed.

With no sign of onlookers, Sally got to her feet. Ben placed a clean handkerchief in the crotch of her panties and pulled them back up her legs. He nestled the vulva comfortably into place. With skirt and coat in place, she turned to face him. She smiled, held her breasts in her hands and showed them to Ben for a few seconds, before placing them back in the cups. She knew just how much Ben loved to gaze at her tits. She stayed in position whilst Ben struggled to put his still rampant wet beast into his underpants. He zipped up and all was as normal.

Who could have guessed that they had just fucked each other stupid? Ben spoke first.

"Sally... was that the naughtiest fuck in the world? Or was that the naughtiest fuck in the world?"

"Ben... that was the naughtiest fuck in the world."

They laughed out loud. It was fifteen minutes before Michael returned with ice creams.

"Enough time to have done it again," joked Sally.

Ben coughed and spluttered.

"Sorry it took so long, there was a queue," apologised Michael.

They sat side by side licking at their vanilla cornets. Ben and Sally held hands beneath the folds of her topcoat. Michael talked more of the cars that he had seen. Ben tried to be an enthusiastic listener, but what he wanted was the impossible. He yearned to sleep in a bed that night with Sally in his arms.

Michael suddenly changed the subject.

"What's your girlfriend's name, Ben?"

He almost replied "Sally".

"Ss-Simone... her father is French."

"And would Simone mind Sally sitting on your lap?" smirked Michael.

The question took Ben by surprise, but he replied nonchalantly, "I'm not sure, but I don't think so. Sally is my friend... and what about your mother, would *she* mind Sally sitting on my lap?"

"Probably," replied Michael.

"Then perhaps we should say nothing to either of them," suggested Ben.

"Agreed," replied Michael, with a fist bump.

Well handled, thought Ben.

"Come on," said Ben. "We've got a long walk to the car. We'll stop for a snack and drinks before home."

They set off down the promenade. True to form, Michael went on ahead, balancing on the sea wall.

"Do you think Michael suspects?" asked Ben.

"I don't think so," replied Sally. "But he wouldn't say anything anyway. He likes you loads and wouldn't risk not spending time with you."

Sally's delicate hand slipped into Ben's warm palm. He gently squeezed her fingers.

A woman of around thirty walked towards them. It was more of a stumble than a walk, as she struggled to master control of her six-inch stiletto heels. She was overdressed and had been too liberal when applying make-up. Her most obvious physical feature was the pair of huge suntanned tits that were bulging from her low-cut top. The appendages lacked any degree of softness – they were rock hard and resisted any possibility of a wobble. They were more like shelves on which her partner could set down a pint of beer. *Useful in a busy bar*, thought Ben.

She ignored Michael's gaze, but smiled satisfaction at Ben's interested evaluation. She passed by.

"Not real," whispered Sally.

"Absolutely not real," agreed Ben. "*Your* breasts are perfection."

"I know," laughed Sally. "Some of the lecturers, or as we girls call them, lecherers, spend enough time looking at them. But don't worry, Ben, they're *your* breasts."

Ben hoped that he would never need to smash the hands of teaching staff.

Back in the car and on the coastal motorway, Michael chose not to talk about cars.

"Be-en," he began. "The woman that passed us on the prom. Do you think her boobs were real?"

The boy was growing up fast.

"Not a chance – silicone implants," Ben replied with authority.

Michael paused for a moment.

"Mmm… You should get some, Sal."

"Never!" Sally screeched in horror.

"What do you think, Ben?" asked Michael.

Ben paused. The Crew suspected that he would have something philosophically important to say on the matter.

"I think that the issue should be defined in law… All breast implants should contain a little squeaky toy!"

Sally and Michael howled with laughter. Ben mused that it would certainly put some fun into foreplay. Sally spluttered through tears of laughter, "I've changed my mind… I want squeaky toys."

Ben smiled as he pictured a group of well-endowed women or drag artistes performing in the televised final of a talent show. With squeaky toys tuned through the musical scale, and concealed within their bras, their rendition of a Richard Strauss waltz would receive rapturous applause. He shared his thoughts with the Crew. Ben had no option but to pull onto the hard shoulder, as the car swerved along with their uncontrollable laughter. Through their tears, it took the Crew some time to explain to the traffic police the urgency of their illegal parking. The police moved them on without fully understanding the depth of the humour.

Ben parked up at a café bar not far from the apartment. Sally immediately went to the toilets. She returned, smelling lightly perfumed. She sat next to Ben and passed beneath the tabletop his wet handkerchief wrapped in toilet paper. He slid it into his pocket, before going to the gents. He took a piss, smelt his fingers, and washed his hands. He returned to the table where brother and sister were recounting squeaky toy humour. Sally was wagging her finger at her brother.

"I know, I know," said Michael impatiently. "We don't talk to Mum about some of the fun we have."

They shared a family-sized pizza with salad and drank lots of cola.

"I don't think that the prostitute had implants," said Michael.

"I think that you're in love," laughed Ben, ruffling Michael's hair.

Sally's mobile rang. It was Margaret ringing from the apartment. It was still quite early, but Sally told her mother that they would be home in around twenty minutes. Ben left the car parked up. He would walk them the few hundred yards to their home. The back streets were quiet. Michael walked ahead, perhaps sensing the undeclared love between Ben and his sister. Sally took Ben's arm in both hands. She stopped to window-shop at a closed-up premises. Her topcoat was fully buttoned. He slipped his hand and then his arm between a gap in the fastenings. His fingers and hand found their way past the elasticated waistband of her skirt. Sally parted her legs, just enough for Ben to nestle the crotch of her panties in his fingers. They walked on with Sally's mound comfortably settled in Ben's hand. He could feel the entrance at her vulva, but made no effort to arouse her. A fuck in a shop doorway would have been pushing it!

When people walked towards them, Ben's hand remained in place and they would turn to innocently indulge in a little more window-shopping. His hand gently cuddled in the warmth of her loins. Michael waited for them. Ben reluctantly removed his arm. They rounded the corner to the apartment block, avoiding physical contact. They entered the foyer.

"Come up for a coffee, Ben," Margaret shouted down the stairs.

Ben was curious and accepted the invitation. He hoped that she wouldn't smell Sally on him. Michael began to enthuse about his day in Puerto Banus, but before long Margaret darkened the mood, droning on about poor Sebastian's misfortune. She related the full details of his "accident". Poor Sebastian had been kept in hospital. He would need at least one operation to repair broken bones and damaged tendons. A doctor had told Rocio that her husband might not regain full use of his hand.

Oh, the drama of it all, thought Ben cynically. *Poor Sebastian!*

Ben wished Margaret no ill. Despite all, they enjoyed a close friendship, but how he wished that she would one day be enlightened. Sally had stayed in the background during her mother's storytelling.

"So he'll not be moving filing cabinets for a while," said Ben.

Margaret didn't question Ben's apparent lack of sympathy. Michael tried once more to involve his mother in the joy of his day, but she simply harped on about the distress that Sebastian's wife and parents were suffering. Ben thought back to when Margaret had no compunction about destroying the family life of Cliff and Jenny. *If it came to it,* he wondered, *could she summon the same vitriolic hatred for the brother of her beloved Miguel.* Sally was right – her mother was deluded, fragile, and susceptible to total destruction. Ben had to get out of there.

"I'm sorry to hear about all of this tragedy, but I really must go," said Ben.

"Of course, the cats," said Margaret. "I haven't made you a coffee."

"Don't worry, I'll have coffee at home."

"I'll see you out, Ben," said Michael.

Sally followed. Margaret stayed in the apartment, absorbed in thought, drumming her fingers on the table. The others said their farewells in the foyer.

"Great day, Ben, thank you," said Michael.

Ben gave him a little man hug.

"Great day, Ben, thank you," said Sally.

She gave him a high-five and a fist bump, laughed, and followed up with a hug and light kiss to his cheek. Her lips involuntarily brushed briefly onto his. Michael observed, but chose not to comment.

Ben walked to his car, smelling the toilet paper package that Sally had passed to him. How he loved her smell – More material for his pillow.

As always, the cats came running at the sound of tins being opened and crunchies being tipped into bowls. Ben went to the boot of his car, retrieved the fake gun and baseball bat, and dumped them in his rubbish bag to be collected the following day.

He lay in his bed, being certain on various matters of the day. He was certain that Margaret was in a state of total delusion. He was certain that he would do whatever it took to protect Sally. He was certain that he loved Sally beyond reason. He was certain that he would never want to make love with anyone other than Sally. He was certain that Michael would fantasise about his prostitute lady. He was certain that Michael would wank himself daft.

His telephone rang.

"Hello bed sheets," said Ben quietly.

"Hello my special friend – I love you… I'll ring you tomorrow," whispered Sally.

Ben whispered back, "Goodnight sweetheart – I love you too… so much."

Chapter 16

Ben spoke to his beast as he washed it in the shower the following morning.

"*You* had a wonderful time in Puerto Banus yesterday, didn't you?"

Just like Scampi, it didn't reply, but seemed to nod confirmation through a cloud of soapsuds.

Ben felt good. He enjoyed a full breakfast with several cups of tea. He was disappointed when the first call was from a friend suggesting a game of golf later that day. Ben lied about having sprained a wrist during gardening and declined the offer. He urged the caller to get off the line, claiming that he was expecting an important call. Sally didn't disappoint.

"Hello darling, could you collect me? I'm at the railway station."

"Of course," enthused Ben.

He hadn't expected to meet with Sally that day and was excited at the prospect of being with her, without the need to sneak around looking over shoulders. She beamed her wonderful smile as Ben's Ferrari roared menacingly to a halt. She was equipped with sports bag and tennis racquet. Ben had no need to ask what her mother thought her daughter was doing that day. He placed her bag and racquet in the boot. Young men watched as she took her place alongside Ben and fastened her harness.

Were they admiring the sleek lines of his motorcar or the way in which the cross belt parted her lovely young breasts?

He drove off, but pulled into the kerbside just a hundred yards further on. He released his harness, leaned across, took her in his arms, and kissed her open mouth passionately. Sally responded with a wriggle of her tongue. Her sweet breath smelt of mint chewing gum.

She pushed Ben away slightly.

"Ben, my period started this morning. I just wanted to be with you. I hope you don't mind."

Ben didn't mind – he would be happy to spend hours just looking at her.

"It's wonderful to be with you at any time," Ben reassured.

In the front garden Sally played with the cats for a few minutes before joining him in his kitchen. Ben was pouring fresh orange juice into tall glasses. He stopped to take her in his arms. They held on closely, enjoying each other's freshness of shower gel and shampoo. Ben took her face in his hands and leaned back to look at her. Not a trace of make-up – her young face needed no enhancement. He felt that he could drown in the loveliness of her large blue-grey eyes. He looked down at her slightly parted mouth and planted gentle kisses. She returned them with an occasional movement of her tongue around his lips.

Sally was dressed in a pink one-piece tennis dress, white ankle socks, and plimsolls. To protect her modesty during her train journey, she had chosen to wear a mid-length skirt over the tennis dress. She unzipped the skirt, stepped out of it, and threw it to the back of a chair.

"Anyone for tennis?" she laughed.

Ben laughed with her, but was mesmerised by her beauty in the simple but perfectly fitted attire. Sleeveless, with a high neck and collar, zipped at the back from neck to mid-buttock, the dress revealed little for the eyes, but a lot for the imagination. It *did* reveal her beautiful slim legs. The tiny skirt fell beautifully from her rounded buttocks and settled just four inches below. Sally put her arms around Ben's neck and settled her body against his. Ben responded with a grasp of her buttocks into his hands. He pulled her upwards; close and hard. He pictured spectators gathered around her local tennis courts. Spectators with no interest whatsoever in the game of tennis. What right had he to love this girl and have her return that love? She could take her pick of any man.

They took their drinks to the lounge.

Ben had been watching one of the series of Formula One Grand Prix when Sally had telephoned and had forgotten to switch off before leaving to collect her. He reached for the remote, but Sally stopped him.

"Leave it on, I know you like to watch motorcars," said Sally obligingly. Ben obeyed, but muted the audio.

Sally curled up alongside him and he cuddled her, as he would a child. Ben smelt at her hair and kissed her head as they talked of their love and what the future might hold for them.

"I wish I could live with you, Ben," she whispered.

Ben wished for the same. He was unsure of where their long-term relationship was going, but knew that, at this stage, cohabitation was out of the question. Sally winced.

"Period pain," she groaned.

Ben stood her up and then settled her on his knees facing the television. He unzipped the full length of her dress. His hands had never done manual labour, but they were strong. Sally enjoyed their warmth, firmly massaging her shoulders and neck. Ben skilfully used his thumbs to apply pressure to her shoulder blades and upwards into the nape of her long neck.

"Mmm… that's nice," she murmured quietly.

Ben moved the attention of massage to her back and sides, his thumbs applying pressure to either side of her spine and down firmly to the upper area of her buttocks. Sally's hands reached around and released the clasp of her bra. To Ben's eyes, the form of her naked back, reducing to a slim waist before curving outwards again to a rounded rump, was almost as sensual as her front. Ben had a swelling and needed to have her breasts in his hands. His head swam with desire as he cupped their firmness. He kissed her back as his fingers moved to her swollen nipples. Sally winced more strongly than before.

"Damned periods," she said.

"I'll get you a painkiller," said Ben.

She didn't object and followed him to his bathroom. She swallowed the pill and washed it down with a little water.

"It will help to stand for a little while," said Sally.

Ben cuddled her gently for a while, before lifting her to stand on the surround of the shower base. Her eyes were now almost level with his and she placed her head on his shoulder, with arms beneath his armpits and around his back. Her abdomen pressed against his. She could feel the swelling in his pants and pressed her mound firmly against it.

"I think I could come just rubbing against you," Sally whispered.

"I'm surprised that there's an orgasm left in you after yesterday," Ben teased.

Sally giggled.

"Yesterday was wonderful, Ben. But I think I'll always be able to find another climax for you."

She continued to use Ben's beast to pleasure herself.

"We can do better than this," said Ben, returning her feet to the floor of the bathroom.

"If you're wearing a tampon, take it out," he added, as he left the room.

He returned with a small plastic footstool that had been in the shower cubicle of another bedroom. His own cubicle contained an identical stool. The toilet cistern was filling with water. The restrictive article had already been washed away. Sally looked at the stool in Ben's hand and wondered what he had in mind. She trusted him implicitly. Ben slid the dress from her shoulders and dropped it to the marble flooring. Sally stepped out of it and it was joined by the loosened bra. Her panties were already on the floor. Ben speedily removed his own clothing as Sally removed footwear. He stepped into the shower cubicle and positioned the two footstools in the corners of the narrowest end of the base.

He took Sally by the hands and invited her in. He lifted her naked body and placed her, one foot on each stool. Now positioned with legs straddled, her head was a few inches higher than his. She placed her hands on Ben's shoulders. His mouth moved urgently to her breasts and nipples. He loved those hard tits so much he wanted to bite them off. She moaned pleasure as her nipples and labia swelled. The removal of her tampon had left her vagina a little dry, but her sliding juices were already beginning to lubricate her cavity. Ben's beast was at full tilt, but he knew he must be gentle. He took the throbbing flesh in his hand, bent his knees, and worked the helmet around her vulva and fanny lips. Straddled as she was, across the width of the cubicle, the entrance to paradise was slightly open, but Ben waited until he could feel the first welcoming texture of lubrication on his helmet. It soon came and he straightened his legs slowly to satisfy his helmet's insistence.

Sally groaned with pleasure.

"Is it alright to do this, Ben?" she asked.

"It's alright with me, if it's alright with you. I'll stop if you have period pain," replied Ben.

"Ooh. It's fine with me," she sighed.

Ben returned his mouth to her breasts. He licked their roundness and worked his tongue around large pink nipples. He felt that he wanted to be suckled. They moaned and gasped desire. The beast was halfway home and wouldn't be denied the delight that full penetration would bring. Ben looked down at their union. A little blood seeped from Sally's vagina and trickled down her inner thigh. He took Sally by the waist and supported her weight. She bent her knees slowly and slid gently down to engulf the whole of Ben's animal to its base. She stayed there, impaled, and groaned loudly.

"Oh Ben... I adore you."

"If you knew how much I love you," gasped Ben.

For some time they stayed locked, kissing gently, with tongues working a gentle rhythm. The intensity of love spread through their fused bodies and their loins demanded action. With straightening and relaxing of the knees, Sally worked her clitoris along the available seven inches. She looked down. The blood was running down her legs. Her rock-hard magic button hadn't been exhausted the previous day.

"I have to stop already, Ben," she pleaded. "I'm coming."

Ben allowed her to rest.

"We'll do it slowly and full length," suggested Ben.

Sally lifted off; Ben bent his knees and withdrew to the point of helmet at vulva. They synchronised their movement of up and down, in and out, and continued with slow penetration from helmet to base. Sally gorged her desire on the full length and girth. Her vagina sucked at the seven inches of length and the six-and-a-half-inch circumference that stretched her entrance tight. They murmured pleasure.

Sally spoke.

"Slower, Ben, or I'll come… I want it to last forever."

Ben obeyed. He watched the reflection of her movements in the glass screens. She looked like a lap dancer that actually enjoyed her occupation. The tactic lasted only a couple of minutes, until a nerve ending in Sally's clitoris decided it would wait no longer.

"Aah… aah… same speed, Ben… aah… aaaah."

Ben kept the same rhythm. Sally's climax went on and on. She screamed throughout. Her screams settled to groans as her orgasm subsided. At full penetration, with circular gyrations on the base of the beast, her mound pressed hard against Ben's pelvic bone. Her full body weight collapsed into Ben's arms.

"Why did I apologise for having a period? That was fabulous," she panted.

Ben smiled and kissed her lips gently. They looked with pleasure at the union of genitals. There was menstrual blood everywhere; down their legs and into the shower tray.

Always quick to see the funny side of things, Ben spoke.

"Fucking hell, Sally – it's like a scene out of *Psycho!*"

Sally laughed and laughed, and with each convulsion, her vagina grabbed him harder.

"I want to see my penis enter you," said Ben.

He bent his knees, withdrew his erection, and lifted her from the stools to the shower base. More blood flowed down her legs. He turned her to face the tiled wall. She grabbed a wall handle with both hands, arched her back downwards, parted her legs, and offered up her vagina to the beast. Her labia were swollen and red with blood. He bent his knees to gain entry and went to full penetration. He stopped to enjoy the moment.

"Does that feel nice?" murmured Sally.

"You have no idea," replied Ben quietly.

A few long strokes and Sally spoke again.

"I know it's greedy, Ben, but if you do it slowly, I might come again."

"I'd like that… and I have no doubt that you *will* come again," said Ben.

With knees bent and his bollocks swinging in fresh air, he had the stance of a large dog desperate to shag the arse off a small bitch on heat. That didn't matter – it was pure animal lust. Ben took her hips in his hands. The length of his erection moved slowly in and out. With each inward thrust, Sally's labia sought sanctuary within the confines of her vagina. On withdrawal, the swollen lips reappeared. He pictured a sea anemone hungrily devouring its prey. Happy to be consumed, the beast would *not* put up a fight. Ben gazed in awe, as he used the fabulously curved body before him to satisfy his shameless craving. He moved his hands to lightly cup her breasts – they were firm and swinging gently in sync with the rhythmic thrusting of his loins. Sally's nipples had either not settled or were re-aroused. They were large and rock-hard. Sally was moaning again. She too shamelessly enjoyed the animal desire.

"I'm going to come soon," gasped Ben.

Sally whispered breathlessly her reply.

"Yes. You come, my love… I'll come with you."

Ben kept the strokes long, but quickened the pace. Both began to howl as clitoris and helmet enjoyed the friction. Ben ejaculated first. He grunted like a pig as he climaxed and his semen poured and oozed into her vagina. It felt that the spunk was being sucked from him.

Sally urged him, "Fuck me, Ben… fuck me hard… fuck my cunt!"

With due deference to Ms. Greer, there are times when the "C" word is not offensive – often used with contempt, but sometimes with love and desire.

Ben straightened his trembling legs, lifting her feet from the shower base. She couldn't have escaped had she wanted to. She squealed like a stuck pig, her legs thrashing in mid-air, as her cavity ravaged his penis. She blissfully achieved the second orgasm that she so wanted. Ben withdrew, turned her to face him, and lifted her back onto his organ. Sally wrapped her legs tightly around him, her arms around his neck, and her breasts pressed to his chest. She clung in that position as Ben sat onto the porcelain base of the shower cubicle. They panted approval of each other. They gathered their breath.

"Not as naughty as yesterday," said Ben.

"Have we just been a bit dirty?" asked Sally.

"Absolutely not," retorted Ben. "Some people might find it offensive, but there is nothing that you can do or say that would disgust me. I love you... I love every cell of your body."

Ben looked around the porcelain base.

"Especially your *red blood* cells."

Sally laughed. She loved his sex. She loved his humour. She loved Ben.

They sat in a mix of love juices and Sally's blood for ten minutes whilst the beast softened. Ben lifted her off and sat her facing him on his thighs, her legs straddled wide.

He reached for the flexible hose and ran water from the showerhead directly into the waste until it was lukewarm. He directed water at Sally's loins. She parted her legs further and more blood and liquids of love trickled from her vagina. The sprayed jet of water washed them from within her body, forming a swirling vortex beneath them. He directed the jet at his softening penis. It looked as though it had been in a cockfight. Sally lifted her hair and Ben washed her tits; bloodied from Ben's handling of beast and breast. They sat, surrounded in pooled pink water. They got to their feet and hosed blood from Sally's buttocks and each other's legs. The water turned a deeper shade of pink.

"Perhaps I'll just leave it and tell Juanita I cut myself shaving," said Ben.

Sally laughed loudly and more blood was pushed from her vagina.

"Maybe I'll name this en-suite 'The Abattoir'," he joked.

Sally laughed louder. The water drained and they hosed their feet.

"The weeping of a disappointed womb," philosophised Ben.

"Aw Ben... what a lovely way to describe a woman's period," said Sally quietly.

They dried off and Ben redressed in underpants and slacks.

"Ben, would you get my sports bag from the car please?"

He knew, of course, what she needed. He returned a few minutes later.

"Let me do it," he suggested.

Though there were no holds barred between them, Sally was a little surprised that Ben would want to replace her tampon. She agreed

146

without question. This was a first for Ben and he willingly took instructions from Sally. She sat straddled on the toilet whilst Ben gently inserted the tube. He withdrew it slowly, leaving the white string hanging from her vulva.

"Perfectly executed," he boasted. "Oh look, Sally, your pussy has gobbled up a little white mouse. Its tail is hanging out."

Sally giggled. Ben put the tube behind his ear.

"I'll smoke that later," he added.

Sally laughed and laughed.

"Ben, you're crazy... and I love you for it."

Ben loved the sound of her laughter. More than for anyone he had known, the joy of life was long overdue. Sally positioned a fresh liner and pulled on her panties. Ben removed his slacks, took her by the hand, and led her to his bed. They lay in each other's arms, perfectly content to be silent.

A while later, Ben realised that Sally had become very still. She had fallen fast asleep. He released his arms from around her and sat at the end of the bed. She had the innocent beauty of a child at rest. What a beautiful sight. He fetched his digital stills camera and framed her face and shoulders in the viewfinder. The natural light from his bedroom window added a softness to the lovely image that he captured. He looked at her body for some time. He had viewed every square inch of her and at no time had he seen a single imperfection; not a mole, not a freckle. Even her small, perfectly manicured feet invited sensual attention. She was perfection.

He should wake her, but allowed her to sleep. He dressed and went to the kitchen to brew tea.

Time passed and Ben thought perhaps Margaret would be fretting. He found Sally, still in a state of contented rest, but woke her with gentle words and light kisses to her mouth.

"Mmmm," she sighed as she came around.

She didn't start or jump. She recognised his presence immediately. She *did* jump when she saw the time on the bedside clock.

"I must be going," she said, a little blearily.

Sally was one of those fortunate people who are wide awake soon

147

after sleep. She dressed quickly and joined Ben in the lounge. She was thirsty and drank the orange juice that Ben had poured three hours earlier. Ben showed her the photograph that he had stolen whilst she slept.

"You are gorgeous," he whispered.

Sally smiled.

Ben decided that he would drive her home, but park away from the apartment block. To avoid attention, he bypassed the Ferrari and picked up the keys to his Audi. He gave Sally instructions as he drove.

"Tomorrow, I want you to leave college at lunchtime. Severe period pains would be a good excuse. I'll collect you and we'll open a bank account in your name. Your uncle's cheque must be cleared as soon as possible."

"Ben," Sally began. "You remember that I told you that some of the lecturers leer at us girls..."

Ben looked concerned.

"I haven't said anything to you because I didn't want you to worry. But I think one of them is stalking me."

Ben listened. She continued.

"I have seen the same man several times when I get home from college, sitting in his car, parked near to our apartment. He was there again today when I left. I think I've also seen him at the tennis courts. He always wears a cap and sunglasses. I'm not in any of his classes, but I'm almost sure that it's one of the biology teachers from the later grades."

Ben was silent and deep in thought, but eventually spoke, with a little anger in his voice.

"Firstly, Sally, if ever you feel threatened in *any* way, you *must* tell me *immediately*! How can I protect you if you keep me in the dark? ...Now then, the next time you see him, telephone my mobile. Tell me the colour of his car and try to get at least part of his car registration number. Stay outside the apartment and sit on the bench in the courtyard. Leave the rest to me."

Sally was worried.

"Ben, you won't get yourself into trouble, will you?"

"Don't worry," said Ben.

"If it's who I think it is," said Sally, "it's a yellow car and the number I can get from the staff car park."

Jesus Christ, thought Ben. *Why won't these perverts leave her alone?*

He had promised himself that if Sally were ever at risk again, he would take her from the family home. He must know the truth of what was going on and take the necessary action.

They arrived near the apartment. Sally pointed out the spot where the yellow car normally parked. They hugged, kissed their farewells, and arranged to meet the following day to open Sally's bank account.

*

"Where have you been?" demanded her mother, as Sally entered the lounge. "Your friend Maria telephoned asking why you hadn't turned up for tennis today. She rang your mobile, but it has been switched off all afternoon."

"It wasn't a definite arrangement," replied Sally. "I *was* going to play, but changed my mind, I didn't feel well enough."

"So where have you been?" her mother demanded again.

"I have been walking. We all have needs, Mother, and sometimes I need to be alone," came the terse reply.

Margaret wouldn't let it go.

"So who have you been with?"

Sally became angry at the inquisition.

"I am not a child, Mother. I have been alone. Where do you *think* I've been? – Off having sex during a heavy period?!"

Sally almost choked on the words. Margaret felt guilty that she had doubted for one moment her daughter's integrity.

"I'm sorry, darling," said her mother quietly.

"I'm sorry I shouted," replied Sally, kissing her mother's brow.

There was a long pause, whilst Sally removed items from her sports bag.

"Talking of sex," said her mother. "Are you at a time when you should be on the pill?"

"Mum, I'll know when it's time."

Sally went to her bedroom, regretting the list of lies she had been forced to tell.

*

Ben was restless that evening. Other men's devious lusting troubled him greatly. He imagined Sally in similar circumstances to those with her uncle. If he were not careful, the only time that he would get to see Sally would be during prison visiting hours. He must think long and hard about what action to take. He felt more relaxed after they had spoken their nightly bed sheets words of love. He reminded Sally to bring her passport and Spanish NIE registration number. They would be needed to open an account.

Chapter 17

The following day, Ben visited Casas a la Moda. A notice in the window read:

APOLOGIES FOR THE INCONVENIENCE.
TEMPORARILY CLOSED DUE TO ILL HEALTH.

Sebastian was evidently still hospitalised or laid up at home. Ben dialled the mobile number advertised on the office frontage, hoping that it would be Sebastian that would pick up. Ben recognised his voice and spoke calmly and deliberately.

"Today, Sally will be banking the cheque. If you receive a call from your bank, you will confirm that everything is in order. Do you understand?"

"I understand," came the subdued reply.

Ben and Sally met, as arranged. She looked as sensuous in plain daywear as she did in a tennis dress. She jumped in alongside Ben and passed to him the information that he needed on the yellow car. They had begun to throw caution to the wind and embraced passionately. Ben inhaled the smell of her lightly perfumed body and kissed her gently around her mouth. It was a mouth that invited the caress of lips, just as much as it invited urgent pressure. He broke away from their loving; there was business to be done.

Ben had studied the cheque. He drove off and ten minutes later was parked near the very branch that Sebastian used. He explained to Sally that he had spoken with her uncle earlier and assured her that there would be no problems. He coached her on what she should say, but Sally was having second thoughts. She was reluctant to cash the cheque; she didn't want her uncle's money.

Ben insisted.

"Even if you never cash one cent of this money, it's important evidence of his guilt."

Sally understood the importance, because she had been dwelling on the possibility that her uncle may one day make trouble for Ben.

She approached the cashier nervously and handed over the cheque, her passport, and her NIE number.

"I'd like to open an account please," she began confidently.

"This is quite a large amount," the cashier said, eyeing the cheque and then Sally's youth.

"Yes – it's a gift from my very generous uncle, to help through my four years in teacher training," said Sally, trying desperately to remain calm. The cashier walked off and spoke to a more senior employee. Sally became twitchy. The cashier returned.

"I've spoken with the manager. We'll accept the cheque and do the paperwork, but because it's a large amount, we'll have to check with your uncle before we can transfer the funds."

"That's fine," said a relieved Sally. "You'll have to speak to him on his mobile. He had an accident and he's in hospital at the moment. He hurt his hand badly, but I'm sure he could take a call. I have his telephone number if you want it."

The cashier left and spoke with the manager again. Was it Sally's imagination or was this woman very suspicious? She wanted to run from the building, but held her nerve. Sebastian operated a successful business and was known at a personal level in that small branch of a large bank. The manager made a call whilst the paperwork was being prepared. Some minutes later he approached. He smiled at Sally and instructed the cashier.

"A nasty accident your uncle has had. Everything is in order."

With paperwork completed, the cashier smiled and spoke to Sally.

"Do you want monthly or quarterly statements?"

"I'll not need statements," smiled a relieved Sally.

"Your passbook will be ready at the end of the week. Enjoy college."

"Thank you," said Sally and smiled back.

She left the bank and gasped a sigh of relief. She ran to Ben's car.

"Oh Ben, that was terrible. I thought I was going to faint!"

Her hands fanned her face as she related the incident to Ben.

"Well done, you're very clever," praised Ben.

They moved to the rear seat of the car, Sally curled up and they cuddled behind the dark tinted glass of the doors.

Ben felt the need to lighten the mood. He moved his hand up Sally's thigh and took her liner-protected mound in his hand.

"Sally?" he asked. "What do you young ladies call your girly bits these days?"

"All sorts of things," she replied, not knowing where the conversation was going. "And as you well know, Ben, when you got me very excited, I even used the 'C' word. Why do you ask?"

"Well, I've been thinking. Perhaps I should give her a name."

"What have you got in mind?" giggled Sally, anticipating some of Ben's humour.

Ben described what he had always known as a "Fairy Cake" – a small cup cake topped with two sponge wings, usually nestled in butter cream.

"Your lovely labia become firm, swollen wings when you're aroused, so we could call her Fairy Cake."

Sally looked at him with open mouth and eyes wide, but said nothing. Ben continued.

"Alternatively, you know, of course, the story of Peter Pan?"

Sally nodded.

"And who was it that loved Peter Pan?"

"Tinkerbell!" screamed Sally. "And she has wings! Oh yes, I love that. Call her Tinkerbell."

They laughed. Sally's girly bits now had a name! They cuddled and all went quiet for a while. Sally broke the silence.

"There's a problem Ben... we need a name for yours, but we can't call him Peter Pan... Peter Pan never grew into a big boy!"

They laughed and giggled together. Ben looked at his watch. Sally must go home; she had left classes feeling unwell and must be at home when her mother returned from work. They kissed and Sally promised to be in touch as soon as possible.

That was sooner than he had imagined. Five minutes into his drive home, his mobile rang. It was a concerned Sally.

"Ben, he's there now!"

Ben felt sick; life was a series of highs and lows. The mood had suddenly darkened.

"Stay outside, sit on the bench, read a book, and try not to look at him," urged Ben. "Go inside only when you see me get into his car."

He turned his car around and sped off. He parked up, but not too near the apartment block. In the distance he could see Sally seated. She was reading, but taking the occasional glance upwards. Ben tried to keep his walk casual as he approached from the side and rear. He took the paper from his pocket and checked the registration. Yes – it was the offending lecturer. As he neared the car he crab-walked on hands and feet to the side of a rear door. Reaching upwards, he grabbed the handle and in an instant he was inside. What he witnessed sickened Ben – a perverted man in his mid-fifties, eyes fixed on Sally, and grunting with cock in hand, his other holding tissues to receive his imminent ejaculation. Ben slammed his clenched fist into his temple. The filthy bastard's chin fell to his chest. Ben had knocked him out cold. Sally remained seated on the bench. It had all been so swift that she hadn't seen Ben get into the car. He stood from the car and motioned Sally to go inside. She saw him and obeyed. Ben returned to the rear seat. He grabbed the pig's hair and violently pulled his head backwards. He was starting to come around. Ben spat his words.

"Now then, wanker – first of all, put your filthy prick away."

Ben tugged at his hair as the offending organ was hurriedly pushed into its pants.

"You just came very near to being dead. You are a disgusting shit that shouldn't be anywhere near young women. You are a sick voyeur and only one step away from being an abuser… Are you also stupid?" he yelled. "Do you know what will happen if I now call the police? Look at the wedding ring on your finger. If your wife and children could see you now! You are on the verge of destroying your career, your life, and the lives of your family. More importantly, you are a threat to others."

Ben trembled with anger.

"You will stay well away from that girl and any other young women. Do whatever it takes to get rid of those sick thoughts in your mind… I suggest that you get help. But above all, remember this, I know *who* you are and *where* you are. I will be keeping a very close eye on you... now FUCK OFF!"

He slammed the stalker's head forward onto the steering wheel. The bone cracked and blood gushed from his nose. Apart from a cry of pain, the voyeur hadn't uttered one word throughout the confrontation. Ben returned to his car, but waited until the bloodied stalker had left before going home.

*

Margaret was sympathetic and loving when she discovered that her daughter's period had ended the day prematurely. It was no great surprise, as it had happened once or twice in the past. Sally managed to slip out later to telephone Ben.

"What happened?" she enquired urgently.

Ben reassured her.

"Don't worry, precious, nothing much. But he'll not be bothering you or your friends in the future."

"I *do* love you, Ben... thank you for looking after me. I'll ring you from my bed later... Bye."

He recalled his silent vow to take her from her home if she were ever threatened in the future. Sally had overlooked or dismissed her opportunity. Had she said the words, he would have told her to pack a bag. In reality, it would take more than her threatened security for Sally to summon the courage to inflict deep hurt on her mother. If she were to leave home, it would have to be Sally's choice – at a time of *her* choosing and not his. It must be *her* choice to divulge as much or as little information that would threaten her mother's delusions. It would be a momentous move in her life. It must only ever be Sally's decision.

Ben was satisfied with what he had achieved that day on behalf of Sally and her fellow students, though he didn't perceive it as his duty to crusade for the safety of *every* young woman in Spain. His concern was solely in the interests of his lover. He passionately loved her and loved her with compassion.

Sally whispered from beneath the bed sheets.

"Sally adores you and Tinkerbell sends her love."

Ben teased her.

"Tell Tinkerbell that I adore her and that I like Sally a little bit."

"Ooh you," giggled Sally. "By the way, I've thought of a name for yours, I'll tell you next time."

"Goodnight Ben." ... "Goodnight Sally."

Chapter 18

Ben thought through the events of the previous day. He recalled saying to Margaret that her daughter's beauty may one day be her greatest asset. In the few short months that he had known Sally, it was proving to be her downfall – but why should that be so? Spain was full of lovely young women. Were they also the targets of unwelcome incestuous or perverted attention? How could he help her, other than deal with each situation as it arose? If he could summon the courage, should he end the romance in their lives, remain friend and protector, and allow her to move on? Would she allow that? – No. Is it what *he* wanted? – No. In any event, they were too deeply involved to throw her life into chaos during a period of important education. Nothing must happen to jeopardise her assessment by peers that would decide her future.

Ben was becoming very frustrated with their relationship, even though it was *he* that had laid down the ground rules of secrecy and discretion. He knew that Sally was suffering the same pangs, but for how long could they go on with the pretence? Not knowing when they could next meet was ripping their emotions to shreds. Ben knew too well how it affected *his* daily life, but perhaps the demands of study and the companionship of fellow students made things a little easier for Sally. The worst-case scenario was that her ambition would fall apart. He could never forgive himself if that were to happen. Was he in danger of undoing the very thing that he had promised to Margaret? – The promise that he would never hurt her daughter. It would never have been deliberate hurt, but their romance had certainly complicated her life. He could never abandon her, unless a day arrived when she didn't need him. He wanted that day to never arrive. The questions swirled in Ben's head in no particular sequence.

Despite honourable thoughts of what to do for the best, it was Monday morning and yet another day without plans in place to meet with Sally. He was very uncomfortable with that. He decided to ring Alan and shamelessly conspire to use Michael.

Alan was the quintessential London East-Ender. The liberal use of fackin' was obligatory. Alan would split the infinitive to insert a fackin' or two. Ben had met him three years earlier, just a few days after moving into his villa. He was a friendly and considerate man that pulled up at Ben's gate to warn him of the dangers posed by the caterpillars that were emerging from their nests in his pine trees. It was a breed of caterpillar that posed a serious threat to animals. When disturbed, their defence mechanism was to shed a cloud of very fine hairs that could asphyxiate a large dog or cat. Ben was grateful for the information and Alan joined him for a couple of cans of beer in the garden.

Ben, Alan, and his wife, Shirley, became soul mates. The kind London couple housed twenty-six abandoned cats in a purpose-built outbuilding. They chatted for an hour or so in the garden and, without delving into Alan's past, Ben gathered that his visitor wasn't short on wealth. Alan had all the trappings of success.

A few days later, Ben was watering plants when Alan pulled up again. He noticed that Ben's car was missing from the drive.

"Where's your fackin' car," Alan demanded.

"In for clutch repairs," Ben shouted down the drive.

"Fack me, why the fack didn't you say?" Al shouted for the whole neighbourhood to hear.

With that Al was fackin' gone. Fifteen minutes later, there were two cars outside Ben's house – one driven by Alan, the other by his wife, Shirley. Al jumped out and threw a set of BMW car keys to Ben.

"Green gate, house round the corner, Number 1180. Let me have it back when you've finished with it. No fackin' rush."

Al jumped in alongside his missus, she waved, and they left. At that time Ben didn't own a second car and the gesture summed up the kindness of the man. Ben never socialised with Alan beyond a few beers in the garden, but came to know him as a good earthy mate. He regretted that some months later, Alan and Shirley moved to a village around twenty miles away. As so often happens, they lost touch.

Ben telephoned, hoping that Alan was still on the same mobile number.

"Hello Alan, it's Ben."

Al recognised his voice.

"Fackin' 'ell Ben, how the fack are ya? Long time no fackin' see. Jus' the other day, me an' Shirl were talking about ya. We should contact the ol' facker, get tagetha an´ 'ave a piss up. What's up, what can I do for ya?"

"Well, Alan, I feel guilty that after all this time my first contact is for a favour," began Ben.

Alan interrupted.

"Of course, me ol' sunshine, no problem, wa' is it you want?"

Ben continued.

"Several times you said I could borrow it, but I never took you up on the offer – have you still got your Jet Ski?"

"Yeah, man, course you can borrow it, course you fackin' can, any fackin' time. But the sea's going to be a bit cold now, in late September."

Ben pushed Alan's generosity.

"Problem is, Alan, my car hasn't got a tow bar."

Al anticipated the rest.

"No fackin' problem, pal, when you're ready, I'll 'itch the trailer to the Range Rover an' just take the facker away. When d'you wan' it? – Ta-fackin'-morra?"

This man is so generous, thought Ben.

"No, no. The weekend if possible. A family I know have got a young lad and he'd love a ride. It *is* a two-seater, isn't it?"

Al confirmed with his usual Cockney enthusiasm.

"Course it fackin' is. Get two arses on that – no fackin' problem. Jus' let me know when you wanna collect the facker. It'll be good to see ya – been too fackin' long."

"Thanks, Alan, you're a pal," said Ben. "Love to Shirley, I'll ring you later in the week."

Part one of the plan had gone perfectly. Now for part two – Michael

159

must be used again. It was during Sally's lunch break that her mobile jingled.

"Hello Ben, you must have known that I was just thinking of you. I wish we could meet, but there's a problem. I don't think that Mum has any evening lessons this week, so it will be difficult to get away. I miss you."

"I know, sweetheart, that's why I'm ringing – I'm hoping to plan something for the weekend."

"Damn," Sally interrupted. "The bell has just rung, I have to go."

"O.K.," Ben replied urgently. "I'll be quick. Ring me from your mobile when Michael is home from college. I want to speak to him. When I know that he is there, I will ring on your landline. *You* answer the phone if possible. It doesn't matter if your mum is there. Love you lots – bye."

The call from Sally came later than he anticipated – Michael had gone off to kick a ball around with his mates. Sally spoke quietly into her mobile.

"He's home now, bye."

Ben dialled the apartment and Sally picked up.

"Hello Sally, is Michael there?"

Michael came to the phone.

"Hello Ben, how are you?"

"Michael," started Ben. "Have you ever been on a Jet Ski?"

"Yes. During the summer, my pal and I hired one for an hour. It was expensive but brilliant."

Ben continued.

"Well, you would need your mum's permission, but a friend of mine has a two-seater that I can borrow next Saturday if you're interested and you could invite your friend as well if you want to."

"Fantastic!" yelled the lad. "I'm sure that it will be O.K. with Mum. I'll speak to her and ring you back."

No more than five minutes passed before Ben received the call.

"Hi Ben. Good news and bad news. The good news is that Mum says it's O.K. The bad news is that Sally wants to come."

"Well," hesitated Ben. "I suppose we'll have to put up with her. I guess that we should be fair, tell her that she can bring one of *her* friends. I'll ring later in the week to fix a time."

"Great! Thanks, Ben, see you on Saturday."

It was during lunch break the following day that Sally telephoned Ben.

"Hi Ben. Great! We meet on Saturday. I've never ridden on a Jet Ski; I'm quite excited. You *will* look after me, won't you?"

"Of course," Ben assured her.

Sally continued.

"I've invited my friend Maria to come along. She's excited too, if her parents give her the O.K."

"Maria is your best friend, is she?" enquired Ben.

"No, Ben – you are."

That statement was as special to Ben as the words "I love you".

"Maria is very beautiful, so I will be keeping an eye on you!" laughed Sally. "Michael has invited his friend Juan. He's already spoken with his parents and has the O.K. – I can't wait to see you again, Ben."

"Same here," Ben replied. "Can't wait, but study hard in the meantime."

"I must go," Sally apologised. "I will speak soon. Love you."

"Bye, precious," said Ben quietly. "Ring me when you can."

Ben was lifted by Sally's call, but became gloomy knowing that unless Margaret was otherwise engaged one evening, it would be five days until he could be near his woman again.

The week passed slowly. Several hurried phone calls and the regular call from Sally's bedroom was welcome, but no substitute for being together.

Chapter 19

The anticipation built in Ben as he drove to collect the Jet Ski. He found the villa without much difficulty. Alan was in the driveway when Ben arrived. His Cockney friend remembered that Ben was from Wales and greeted him accordingly.

"Hola Taffy Sheep Shagger, how the fack are ya?"

"I'm well," replied Ben, shaking Alan firmly by the hand.

Shirley appeared from the house and they exchanged greetings, giving each other several warm hugs. Alan led Ben to the enormous garage, hit the remote, and the electronic door lifted to reveal the gleaming powerful machine, already loaded onto a trailer and hitched to an equally pristine Range Rover. Alan loved his toys and spent hours ensuring that they were always in immaculate condition.

Ben listened intently as Alan gave him launching instructions.

"There are two fackin' lifejackets and a Gerry can o' spare fuel in the car – got it from the fackin' petrol station this morning," Alan instructed.

The man's kindness and generosity were boundless – Ben's kind of man.

"So you're giving a lad a fackin' treat on the ol' Jet, yeah?" asked Alan.

"Yes, and his sister," admitted Ben, choosing not to talk about the additional guests.

"An' how ol's the sister?" asked Alan.

"Eighteen," replied Ben awkwardly.

"You fackin' 'er?" Alan abruptly asked with a smile.

Ben found himself talking as though he had been reared in the East End.

"Don't be fackin' stupid, I'm old enough to be her father."

"Since when was that a problem to any fackin' man?" joked Alan.

"Fack off, Alan," Ben retorted, giving him a playful punch.

Alan didn't realise the significance of his words of jest. Ben knew him to be a good-hearted man. He also knew that his friend, though not having children of his own, would be second in the queue to kick the shit out of the three men that had abused Sally.

Alan insisted that they have a morning beer together before Ben was allowed to leave. Ben thanked him with huge sincerity.

"Keep it for the fackin' weekend," insisted Alan. "Let me 'ave it back next week. No fackin' problem. You can borrow the speedboat next summer."

Ben gave his car keys to Alan, should he need use of the car. Alan assured him that it wasn't necessary, but he left them anyway. He drove carefully, not having towed a trailer for some years.

During his drive, Ben pondered on the poignancy of Alan's macho words and the injustice of pain that the innocent often suffer. To lighten his thoughts, he mused on how strange it was that great care must be taken when referring to somebody's country of origin as a soubriquet. Yet the man he had just left was free to brand him a Welsh Taffy with a penchant for the arse end of a sheep. No offence was intended or taken, but "Sheep Shagger" was hardly a label to proud of! He smiled as he pictured the personal damages case of Benjamin versus Alan being read in the High Court.

"Where are you from?" the judge would enquire.

"From Wales," Ben would reply.

"Case dismissed… Full legal costs awarded to Alan."

Something wrong with equality in political correctness these days, thought Ben.

He phoned ahead from his mobile to warn the Crew of his imminent arrival. He would want the Crew and guests waiting outside. Alan's toy must be guarded with his life – it must *not* disappear during the few minutes that he may be exchanging pleasantries in Margaret's apartment. All were excitedly waiting outside the block as Ben pulled in. The boys immediately disappeared to the trailer, enthusing "Wows" and "Coors" as they admired the sea-going charger.

Courtesy demanded that Ben should first approach Margaret to accept a continental kiss. Sally beamed and gave Ben a light kiss on the cheek. She beckoned her friend Maria, who was very comfortable with the traditional two-cheek Spanish introduction. It was a beautifully warm, late-summer day, but all were dressed in tracksuits or similar, in preparation for the cooler temperature expected later in the day. Ben's man thing could evaluate only Maria's face at that point. Sally had not exaggerated – Maria was a beautiful girl. She was beautiful in the purebred female Spanish sense – fine features, jet-black hair, perfect white teeth, and those large, dark brown eyes as deep as wells.

Margaret scolded Michael and reminded him of courtesy before Juan was introduced. Ben wasn't offended; they were excited young men! Juan was a handsome young man that probably had young British female tourists wetting their knickers. Michael too was moving on; his corrective brace had been removed that week to reveal a very good set of teeth. He seemed to have shot up in height and was now several inches taller than his sister. He could well be suffering the physical pain of limb growth.

Bags containing sandwiches, soft drinks, and towels, et cetera, were loaded up and Ben gave Margaret his faithful promise that the young people were in good hands. They would come to no harm. Strangely, Michael was content to allow Sally to take the front seat. Was that to be seated with his friend or to be near Maria?

Ben drove to the adjacent resort. Alan had advised him that there were better launching facilities and secure, supervised parking for car and trailer.

The moments of exhilaration were near. The car and trailer were parked up, additional fuel was with the bags on the beach, and the Jet was lolling on the gentle lapping at the shoreline. The ignition key was securely zipped in the pocket of Ben's tracksuit. The boys helped Ben to drag the machine a little onto the sand.

Top-clothes removed, the boys were soon ready for action in their fashionable baggy swimming trunks. Michael's and Juan's eagerness to get astride 1000cc of power was delayed by their interest in the spectacle of Maria removing her tracksuit. Ben was sure that she made more of

164

a meal of it than was necessary. She sensually revealed a body equally desirable as Sally's. It was a taller and less delicate body, but perfectly contoured and more heavily suntanned. Sally's bronzed skin looked quite pale in comparison. Michael had reached a period of development where the man thing was beginning to take over. Ben observed the young men's delight, as a temptress revealed her rounded flesh covered only by a tiny white bikini. Michael and Juan watched Maria, Ben watched Michael, Juan, *and* Maria, and Sally watched Ben.

Sally caught Ben's attention, screwed up her eyes and wagged a finger at him – but smiled. For now, Sally preferred to stay dressed; she wasn't the extrovert that Maria was. Here was evidence that opposites attract. For public eyes, Sally was delicate, demure, and refined. Maria was full on, upfront Spanish – loud in voice, loud in gestures, and approached everything with passion – but beautiful with it!

A few minutes of fantasy and the lads were ready for excitement. They made for the Jet.

"Bugger it," murmured Ben. "I've left the lifejackets in the car."

"We're O.K. without them, Ben," insisted Michael. "Don't worry, we've been on a Jet Ski before. Besides, we'd look like a pair of sissies!"

Ben reluctantly agreed to allow them out without jackets, but not before delivering a five-minute lecture, with the closing words, "Any stupidity and I will have the key from you, and that will be it. I want you back here in twenty minutes. We'll take it in turns... Understand?"

Ben secured his waterproof watch on Michael's left wrist. He checked the safety feature of ignition key strapped securely between the machine and Michael's other wrist, the engine spluttered into life and the pair roared off into the Mediterranean.

Ben watched them for a while. He needn't have worried – they seemed to be in total control of what they were doing, but he *was* concerned that he'd allowed them to speed off without safety jackets.

Sally arrived at his side to watch. Removal of her tracksuit revealed a one-piece lemon-coloured swimming costume. It was a colour that complimented her lovely skin.

"You look fabulous," Ben whispered.

"Thank you," Sally smiled.

She took his arm in both hands, reached up, and kissed his cheek. To Sally's annoyance, Maria arrived at Ben's other side and linked her arm through his. Sally was already regretting that she had invited her friend. *But nothing to worry about*, she thought. *This was the normal gregarious Maria who knew nothing of their clandestine relationship.*

Ben sensed that Sally was uncomfortable and broke away to point out a powered paraglider who was approaching. Sally loved him for his gesture of understanding. Whenever Sally made movements of friendship or affection towards Ben, it followed soon after that Maria was on hand to crave similar status. Ben asked himself if the apparent female competition was entirely healthy. He did his best to avoid the situations where it might occur. It pissed him off that, to achieve that, he was distancing himself from Sally; the very person that he wanted to be close to. He too was regretting Maria's presence.

Hollers of delight announced the arrival of the boys after thirty minutes. Ben hadn't expected them to observe the twenty-minute arrangement. He checked the level of fuel, climbed aboard, and before Sally could make a move Maria clambered up behind him. Sally pulled a face of frustration. Ben pulled the same face in return.

"Can I drive?" Maria yelled.

"Shortly," Ben replied. "Won't be long, Sally."

Sally watched as they sped away with Maria holding on tightly, her chest pressed over-close to Ben's body. They travelled at speed a few times back and forth across the bay. The engine roared and the Jet vibrated.

"It feels nice between the legs," Maria shouted above the noise. Ben was unsure that he had heard correctly.

There was a slight swell on the sea, but not difficult for a beginner like Maria to master. He shut down the engine.

"Now me please," pleaded Maria.

Changing positions was a complete disaster. Maria fell into the cold water and she squealed at the sudden change in temperature. Ben laughed and reached out to pull her aboard. She was taller and heavier than Sally. He held onto the steering bars and placed his arm around her torso to haul her upwards. The whole operation was less than athletic and her breasts slipped from under her top in the process. She regained a position behind Ben but left her breasts exposed. They were perfect young tits and the same colour as the rest of her body. Ben wondered if there were *any* pale bits. They were well away from the shore, with Maria's back facing towards the beach.

With one foot on the runner board, Maria raised and rested the other onto the seat ahead of her. During her recovery, the fabric of her bikini had found its way into the cleavage of her buttocks. She dropped her knee to one side, exposing the side of a hair-free mound, almost to the point of revealing labia. Ben's eyes refused to be averted. He decided that the exposure was deliberate and nor was she in any hurry to put her tits away.

"Ben," she began in her broken English. "Do you think I'm pretty?"

He paused.

"No, Maria, you are not pretty. You are very beautiful... and I am too old for you. Now cover yourself up."

Ben knew not why, but younger women had often found him to be an attraction; perhaps because he treated them as more adult than their years. However, this was ludicrous; Maria barely knew him, but here was an eighteen-year-old teenager blatantly offering up her body. He quickly concluded that she was insecure and needed to be the centre of attention. *She has no genuine interest in me*, Ben thought, *only that his interest must be diverted from Sally to her – at any cost.*

A second attempt to put Maria in the driving seat was clumsy but successful. She set off at speed, her loins enjoying the vibration of the power beneath her.

Heading in the direction of Egypt, she removed Ben's hand from her waist and placed it firmly onto her breast. Ben summoned all that he had in self-control and returned his hand to her waist. *If she's going to orgasm*, he promised himself, *the source of pleasure must be the machine vibrating between her straddled legs.*

Maria set off across the bay, gyrating her hips. What was causing her screams of pleasure? Was it the excitement of the ride or the angry 1000cc of power pleasuring her fanny? Uncertainty was answered when her left hand dropped to her crotch. Importantly, Ben had resisted temptation and remained loyal to Sally.

Jesus Christ, thought Ben. *This girl is dangerously red hot!* Had there not been Sally in his life, he would readily have taken her approaches to the logical conclusion.

Sally had seen from the shore the antics of changeover, but mercifully wasn't privy to the hit that Maria had made on Ben.

"Come on, Sally's turn," insisted Ben.

Maria jumped off the Jet into waist-high water as they approached the shoreline. Sally viewed her with suspicion, unable to ignore that Maria's nipples were making every effort to burst through the thin fabric of her bikini top.

The boys were keen to retake possession of the toy, but conceded that it was fair that Sally should now take the reins. Ben topped up the fuel to full. He had planned this ride the day before. He placed Sally at the driving position from the off. He started up the engine and placed her hand on the throttle. His hand joined hers and they gently powered off from the shore. Sally screamed excitement as the speed picked up. She too was probably feeling the effects of vibration beneath her. Ben caressed her breasts as they moved on at a moderate pace. Sally murmured pleasure.

"Just keep heading for North Africa," said Ben.

He moved his hand down and took her crotch in his hand. He fondled her quim through the fabric of her swimming suit. He turned to look back – they were now far out to sea. Ben cut the engine. It was that time of day when the Mediterranean often becomes a millpond. The excited bustle of the beach had been left far behind. The sudden near silence was quite eerie. Sally leaned her head back onto Ben's shoulder.

"What went on with you and Maria?"

"Absolutely nothing," Ben assured her.

"So how come she came back with huge nipples?" questioned Sally.

"That was probably the cold water when she fell in or maybe the excitement of the ride – just as your nipples are aroused now."

"Oh, I see," laughed Sally. "Nothing to do then with the fact that you've been fondling Tinkerbell. Oh, I must tell you my name for your big boy."

Ben stopped her.

"Sally, tell me later. It's been six days since we made love… I need you so badly."

"I know," said Sally quietly. "I need you too."

She wondered what was about to happen.

Ben unfastened the clasp at the nape of her neck. In a swift movement, he pulled her swimwear downwards, she lifted her buttocks and the fabric slid down her thighs and over her ankles. Ben tied the suit firmly to the steering bar. In less than fifteen seconds, she was now totally naked, floating on an unstable platform in the middle of the Mediterranean Sea.

"Stand up, precious," said Ben.

Sally followed his instructions to the letter. Ben twisted onto his back, moved down the length of the seat, and hung his legs over the back of the Jet. He lifted her buttocks. With her loins now directly above his head, he looked up in adoration of the parted labia, already offering a taste of the pink. He pushed two fingers into her vagina, removed them, and licked the taste of her juice into his mouth. His thumbs stretched her labia apart. Sally looked down past her belly, in awe of Ben's love for her. He offered her vaginal cavity a waggling tongue. Sally watched as she lowered herself onto the eager little snake protruding from Ben's mouth.

"Tell him to find my clitoris, Ben," urged Sally.

"He will. Have a nice time, but don't come," said Ben.

Sally gyrated her loins in a circular motion for a few minutes, groaning pleasure as her clitoris found variable degrees of contact with the wriggling muscle. Ben's arms stretched out to fondle her breasts and to squeeze nipples.

"I want to come, Ben," she pleaded.

"Not yet," Ben insisted. "We will come together soon."

She became frustrated when Ben lifted her buttocks and removed his mouth from her entrance. He twisted himself back into a forward-facing position. He stood on the runner boards behind Sally. She was in a perfect position. She held onto the steering and arched her back downwards. She stood on the runner boards, her legs straddled across

169

the wide machine. She arched her spine further, forcing her buttocks upwards. Ben gazed at the perfect curvature that swept up from her small waist. How he loved that glorious sight. He released his penis and balls from his trunks, hooking the waistband beneath his scrotum. His helmet was at explosion point, but before satiating the animal, he bent his knees to take Sally's open vulva in his mouth. His nose settled in the cleavage of her buttocks and his tongue worked feverishly inside the warmth of her cavity. Sally yelped each time it crossed the path of her swollen clitoris.

"I want to come," Sally insisted.

"Not yet... It won't be long," Ben assured her.

He was referring to time and not length. He took the beast in his hand. It was at full stretch and beyond. He worked his helmet around the vulva and labia – but briefly. She would climax uncontrollably with too much more attention to that area. With gentle thrusts of no more than half an inch each time, his penis began the sensual journey to full penetration. Ben had no control over the final urgent thrust of three inches.

Both gasped delight at the moment that Sally was fully impaled. Sally allowed her libido to settle whilst they enjoyed a minute or two of locked and total fusion. Ben leant back to admire their union; he loved the sight of her labia stretched tightly around his erection.

"Slowly when you're ready, darling... I'll try to hold back, I want it to last for hours," Sally whispered.

"I wish," gasped Ben.

He watched as the labia disappeared and reappeared during the long, gentle thrusts from base to helmet and back again. Her labia and delicate pubic hair were soaked with the juices that appeared from around her tightly stretched vagina. Sally's bum hole quivered a little. Ben slowed his thrusting. The contractions of her vagina seemed to be sucking at him. It was glorious.

Sally murmured, "Oh Ben, it feels so big... it's wonderful. I need you to have me every day... thank you for not letting me come."

"It's been six days," said Ben. "It's been hell."

He knew that he couldn't hold back for too much longer. He also knew that one explosive climax would be enough for him. Sally was blessed – she could enjoy multiple orgasms. Sally realised the urgency of Ben's desperate need to unload.

"If you're ready, Ben, fill me with your spunk... squirt into me."

Her words triggered an electric storm in Ben's brain and a six-day build-up of his fluid shot out under pressure. He grunted delight.

"Ooh. I felt your juice come into me, Ben... Oh, ooh... I'm coming... I'm coming," she screeched.

The orgasmic contractions of her vagina sucked at the remnants of fluid that Ben had to offer. Ben groaned and Sally squealed through a climax that went on and on. Their legs trembled as they stayed locked in their coital embrace. They needed to express their deep love for each other. Ben withdrew his satiated beast, turned Sally onto her back, supported himself above her, and re-entered her vagina. They embraced and kissed passionately. Sally threw her legs around him, trapping his still rock-hard penis within her body. They quietly spoke of their love and commitment. They wanted hours in that embrace, but others awaited their return to the shore.

If her body could handle it, Ben decided that he could pleasure Sally on their return journey. She awkwardly re-dressed into her swimwear. They returned to a locked embrace, but now both facing forward. Sally sat upon Ben's lap, her legs wide apart, and feet anchored on the runner boards. She lifted her buttocks and Ben released his still erect penis and balls from inside the leg of his trunks. Sally pulled aside the fabric covering her mound and the erection was thrust deep into her body. The contact was aggressive; her mound hard onto the base of Ben's beast.

Ben took control of the steering and started up the engine, which immediately excited Sally. He zoomed off into a series of swerving motions. The action pressed Sally's rubbery labia viciously against his base and clitoral needs were served by her gentle gyration. She dropped her head forward to observe the pleasure they were providing each other. Ben controlled the Jet with one hand, using the other to fondle breasts through fabric and to squeeze hardened nipples.

"Stay on my tits, Ben," urged Sally, as she placed her middle finger to caress her clitoris. "Oh fuck, I'm coming again... Big time."

She gasped through another climax.

"Oh Ben," she panted.

Ben was nearing the beach, but did a swift turn back out to sea.

"I can't believe it," he gasped. "Me too... *I'm* coming again!"

He couldn't recall having had a second climax so soon after the first. It was good! They had exhausted each other.

They put their love bits away, Ben washed love juices from the seating, and they set off to an impatient Michael and Juan. They approached the shore slowly. Sally leant back to be close to Ben's body. Her insecurity surfaced again when she pleaded with such sincerity, "I adore you, Ben... can you promise that you will never love another woman the way that you love me?"

Ben replied with genuine warmth.

"Sally, I can do better than that. I can promise you that I will never love another woman – period!"

Sally beamed.

"I am going to have to jump into that cold water to do something about this erection," Ben laughed. "It won't go to sleep."

"I'll jump in to wash Tinkerbell," added Sally. "Oh yes, and that reminds me. Yours is now called 'Big Ben'. Get it? – A clock tower, tall and straight, and its timing is perfect!"

They laughed happily as Ben cut the engine and glided to the shore. They held hands as they jumped into waist-deep, cold seawater. Both stumbled and fell forward to shoulder level. They screamed in unison at the sudden cold shock. Within thirty seconds Ben's angry beast was the size of a cashew nut. Sally disguised her attention to girly bits beneath the water.

The boys had moved the bags and fuel to soft, warm sand nearby and Maria was reclined on a ground sheet that had been packed. Ben sensed that she was sulking. Not before another lecture, Michael and Juan were soon aboard again, the machine snaking and swerving, thrashing up foaming white water from the surface of the sea.

"Good ride?" Maria asked, as Ben and Sally approached.

"Fantastic!" replied Sally, with a little wink at Ben.

The three settled to chat in the warm sunshine. Sally sat in an upright, slightly demure position, her crossed hands placed across her crotch to deprive the leering eyes of passing male admirers. In contrast, Maria chose to lie back opposite Ben, her upper body supported on her elbows, her heels planted, and her knees apart, seeking admiration of her crotch. Sally disapproved of her sensuous flirting and, with difficulty, dismissed the brief look that Ben had taken between Maria's legs. It was, after all, simply the way that Maria always behaved; she had no knowledge of Ben and Sally's love for each other and it was *her* vagina that was seeping Ben's spunk – not Maria's!

Maria took over conversation with her broken English.

¨Me and Sally are such good friends. Ever since we were in school together I have wanted to have lots of time with her, so that I can improve my English.¨

As in many friendships, Maria had chosen to follow Sally into a career of teaching. She spoke at length and, to be politely helpful, Ben corrected her grammar and pronunciation as she continued to talk about unimportant things. Unimportant things to Ben's ears, but things that were important to Maria – always about Maria, Maria, and more Maria. She revealed herself to be immature, insecure, and incredibly vain.

This girl needs help, thought Ben. *Something in her life has turned her into an attention seeker in the extreme.* He pondered further; *I wonder how many men have enjoyed her body in return for a little flattery? – Or did they run from the way in which she demands and consumes? Despite the apparent promiscuity, she could still be a virgin.*

He felt a degree of sympathy for her, but had no intention of stepping in as helpful therapist. His thoughts led him to ask a question.

¨Do you have a boyfriend?¨ he asked casually.

¨Not at the moment, but you know what boys are. They only want us girls for sex. They are only *really* interested in football, cars, and motorbikes.¨

With that, she jumped astride him, hugged him close, and firmly kissed his cheek.

¨What I need is an older man that can teach me English,¨ she laughed. Over Maria's shoulder, Ben looked at Sally with widened eyes and raised eyebrows. Sally returned the expression and interrupted the proceedings.

"Come on; let's have something to eat."

A good move, Sally! For a few short seconds, Maria's fanny had been in contact with Ben's loins and her hug had almost released firm breasts from a tiny bikini top.

Maria positioned herself uncomfortably close to Ben as they ate sandwiches and drank from cans.

"I'll check on the boys," announced Ben, releasing himself from the situation. With sandwich and can in hand, he walked to the water's edge, soon followed by Sally.

"For God's sake, Ben. She's throwing herself at you," Sally complained.

"I know," he replied. "But don't worry, it's only insecurity. She needs to outshine you or any other woman when there's a man around."

"I can easily put her in her place if I tell her about us," Sally came back.

Ben replied with urgency in his voice.

"Whatever you do, do *not* do that… I think she's probably quite a dangerous girl to have as a friend."

Sally wasn't aware of Maria's behaviour on the Jet Ski and didn't understand the true depth of Ben's warning.

Predictably, Maria was soon at their side, but Ben was rescued by the boys' arrival.

"Jump on, Maria," Michael shouted.

With testosterone and other hormones racing through his system, he would have enjoyed the pressure of breasts on his back.

"Perhaps later," she shouted back.

He was visibly disappointed and would have to settle for fantasy and a wank in his bed later that night.

"Come and eat," Sally shouted to her brother.

The boys helped Ben to secure the Jet on the sandy shore and welcomed food, drink, and the warmth of large towels wrapped around their wet, shivering bodies.

Despite their discomfort, Michael and Juan were keen to grab every moment available on the machine. They ate heartily and, much to Michael's chagrin, Maria accepted the offer of a brief spin with Juan. Ben topped up the fuel, gave Juan yet another lecture, and the two set off. As Ben returned to the Crew, Sally was removing a long fabric modesty cape from her bag – a loose, tent-type garment, to be tied at the neck and perfect for ladies to remove wet swimwear away from prying eyes.

"I'm feeling a bit chilled. Are you cold, Ben?" asked Sally.

"A little," he replied, anticipating what his insatiable lady was about. He joined her inside the garment.

Michael ignored their intimacy, as his sister stood with her back close to Ben's chest, their bodies cocooned in fabric. They sat onto the groundsheet, Sally's buttocks cuddled close to Ben's penis – the cashew nut envisaged a life hanging from a palm tree. It swelled automatically at the first touch of her amazing body.

"I'll leave you two lovebirds to it then," said Michael smiling, and walked to the water's edge.

It was his first open acknowledgement that his sister was in love. Sally smiled at him.

"Just to be close to you is sometimes enough," Sally whispered. Ben knew that it wouldn't be enough as he slipped his hand downwards. He took her crotch in his hand. She raised her knees and planted her heels. Ben glanced around to confirm their relative privacy. Her knees parted as Ben's adept fingers lifted away the elasticated leg of her swimsuit. In one move, the vulva and labia were nestled in his hand. His middle finger reached under and pressed on her bum hole, then quickly upwards to join two other fingers. All three were thrust rapidly into her vaginal cavity. Sally gasped at the urgency of it all. Earlier arousal and the contents of Ben's testicles had left her vagina flowing with juices. Sally's hips responded to the beckoning motion of his fingers over her G-spot.

"Don't move," Ben insisted. "People will know what we're doing. Just relax. I promise it will still be nice... open your vagina."

Sitting lotus-style, Sally's fingers pulled her labia wide apart. Ben's three fingers moved to her waiting clitoris and massaged it in a slow circular motion. Her climax built steadily. Ben took the appendage between finger and thumb, squeezed, and caressed. Sally´s orgasm followed almost instantly. She dropped her head, holding back the screeches of delight that wanted to escape from her mouth.

"Oh Ben," Sally complained.

"I know," said Ben quietly. "The problem is that we grab every possible opportunity, not knowing when we'll next see each other… We find time to *make love*, but rarely have time to *show love*."

"It won't always be that way, will it, Ben?" asked Sally quietly.

"I hope not… I do hope not," Ben replied.

It had been rapid, it had been urgent, and for Sally a memorable orgasm. For Ben, it had left him with a re-aroused erection that had nowhere to go.

The image of her friend and Ben cuddled in their tent of love was not welcomed by Maria as she approached. She all but glared at Sally.

"What are you doing in there?" Maria demanded.

"We were feeling a little cold," Sally reluctantly offered as an explanation.

"In fact, I think I'll get dressed," interrupted Ben, fearful that Maria would think it a good idea to join him inside the garment.

They got to their feet, Sally slipped downwards from inside, leaving Ben to remove his swimwear. He dropped his trunks, but bent forward and swivelled to one side, disguising the presence of an erection that was determined to convert the modesty garment into a circus bell tent.

"Behave yourself," scolded Sally, as Maria playfully made to peek up the garment whilst Ben struggled into underwear and tracksuit trousers. How she wished that she had never invited Maria to join them that day.

Ben pictured Sally's nudity, as she too stripped within the cape and redressed. He wanted to be inside that fabric with her, on his knees, her loins pressed to his face. As expected, Maria made more of a show of her stripping, using only towels to vaguely preserve modesty. Ben ignored the performance, but it was much appreciated by the younger Michael and Juan.

After a final session on the Jet, the boys made no objection to the idea of calling it a day. Limbs shivered and lips were blue. They were now cold and tired out.

"Great day, Ben," Michael trembled. "Shall I come with you when you return the Jet tomorrow?"

Ben bit his tongue as he replied, "I've got it for the weekend, I won't be taking it back until Monday or Tuesday."

He would, of course, have welcomed another day with Sally and Michael, but his lapse in concentration had opened up another opportunity for Maria to make herself available. He wished Maria no harm, but she was a serious intrusion into his and Sally's closeness.

"Can we do the same tomorrow?" begged Michael.

"That's between you and your mum – I'll be here from two o'clock," said Ben.

Everything loaded, Ben drove from the resort hoping that geography would dictate that Juan and Maria would be dropped off first. He did *not* want to be alone with Maria. Sally knew that geography would dictate that Maria *would* be the final drop-off and was equally uncomfortable with the thought of Ben being alone with her flirtatious friend.

*

Margaret had spent much of the day brooding on how unfair it was that Sally and Michael couldn't have spent the day with their father. She watched uneasily from the window, as her children hugged Ben warmly during their goodbyes.

*

Maria insisted that Juan be dropped off first. Ben pulled in at the end of Maria's road. He tried to make his goodbye slightly formal, but she would have none of it. She pulled and locked his face onto hers, her lips parted, her tongue seeking his. Ben broke away.

"No, Maria. I told you. I am too old for you."

"You're not too old for Sally," she replied angrily.

"You've got it all wrong. Sally and I are friends and you too are supposed to be Sally's friend," Ben replied tersely.

He unloaded her bag and brushed her to one side as she attempted to embrace him.

"Shall we meet again tomorrow?" Maria pleaded.

"I don´t think that´s a good idea," was Ben´s firm reply.

He drove away, both flushed and nervous. *This is one dangerous young lady*, he thought. At that stage, he didn't know just how dangerous she could be.

*

Ben took the call on his mobile as he drove home. It was Michael.

"Sorry, Ben, I've still got your watch."

"Don't worry about it," assured Ben. "I'll have it next time or I'll call in if I'm passing."

"About tomorrow. Mum's playing up, but I'm working on it," complained Michael.

"I'll leave it with you," Ben smilingly replied.

Sally was also taking a call on her mobile.

"Hi Sally, it's Maria – you must let me have Ben's number. Older men are so hot, aren't they? He kisses so passionately."

Sally fumed with anger as Maria droned on, but she kept her cool. She sensed that it was Maria's envy stirring a hornet's nest. The call nevertheless upset her and irrational jealousy led her to make a serious mistake. For the first time since their declaration of love, she failed to telephone from her bed that night.

At home, Ben pondered on the potential complications that Maria could create in their lives. He decided that when Sally´s call came from her bed that night, she should be warned of the dangers that her friend presented. He would tell all; including Maria's behaviour on the Jet Ski.

That call never came.

Chapter 20

"Why not?" pleaded Michael.

"Because one day over the weekend is quite enough," shouted his mother.

Margaret was still smarting from the affection shown to Ben the previous day. The argument had raged between Michael and his mother all morning and through lunchtime, but she would not back down. She was determined to keep her children and Ben apart that Sunday. Sally avoided becoming involved. Her thoughts revolved around any possible truth in Maria's phone call and her regret that she hadn't called Ben the night before. She must confront the truth, even if the truth hurt.

"I'm fed up with this arguing. I'm going for a walk," she announced.

She didn't walk – she ran to the coastal train railway station.

*

Ben had dumped the car and Jet in secured parking. He had no intentions of launching, unless Sally and Michael turned up. Instead, he hired a sun bed and waited anxiously. He fretted that he hadn't received a call the previous night, but convinced himself that Sally had been careless and not topped up her mobile.

"Oh fuck," he murmured, as Maria appeared on the scene.

"Hola Ben," she enthused with a broad smile.

He greeted her with friendship but without enthusiasm. Maria sat beside him on the bed.

"About yesterday," started Ben.

Maria stopped him.

"What has *she* got that I haven't got? Wouldn't you like to fuck me? – The way you fucked Sally yesterday."

Ben swallowed hard – had Sally disclosed their secret love to Maria?

"What *are* you talking about?" questioned Ben.

Maria pointed to the coin-operated binoculars along the promenade.

"I was watching... you were a long way out to sea, but I could see what was going on."

Ben remained unflustered.

"Maria, you are mistaken. Those binoculars are rubbish. You saw us fooling around changing over positions, not having sex. Sally and I are very good friends – we are not lovers."

Maria looked unconvinced.

"Well, will you make love to me anyway?" asked Maria.

"No, I will not," he answered angrily. "Now listen to me. You are not interested in *me*. You are interested only in being more popular or more desirable than your friends. I don't want to be unkind, but you have a big problem of insecurity, to a point where you must be the centre of attention at all times, regardless of who you hurt. You are a very beautiful girl, but not every man in the world has to fall at your feet. You demand too much... Let a man fall for you, instead of you insisting on his attention. You need help, Maria, I feel sympathy for you, but I am not a therapist. I can't help you. You want me to believe that you are very experienced in the ways of love, but you're not, are you?... Virginity is not something to be ashamed of. Don't lose it to me or any other man for the wrong reasons." Ben paused. "You *are* a virgin, aren't you?"

Too many of Ben's points had struck a chord. Genuine tears of distress welled in her eyes. Ben took her in his arms to comfort her.

"I'm sorry... I've been unkind – I didn't mean to hurt you," comforted Ben.

*

Sally arrived at the sea wall. She saw not an embrace of comfort; she saw the embrace of romance. She felt that she had been stabbed. She wanted to throw up. She almost fainted, as her head span with confused emotion. Sally was heartbroken. She turned in a daze and scurried back to the railway station, hiding her tears from passers-by. She had seen the flirtatious Maria in operation, but how could Ben do this to her? How could he so casually betray her? She was hurt beyond belief. Despite their declaration of love, was he no better than the other men in her life – driven by nothing more than sexual desire? Was there *any* man in this world that she could trust?

*

Ben released Maria from his embrace.

"There are people who can help you, Maria," Ben whispered.

She sniffled, got to her feet, and left without saying a word.

Sally sat waiting for the train, resisting the temptation to ring Ben to demand an explanation or at the very least to express her contempt. Her self-esteem and dignity prevented her from making the call.

At 5.00 pm Ben conceded and accepted that he wouldn't be seeing Sally that day. He returned home. If only Sally had dialled his number.

*

"I'm going to do some revision, Mum," shouted Sally, as she entered the apartment.

Mother's intuition kicked in and, seeing that she had been crying, Margaret followed Sally to her bedroom.

"What's wrong, darling? – Nothing bad has happened?" she asked.

"No, it's nothing... sometimes I feel a bit sad, that's all. Leave me now, I have revision to do."

Her mother explained away her daughter's emotion to the occasional depression caused by her unfortunate history and left her to study.

Sally's mobile jingled. The screen read Maria. She didn't pick up and switched the phone to off. Sally didn't revise. She lay on her bed and wept.

*

Ben threw caution to the wind and rang Sally's mobile. It was switched off and, in any event, just as children do, she had escaped from her distress into sleep. Powerless to achieve any result, he set about hosing down the Jet Ski and Range Rover. He checked for incoming calls before wiping down and vacuuming the interior. Alan wouldn't expect it, but Jet and car must be immaculate when returned. He telephoned Alan to arrange the return of his motors the following morning.

His cats reminded him that they had been neglected. He apologised frequently as he fed them. Ben waited anxiously that night for a call that didn't happen. He had a feeling of foreboding. Something was wrong and he sensed who was behind it. Something must be done and quickly.

Chapter 21

Ben was at the garage early the following morning to fill up both car and Gerry can. He had woken anxious, with nerves twitching, but forced himself to drive carefully. He pulled into a lay-by at the time that Sally would be travelling to college. Her mobile remained switched off.

*

During that morning, Sally's and Maria's paths crossed in the corridor. They ignored each other. Maria gregariously continued on, giggling amongst a group of other students. All looked in Sally's direction. There was laughter, Sally thought, at her expense. She fought back tears of sadness and depression.

*

The electronic gates slid open and Ben drove Alan's car and trailer to the garage doors. His friend greeted him enthusiastically, but didn't object when Ben feigned illness and wanted to leave. Ben couldn't handle drinking beer in Alan's garden at 9.15 am when there were urgent matters on his mind.

    "Alan, the lad and his sister send a big kiss. They had a fantastic time and send the message thank you, thank you, thank you. But I must go, I feel like shit. That seawater was cold – I'm coming down with something. It feels like flu," Ben apologised.

    "Don't fackin' kiss me goodbye then. Go on, fack off. Give me a ring an' we'll 'ave a night on the piss."

"I will, Al, thanks a bunch. I'll be in touch," said Ben, hugging his friend warmly around the shoulder.

Ben jumped into his car and set off to address urgent problems. His stomach was in knots.

He drove home at some speed, but wasn't surprised that there were no incoming messages. Ben became more and more agitated with repeated failure to get through to Sally's mobile. He recalled that he had an excuse to turn up at the apartment – Michael had his wristwatch.

It was mid-afternoon when Ben parked in view of the apartment block. A dejected-looking Sally arrived and Ben intercepted her as she punched in the code to the main entrance door. She was a little startled.

"Give me five minutes," said Ben. "If you then want me to walk out of your life, I will."

"Come in," said an unhappy Sally.

Ben made no effort to have physical contact with her and sat opposite her at the dining table before speaking.

"Sally, if you want to end things for any good reason, I will accept that, but I will not allow an insecure child like Maria to destroy our love."

Sally interrupted sharply.

"She's asking for your number! Did you kiss her passionately on Saturday when you dropped her off?"

"No," came the firm reply. "She caught me unawares, she kissed *me* and I pushed her away. Don't you see it, Sally? Maria can't handle rejection and she is doing everything in her power to destroy us."

"But I saw you both at the beach yesterday," Sally protested. "You were cuddling her!"

Ben's eyes widened with relief.

"Oh, I see," he said smiling. "I wasn't cuddling her, I was consoling her and she left just minutes after you saw that. I was going to warn you of the whole situation, had you rung as usual from your bed. You didn't make the call, Sally."

Ben spent the next few minutes detailing everything that had happened, from the moment Maria had jumped on board the Jet with him, through to Sally's misinterpretation of Ben's and Maria's embrace. He told her everything – his rejection of her advances on the Jet Ski, his rejection of her kiss in the car, her claim that she had seen them making love, his rejection of her offer of sex on Sunday afternoon, and the lecture that he had given her, leading to the mild embrace of consolation.

Sally's face lightened as Ben revealed all and everything clicked into place.

"Sally?" asked Ben. "If a young man in college takes an interest in you, does Maria chase after him?"

Sally nodded.

"Every time," she confirmed.

"Doesn't that say it all?" Ben questioned.

Sally closed her eyes and spoke softly.

"Oh Ben, I am so ashamed that I doubted you... it's my insecurity, isn't it?"

"Yes," he replied. "But you have no need to be insecure. Simply remember that I would never give you reason to doubt my love for you."

They stood, moved to each other, and melted into an embrace of warmth and tenderness. It was an embrace of pure love, without sexuality. They had come through their first crisis. It was an embrace of intense relief and more meaningful than any simultaneous orgasm.

"I was terrified that I would lose you," whispered Ben into Sally's ear.

"I was heartbroken when I saw you together... I'm sorry, Ben, I will never doubt you again," she whispered back.

Ben continued.

"Sally, it hurts me so much when you are unhappy. What do you want more than anything?"

"You know the answer to that, Ben... I want to live with you. I want to be your wife."

Ben paused.

"Have you forgotten that I can't give you children?"

Sally pulled her head back slightly to look directly into Ben's eyes.

"I haven't forgotten," she said with a smile.

Ben sat her down facing him and dropped to one knee. Sally couldn't believe the words that he spoke.

"Sally... We can't continue forever as we are. Despite all the problems that we'll face with your mother, when you decide that the time is right, will you make me the happiest man alive... and become my wife?"

Her jaw dropped.

"Ben, do you mean it? Do you really, really mean it?"

Her face lit up at his reply.

"Yes, precious... I really, really, really mean it."

"Oh Ben, my answer is yes, yes, yes – a thousand yeses."

She kissed and hugged him, then kissed and hugged some more. Ben lifted her delicate body and swirled her in circles.

He set her down and stressed, "I know that you want to tell the world, but it's our secret until you and your mother are ready to handle the situation."

Sally could barely contain her excitement. Ben looked at her deliriously happy face. The happy Sally was back! They were brought back down to earth by the sound of Margaret's door key turning in the latch.

Sally rushed to the kitchen and shouted out, "Is that you, Mum? I'm just making a coffee for Ben, would you like one?"

"Oh, yes please, darling. Hello Ben, what are you doing here?"

Her tone wasn't over-friendly, but nor was it suspicious.

"I was in the area and decided to call in for my watch," he replied.

"Well, you're a lot more cheerful than you were this morning," she said, as Sally joined them.

"Yes, Ben's been telling me a couple of jokes," Sally lied. "He *is* funny."

"How is your brother-in-law?" Ben enquired.

Margaret was pleased that Ben had taken the trouble to ask after the health of the Spanish side of the family. Ben drank his coffee and sat through the tedium of Margaret expressing concern over the slow progress that Sebastian was making.

He eventually released himself with the words, "Sorry, must go – cats to feed."

"Of course," said Margaret. "What would they do without you?"

"Starve!" joked Ben.

They laughed.

"I'll see you out, Ben," Sally offered.

He deliberately left without the watch that he had "come to collect". At the foot of the stairs, Ben took his woman into his arms and briefly but passionately kissed her.

"I adore you," he whispered.

Sally simply beamed her lovely smile and kissed him back with the words, "I'll ring you later."

*

Sally didn't study that night. Her books lay on her desk and she lay on her bed, her head nestled into her "Te quiero" cushion. She smiled as she contemplated the wonderful life that lay before her. She would give all to spend that night in his arms. She loved Ben for wanting her as his wife, without a need to delve deeply into the detail of her past. They were memories that she wanted buried. She wanted time to pass quickly – to a time when she could be his wife.

*

Twenty miles away, Ben felt elated that his proposal of marriage had brought a form of closure to his future with Sally. He knew that there would be many hurdles to negotiate, not least of all the reaction of Margaret. He was content that Sally had returned to the fold, but regretted that her fragility had given credence to the malicious activity of Maria. *It's now history*, he told himself. *I'm strong enough to face any amount of objection, disapproval, and bigotry that will be thrown our way. Will Sally have the same strength?*

Sally's call from her bed was a little different.

"Hello fiancé… I love you lots."

"Hello, precious," Ben whispered. "Are you allowed to wear jewellery in college?"

"A little, but an engagement ring might be a little too much upfront," she giggled.

187

"That's true," agreed Ben. "But we could choose one together in the meantime, couldn't we?"

"That would be lovely," she whispered dreamily.

Chapter 22

It was a different Sally that went off to academic study the following day. The previous day it had been a depressed teenager. Today it was a confident and vibrant young woman, with head held high, that approached a group of friends in the college grounds.

"Hi guys, hi Maria – everything good?"

All but Maria returned her morning greeting. She was bemused and disappointed to see the overnight transformation in Sally's demeanour. She must conspire and scheme to undo the happiness that Sally enjoyed. She had already begun the process the previous day.

Sally was a student eager to achieve and it came as no surprise that she was able to concentrate even more attentively and enthusiastically during classes. With uncertainty out of her life, replaced by a direction and a goal that she so wanted, she was ready to achieve her ambitions with more gusto than ever. It's what Ben would want, if only to reinforce the point that their love wasn't a destructive emotion.

It was mid-afternoon when Sally was summoned from class to the office of her principal.

"Come in, Sally – take a seat."

Mrs. Sanchez, a middle-aged and kindly lady from Hertfordshire, had studied languages at Oxford University, met and married a Spanish national, and settled in Spain. The education system in Spain had snapped up her multi-lingual talents when she had applied for a post fifteen years earlier. She had progressed quickly to the position of Head of Teaching Faculty.

The personal file of Sally Perez lay on her desk.

"Sally... you are not a child and in theory I have no right to interfere in your private life, but I sometimes have to look beyond academic and personal skills to assess the suitability of students for their chosen career. I'll come straight to the point. I am concerned that a rumour has quickly reached the ears of members of staff that you are having a relationship with a much, much older man."

The new confident Sally was quick to respond.

"Oh, I see, Miss. This, of course, has come from Maria. She is talking about Ben. He is a close friend of the family. At the weekend, my brother, his friend Juan, my so-called friend Maria and I met up with him at the beach to use his Jet Ski. It was a brilliant day, spoilt only by Maria embarrassingly throwing herself at Ben. He is nearly old enough to be her father and, of course, he rejected her flirting."

Mrs. Sanchez listened without interruption, nodding her head knowingly throughout. Sally continued.

"Miss, I don't know how well you know Maria, but when men are around, she *has* to be the centre of attention and does *not* handle rejection very well. It's obvious that she has chosen to turn my friendship with Ben into something entirely different – Ben is a lovely, lovely man and, if anything, is more of a father figure to me."

From the file, Mrs. Sanchez knew of the death of Sally's father. She also knew from past staff meetings of the flirtatious lengths to which Maria would go in order to be a favourite with male lecturers. She had no difficulty in believing Sally's version of events.

"O.K., Sally, thank you for explaining. Off you go, work hard."

Despite Maria's actions, Sally was not a vindictive person. She stopped at the door, turned and spoke.

"I know you mean to help, Miss... don't think too badly of Maria – she's not an evil person; just a little insecure. It's Maria that needs your help, not me."

The Head smiled. Sally moved to leave, but stopped again.

"One more thing, Miss... I'm sure that the girls won't mind me speaking on their behalf. Older men, glancing occasionally at the young, developing female body is normal – I think it's called the man thing? We understand that, but, without naming names, we're not too comfortable with *leering*. Perhaps you could bring it up at the next staff meeting?"

"I will," came the reply.

Sally walked out of the office, leaving Mrs. Sanchez dumbfounded by Sally's polite arrogance.

Sally walked back to class, congratulating herself on how well she had handled the matter, with her combination of truth and the one big lie. It was a necessary part of the deception that she and Ben were living.

*

Maria was summoned.

"Come in, Maria – sit down."

Maria nervously obeyed and the Head continued.

"Now then, Maria. The spreading of malicious gossip will not be tolerated in this college – do you understand?"

Maria moved to fight back. Mrs. Sanchez stopped her in her tracks and repeated.

"It will not be tolerated! – Do you understand?"

"Yes, Miss," came the sheepish reply.

Mrs. Sanchez added, "I suggest that you apologise to Sally. You can go back to class now."

As Maria moved to the door, her headmistress added a final word.

"Maria… we are here to help students in all sorts of ways. If ever you need my help, you know where I am."

The tears welled in Maria's eyes and then flooded down her cheeks. The poor girl perhaps had problems far more deep-seated than Ben had pondered. The firmly handled interview softened. The Head beckoned Maria, took her in her arms, and comforted the teenager, as she would her own daughter. The rest of the college day became a confidential period of talking woman to woman.

*

Mrs. Sanchez watched from her window during the mayhem of students leaving the faculty. She spotted Sally's approach towards Maria and dreaded the start of a catfight.

191

"I don't know if he will be interested, Maria, but you wanted Ben's number," Sally offered.

"I won't need it. I'm sorry, Sally." Maria sniffled with tears welling. Sally held out the hand of friendship.

"Let's not be enemies, Maria."

They hugged each other and walked to the gates arm in arm.

The Head of Department pondered – another day and yet another incident that has nothing to do with education. *What am I... a teacher or a counsellor? – Or both?*

*

Sally rang Ben before entering the apartment block. She told him of the day's drama. He was proud that she had handled her first test of public opinion so well, but hoped that the gossip wouldn't extend beyond college boundaries into the homes of other students.

Ben praised Sally.

"The kindness that you showed to Maria at the end of the day – it makes you very special."

Sally found the opportunity to ring Ben later in the day.

"Hello my lovely man. Mum has a staff meeting after school tomorrow and Michael will be at football practice. Come and collect your watch... again!"

After their nightly goodbyes, she fell asleep dreaming of her life ahead.

Chapter 23

A call from Sally later the following day confirmed that they could meet. Ben was already parked and waiting when Sally opened the main entrance door. They moved swiftly up the stairs, hand in hand, and burst into the apartment, almost tripping as they fell into each other's arms. They held on tight and kissed passionately, loins pressed hard together.

"Do we have time to consummate our engagement?" asked Ben.

Sally smiled as she answered.

"I thought you'd never ask. But, first, I need a wee."

She moved quickly to the bathroom, relieved herself, threw her panties into the Ali Baba, and sat astride the bidet to freshen her loins.

"In here, Ben," she urged. "We will have to keep watch."

She led Ben into her bedroom, where slightly open Venetian blinds would allow sight of the courtyard below, but afford the privacy needed.

"I really want to face you, Ben, but I'll have to watch for unwelcome visitors," apologised Sally.

She turned her back, unclasped her bra, placed her hands on the windowsill, and unashamedly offered up her rear for the attention of Ben's desire. Sally used a hand to push her bra upwards and Ben's eager palms were already in position to receive breasts as they fell. Ben murmured satisfied delight as he fondled their firmness. Sally's murmurs blended with his, as he first stroked, and then gently squeezed her aroused nipples. There was uncertainty as to when Margaret would arrive, so there was pressure to take their loving to a swift closure. Sally parted her legs and spoke.

"Make beautiful love to me, Ben… put Big Ben inside Tinkerbell."

Ben lifted her skirt and placed it on her back. Despite her ongoing education, he thought of Sally as a woman and would never tire of the joys of her submitting her body to his love. He dropped everything to his ankles and pulled her labia apart to take in the intimacy of her wet pink. His helmet homed in and he held her apart as his rock-hard penis slowly slid the length of her cavity. They groaned the ecstatic pleasure of full penetration. It felt different. The declaration of a future together somehow induced a gentler emotion into the union of their bodies. They stayed locked and fell into an abyss of adoration. Over time they had been captured by mutual love. They were now consumed by it. It was sublime. With hands returned to Sally's breasts, the need for orgasmic satisfaction began to build. There was love, desire, and emotional commitment from every long stroke of penis in vagina.

"Oh Ben... It feels so big, I could explode with love," Sally gasped.

"I wish I could give you babies," Ben said quietly.

Ben was not without his own insecurity, but Sally reassured him.

"I have *you*... that's what matters."

Ben bent his knees and thrust upwards into her body. Her buttocks lifted automatically, to receive a more direct contact with her clitoris. Before Sally could request a slower arousal she was gripped by the urgent need to climax and muffled cries as her body trembled through an intense orgasm. Ben set about satisfying *his* urgent need. With each long rhythmical stroke the fire in his helmet burned with a fury that couldn't be contained. The moment arrived and with small thrusts at total penetration, his liquid of love poured deep into her vagina. He groaned with pleasure.

"Was that nice?" Sally sighed.

"If only you knew," Ben panted.

"Oh, I do," she replied. "I love you so much, Ben."

She stood and leant back against Ben. One hand took her by the mound, the other by her breast, and he pulled her to tiptoe, hard against his body. His wrist could feel the huge penis inside her, insisting on escape through the abdomen wall of his delicate woman. They stayed locked for some time, whilst Ben planted gentle kisses on Sally's neck and ears.

"Ben," whispered Sally. "I wish we could stay like this for hours, but if you leave now, you could collect your wristwatch over and over."

"Good thinking," said Ben.

Ben kept watch whilst Sally sorted herself out in the bathroom.

"Do you want to wash?" asked Sally, as she returned.

Ben showed her the penis mummified in a handkerchief.

"No. I want to sleep with the smell of you tonight."

"Is there anything that you don't like about me?" she smiled.

"Nothing," came the firm reply.

They cuddled and quietly expressed their mutual love before Ben made a hasty retreat avoiding Margaret's return.

Sally blew a kiss to Ben as she said goodbye from the top of the stairs.

"I'll ring you later."

Her words prompted Ben to rush back to Sally. He pushed a pile of notes into her hand.

"Top up your mobile."

Uncle Seb's pay-off lay untouched in Sally's account.

*

A call that night came sooner than expected.

It was Michael.

"Hi Ben. Will you have a word with Mum? I've told her that I'm sure you wouldn't mind."

Margaret came to the phone.

"I'm sorry, Ben. It's Michael being silly. I've had some bad news from England. My father has had a serious heart attack and is in hospital. I've just booked a flight to go over tomorrow. Michael wants to stay with you, but I've told him that it's out of the question. Sally's a big girl now and they can look after themselves while I'm away. It would be a bit too much for the grandparents, but I'm sure that Rocio and Sebastian would step into the breach if she needed any help."

Ben's heart leapt – he was not having Sebastian anywhere near Sally. Ben stopped her.

"It has to be your decision, Margaret. I don't know how long you will be away, but Michael's suggestion isn't as silly as it sounds. I can get them to college or to a rendezvous point with the college-run mothers

195

each morning. With their studies, they don't need the hassle of preparing meals, washing, and ironing, et cetera. Simone and Juanita will happily put some meals together and generally look after things. On top of that, I have a deal with the telephone company where my calls to the U.K. cost absolute buttons – you can talk with your kids as often and for as long as you want. Give it some thought, but in any event, ring me back with your flight details and I will get you to the airport tomorrow."

"You're too kind, Ben, I'll speak to them and ring you later."

It's true that kindness came easily to Ben and he would have offered the facility regardless, but throughout his conversation, the ulterior motive had been in his mind.

Michael punched the air when his mother agreed and Sally worked hard at containing her excitement.

"Remember," lectured their mother. "You are not going on holiday. You will study and revise as normal. I will be checking with Ben that you are behaving yourselves and working hard. You must treat every day as a normal learning day."

Margaret put Ben out of the misery of waiting for the phone call.

"Thank you, Ben. Michael and Sally *would* like to stay with you. They are packing their things now and if it's no trouble I will accept your offer of a lift to the airport. You are so kind to this family."

Ben felt guilty accepting her praise and gratitude, but relieved; had Margaret refused her children's wishes, he would have had no option but to reveal his refusal to risk any contact between Sally and her uncle.

They discussed arrangements and agreed that Ben would collect them all from the apartment, load up suitcases, and wave Margaret off at the airport as she left on her early evening flight to Nottingham. Ben insisted that it would be more convenient to forego the existing shared college-run arrangements in favour of him taking responsibility for transport. He left Margaret to inform the other mothers involved.

Sally rang from her bed.

"I'm sad that Granddad is not well, but so excited that we'll be together."

"I know, precious. I can't wait," whispered Ben.

Chapter 24

Throughout the drive to the airport, Margaret continued to lecture her brood on good behaviour. Ben, in turn, assured her that he would keep their noses to the grindstone and that they were in safe hands. She hugged her children warmly as they said their farewells. Sally passed over a letter that she had written for Grandma and Granddad. Margaret had been to the bank that morning and gave to Ben an envelope containing quite a large sum of money. He immediately pushed it into her handbag.

"We'll talk about it when you come back," insisted Ben.

Sally waved back to her mother as they drove off.

"Right, tenpin bowling!" laughed Michael.

"Bugger off, studies!" replied Ben.

Ben left them to settle into their bedrooms whilst he collected fried chicken and chips from the local take-away. They revelled in each other's company during their first evening meal, but Ben dutifully sent them off to study whilst he cleared up and fed the cats.

Ben reminded them, "Be sure to ring Mum later. No doubt she will visit your granddad this evening, but I would think she could be at home by around ten."

An hour and a half later, Michael insisted that all revision was complete and begged a bit of footie in the garden.

"See you down there in five minutes," said Ben.

He went to Sally's room. She lay on the bed studying a textbook. He knelt across her and kissed her mouth gently.

"A bit of football with your brother… see you shortly."

Sally smiled. She watched the two boys at play from her window for a little while, pondering on what a lovely father he would make. If she

197

didn't love him as a man and as a friend, she would happily have him as a father.

Michael's youth eventually tired Ben and, after a shower, he threw on a comfortable tracksuit. Sally was already in thin fabric pyjamas, curled up on the sofa when he walked into the lounge. The television was switched on but the audio muted. She was scribbling notes and deep in study from one of her textbooks. He was determined not to undermine her obligation to learning, but couldn´t resist sitting beside her.

"Test me," insisted Sally, passing over her textbook.

Ben would be content to spend any amount of time sitting with her and simply admiring her beauty. They were joined on the sofa by two cats, each one choosing a lap on which to purr. He sat holding her hand, stroking a furry animal, and marvelling on the good fortune of being loved by this young woman.

Michael arrived from his shower, flicked through the T.V. channels, and considerately set the volume to a low level. Sally pushed her books to one side and, without consultation with Ben, spoke openly with her brother.

"Michael... do you know that Ben and I are in love?"

"Of course, Sal, I'm not entirely stupid." He smiled. "I always suspected that Simone didn't exist."

Ben was surprised by her next revelation.

"Michael, what you don't know is that when the time is right, we are going to get married."

Her brother narrowed his eyes and pursed his lips. There was a long pause before he responded.

"Just make sure that I'm not around when you tell Mum."

They all laughed. Sally continued.

"I want *you* to know, because for months we've been ducking and diving. Fate has stepped in and we now have some special time together. I would prefer not to be sneaking around."

"I'm ahead of you," Michael interrupted. "You'll be having an early night then?"

"Probably," laughed Ben.

Sally got to her feet, took her brother's face in both hands, and gave him a sisterly kiss on the lips. Michael immediately wiped the affection from his mouth. She curled up in Ben's arms and the threesome watched television together.

Impervious to his sister's fragility, Michael suggested, "Ben... why don't you marry Mum instead?"

Sally playfully slapped his head and scolded him.

"Because he's mine!"

"Besides," Ben added, "I couldn't handle having you as a step-son."

They laughed and exchanged a high-five.

"Talking of Mum, give her a ring now. She may be home from the hospital."

There was no response. Sally spoke after the beep.

"Hi Mum. You are obviously still with Granddad. Time is getting on here, so we'll be going to bed shortly. I will ring you tomorrow evening. Give our love to Granddad and Grandma. Ben sends his regards. Love you, we'll speak soon."

"Don't stay up too late, Michael," said Ben, as he and Sally fed the cats before going to bed.

They slipped naked beneath the covers. He left the bedside lights on. Ben spoke lovingly.

"I have shared this bed with only one woman... do you remember the first day that we made love?"

Sally threw herself into his arms and held him so tightly they could barely breathe. They kissed with affection rather than passion. These were the moments they had longed for. The moments that could last for as long as they wished, without a thought of being judged. The moments that would last for as long as swelling body parts could resist the craving and the demands of sensual satisfaction.

In time, penis, labia, and nipples swelled. Juices began to flow and tongues began to gently search out a partner. Ben pushed back the covers. He knelt and gazed upon Sally's flawless skin bathed in the warmth of artificial lighting. Her curves were accentuated by soft shadows. He turned her onto her tummy. Sally submitted to whatever was to come, safe in the knowledge that Ben would never fail to pleasure her, and safe in the knowledge that his love would never echo her unfortunate past. He lifted her long hair to one side and kissed her neck and face. He whispered adoration into her petite ears. She giggled as he occasionally licked. His kisses travelled downwards; planted, first, on her shoulders and back, then down further to her buttocks. She jumped as his tongue thrust out to have brief contact with her clitoris. Sally murmured pleasure as the kisses continued the length of her legs to her ankles. Ben turned her over and she reached to hold the enormous hard prick that towered above the level of her lover's belly button.

"Not yet," whispered Ben.

He kissed her legs from ankles upwards. Sally parted her legs to receive kisses on her inner thighs. The tip of his tongue tickled the swollen vulva. Full tongue licked parted labia, before plunging into her vagina, seeking out a few caresses of her eager clitoris. She moaned and gyrated her hips. Her skin smelt of shower gel. Her Tinkerbell tasted of Tinkerbell. How Ben loved the taste of Tinkerbell.

His mouth moved swiftly to swallow her nipples. His tongue thrashed furiously, arousing them to bursting point. Sally caressed Ben's erection with both hands and her desire could be denied no longer.

"Ben," she begged. "Tell me that you love me and then join our bodies."

"You know I love you, Sally… beyond reason," Ben said quietly.

He kissed her lips gently and leaned back. He knew that if he entered her at that moment, they both would orgasm in an instant. He looked into the depths of her lovely eyes, smiled, and kissed her hands for a while. He propped another pillow behind her head so that she could watch the union. Heels planted and legs wide apart, Sally took the erection in her hand and watched wide-eyed as she fed it slowly into her body. She gasped as her vagina slowly swallowed the enormity of his muscle.

"Oh God. There isn't a feeling like it. It's wonderful," she sighed.

Ben's eyes smiled as she continued.

"I want it to last and last, Ben, but I may lose control."

"That doesn't matter, precious, come when you want to. We have days ahead of us… and in the future, years."

Sally smiled.

"Oh Ben… make love to me gently. Fill me with your love."

Ben withdrew almost to the point of complete withdrawal. Soaked in her fluid, he slid in and out, her vagina gripping tightly. He moved more slowly than they had ever loved before. The urgency was no longer there and, with control, they could bask in love, as well as their animal desire. Sally's attention wandered between the adoration in Ben's eyes and the slow pumping of love into her very being. She was in a swirling, dreamy world and felt that no two people could love each other more. Ben was alongside her in that same world.

For a full fifteen minutes they enjoyed the slow build-up, but when Ben took her breasts and nipples in his hands, Sally's vagina demanded more.

"Whenever you want to, my love," Sally gasped.

The synchronised climax that followed was beyond anything that they had experienced. They buried their heads in each other's shoulders to muffle the squeals and groans. Ben wanted to eat her and Sally thought she would faint. The need to protect Michael from the vocal intimacy of their orgasm was the only consideration that prevented them from declaring the moment throughout Spain.

Ben sat back on his haunches and pulled his beautiful woman astride him. Sally clung tightly to him, her breasts pressed hard against his chest. He was so deep inside that he felt that he could damage her. Sally felt otherwise as she pressed her labia firmly onto the base of Ben's erection.

"I can't find the words," sighed Sally.

"Nor I," panted Ben.

After some time, he lifted Sally's loins from Big Ben. The big boy settled in the cleavage of her buttocks. They held each other whilst the liquids of love dribbled from her body into Ben's pubic hair.

They kissed and cuddled at length, before Sally enjoyed again the pleasure of being astride a bidet, her lovely man washing her every intimate part. They were so comfortable with mutual nudity. It felt completely natural to them. Cleaned up, they returned to the love nest. Sally laid on her front, whilst Ben gently massaged her neck and shoulders. Her "mmm"s gave way to a soft deep breathing. Just like

Scampi those years before, Ben's love had sent her into a deep sleep. He looked at her adorable young face for a while, set the alarm, and joined her under the covers. He kissed her shoulder, whispered "Goodnight", and killed the lights.

Before sleep, he marvelled at her brother's adult acceptance of their love.

Michael, he thought, was probably cock in hand, fantasising over Maria or the Puerto Banus prostitute.

Chapter 25

The insistent beeping of the alarm clock threw Ben into a world of surrogate fatherhood. He was not at his most lively first thing in the morning, but forced himself to the bathroom and cleaned his teeth. Sally stirred only slightly when he switched the alarm to radio mode. Ben kissed her gently on the lips.

"Come on, precious… time to get up."

Sally knew immediately where she was and murmured, "Come back to bed."

"I wish!" said Ben. "Come on. I'll start breakfast. You can drag Michael out of his bed."

Ben quickly threw on a dressing gown and banged on Michael's door as he passed.

"Come on, Michael, rise and shine."

The lad groaned a response.

Ben set about laying the table in his kitchen/diner. He was setting the last of the fruit, cereals, and orange juice when Sally appeared in the kitchen. She looked as though she had just stepped from a beauty parlour.

"Good morning, my lovely man," Sally enthused, kissing Ben's unshaven face.

She had only ever seen Ben in ship-shape and scrubbed-up condition.

"Do you think you can live with this?" Ben asked, drawing attention to his bedraggled appearance.

"For ever." She smiled, kissing his lips gently.

Demanding cats meowed, circled, and brushed against their legs. She pushed Ben out of the kitchen.

"You get dressed while I feed the furry things. Then I'll make tea and toast."

Sally was enjoying her new role as surrogate mother to Michael and pretend wife to Ben.

It was a showered, shaved, and rejuvenated Ben that joined his new family for breakfast. He had never been a breakfast man, but found himself enjoying not just the food but also the loud banter between them. Sally interrupted the proceedings in an organisational tone.

"Now then, we normally take lunch boxes to college, Ben. I'll get that set up for tomorrow onwards and before you ask – yes, we do have money for the canteen today."

Ben smiled and touched her hand. He thought the task of preparing lunch boxes to be unnecessary hassle, but didn't argue the point.

"As you wish," he agreed. "And if you need any between-meal snacks, the goodies are in the left-hand drawer of the fridge. Whilst you're my guests, help yourself to whatever you want."

Michael immediately investigated and helped himself to a couple of chocolate bars, before running off to collect briefcases and sports holdalls. Sally moved to clear the table and wash up. Ben stopped her.

"Leave that," he insisted. "Juanita will be here later."

"But I want to look after you," she pleaded.

Her mind tingled with anticipation at his response.

"When you are my wife."

After manic searching for Michael's football boots, they were soon on their way. Michael had become considerate and relegated himself to the rear seat. Sally rested her hand on Ben's thigh as he drove. Half an hour later, they were at the college where dozens of other drivers were delivering hungry minds.

"I love you, Ben, think of me," Sally said quietly.

"I always do," Ben replied.

Mock vomiting sound effects came from the rear. The lovebirds fought off the temptation of even a continental kiss farewell. They waved and Ben drove off to enlist Juanita's more committed help.

His Argentinean lady had been entrusted with a set of house keys and was already clearing breakfast things when he arrived home. Ben sat her down and explained the situation in detail. Juanita was ahead of him and enthusiastically offered any amount of help he may need whilst Margaret was in Nottingham. Juanita agreed to mother them all, for as long as was necessary. She would prepare evening meals Monday to Friday, in addition to her usual washing, ironing, and cleaning. The subject of payment wasn't discussed. Juanita would welcome the extra income and knew Ben to be a fair and generous man.

Ben left his helper working in the kitchen and hurriedly messed up the unoccupied bed from the previous night. That deception would be necessary throughout the length of his guest's visit.

*

It was late that afternoon when Sally was summoned to the office of her Head again.

"Hello Sally, come in and sit down," said Mrs. Sanchez smiling. "I'm afraid that the rumour that we talked about has reached the ears of one or two very protective parents. It's ridiculous, I know, but they are concerned that their daughters could be contaminated with liberal attitudes. I have assured them that it's a storm in a teacup and a story circulated for all the wrong reasons. They have accepted my explanation, but because parents have become involved, I wonder if I have an obligation to inform your mother of what's going on."

Sally's heart raced as she spoke with urgency.

"You can't, Miss. My mother is in Nottingham. My grandfather has had a serious heart attack and Mum has gone to visit. This would be the last thing she needs right now."

"I'm sorry to hear that, Sally. How is your grandfather? And how are you and Michael managing?"

Sally ignored the first question and flushed heavily as she answered the second.

"We are staying with Ben and his housekeeper is looking after us all."

Her principal was a kind woman whose only agenda was to help. A surge of guilt ran through Sally, having deceived her during their previous meeting. By necessity, she and Ben were living a life of deception, but brought up to be an honest girl, she had an overwhelming need to come clean. Tears welled a little.

"Miss… please forgive me. I owe you an apology. When we spoke before, every word that I told you was absolutely true – except about me and Ben. Maria had no idea how near to the truth she was when she spread that rumour. I'm sorry that I had to lie to you. Of course, my mother doesn't know about us and I want it to stay that way until she is in a better frame of mind to handle it."

Mrs. Sanchez smiled.

"I understand. Thank you for being completely honest and thank you for the apology."

Sally wanted to unburden and continued.

"Miss… let me tell you about Ben. At thirty-six he´s twice my age, but it's too easy to assume the worst about big age-gap relationships… You don't need to know the details, but I've had my fair share of unhappiness. Then Ben came into my life. He has been the only person that I could open up to. He listened, but didn't judge. He's been there for me ever since. The family have known him for around six months. In the early days, he treated me like a protective father would care for his daughter, but I began to fall deeply in love with him. At first, he rejected my attention, just as he rejected Maria. He *had* fallen in love with me, but wouldn't admit it. I'm so happy that he eventually gave in to his feelings. He's a clever and very responsible man. He insists that I do well with my career and go on to even higher education if it's what I want. He wants to hold my life back in no way whatsoever. I know all of the downsides; he's twice my age, but he is the kindest and most loving person I have ever known. Miss, unfortunately, I know more about the difference between lust and genuine love than most girls my age. My head is not in the clouds. I am not in the middle of a teenage romance and when the time comes we *will* get married. In private, I sometimes cry with happiness… Surely it can't be wrong."

"Let me think for a moment, Sally," said the Head.

There was a long pause whilst Sally sat with head bowed.

Mrs. Sanchez eventually rose and placed the "Do Not Disturb" sign outside. She moved to a comfortable chair at a coffee table and invited Sally to sit opposite.

"Sally," she began. "My principal role in this academy is to ensure that all students leave with as good an education as possible. It's my duty to prepare them, where possible, for specialising in rewarding careers. It's an obligation that I have to students and to their parents. It's a role that I enjoy. I am so lucky that I look forward to every working day. In your case, being fluent in both English and Spanish, you are perfectly placed to carve an excellent future in teaching... Never forget that. Now let's have a confidential talk, woman to woman. When I was twenty-four, I fell in love and married a man that was thirty-five. A gap of eleven years – not the gap of eighteen years between you and Ben and I *was* six years older than you are now. But even so, I was put under huge pressure to end the relationship. Everyone, from my parents through to the milkman, had an opinion on how I should spend *my* life. It seemed that *they* wanted to live it for me. The marriage was destined to fail, I was warned. Six years later, my parents divorced... I have found that the love of an older man is absolutely wonderful. The love of an older man is more mature, more considerate, and often, I believe, more sincere. I don't know your Ben or his background and I can neither condemn nor condone your relationship with him. I would be wrong to encourage or discourage your feelings for him. You, and you alone, can make those decisions. Your file tells me that your eagerness to learn is second to none and that you adore young children. The teacher in me wants you to go on to enjoy huge vocational success. The woman in me says this... *Sacrifice happiness... for nothing*. If, in the future, you can feel fulfilled by combining a rewarding career with happiness in your personal life, you have everything."

Tears of gratitude welled in Sally's eyes. They stood and the arms of a worldly wise Head welcomed the embrace that Sally gave.

"Thank you, Miss," Sally murmured into a shoulder of compassion. The bell sounded end of day.

"Sally, I'll not make contact with your mother when she returns and we have *not* had this conversation," was said with a smile. "Now off you go – work hard and be happy."

"I will," confirmed Sally knowingly.

"You know where I am if you need me." The Head smiled.

Mrs. Sanchez sat back in her chair and contemplated the problems that Ben and this sweet young woman would face when they declared their love to the world. She'd had first-hand experience. She wondered what Sally's declaration of "my share of unhappiness" could entail. Why was it Ben, and not her mother, that Sally turned to? She had chosen not to press Sally on the matter. Had Sally unburdened all, she and the compassionate Mrs. Sanchez would have wept floods together.

She watched from her office window. Michael had involved Ben in conversation with Juan and other friends. Ben readily joined in with a bit of kung-fu play-fighting. *How sad that their father died*, she thought.

*

After brief farewells to her friends, Sally joined them and Ben placed a fatherly arm around her shoulder. Maria rushed to the group and exchanged a continental kiss with Ben. Animated re-living of riding a Jet Ski followed. Friendship seemed to have replaced competition. The young men and Ben exchanged high-fives and fist bumps, bags were loaded, and the three set off for home.

"I forgot to say," said Ben. "If either of you have after-college activities, let me know and I can either collect you later or you can jump on the train and I'll collect you at my local station."

Michael rattled off a reply.

"That's great, I sometimes play one sport or another after college, Ben. I could ring you from the train. What's for dinner?" he demanded, with his pleasant abruptness.

"Juanita is cooking our evening meals," replied Ben.

"Oh no, not Spanish shit!" complained the lad.

Sally scolded his rudeness and ingratitude.

"No, Argentinean shit!" laughed Ben.

It was neither. Ben had warned her that his guests liked basic foods and were not over-fond of Spanish cuisine. Juanita was busy preparing soup starter, fillets of pork with all the trimmings, followed by custard-filled doughnuts with ice cream.

The introductions to Juanita were manic. She didn't stand on ceremony and hugged her new responsibilities warmly.

"Oh Ben," she exclaimed. "They are so beautiful. Muy guapa, muy guapo. Very beautiful, very handsome."

Sally accepted the compliments gratefully, but slightly resented Juanita's presence on her new territory. Michael seemed not to have a problem with being cuddled into the large tits bursting from a low-cut blouse. His man thing forced his eyes to the inviting cleavage.

Sally went to her room. Ben followed.

Sally spoke furtively.

"She is very attractive, Ben."

Ben stopped her.

"No, I haven't and nor will I. Have you forgotten? I will never—"

Sally finished the sentence.

"—give you reason to doubt my love for you."

They smiled at each other, Sally threw herself into Ben's arms and they kissed with passion. There was still much work ahead to overcome her insecurity. Ben brought the clinch to an end.

"If I don't feed the cats now, you will be on your back on that bed."

Sally loved the cats and insisted, "I'll get changed and help you. Then I'll ring Mum."

Sally reappeared in the kitchen wearing a cosy one-piece suit designed for comfort rather than appearance. It hardly mattered – she would look gorgeous dressed in a potato sack.

"Muy guapa," repeated Juanita, pinching Sally's cheek.

The now secure Sally smiled and graciously suggested that Juanita should stay to eat with them. That was impossible, as her husband and two young children would need to be fed.

"Sally, I will feed the cats. You can love them later," Ben insisted. "Go and ring your mum."

Sally called Michael to be part of the conversation and telephoned Nottingham. Ben stayed away from the call and got under Juanita's feet trying to be helpful. He was eventually called to speak with Margaret.

"I'm so grateful, Ben, are they behaving themselves?"

Margaret rattled on for some time, Ben feeling more and more uncomfortable with her gratitude. It was *he* that should be thanking *her* for making available her lovely daughter.

He interrupted.

"The Crew will ring you every day and they'll keep me posted on your father's progress. Juanita will be serving up a meal shortly. I'll pass you back to Sally."

Ben escaped from the phone and listened as the family exchanged fond and loving goodbyes. Sally's final goodbye was a tearful expression of love to her grandma. She missed her grandma. She thought of her as a big cuddly teddy bear.

"Juanita, this looks delicious," exclaimed a seated Michael, as starter and main course was set before him.

"Gracias, Michael," Juanita thanked him, hugging his face into her large breasts.

"Juanita, this looks delicious," smiled Ben.

Ben received the same facefull of tits.

"Juanita, this looks delicious," exclaimed Sally.

Juanita picked up on the significance of what was going on and they all laughed. She placed her hand on Sally's head and warmly kissed her brow. As she left, Juanita was called back to the kitchen.

"This really *is* delicious," said Michael with a smile.

She narrowed her eyes and wagged a forefinger.

"Naughty boy! No more Num-Nums until Monday! Adios guapos."

The family laughed and settled into their meal.

"Before you ask, Michael, I think they are probably real," said Ben.

They spluttered food as they joked and laughed.

"Sal, have you brought a dress for next week?" asked Michael.

"I wasn't planning on going," replied Sally.

Michael went on to tell Ben that it was the end of term disco for first-year students the following Friday.

"You *must* go," insisted Ben. "You'll have fun with your friends and they would expect you to be there."

Sally pulled a face of reluctance. Michael jokingly assured Ben, "She's a bit of a flirt, but I'll keep an eye on her."

"Ben knows me better than that," protested Sally.

"Only joking," laughed Michael, as his delicate sister clipped his ear.

"I've got an idea," said Ben. "I've been wondering about your Christmas presents. It's Saturday tomorrow, suppose we go into Malaga and I'll fix you both up with new outfits for the disco."

"Cool," agreed Michael. "Will we be anywhere near a bowling alley?"

"Perhaps," said Ben smiling. "Come on, eat up, and then get study out of the way. Leave the weekend clear for fun."

Chapter 26

Margaret answered the phone; as promised it was Sally ringing from Spain.

"Hello Mum, how's Granddad?"

"A lot better, very tired, but now stable, and thankfully through the danger zone. The doctors say that he can probably return home sometime during next week. I was thinking I could perhaps ask Ben to have you both until next weekend, so that I could help Grandma to settle him in before flying back to Spain."

Sally interrupted.

"Ben... can you put up with us until next weekend?" she shouted through to the kitchen.

"No problem," came the shouted reply.

Michael was called to the phone. Mother, grandma and grandchildren passed the phone amongst themselves for over an hour before saying their goodbyes.

*

"So tell me about Ben," said Grandma to her daughter.

Margaret related all that she knew of him. How they first met, his kindness and generosity, their combined lottery win, how her children loved to be in his company, and how he enjoyed being with them. She painted a picture of a man that was rather wealthy, young at heart, and fun to be with.

"He sounds like a very nice man. And how do *you* feel about him?" asked Grandma.

"Oh! Out of the question," huffed Margaret. "No man could replace Miguel; as husband or father."

Grandma was a wise, educated woman, with a mind like a razor blade.

"For the children's sake as much as your own, why don't you at least allow yourself the *possibility* of moving on?" she asked in a kindly manner.

Intrusion into her world of obsessive mourning offended Margaret and she chose to digress.

"I used to be concerned that Ben might have desires on Sally, but I'm more relaxed now."

Grandma interrupted.

"Sally is growing into a woman. She wouldn't be in his house if she felt threatened. When the time comes, we all hope that she chooses wisely, but it will be her choice. Never forget, dear, that your father and I didn't exactly welcome Miguel with open arms and when it comes to sex, if Sally chooses to have an affair with a twice-divorced, drug-addicted low-life, it will be her choice – not ours."

Margaret was astounded at her mother's outspoken and liberal attitude.

Grandma answered the phone.

"Oh Sally, you darling girl... yes, he's well enough to take a call. He would love to hear from you, how thoughtful of you... Your mum and I will be with him at around eight o'clock this evening if you would like to ring then... He is on Victoria ward... Bye bye, precious... bye."

"What a lovely thoughtful girl, Margaret," sighed Grandma. "Now then, where was I...? Oh yes, I've been thinking. If there is nothing to hold you in Spain, why don't you come home? Live here with us; the house is too big for just your father and me, and it will one day be yours anyway. The standard of education is better; job opportunities for the children are better. You often complain about it being too hot in Spain. You can put the proceeds from your house sale in the bank and we have savings that will go to you and the children when we are gone... We could live a comfortable life."

"I do love you, Mother," said Margaret quietly. "You make me wonder why we ever moved to Spain."

After further discussion, a more or less spontaneous decision was made that a return to the U.K. was the way forward.

Chapter 27

Ben cleared the kitchen and left Michael studying at the dining table, before disturbing Sally's studies. She was making notes in one of several books spread across the dressing table. He approached her from behind, leant forward, and encircled her torso in his arms.

"Hello precious," he whispered in her ear.

"Grandma calls me precious too," she whispered back.

"Then we can't both be wrong, can we?"

"I suppose not," laughed Sally. "I *must* be precious."

She unzipped her "baby-grow" to waist level. She was bra-less.

"You love these, don't you, Ben?"

He didn't answer and took her breasts in his hands. He stroked and squeezed their roundness, then with thumb and forefinger teased the nipples into swollen firmness. Sally unzipped to crotch level and moved his hand downwards.

"Just a little love to keep me going," she pleaded.

Ben hadn't intended to interrupt important study, but couldn't deny her or *his* need for pleasure. His hand went into her knickers; he thrust his fingers inside her and beckoned her G-spot. She wetted immediately and parted her legs further. Ben swivelled the chair to face her, unzipped his pants, and offered his partly aroused penis into her hands. It became gorged with blood as she rubbed it hard across her breasts. His fingers moved to her clitoris. He teased, rubbed, and squeezed. His helmet, now the size of a large plum, stroked nipples and eagerly attacked the cleavage of her breasts. Sally was about to witness the boy in action. Ben felt the semen rushing up from his balls. It ejaculated fiercely and in quantity over her breasts and into the valley between. Sally gasped in

214

delight and Ben moaned as his helmet spread fluid across her chest. She pressed and passed his helmet across lubricated nipples. Ben's fingers worked with expertise. The fire in her clitoris sent a tremble through her vagina and into the whole area of her loins. Through her orgasm, she muffled squeals of pleasure. She settled herself.

"Ben," she panted. "One minute I'm studying – now look at the state of me."

"Sorry," gasped Ben.

"I forgive you."

They kissed tenderly as they showered together.

The past urgency of their meetings would have led to continued sexual arousal, but for now they could relax in the comfort of an uninterrupted, almost normal relationship of deep love.

"Don't forget to ring Granddad," Ben reminded, as he left the bedroom.

The three re-grouped later. An emotional call was made to their granddad's bedside in Nottingham and they settled into an evening of chatter and television. Sally manicured her finger and toenails before curling up alongside Ben and a couple of cats. The cats purred, the lovers cooed, and Michael took the piss. There was an air of warm contentment, but the lovers were all too aware that the bliss would cease the following weekend.

"Michael," began Ben. "After we have sorted some outfits for you both tomorrow, Sally and I need to do some food shopping. How do you feel about us picking up your friend Juan at Malaga railway station at around two o'clock? We could drop you off at the bowling alley and join you later."

"Great idea!" enthused Michael, rushing to the phone to ring his pal.

Ben winked at Sally. He had something in mind, but Sally knew not what!

"We'll have an early night and set off early," suggested Ben.

Sally made hot chocolate and they demolished a packet of digestive biscuits before going to their beds. Partly due to satiation, but mainly down to contentment, Ben and Sally chose not to make love that night. They were happy to talk and lay naked in each other's arms.

She confessed to Ben the circumstances that led her to tell Mrs. Sanchez of their love. Ben was concerned but reassured by Sally.

"She's a very understanding lady, Ben. She was in a similar situation when she was a young woman. She couldn't exactly give us her blessing, but she did say four wonderful words… *Sacrifice happiness, for nothing.*"

Their lips met gently, their bodies curled to a close foetal position, and they slipped into deep slumber.

Saturday morning traffic delayed their arrival in Malaga. Choosing an outfit for Michael was easy. He knew exactly what he wanted; new jeans, new trainers, and a trendy American-style bomber jacket with an enormous number on its back. Ben threw in a couple of T-shirts. Sally was successful in persuading her brother to tone down the colours to a co-ordination that looked less like a circus clown. For the young men at the disco, casual dress was the order of the day. Michael inspected his new persona in a full-length mirror and compared himself to the dog's private parts.

In contrast, the young ladies would be dressed in their finery – not necessarily to attract the boys, but simply to look beautiful. Sally guided them to a store for the modern young woman. She set about leafing through the racks of cheaper dresses. Ben made his way to the more expensive wear and immediately saw the cocktail dress that his lady should wear. He returned to her side, amongst the cheap stuff.

"I'm very undecided," said Sally.

"Not a problem, because I think I've seen something," Ben replied. He led her to the appropriate rack. She went straight to it.

"This one?" she questioned.

Ben nodded. Sally looked at the price tag.

"Oh no, Ben, it's a designer label and far too expensive."

"If they have it in your size, try it on," Ben insisted.

Dressed in a purple glittering lame dress, Sally walked from the changing rooms with the grace of a professional model. The dress had a tight-fitting bodice, which flared slightly to a level just above the knee. With a deep-cut back, it was designed to be worn bra-less. The bodice was held by two delicate straps tied in a bow beneath her hair at the nape of the neck. She looked fabulous. A dress designer couldn't have fitted the garment to her body more perfectly. Even Michael remarked that she looked cool.

"It's lovely, Ben, but I can't let you spend this amount," whispered Sally.

"Take us to the shoes," Ben instructed the assistant.

Silver sling-backs, with delicate two-inch heels, were chosen to complete the outfit. Though not a tall girl, her natural elegance in that dress was a sight to behold. Sally hugged and kissed her thanks as dress and shoes were bagged.

As breakfast had been skipped, sandwiches, fruit juices, and coffee were enjoyed before collecting Juan from the station. Ben provided Michael with adequate cash to get the two lads through several sessions of bowling, with drinks in between. Sally took her brother to one side.

"Michael. Our love is a secret love."

"Of course, Sal. Don't worry; I'll not say anything to Juan," Michael assured her.

"We'll catch up with you in a couple of hours," shouted Ben from the car.

"What food do we need, Ben?" asked Sally, as they drove away.

"Not food," whispered Ben. "Diamonds!"

Sally's mouth dropped and her eyes widened.

Arm in arm, they strolled the main shopping area of central Malaga. There was much discussion on the type of engagement ring that would best suit Sally's hand. She had style and dismissed any thought of a large, gaudy cluster being suitable for her slim, delicate finger. Ben avoided offering guidance as they window-shopped.

"My love doesn't need an advertisement. A cheap, simple ring is all I would want," she insisted.

They paused at a stylish jewellery shop frontage. None of the rings in windows bore price tags and she had no conception of prices when it came to precious stones.

"Just choose a design that you like," said Ben, "and we'll take it from there."

"That's nice," she said, pointing to a miniscule solitaire.

"Not as nice as the one on the shelf above," said Ben.

He pointed out what he thought to be a medium-size, high-quality diamond solitaire in a claw setting. He suspected that it wouldn't come cheap, but that was of no importance to him.

"It's lovely," drooled Sally. "But that could cost hundreds."

Sally had never taken an interest in the value of jewellery and Ben smiled at her delightful naivety.

"Come on, try it on, but you must *not* ask about price," insisted Ben.

Sally took an assistant to the window, they returned to Ben's side and the ring was presented for trial. Another assistant nudged the shop manager and, with eyebrows raised, nodded in the direction of the loving couple. It was a taste of things to come. A mirror gave Ben full view of the judgemental proceedings.

"It's perfect, Ben, but how much is it?"

Ben stopped the reply with a single gesture.

"Write it down," demanded Ben.

The manager took over, as the paper bearing the price was slipped to Ben. The note read six thousand euros.

"Twenty euros is a bit heavy," gasped Ben with a sharp intake of breath. "But if you like it, it's yours."

Sally wasn't *that* naive, but didn't press Ben any further.

"As long as *you* like it, I think it's perfect," whispered Sally.

"Size the lady's finger, please," Ben instructed.

Finger diameter measured, the choice of engagement ring had taken no more than fifteen minutes. The jewel would be ready for collection the following Friday, together with valuation certificate for the purpose of insurance.

"Wait outside for me, Sally ," said Ben.

She beamed and kissed him gently before leaving.

"Now then," said Ben to the manager. "Without the performance that took place between you and your assistant, I would have been prepared to pay full price for this ring. But as a penalty, I now want a twenty-five per cent discount."

The manager made to protest innocence. Ben stopped him.

"Don't speak," said Ben calmly. "It's twenty-five per cent or I walk out of the door."

Ben knew that a similar discount could easily have been negotiated regardless of the incident, but felt he had to make a point. The manager and assistant blushed heavily and Ben's terms were agreed.

Ben used plastic to pay a deposit. Before leaving, his latent anger forced him to approach and speak to the offending assistant.

"Talking of percentages, if you and your partner enjoy twenty-five per cent of the love that exists between me and mine, you are a very fortunate couple."

She coloured up even more, but said nothing. Though determined to make his point, Ben suddenly felt guilty that he had embarrassed her for a second time. At the door, the manager graciously apologised.

"Have you spotted something different?" asked Ben, joining Sally who had continued to window-shop.

"Absolutely not! I couldn't hope for a more beautiful ring."

"Before you ask, I managed to knock them back to fifteen euros," Ben warned.

"I worry that you spoil me. Tell me the truth," insisted Sally.

"The truth is this," said Ben. "A special lady deserves a special ring."

Sally clung to his arm as they wandered the main shopping area. They enjoyed tea and cream cakes before setting off to meet with the boys.

Their arrival was greeted with huge relief. Juan, it transpired, was no mean bowler and Michael hadn't had things all his own way. An arrangement that the lads would take on Ben and Sally rescued Michael from a humiliating three–two defeat. His competitive nature could handle a two-all draw – but not defeat.

Ben and Sally were careful to stay well apart in Juan's presence. Any words, or touches of affection, were brief and secretive. They longed to hold each other, but they had learned to handle the frustration. The thrashing that they suffered on the rink was of no consequence, though for the boys' benefit, Ben pretended irritation and bad sportsmanship. All were a little tired as they settled down in a nearby burger bar. Sally and Ben were not overly hungry, but the boys had very healthy appetites. They managed chocolate cake with cream to follow a meal fit for grafting manual workers.

A rested Michael decided that some time in the amusement arcade would complete his enjoyment of the day. Ben furnished the funds and he and Sally watched as they liberally added to the profits of the establishment. Embarrassed by their apparent disregard for the depth of Ben's pocket, Sally eventually persuaded the lads that it was time to leave.

"Juan, see you at football practice tomorrow," said Michael to his pal, giving him a high-five at the railway station.

That was music to Ben's ears. He and Sally would have much of the day to themselves.

After the call to Nottingham that evening, the Crew decided that they were content to spend time playing board games – Michael because he had football the following day; Sally because she wanted nothing more than to sit contentedly with her man. Later, Ben returned from town with an assortment of take-away Chinese fare. He found Sally stood in her new dress before a full-length mirror.

"It's beautiful, Ben... thank you so much."

"It's only a dress," replied Ben. "It's the model that makes it beautiful."

Sally smiled and they embraced with tenderness.

Over dinner, Ben made an announcement.

"Now then, Crew. It's traditional in Spain that from a very early age, all of your Spanish girlfriends have been taught by their mothers to dance Salsa and Sevillana."

"What's Sevillana?" interrupted Michael.

Ben explained.

"It's rather like a line dance in four parts. Danced in pairs, I suppose you could call it the people's Flamenco. If you really want to impress, you occasionally pull a 'stepped in dog shit' face – just like a professional Flamenco dancer."

"What's a 'stepped in dog shit' face?" the lad chuckled.

Ben demonstrated as he spoke.

"Head turned slightly to the left, chin up, frown, look down your nose, and stretch your lips downwards."

The three fell into hysterics as they practised the "face". Tears rolled down cheeks and Sally needed a change of knickers.

"Anyway," scolded Ben. "Lessons start tomorrow!"

The couple indulged themselves in glorious gentle love that night. Sally wept onto Ben's chest.

"Happy tears," she whispered.

Chapter 28

Ben left Sally dozing in bed as he prepared breakfast for Michael and himself. A sleepy-eyed Sally appeared as they loaded sports kit into the Ferrari. Michael had pleaded an arrival at the pitch in style.

"Good morning, precious. Dance lesson when I get back," said Ben as he kissed her goodbye.

As they drove, Michael was the first to speak.

"It's going to be difficult when Mum is back. If you need me to cover for you both—"

Ben stopped him.

"It's kind of you, pal, but we'll try not to involve you."

If only Ben could anticipate the same acceptance from Margaret. The Ferrari's arrival at the football pitch made the impression that Michael had hoped for. His friends, headed by Juan, gathered around to admire the sleek lines. Ben checked that his friend had money and arranged to collect him from the local railway station on receipt of a call. As instructed, he blasted the angry engine as he left for home.

What had been a sleepy thing had transformed from caterpillar into butterfly. How could she be so gorgeous so soon out of bed? Sally finished the task of feeding demanding cats, made tea for her man, and talked dreamily of their future together.

"On Friday, the ring will seal our promise," said Ben. "But now a dance lesson."

Two hours of practice loosened stiff muscles from the previous day's bowling, but left them sweated up. The shower that they took together was sensual but not sexual. They lay side by side on the bed, hand in hand. Ben moved onto one elbow, kissed her breasts, and Sally watched as his lips moved to her mound.

"Ben," she said thoughtfully. "Some of the girls remove their pubic hair... do you think I should do the same?"

He sprang to his knees and knelt astride her, his face just inches from her vulva. Sally wondered what his verdict would be.

"Hmm... definitely not. I think *I* should do it."

Sally laughed as Ben appeared from the bathroom carrying the tools of his newfound vocation. With widened eyes and the manic grin of a Sweeney Todd, he fooled around, brandishing a comb and clacking the blades of nail scissors. He laid a towel beneath her bottom and set to work.

"No laughing," he urged. "Or I could remove Tinkerbell's wings."

Her pubic growth was neither abundant nor coarse. She didn't need hair removal – it was just one of their little adventures. Ben cut as close to skin as he dared, followed by very light strokes from a safety razor. He kissed her vulva gently. He massaged a little skin cream into the flesh of Venus before carefully applying his electric razor.

"Ooh," Sally murmured, as the spinning blades buzzed near her labia.

Ben's dormant penis began to swell. He stepped back to satisfy himself that he had achieved the perfect full removal. He clipped the plastic head protector to his razor and set the blades spinning again. He placed pillows beneath Sally's head so that she could watch herself being pleasured. She fondled her nipples as the clever improvisation took labia to fullness. She spread her legs as Ben eased the covered spinning blades past labia to the pink beyond.

"A little deeper... that's it... hold it just there," she said quietly.

Her hips lifted and gyrated to force contact against her begging clitoris. Sally thought wrongly that she could control the timing of her orgasm. She lost it and one tingle too many led her rapidly into an explosive climax. She screamed pleasure, as she took Ben's hand and pressed the device hard against the swollen organ demanding satisfaction. Her arousal had moved Ben to full erection.

"I'm sorry, Ben," she sighed. "It's much better with you inside me... but it *was* nice."

"I'm not offended," he assured her. "After all, there's someone else in *my* life... I'm in love with a Brazilian."

Sally gasped a laugh as he spread her legs wide and urgently thrust himself into her. A follow-up climax for Sally was out of the question. Almost instantly Ben's liquid poured into her depths. His grunted orgasm almost drowned the sound of the insistent telephone ring tone. Sally's legs encircled his torso and pulled him to her open shaven mound. They clung to each other and ignored the bedside telephone.

"I love you, Ben."… "I love you, Sally."

The second ring couldn't be ignored. It was Michael.

"Hi Ben, I'm at the station."

"Stay there. We'll collect you and go for Sunday lunch at the Carvery," panted Ben.

"Sorry," laughed Michael. "You're out of breath, did I interrupt something important?"

"Yes, you did, a dancing lesson – you cheeky little bugger," said Ben smiling. "We'll see you soon."

Sunday evening was spent preparing for college the following day, watching television, stroking cats, and Michael cheating at cards. The evening was warmly pleasant, but Monday would bring the intrusion of academic study and end the joy of being together throughout the day. Their daily lives for the next five or six days would be a blessing, but somehow, not quite enough.

"It's wrong to wish my life away, but I wish I could see the future," said Sally, as she cuddled into bed with Ben.

"Concentrate on study… time will soon pass. Though I'm not sure what will ever achieve your mother's acceptance," Ben comforted, without any true conviction.

Sally didn't reply.

The family settled into a daily routine over the next five days – breakfasts together, Ben's commitment to college runs, the feeding of cats, Michael's admiration of Juanita's breasts, nightly calls to Nottingham, study, and dance lessons. Ben spent lonely hours during the day, but relished the evenings with Sally. He craved night time, when their bodies came together to make love – sometimes with abandoned passion, sometimes deep in the abyss of adoration.

Chapter 29

Friday arrived – disco night. Sally had mastered the Sevillana routine quickly and her young brain easily remembered the sequence of steps. She would, nevertheless, need spare knickers if she had any intention of pulling the "face". The attempt to instil dancing prowess into Michael was less successful.

After the morning college run, Ben collected the ring from Malaga. It was more impressive than he remembered. Before leaving the shop he handed a gift-wrapped box of chocolates to the assistant. It had played on his mind that perhaps he had been too unkind during their previous confrontation. She rewarded his wink with a smile.

*

He placed the blue velvet box on Sally's dressing table. Ben had arranged for Juanita to prepare an early meal, giving Sally and Michael plenty of time to prepare for their night out. He had briefly considered hiring a stretched limousine for their arrival, but decided that it would be tacky and over-pretentious.

Whilst Michael showered, Sally put final touches of clear varnish to manicured finger and toenails. Her delicate hands and feet needed nothing more than a natural look. Michael was the first to appear fully prepared.

"Cool… you'll pull tonight!" remarked Ben.

The lad had developed into a handsome young man. With shoulders back and head held high, he strutted with the confidence of a peacock displaying its courtship plumage.

Sally needed no lessons in deportment. Ben caught his breath as she entered the living room. She had applied a little eye make-up and rolled a slight swirl to her long, dark hair. Though slight, the teenager had disappeared and become a woman.

"What do you think?" she asked shyly.

"Oh Sally… you look stunning," Ben gasped.

She blushed heavily as Ben kissed the diamond on the finger of her right hand.

"My engagement ring," she beamed to Michael, offering her hand for inspection.

"Mmm… nice," he casually replied. "Don't let Mum see it."

His remark defined the reality of their situation.

"Can I wear it tonight?" she asked Ben, with pleading eyes.

"It's your ring, it's your decision," he replied kindly. "But two things… number one, the ring finger for us Brits is the left hand. Number two, it will not go unnoticed if you spend all night looking at it."

"I'll try not to look at it." She smiled, moving the ring to her left ring finger.

As they drove to the college, Michael chattered excitedly, but Sally was a little pensive.

"I wish you could be with us tonight," she said quietly.

"Not possible. But don't worry, I've got plans for when I collect you at midnight." Ben smiled.

Sally's eyes lit up.

As she got out of the car, a group of girlfriends rushed over, squealing admiration of her dress. She was embarrassed by their attention, but obligingly threw her head back and, with a laugh, gave them a twirl. Ben watched the group whilst talking with Michael and his friends. Sally stood out from the rest. Her friends were mostly dressed in tiny mini-skirts or hot pants. Most were beautiful, but it was only Sally that carried an air of demure and sophisticated elegance.

"Ben, I can't remember any of the steps," laughed Michael. "But I've got a 'stepped in dog shit' face to die for."

Both laughed, as the lad made off with his pals. He waved to Sally as he got into his car. She rushed over to say goodbye.

226

"They all want a dress like mine!" she enthused.

"We can't have that. Tell them you found it in a skip," he joked. "Have a great night, precious, I'll see you later."

She kissed his cheek and rejoined her friends. Mrs. Sanchez stood with a group of teachers and observed their affection.

Ben drove off to prepare for an extension of their night out. With four hours to kill, he first spent some time in a café bar, drinking coffee and just one large brandy. Though not a jealous or possessive man by nature, he did ponder on how many young men would want to get between Sally's legs that night. *Forbidden territory*, he thought. He wondered if the leering eyes of the voyeur would be hard at work. The thought disturbed him. He dismissed the idea from his head and drove home.

*

Meanwhile, things were heating up at the disco. On-site regulations demanded that only soft drinks were available, but it didn't restrict the young people's enthusiasm to throw themselves into the occasion. Unlike the young people of some other European countries, most Spanish teenagers didn't view being drunk as a prerequisite for enjoyment. Spanish, American, and British pop and rock blasted from zigawatt amplifiers, through speakers the size of rubbish bins. The acoustics of the large hall were terrible and delicate tympanic membranes within young ears screamed for mercy. The disc jockey ensured that no mercy was offered.

*

Ben showered, shaved, and dressed himself in a beautifully tailored, navy blue lounge suit, set off with a crisp white shirt, fastened at the cuffs with gold links. A silver-grey tie and black shoes completed the ensemble. A little aftershave was splashed to his lightly tanned face. He looked in a full-length mirror and decided that he could easily be considered for the leading role in a James Bond movie.

*

The disco was in full swing. The young students eagerly imitated globally known dance routines from *Grease* and *Saturday Night Fever*. It was mainly groups of girls who would dance together, though some of the more extrovert young men would join them. The order of the day was having fun rather than finding romance. Sally's ring sparkled beneath the flashing disco lighting and one or two of her friends showed a little too much interest for comfort. She boasted that it was nothing more than costume jewellery and had cost the princely sum of five euros from a looky-looky man on the seafront. In the subdued lighting, her lie wasn't queried. The music cross-faded to Sevillana and students rushed in pairs to form a line. Most were accomplished dancers of the folk Flamenco and moved with some panache. Others were caught up in the humour of Sally and Michael pulling "stepped in dog shit" faces and it became competitive. Barely a few steps were danced before a dozen young women were screeching with laughter at each other's efforts to pull "the face". Mrs. Sanchez and others laughed with them, as they watched from tables on the sidelines. Another cross-fade and Sally danced a creditable Salsa with one of her girlfriends, before sitting to rest.

Yesterday's beautiful teenager engrossed in study had become a stunning exotic flower in the jungle of life. Her magnetism had not gone unnoticed by a young married lecturer in his mid-thirties. Perhaps he had been lacing his cola with alcohol – perhaps not. Regardless, he decided that he must get to handle her. She was pulled from her chair to dance a Salsa. Surrounding students cheered as she was led to the dance floor. The teacher was no dancer. He wanted only to shuffle around without rhythm, his body close to hers. The cheering became louder. The Head's attention was caught by the activity and she stood to investigate. Sally was flushed with the embarrassment of so many eyes upon her, but more importantly, visibly uncomfortable with his efforts to pull her body close. His right hand rested at her side and was noticeably close to making contact with the side of her left breast. Mrs. Sanchez moved to a strategic position. Sally caught her eye and the dedicated protector realised the young woman's discomfort. The dancing couple swivelled and the teacher came face to face with the one person whose opinion would dictate his future. She simply looked at him. It was an expressionless look. Not even her eyes expressed disapproval. The fixed deadeye stare was enough for him to get the message. Amidst boos from onlookers, he thanked Sally for the dance and returned her to her seat before the number had finished.

"Thank you, Miss," said Sally to the Head as she made her way to the toilets with a group of friends.

Mrs. Sanchez smiled warmly. She had handled the situation delicately and returned to the staff table, where she surreptitiously sniffed at the glass from which the teacher had been drinking. Alcohol was forbidden for both students *and* staff. He left the disco soon afterwards. No doubt, a verbal warning would follow at a later date.

*

Ben glanced at his watch frequently as he drank coffee and a liqueur in a nearby café bar. He genuinely hoped that Sally would enjoy the evening with young friends, but nevertheless was keen to be with her again. He would *not* have wanted to know of her brief predicament earlier. For some reason, it certainly seemed that her aura sometimes attracted male craving of the wrong kind. Would her loveliness be a problem throughout her life? It should surely be an asset rather than a liability. With his involvement in her past problems, Ben had pondered that very point over the months that they had been together. He had convinced himself that with growing confidence and experience, she would learn to anticipate and handle most of what came her way. Besides, from here on in, he would be there to guide and protect her.

The grounds were heaving with noisy, excited young people as Ben pulled up soon after midnight. He stood and leaned against the car door, amongst parents there to collect sons and daughters.

"Ben, come and meet my friends," shouted Sally from the throng.

She ran to him, kissed his cheek, took him by the hand, and pulled him to a group of lovely young women. He was introduced and greeted by each with a continental kiss. Maria ran to the group and her kiss was followed by a close hug. Maria told them all of the great day that they'd had with Ben and his Jet Ski.

229

"Ben's got a speedboat and water-skis for the weekend next summer," added Michael, as he joined the group.

Sally frowned at her brother's indiscretion and apparent open invitation.

"Yes, you must all come," confirmed Ben.

The girls squealed excitement.

Safety in numbers, thought Ben.

He moved on with Michael to *his* group of friends and talked football as best he could. It was half an hour before farewells were exchanged between the groups of students.

Sally joined Ben and Michael, soon followed by Mrs. Sanchez.

"Miss, this is Ben," said Sally. "He's been looking after us whilst Mum has been in England."

"They've worn me out," joked Ben, as he shook hands with the Head. She smiled warmly during the introduction.

"How *is* your grandfather now?" she enquired.

"Much, much better," Sally thanked. "Mum is coming home Sunday."

As they chatted, Mrs. Sanchez appraised Ben and appreciated how her student had been drawn to this handsome man. She glanced at the ring on Sally's ring finger and hoped that she hadn't been seduced by only his wealth. As the group parted, Mrs. Sanchez took Sally to one side.

"Very expensive. You'll not wear it in college next term, will you?"

"Of course not, Miss. Goodnight and thank you," said Sally smiling.

Ben waited at the car whilst Sally and Michael exchanged final farewells with friends.

"You've changed clothes, Ben, you look so handsome," admired Sally.

"The night is young!" was Ben's reply with widened eyes.

"So did you pull, Michael?" asked Ben, as he drove away.

"I certainly did!" came the proud reply. "Her name is Ana-Belen. She's studying law and we're meeting at six o'clock on Sunday, after football."

The lad had yet to sort out his priorities! Sally placed her hand on Ben's thigh.

"It was good fun, but I wish you could have been with us." She smiled.

Sally and her brother talked Ben through the highs of the evening, but she chose to say nothing of her uncomfortable incident.

Back in his hometown, Ben parked up to take them to a bar that he had rarely visited since first meeting Margaret and family. It was a particular favourite of his, the clientele being mainly young Spanish couples in their early twenties through to married couples in their early forties. He couldn't recall meeting anyone there other than Spanish locals, who readily welcomed him into their fold. Importantly for Ben, the weekends brought out the fun people, who, in the early hours, would take to the floor for Salsa and other Spanish routines.

Sally was unnerved by the hugs and kisses that Ben received from young women, rushing to greet the "prodigal son". She relaxed when their boyfriends and husbands hugged him with the same warmth. She was proud and not surprised that Ben was such a popular man. He jokingly introduced Sally as his new girlfriend and Michael as her brother that they couldn't shake off. The ladies raved about her dress. She was taken by the hand and led off to be seated with them. Fluent in Spanish she was soon taken under the wing.

"Muy guapa! Muy guapa!" they all exclaimed.

Sally was delighted, but blushed with embarrassment. She chatted along with them and Ben lost her to the group of new female companions. Michael was similarly lost to their grouped men, who traditionally talked all night about cars, motorbikes and, of course, the wonderful game. Traditionally, the women would talk about each other.

Ben supplied Sally with a large gin and tonic and requested a waiter to repeat the group's drinks. Michael was supplied with a beer, drunk like an aficionado, through a slice of lemon stuck in the neck of the bottle. Now deserted, Ben drank rum with cola and talked at the bar with the boss and his lovely, fat wife. He watched with fondness the animated opinions on football being played out by Michael. He watched with adoration the enthusiasm of Sally with her gathering of new, more adult friends. She occasionally looked across and smiled. He would smile and wink in return. He noticed that one friend had taken Sally's hand in hers and was talking admiringly of the ring upon her finger. Sally spoke in return and Ben wondered if she was revealing the significance of the precious stone. He didn't really care. It wasn't a bar frequented by gossiping British ex-pats and most of the women would be enthralled by the romance of it all. Their men would perhaps express envy, but not disapproval.

Michael was already on his third beer when Sally approached Ben to request a second G&T. It was 2.00 am and the bar wouldn't close before 4.00 am. Ben suspected that there would be three hangovers in his house the following day. *Their mother would be furious*, he thought.

One of the ladies grabbed Sally for a partner, as women rushed to the floor when Sevillana blasted from the speakers. She had forgotten some of the sequence, but had everyone in stitches of laughter as she demonstrated the perfection of her "stepped in dog shit" face. The fourth section finished and she moved to Ben, pulling him to the dance floor.

"Come on, Ben, Salsa," she urged, as the music cross-faded.

Just as he had done when teaching her, Ben talked her through some of the moves as they danced. She had a natural sense of rhythm and their bodies worked in harmony. The men paused from their talk of football to watch as her dress occasionally swirled to reveal slender thighs.

Her movement revealed less than many of the tiny skirts that were being worn – but it's what you don't see that excites. The song finished and she fell into Ben's arms panting for breath.

"I love you so much, Ben," she gasped. "Your friends are lovely and I'm sorry, please forgive me… I've told them that we are engaged."

Ben smiled his reply.

"It doesn't matter if my Spanish friends know."

Sally put her arms around his neck and firmly kissed his lips. That kiss removed any doubt in the minds of onlookers.

Through the early hours, dancing skill became less impressive as more rum, gin and beer was consumed. Sally's eyes became a little glazed, Michael began to speak fluent gobbledygook, and Ben was way over the limit for driving. He phoned for a taxi at 3.30 am. A few hungry, nocturnal cats came out of the shadows when they arrived home.

Michael didn't waste any time in going to his bed. His system wasn't accustomed to alcohol and Ben helped the wobbly lad in the direction of his bedroom. He regretted that he had allowed him to drink to excess. Sally, meanwhile, had flopped onto the sofa. She was exhausted and a little tipsy, but sure-footed, as Ben led her to their bedroom. She leant heavily against him as he untied the bow at her neck. She sighed as the zip travelled full-length to a point above her buttocks. She straightened her back; the fabric fell from her shoulders and glittered in the artificial lighting as it fell to the floor.

"I must hang my dress," she murmured.

"Don't worry, I'll see to that," whispered Ben.

She stepped out of her prized garment; Ben placed a hand beneath her bottom, held her body close, and laid her onto the waiting sheets. He slipped the shoes from her feet, adjusted her almost lifeless body into the bed, and laid her head to the soft pillow. She slept soon after the duvet was placed to conceal her near nakedness. He returned her dress to a hanger in the wardrobe. Ben was mindful of his responsibilities towards his four-legged friends and returned to the kitchen to silence their insistent meowing.

He made hot chocolate and sipped at a brandy nightcap, musing on the good fortune of having such a gorgeous creature in his bed below. He marvelled that she loved him so deeply.

He cleaned his teeth before checking that all was well with Michael. The boy was snoring like a walrus. Sally had kicked the cover from the bed and she lay invitingly, almost naked before him. One-sided sexual satisfaction would have been an insult to their love. His lips kissed the thin cotton that covered her vulva, before moving to briefly caress her breasts and nipples. His mouth gently settled onto hers.

"Goodnight, my treasure..." he whispered. "I love you so much."

Chapter 30

At around midday Sally was the first to wake. She felt quite alive, but cleaned her teeth to freshen her mouth from the previous night. She checked that Michael slept contentedly and slipped back under the duvet to be with her man. Ben lay on his back sleeping soundly and didn't react as she laid her head on his arm, and her hand on his smooth muscular chest. She gave in to temptation and took his penis in her hand. Sally moved the bedding to one side. She had never seen or handled "Big Ben" when in dormant mode. It was warm and soft. It flopped from side to side as she fondled it. Was this the animal that had been rammed aggressively into her body so many times? Almost with a kick-start it grew rapidly in her hand. Her fingers encircled the growing muscle, as it became hot and gorged with blood. Her vagina secreted juice, in readiness for the pleasure that it would demand. Ben was soon at full erection and pre-entry fluid lubricated the top of his helmet.

"Sally," he murmured in his sleep.

She removed her panties swiftly and knelt across Ben on all fours. The throbbing pole found its way, first, to her bum hole and then to her vulva. Obliging labia parted and Sally began to lower herself. Ben stirred as the beast began its slide into her body.

"I thought I was dreaming," murmured Ben.

"Good morning, my love," whispered Sally, gently kissing his lips with mint-flavoured mouth.

Ben sighed content, as she used his helmet to apply short strokes of arousal around the vaginal entrance. She groaned quietly as it slid against her hardened clitoris. The strokes lengthened and her vaginal walls clutched at the erection. It slid purposefully to the depths of her cavity. The tube sucked him to full penetration. Light-headed gasps greeted that supreme moment. A little of her juice seeped from her shaven mound into Ben's pubic hair. They stayed fused for a while, Ben's helmet throbbing at the extremity of her vagina. Sally moved to an upright position, sat upon the beast, and achieved an almost impossible depth of penetration. Her pelvis rocked back and forth, grinding her loins against the base of the erection within her. Ben pressed upwards and, with raised loins motionless, allowed Sally to dictate the nature and the timing of her pleasure. With her rocking and gyration, and his helmet grasped within her vaginal sheath, the helmet stroked the inner wall of her abdomen. Sally was fully impaled and using every moment of pressure against her G-spot and clitoris, she drifted into delirium. Ben reached up to take her wobbling breasts in his hands. Fingers and thumbs massaged and pinched her large protruded nipples. She sighed, then panted and gasped, as her clitoris fired up. The climax came quickly. Her insides quivered and her face took on a look almost of distress, as she contained muffled squeals, between gasps for air. She fell forward onto his chest.

"Oh Ben… Oh Ben… absolute heaven," she sighed.

Ben's hands reached downwards to the cleavage of her buttocks and his fingers stroked the wet and swollen, rubbery labia stretched tightly around his penis. He needed ejaculation, but allowed Sally to rest awhile.

She sat up and moved her feet to his sides. She leaned back, her body supported by straightened arms. Ben rested his head on the pillow and gazed at the satiated mound, nestled between her straddled legs. His penis had the vaginal entrance at full stretch, but his thumbs pulled the labia even further apart, to allow sight of the pink and the grateful, swollen clitoris. Sally sat up a little to enjoy the view. She loved the sight of their union.

"They love each other, don't they?" she sighed.

Ben grasped at every opportunity to eradicate remnants of her insecurity.

"Oh yes," said Ben. "Almost as much as *we* love each other."

Sally smiled. Aware of her desire to multiple-orgasm, Ben's thumb worked her clitoris gently.

"Mmm," she responded.

His hand worked throughout, whilst he moved Sally onto her back, legs wide apart. His mouth settled on her right breast, to love the firm rounded flesh and erect nipple. Sally's fingers pleasured the other nipple. Ben took her other hand and placed it to her mound. With his weight now supported by straight arms, his lips and tongue were free to love the breasts that beckoned beneath him. Sally's hips gyrated gently as her finger stroked the magic button within her vagina. Ben began long, slow strokes, briefly removing his erection completely, before thrusting it back to full penetration. It was an unbearable tease and Sally placed her hands around his bum, to each time pull her man back into her body. They whispered love, they panted and sighed, and their excitement grew.

"Stay inside, Ben… I'm going to come again."

Ben had been fighting off the climax for too long and her words were all he needed. The strokes remained long, but more rapid. Juices flowed and seminal fluid gushed from Ben's erection into the depths of Sally's cavity. They buried gasping heads against each other's bodies, as helmet and clitoris exploded together, in a crescendo of absolute love and shameless desire. Their ability to love seemed boundless.

They returned to their love nest beneath the duvet, still fused as one, their juices of love pooled at the entrance to Sally's womb. They cuddled for a long time before Sally spoke.

"Ben… are there lots of different ways to do it?"

"Oh yes," said Ben. "In fact, we're doing a new position right now. It's called 'The Plumber' – you stay in for hours and nobody comes."

Sally laughed so much; Ben thought her pelvic muscles would bite his penis off. She settled and became pensive.

"You're so much fun, Ben, but I feel so guilty. I know she's sometimes a pain, but I do love my mum. It´s wrong of me to wish that she wasn't coming home tomorrow."

Ben's reply was spoken softly.

"I know. We'll have to make the best of it – cheer up, let's take a shower."

*

236

They decided that they would walk the mile or so to collect the car that had been abandoned the night before. Their sexual union had done much to clear slight hangovers. A brisk walk in fresh air would do the rest. A note had been left for Michael, so midway they relished a breakfast of churros dipped into thick hot chocolate. The high sugar content did wonders for their constitutions. Ben graciously accepted the parking ticket that was being placed beneath his wiper blade and they rushed back to feed Michael.

Sally urged her brother to leave the pit in which he was still rotting. She joined Ben in making a full English breakfast for three. Working alongside her man, she enjoyed the feel of apparent marital domesticity. Michael appeared from his bedroom wearing a dressing gown.

"I feel like shit," he grunted.

"Have a look in the fridge, I think there's some left," quipped Ben.

Sally laughed and Michael managed a smile.

"It's either a hangover or you contracted something from Ana-Belen last night," continued Ben.

The mention of his new girlfriend gave cheer to the lad and the normal Michael began to emerge, as he consumed man-sized helpings of bacon, eggs, baked beans, and toast. All three would tire later in the day, but for now they felt rejuvenated.

Juanita had looked after the family as if they were her own. There was little or no washing and ironing to be done and Ben conceded to Michael's need for kicking a ball around in the garden, whilst Sally packed suitcases for their departure the next day. The daily call was made to Nottingham and Sally dutifully confirmed that she had missed her mother and was eager to see her again. Michael was less diplomatic and revealed his wish to move in with Ben.

A quite depressing mood developed during the evening. Ben assured them both that they should spend as much time as possible with him, subject, of course, to their mother's blessing.

"Hmm... that's the problem," groaned Michael.

They knew nothing of the bombshell announcement that awaited them. Ben tried to cheer them.

"Would you like to go out again tonight?" he offered.

Neither was enthusiastic and they settled for an evening of television, card games, and a pizza delivery. Ben taught Michael a few card tricks. Hot chocolate and cookies brought the night to an end and it was a pensive group that said their goodnights.

In their bed, Sally cuddled her naked body against Ben and wept a little into his chest.

"Happy tears? Or sad tears?" asked Ben.

"Both," she sniffled.

"Don't be sad," Ben consoled. "Things will work out."

"I'll need to hide my engagement ring really well," she said sadly.

They made love with some urgency the following morning. Margaret's flight was due to arrive at midday and by necessity their sexual union was intense and over-rapid. It hit hard that their togetherness would end that day. Not knowing when or where they could meet in the coming months cast a dark shadow over the blissful ten days that they had spent as a couple.

Chapter 31

Margaret emerged from the crowd in the Arrivals Hall and waved excitedly when she spotted her waiting children. They rushed to each other and the group hugged and kissed with great affection. Ben stayed in the background and allowed the greetings to subside.

"Ben, thank you so much for looking after them," Margaret enthused, offering both cheeks to receive a continental kiss.

"My pleasure," assured Ben. "They were no trouble at all. How is your father?"

For the benefit of Sally and Michael, Margaret had put on a brave face during calls over the previous week, but now told them of the full situation.

"Granddad is on the mend. He's making a gradual recovery, but it was a very serious attack and he will probably need heart surgery when he is stronger."

His grandchildren were visibly concerned, but their mother assured them that everything would be O.K. in the longer term.

"Come on," announced Ben. "We'll go for lunch before I take you home."

They had becoming regular customers at his favourite carvery restaurant and Sunday demanded a traditional British roast lunch.

"Now then, children," began Margaret, as they settled at their table. "I have some important news for you. I am going to put our apartment on the market and when you have completed your first year in college, we are going to move back to Nottingham to live with your grandparents."

Their mother paused and waited for a reaction that didn't materialise.

Michael looked at Sally, Sally looked at Ben, and Ben looked at Margaret. The lovers knew that Margaret's plans would need adjustment.

"What do you think?" she asked.

Without waiting for a response, their mother talked through all the financial, educational, and family advantages of a return to the U.K. Michael's chuckled response was typically flippant, but also highly relevant.

"I've got a date tonight, Mum, what if I fall in love, decide to get married, and stay in Spain?"

His mother's reply could not have been more specific in detailing what she expected of her offspring.

"You're a bright lad, Michael – you can study in Nottingham, get a successful career, and *then* you can fall in love and get married."

Beneath the table, Sally pressed her leg hard against Ben's.

"Sally?" enquired Margaret.

She responded with a firm confidence.

"It's more important for Michael to have a career than it is for me. I haven't yet decided what I want to do. Perhaps I should have worked for a year after my A-Levels or taken a gap year before going to college, but first of all, let's see what grading I achieve after the first year."

Sally was keen to teach young children, but had spoken the first words of reluctance that came into her head. Margaret was horrified that Sally should think in terms of anything other than what she perceived as the natural and assumed progression in academic and career achievement.

"It will soon be time for you to begin applying for a place in a British college," insisted her mother.

"Mother," interrupted Sally. "It would have been a nice gesture had you discussed these plans with us before making final decisions. I am not a child; I must be allowed to make *important* choices in my life. I would prefer to end up as a happy idiot, rather than a sad and lonely professor."

"Now you're just being silly," scoffed Margaret. "What do *you* think, Ben?"

He would have preferred not to get involved and chose his words as best he could.

"Well… it can't be denied that there would be some advantages if you lived with the family back home. It can't be denied that the standard of education in the U.K. is better than in Spain, with better career prospects."

He reached across, squeezed Sally's hand, and lightened the mood.

"But if Sally has her heart set on being a beach bum…"

All laughed, other than their mother.

"Come on, let's attack that food," insisted Ben.

Sally and Ben held back as they made their way towards the sizzling joints of meat. Ben whispered in her ear.

"It will soon be time to come clean. Nothing will affect our plans."

Sally smiled relief.

Margaret's next announcement over lunch wasn't warmly welcomed.

"It's impossible for your grandparents to travel with Granddad being unwell, so, as a gift, they have paid for flights so that we can visit them for Christmas and the New Year."

"Great! Carpet slippers and mince pies!" complained Michael. "I'll stay here and go clubbing with Ben."

His humour wasn't appreciated by Margaret and such declarations of friendship did nothing to help acceptance of Ben into their lives. Despite Ben's kindness towards her son, she still harboured deep-seated suspicion and resentment of their closeness.

"Don't be so ungrateful, Michael," scolded Margaret. "Besides, Ben wouldn't want you spoiling his time with Simone, which reminds me, Ben, you must give me her telephone number, so that I can thank her for helping with the children."

Ben was caught unawares and had forgotten about the story of Simone's involvement. He was forced to respond quickly with further lies.

"As it happens, only Juanita was able to help. Ironically, Simone also flew off to be with her parents. Her mother suffered a fall and broke her hip. She visits her parents regularly anyway. You could ring Juanita if you wish or perhaps a small box of chocolates."

The Crew came to the rescue and Michael assisted Sally as they enthused about the lovely Juanita, detracting attention away from

Simone. It served to draw Margaret's mind away from any possible thought that Ben had spent ten days fucking her daughter, in the absence of the fictitious Simone. The conversation switched to the great time that they had enjoyed at the student disco. No mention was made of the new outfits that Ben had provided.

"That reminds me," urged Michael. "Football, then my date!"

*

As they drove to the apartment, Margaret interrogated her son about the young Spanish lady that he would be meeting later.

"Behave yourself," she demanded, conscious of the liberal attitude towards young consensual sex.

"Don't worry," he assured her. "I'll drop off at the machine before I meet her."

Michael enjoyed the humour of winding up his mother. She had always accepted his taunting, ignoring for now that, one day, he really would be dropping off to buy condoms. In the context of coming of age, it's strangely true that parents are more protective of daughters than they are of their sons. A son that devotes his time to getting between the legs of a multitude of girlfriends is often perceived as nothing more ominous than "a bit of a lad". Parents forget, or ignore, that those girls are somebody's daughters.

Ben unloaded suitcases and carried them to the apartment, but declined the offer of coffee. He was nervous of questioning from Margaret that could be uncomfortable, leading him into an even more elaborate web of deceit. He firmly and categorically refused the money, which she pressed him to accept. She had no option but to graciously accept his generosity. Their farewells were warm and sincere. Sally fought against her emotion and Ben left for home without taking her in his arms.

As he drove, he felt utterly deflated. Their ten days together had been wonderful. He felt now that he was grieving. He entered a house that had been full of happiness, love, and laughter. It now felt like a mortuary: cold and lifeless. His previous joy turned to misery. As though

242

sensing his distress, three cats jumped onto the sofa and sat with him. Ben stroked them and wept a little. There could be no closure until he and Sally were together.

It was a tearful Sally that called from beneath her bed sheets.

"Oh Ben, I feel so sad... I feel so lonely."

"I know, precious, it's the same for me. But hang in there. With your mother's announcement, we are going to have to make some decisions. Sooner rather than later."

That didn't happen. Sally's consideration of her mother's feelings remained paramount and each week that passed seemed more like a month. Each furtively stolen meeting would feel more like a reunion. Far too often, he would rely upon a pillow to his face, breathing in the scent of her hair or the smell of a handkerchief.

Chapter 32

The Christmas holiday period arrived. Ben collected the family and delivered them to the airport. The Departures Hall was buzzing with families anxiously looking forward to family reunions. Margaret was excited by the prospect of spending time with her parents, dismissive of the grudgingly accepted boredom that awaited her children. Sally was distressed by the thought of Ben spending Christmas alone. The previous day they had grasped at a brief opportunity of making love in Ben's car. With their imminent separation, it had been emotion expressed with urgency. Their bodies and souls had bonded with furious intensity.

"Open it on Christmas day," she whispered, slipping a small package into his pocket.

Ben put on a brave face as he said his goodbyes to the family. Michael distracted his mother and the lovers' lips met briefly. It would be only a week, but it felt that they were parting for a lifetime. It was a period when loved ones should be together; a week of celebration when Sally and Ben should not have been apart.

Ben forced a smile as he left to return to his lifeless home. He ignored Sally's instructions, untied the ribbon, and opened the package. The small card inside read "Ever yours". He opened the gift box to reveal a gold teardrop inscribed with the single letter "S". It hung from a fine link, gold neck chain. He was touched by her expression of devotion, but wondered if she had bought the lovely gift from savings or from the account provided by her uncle.

As he stroked the tactile gold, he pondered on the multiple significance of that "S". It could be Sally, it could be Sad, it could be Soul Mates, and, for the benefit of Margaret, could even be Simone.

Their happiness was often marred by sadness, but they would always be soul mates. His mind wandered to a time when a young child had asked him the meaning of the word "soul". It is not an easy word to define and, not being a religious man, he had taken a moment or two to come up with an answer that the child could accept.

"In the film *E.T.*... When the extraterrestrial goes home and when Elliott says goodbye to his little friend from outer space, if you can watch that without crying or getting a lump in your throat... you don't have a soul."

The child was pleased with his inaccurate definition. Ben had a soul and felt the need to cry. He considered booking a hotel room and flight to Nottingham, but dismissed the idea, knowing that it could be difficult for Sally to get away.

The telephone rang. It was his brother urging him to fly over to have Christmas with his family. Ben declined the offer, feigning flu-like symptoms, but was cheered by a lengthy chat reminiscing about his brother's wonderful dog "Zak".

The husky's great pleasure was to lick the salty flavour from between people's toes. It didn't compare to the pleasure that willing people enjoyed by submitting to the animal's demands. His brother often joked that he could have been a very wealthy man had he trained his pet to lick fanny.

Throughout the week, Ben used the same excuse of impending illness to decline invitations from Spanish friends to join their families' Christmas activities. It was ungracious of him, but if he couldn't be with Sally, he wanted to be alone. He felt lonely and miserable, and wouldn't have been good company.

It was remiss of him not to have had further contact with Alan and Shirley and pushed himself to arrange a pre-Christmas night with them. His heavily tattooed, Cockney friend enjoyed the basic pleasures in life, so Ben treated them to steak and chips in their local café bar. Alan washed down a huge fillet steak with an ocean of bottled beer and Shirley consumed a bottle of Rioja. Ben thanked them again for the use of the Jet Ski and Alan confirmed that it, and his speedboat, could be borrowed at any time during the following summer.

Ben's good intentions of drinking moderately were dashed when he accepted the offer of a nightcap at their home. A half-full bottle of vintage brandy was produced and Shirley helped him to all but empty it. In no fit state to drive, Ben went comatose in one of their spare bedrooms.

Nursing a horrific hangover the following day, he welcomed coffee, but declined breakfast. There were cats to be fed and he left a lively Alan enjoying bacon sandwiches and a can of beer.

On Christmas day, he abandoned discretion and called Sally's mobile.

"Oh, hello Maria," Sally enthused. "A Merry Christmas to you too! Hold on, I'll go outside for a better reception."

In protection of their relationship, the need for deceit had become second nature. Ben thanked her for the gift and they whispered mutual love. Michael received a similar call from Ana-Belen and he too escaped from the adults. *His* call was prompted by friendship and perhaps contained the seeds of first love.

To occupy his lonely mind, Ben played golf more than usual that week. Each night, he caressed the teardrop hung from around his neck and intermittently gazed at the photograph that he had shot whilst Sally slept. He consoled himself that Sally would not return to Nottingham with her mother; regardless of the current situation, they would be together in a maximum of six months.

Until the arrival of New Year's Eve, the time passed slowly. Remembering that Spain is one hour ahead of U.K. time and allowing for family embraces, Ben left it until 1.30 am local time, before calling Sally.

She excused herself from the adults to take her call from "Maria".

"Happy New Year, precious," whispered Ben.

"It will be, when we are together," she whispered back. "Will you be dancing with all those lovely girls at the bar later?"

"No," laughed Ben. "I'm worn out. At midnight I was dancing around with the cats."

"You should go out and have fun," said Sally, without any true conviction.

She felt for Ben in his solitude, but didn't really want him in the jaws of temptation. She was quietly relieved that he would suffer the same loneliness, on a night when lovers should be together. They talked briefly, looking forward to the family's return in a couple of days.

Ben watched television and drank brandy, brooding on what a different night it could be if Margaret were in Spain with her in-laws and he, Sally and Michael were having a blast with their young friends in his local Spanish bar. He vowed that when all was out in the open, he would fill Sally's life with fun. He drank too much, got a bit wobbly, and went to bed.

The following day's hangover was briefly relieved by the consumption of bacon sandwiches and a pot of tea. Ben called Nottingham on the house telephone line. He spoke with Margaret and arranged to collect them from the airport at around 11.00 am the next day. Margaret and the grandparents were a little perturbed by the children's enthusiasm to be returning to Spain. Grandma wondered if she had acted a little selfishly when encouraging the return to the U.K. Had she given sufficient thought to her grandchildren's wishes? Meanwhile, Ben was wishing his life away.

*

Ben stood in the Arrivals Hall, searching for sight of his lover amongst the hundreds of travellers returning from throughout Europe. The distressed young woman whom he had left a week earlier hung back from her mother and brother. She caught his eye, beamed, and waved furiously, blowing kisses in his direction. His enthusiastically returned wave was acknowledged by Margaret, believing it to be a greeting for her. Michael's embrace with Ben was warmer than his mother would have liked. Hers was friendly but not close. Sally embraced him and kissed his cheek. She fought against the desire for lengthy body contact, with lips pressed firmly to his. They walked to the car and loaded suitcases. Ben politely enquired about details of their visit and the progress of Margaret's father.

He offered them lunch, but they had eaten snacks during the flight and Margaret agreed only to a coffee en route to the apartment.

"We can't be too long," she announced, as the drinks were served. "We are expected at your other grandparents' later this afternoon."

"That's news to me," retorted Michael. "Besides, I can't come, I've fixed a date with Ana-Belen."

"Who's going to be there?" asked Sally.

"Everyone," replied her mother. "Grandparents, your cousins, aunt Rocio, your uncle Seb."

Sally couldn't stop herself.

"I'm not coming," she said firmly.

"Of course you are, why ever not? It would be so rude not to come," insisted her mother.

"I will be totally bored," Sally replied calmly. "But more importantly, I don't like the way my uncle looks at me."

"Now you're being stupid," scoffed her mother.

Hmm, thought Ben. *If only Margaret knew.*

"And what am I to tell them?" fumed her mother.

Sally remained calm but firm.

"Tell them whatever you like. Look, Mum, you mean well, but you do sometimes treat me like a child; but I'm not a minor, I'm a woman. I tolerate perverted looks from older men. But I don't expect it or accept it from my uncle. Michael's got a date, tell them I have too. Better still, tell them the truth, I'm going to visit my friend, who called from Spain to wish me Merry Christmas and a Happy New Year. Our Spanish family didn't call us, did they?"

Margaret was astounded by the authority in Sally's voice, but avoided a public scene. Ben wondered if Sally had gone too far, but was delighted to assume that it was her intention to spend time with him that afternoon. Absorbed in her own issues, it hadn't occurred to Margaret to contemplate a reason for genuine concern about Sally's refusal to spend time in the company of Sebastian.

The atmosphere was tense as Ben helped Michael to move suitcases into the apartment.

"Could you drop me off at Ana-Belen's?" asked Michael.

Ben looked at Margaret. With raised eyebrows she shrugged her shoulders.

"Me too, please, Ben?" added Sally.

Her children were becoming demanding adults. Margaret had no option but to concede.

"Can I give *you* a lift, Margaret?" Ben offered.

"Thanks anyway, Ben, but I'll do some unpacking. I can jump on the bus or Sebastian will collect me."

"Sorry, Mum," they both apologised, giving her a hug before leaving.

Michael was quickly dropped off and Ben drove at speed in the direction of his home.

"I've missed you so badly," murmured Sally.

"Every minute seemed like an hour," said Ben frowning.

They placed hands on each other's thighs. His hand slid against warm flesh and Sally's legs parted for the crotch to be caressed. She knew where she was being taken and the purpose of the journey. Her hand moved to his loins. He was already at full erection – it was an enormous throbbing animal. She made to move her hand inside his tracksuit.

"Don't touch me inside, I'll come into your hand," warned Ben.

"One night in Nottingham," Sally said smiling. "I was thinking of you and I ended up playing with myself. It was nice, but not like the real thing."

They were flushed and rampant as they pulled onto the drive. In the hallway they kissed feverishly and came close to bruising ribs as they urgently embraced. They rushed to the bedroom, desperately needing their bodies to be naked and fused. They tugged at each other's clothing as though the opportunity could vanish. Sally was first beneath the duvet. Her fingers held her labia parted as Ben's monstrous penis appeared above her.

"Quickly, please, push Big Ben inside me," she urged.

From slight foreplay during the journey, the juices were already flowing. Ben positioned his helmet at the pink and with a single thrust rammed its full length into the furthest depths. Sally screamed and Ben howled as it made contact with the extremity of her vagina. Love and adoration could come later. At that moment, more than anything else, they needed to fuck. They needed the relief of a shameless animal shag.

"Fuck me, my darling… fuck me as hard as you can!" Sally murmured.

Her legs wrapped around her man and he furiously attacked her loins. The action lasted no more than a minute. They groaned and squealed a simultaneous climax. Ben's semen had been in storage, but now squirted and poured into her cavity. It poured and poured.

"What a fuck!" Ben panted.

"What a huge fuck," Sally gasped. "I want to see what's been inside me."

Ben withdrew and knelt on all fours across her. His penis poured a little love juice onto her open mound.

"It's enormous, Ben," she said quietly. "I don't think it's ever been quite so big."

Ben looked and agreed. She didn't need to ask – he slid back into the warmth of her body. Sally closed her legs around the girth of the erection and they rolled onto their sides. They lay still, with swollen, rubbery labia pressed hard against him and her entrance fully stretched. Her extended nipples brushed against his chest and he kissed her brow with tenderness. They rested before Ben spoke.

"I thought you were on the verge of saying too much to your mother today."

"To be honest, Ben, I'm not sure that I can wait. We belong together and it's wrong that we're not. Pretending that we're just good friends is so difficult and it seems so stupid… Would it really matter if people knew that we love each other?" she pleaded.

"I know how you feel," Ben comforted. "I'm ready whenever you are, but only you can decide when your mother is ready to handle it. We know regardless that she's not going to give us her blessing. I will go with whatever you decide, but I suspect that the best time would be when things have moved on a little – when the apartment is sold and when the move to Nottingham is just around the corner. I think that she will be very angry, but she will at least have the support of your grandma. For all her problems, your mum loves you dearly and I hope that her anger will be temporary. Are you sure that you can handle making an enemy of your mother?"

Sally replied without hesitation.

"I'm sure… I do love my mum, but she made *her* choices. I will make mine."

Ben kissed her face gently; her brow, her eyes, her lips. She leant back to receive his lips on breasts and nipples. They whispered their love of each other. Ben's erection softened a little, but remained hard enough for Sally to begin her movements against it. She slid a little further down the bed to achieve heavy pressure against her clitoris. She planted kisses on his chest as her loins worked against the base of his penis. Her orgasm built slowly into a fire around the clitoris. Ben massaged a nipple, Sally fondled the other, his other hand moved to caress her solid buttocks, and then gently finger the entrance to her bum. She squealed and panted, more blood was pumped into his erection, and her body shuddered through her climax. Her bum hole quivered on Ben's fingertip. She lay in his arms and sighed breathlessly.

"Now you," insisted Sally.

She moved to all fours above him. Even with legs straddled astride him, her young vagina sucked and clung to the erection, as it slid slowly and erotically the full length, from head to base. They watched as juices leaked from within her. More urgent movement turned juices to foam and Sally's murmured pleasure led to a second fire in Ben's helmet. His first orgasm had drained his balls of fluid. He thought a second for him would be unlikely. He was wrong; nerve endings in his helmet tingled, then built to a fire, and he groaned a dry climax.

Sally threw her body upright and ground her labia hard onto the base. She rocked back and forth, her hard clitoris demanding more pressure and more pleasure. Ben's skilful hands around her buttocks forced the pressure even higher. She took her breasts in her hands, rolled and massaged them firmly, squeezed her nipples between fingers and thumbs, and screeched a third, subdued but delirious climax. She fell forward onto Ben's chest, panting for breath. They lay for a while; her buttocks nestled in his hands.

"Good?" whispered Ben.

"Wonderful," she sighed. "Never quite like the first, but always nice… I *am* greedy, aren't I?"

"Not greedy," said Ben. "Just blessed with the ability to have more than one come."

Sally lifted off and they giggled as juices, first, dangled and then dripped onto Ben's belly. Before enjoying the bidet routine, Sally pressed her belly to his, gyrated, and spread the liquids between their warm flesh.

It was a satiated but sadly pensive couple that parted that day. Ben watched as Sally waved from the doorway of the apartment block. He knew when her next call would be – it would be from beneath her bed sheets, but wondered when they could next meet.

Sally had listened carefully to Ben's opinion on the least damaging time to declare their love. She wanted to confront her mother that very day, but could see the wisdom in Ben's words. She had no fear that Ben was stalling. She was confident that their needs were identical.

Chapter 33

The next six months were a form of purgatory for them – heaven when they were together, hell when they were apart. It was perhaps more bearable for Sally. She had her college friends, the commitments of a family life, and her genuine desire to succeed in her chosen career. For Ben, every day without her was misery. He abandoned most other personal contacts. His mind only had and only wanted Sally. His love for her had become obsessive. He became more and more introverted, but was intelligent enough to recognise the danger. He forced himself to play more golf. Though not obsessed with the game, it was the one pastime that didn't allow distractive thoughts. Having a few drinks with the boys after a game helped his mindset, though he would, without a doubt, abandon a game midway, should a call be made to signal the availability of a rendezvous.

Margaret wasted no time in placing the apartment with an agent, though it was unlikely that a buyer would be found before the arrival of spring. The occasional Sunday afternoons spent with her Spanish in-laws were welcomed by Sally and Ben, being the one opportunity when they could make love in a private and relaxed way. However, such afternoons only exacerbated the frustration of parting without further plans. Under pressure, Sally and Michael agreed to occasionally visit their Spanish grandparents, but, Sally insisted, only during the working hours when Uncle Seb would not be around. It was a blinkered Margaret that protested frequently that Sally was being stupid and unreasonable, but her daughter would not be swayed. Besides, Sally pointed out; she and Michael were never offered the affection that her purebred cousins enjoyed. Despite Margaret's misplaced loyalty to her Spanish family, Ben was amazed that Sally's continued refusal to meet with Sebastian hadn't alerted her mother to a serious threat. Did she really believe that Sally was over-imaginative and delusional? Would her devotion to Miguel's memory always protect her from the truth?

Michael was growing up quickly; in mind and in stature. He and Ana-Belen remained friends, but he moved on to one or two other young romances. Lovely young ladies enjoyed his company, not least of all because he had become rather handsome. More importantly, he was good fun with a sharp sense of humour; he and Ben sparred verbally at every opportunity. Michael's Spanish friends also used his company as a means of improving their skills in conversational English.

Over the months, Ben and Sally grasped at every brief opportunity to touch hands, to smile knowingly, and to make love. They sometimes met for only minutes, simply to be near each other. Most of the time, their meetings were full of frustrated urgency, and served only to make their future declaration and union more desperate.

The Easter half term arrived, the weather was glorious, and though the sea temperature was cold, Ben borrowed Alan's Jet Ski. Michael showed off his skills to Isabella, a beautiful new girlfriend. Riding tandem, she screamed excitement, whilst pressing her nubile body to his back. The machine jumped the swell, whipped up by a brisk, warm wind. Sally and Ben were content for them to have almost exclusive use of the Jet, but a performance of their past love on the Mediterranean would need to be repeated. Ben waited until the wind abated a little before waving Michael to the beach. He and Sally headed way offshore towards North Africa and Ben cut the engine. Away from the buzz of conversation and play on the beach, the silence was incredible. The sea lapped at the machine's hull, as they kissed love onto each other's faces. The rolling swell made it impossible to make love as before, but they were content to strip naked and fuse their bodies, sinking into their private abyss of adoration. With Sally astride Ben, they made love slowly, until his hot fluid ejaculated past her quivering clitoris. They caressed with deep emotion and, as before, their return journey was slow, with Sally on his lap, her vagina enjoying the deep penetration within her body. The cold seawater was again needed to avoid shocking Isabella with the sight of a rampant erection.

Michael helped Ben to pull the Jet onto the sandy shoreline and the four settled to enjoy conversation and a picnic. The air became a little chilled, so all but Michael decided to dress into warm tracksuits. Michael needed a final solo blast or two across the bay.

Isabella was a lovely girl – quieter than the norm and very polite. There was never going to be the drama that Maria had created. However, the day was not without incident. A British woman, screaming hysterically and running in circles further down the shoreline, caught their attention. A sixth sense in Sally sent her running to investigate. Ben followed. The woman had dozed in the sunshine, whilst her children played at the water's edge with a small beach dinghy. They were missing! Sally's face paled and reflected the anguish that the woman was suffering. Ben ran up the beach as Michael approached the shoreline. He dragged Michael from the Jet, snatched the ignition key from his wrist, jumped aboard, and roared off, fully clothed.

His eyes scanned across the bay as he headed for the horizon. He could see no sign of dinghy or children. He was as far out to sea as earlier, when he and Sally had made love. Surely they would have seen them then or at least heard their cries for help. His eyes squinted against the setting sun as he scanned the horizon – nothing. He feared the worst, but if the children had perished, where was the dinghy? The wind would easily whisk an empty inflatable for miles offshore, but he continued out to sea. The swell was getting higher and restricting his view. He cut the engine to listen. Was it a gull or had he heard the faint cry of a child? He set off in the direction of the sound. The cry became louder and from within the swell, the dinghy briefly appeared. He raced towards it at speed. He approached to find two terrified children clinging to each other. A skinny, nine-year-old boy shook uncontrollably, blue with cold and in shock. His seven-year-old sister was screaming with fear. Ben tried to calm them to little avail. The boy was nearest to the Jet and Ben helped his thin, shivering body to eventually clamber aboard. His sister was frozen in fear and refused to budge.

"Come on, I'm taking you back to Mummy," Ben repeatedly coaxed. She shuffled her way slowly and edged towards Ben's outstretched hand. She stood too early, a sudden swell, and she was over the side. It was a few seconds before her terrified, pleading face surfaced. She was ten feet away and doggy paddling the only swimming stroke she knew. Her face disappeared beneath the water.

"Jesus Christ," screamed Ben.

He dived in. The cold water hit him like an electric shock. He swam to where she had been, dropped beneath the surface of the water, but could see nothing of the child. His legs made brief contact with her body. He dived again, grabbed her arm, and pulled her from beneath the swell. Her face was filled with terror and her mouth gasped for air. Her terrified eyes were like saucers. She clung to Ben, making it difficult for him to swim. The swell had moved the Jet further away. They were now thirty feet from safety and his soaked clothing wanted to drag him under. His life didn't flash before him, but with the encumbrance of a clinging and struggling child, he wondered if he would ever see Sally again. In emergency situations the human body finds amazing reserves of strength. Every sinew of his frame worked against the offshore current. Every effort in his legs worked at reaching safety and a relieved Ben grasped at the runner board of the Jet. The boy was paralysed in fear and shock, and unable to help his sister aboard. Ben screamed at him to assist. The poor lad looked at him with vacant eyes and without response. He swam to the side of the Jet, with the hysterical girl clutched close to him. He lifted her to take hold of her brother's ankle. In a moment of realisation, the boy reached down to take his sister's hand.

"Hold your sister very tight – do *not* let go of her hand," he urged.

Ben moved swiftly to the rear of the machine and, with a final desperate heave, clambered onto the runner boards. He jumped astride the seat, reached down, and with a strong arm around the little girl's waist, plucked her from the sea. In one move, she was astride the Jet, nestled between Ben at the rear and her brother up front.

"O.K., you'll be with your mummy soon," Ben comforted the crying child.

With emphasis on stability, he steered slowly towards shore, the two children shivering shock and cold. A rescue helicopter appeared and hovered overhead, and, in time, an inshore lifeboat escorted them the final two hundred yards to the beach. The police presence cleared access and a weeping, relieved mother ran alongside paramedics, who rushed the trembling children into the waiting ambulance. Ben waved to Michael and the girls, instructing them to go back to their place on the beach. He was shaking violently as he drove the Jet firmly onto the sand. Sally saw that he had been in the sea and realised that it hadn't been a simple pick-up. She had no idea just how dramatic the adventure had been. She rushed to embrace him and pulled his shivering body close to hers.

"Oh Ben, my lovely man, I'm so proud of you," she wept, planting several kisses on his cheeks.

"Careful, Sally, you're getting wet," he trembled.

At their spot, he removed his wet clothing down to his underpants and soaked up the warmth of the evening sun on his flesh. He gratefully accepted the thermal blanket that was offered by a paramedic. A Guardia officer arrived, but Ben declined to give his details. The policeman insisted that providing full information was compulsory in order to complete their paperwork. Ben had no option but to comply. A local television crew had been tipped off and had rushed to the scene of the drama. Ben refused an interview, saying only that parents should never allow children to play unsupervised on rubber dinghies, especially during windy conditions. Wrapped in his blanket, he ignored their insistence and they turned their attention to Michael and Sally. They readily succumbed to the attention, praising the bravery of their friend Ben. He slipped away to collect Alan's car and trailer. The television crew had moved on to the police officers when he returned and, with Michael's help, he quickly loaded up the Jet, hitched up the trailer, and insisted that they should leave. A modest man, he was uncomfortable with the sudden notoriety. During the journey back to the apartment, Sally took a call on her mobile. It was her mother.

"I've been watching you being interviewed on the local news channel!" she exclaimed. "The whole thing is being shown over and over. The drama of it all was filmed from the rescue helicopter!"

Isabella received a romantic but brief kiss from Michael as she was dropped off at her home. He was anxious to get back to the apartment to watch his and Sally's televised interview. Ben pulled in, a quick high-five, and Michael was rushing to the entrance doors. Ben dismissed

Sally's insistence that he should join them to watch the incident. He was still shivering and wanted to drive home with the heater set to full blast. Nor was he prepared to leave Alan's expensive toy unattended.

"I'll speak to you later, my love." Sally smiled, pressing her lips passionately against his. At that moment, she cared not if her mother had witnessed the intimacy.

An hour later, Ben had taken a hot shower and was cocooned in a heavy cotton dressing gown. He was tired and began to doze when the telephone rang.

"Ben, have you watched it?" gasped Sally. "I had no idea that it had been so dangerous. We are all so proud of you."

"Well done, Ben," shouted Michael, from somewhere within the living room.

Margaret inwardly wished that their praise could have been directed to their father. Ben hadn't watched the footage, but played down the heroics.

"I love you, my darling," whispered Sally, before replacing the receiver.

Ben never did watch the television coverage. He didn't want to re-live that moment when he dreaded never holding Sally again. He re-lived it in a nightmare that night. It was a nightmare that would haunt him.

Come Monday morning, the teaching faculty was buzzing with details of the Crew's interview. Maria had seen the television coverage and had been proudly boasting of her friendship with Ben. The Head called Sally over as they passed in the corridor.

"Your friend Ben is something of a hero," she said.

"A reluctant hero," said Sally smiling. "He's very embarrassed by all the fuss."

Mrs. Sanchez pondered on the pair of safe hands that would protect and care for her young student.

*

Three weeks later, Ben's modesty was tested further when during a telephone call he was forced to succumb to the local mayor's insistence that he accept a bravery award presentation at the town hall. Ben thought it would be a quick affair; a parchment certificate, a sandwich and a cup of tea, thanks, and goodbye. He should have known better; the Spanish enjoy notoriety and love to make speeches. To his horror he arrived to be confronted by the town hall committee, representatives from the police force, ambulance service, inshore rescue, offshore rescue, and worst of all, the local television crew. The whole occasion had been engineered to mimic an episode of "Surprise, Surprise". Ben was embarrassed beyond belief. He wanted the ground to swallow him up. Predictably, he sat through endless speeches of praise and gratitude only part of which he understood. His mind wandered to facing the frustration of the Crew upon them discovering that they had not been part of the proceedings. He was shocked back into the occasion with the arrival on stage of Sally and Michael. They rushed to him and hugged his body with huge affection. They had been privy to the arrangements from the start and their mother had agreed to stay at home to record the televised event. They sat at Ben´s side and talked to the host of their pride in having such a fine friend. Ben wondered if viewers, and especially Margaret, would perceive Sally´s hand placed on his, as something more than an expression of friendship.

What began as an award ceremony developed into a contrived ´tear jerker´ when the two rescued children and their mother appeared. He had wrongly assumed that they were tourists, but were in fact Spanish residents. Ben fought back his emotion as the youngsters ran to his welcoming embrace. They seemed to have recovered from their terrifying ordeal. They were followed by their mother who wept shamelessly and held him in a hug so long and so tight that Ben could barely breathe. He became swept up in the emotion of it all and his tears welled a little. Sally did nothing to control her feelings and the tears flooded as she took the children into her temporary care. Instinctively they recognised genuine affection and returned her cuddles.

The show concluded and the mayor beamed delight that he had hosted such fine entertainment. It was a further two hours before Ben eventually freed himself from the stress of it all.

*

"You naughty people," scolded Ben as he settled in the ice cream parlour with Sally and Ben.

"You wouldn't have agreed if you had known anything about the plan," Sally pointed out.

"That's true," agreed Ben.

"You deserved today, Ben," added Michael. "We're very proud of you."

"And we love you," whispered Sally.

"Sal," said Michael with a smirk. "You can leave me here eating ice cream if you need a dancing lesson."

Ben laughed and Sally kissed her brother's brow as they left for Ben's bedroom.

"We'll come back for you in a couple of days," laughed Sally.

Ben's stress at becoming a local celebrity disappeared as he and Sally engulfed themselves in the abyss of heavenly sexual union. Not once in their love for each other had their bodies and minds failed to provide intense and mutual adoration. All too soon it was time to return his lover and his friend to their mother.

*

The following months dragged on slowly. Ben dismissed the inevitable requests from family and friends to visit him in Spain during the summer months on the pretext that his villa was undergoing major internal decorative refurbishment.

A contract was eventually signed for the sale of Margaret's apartment, returning a healthy profit. Glorious union of love and sex was snatched where possible, between the restrictions of family obligation and the need for academic study. Ben began to realise that when able to declare their love, Sally's end of term college grading would be a double-edged sword. Poor grades: their relationship would be blamed for the failure. Good grades followed by Ben and Sally being together: Margaret would accuse him of destroying Sally's future. It could only ever be a no-win situation.

He saw little of the Spanish family in the time running up to the Crew's annual assessment. The week arrived when grading would be announced. He telephoned the apartment to enquire on the level of success. Margaret was neither surprised nor suspicious. Despite Michael's apparent wildness, he was a bright lad and he was confident that he had achieved strong results. To work with young children was so important to Sally, and Ben didn't doubt for one moment that her assessment would reflect her dedication. Both achieved top grading and, in Sally's case, with commendations.

Without consultation, Ben arranged a celebratory dinner at the best of the local restaurants. All were in high spirits as they settled at the sea view table. Margaret rightly basked in the joy and pride of her children's achievements. Her euphoria was dashed by Sally.

"Mu-um... you remember Ben once said 'don't ever let your daughter have a tattoo'... I have a confession to make."

Ben's eyes widened, Michael's jaw dropped, and Margaret's face frowned. Sally turned in her chair and dropped a side of her summer top to one side. Her mother's face turned to abject horror at the sight of what was revealed. Fluttering on her daughter's shoulder was a delicate image of Tinkerbell.

"Wow," said Ben.

"Cool," said Michael.

"Oh my God! You silly girl," choked Margaret.

Sally endured several minutes of criticism from her mother before removing a small packet from her purse.

"Now then, Ben has always said that he enjoys the company of young people... so he can be Peter Pan."

A stick-on transfer was duly applied to Ben's bicep amidst laughter about the wind-up. Margaret was still reeling from the shock of Sally's ruse and refused to be part of the proceedings. Michael ended up with forearms decorated with Captain Hook, Wendy, and the Crocodile.

Sally winked at Ben and was eventually forgiven by her mother. Margaret placed no significance on the love that existed between Peter Pan and Tinkerbell. A fun evening was enjoyed by all; despite the underlying tension of the lovers' issue. The Disney characters would disappear in the shower but it would take more than soap and water to destroy their love.

The university term had ended and hundreds of relieved students began to enjoy a summer of relaxation. Sally and Ben couldn't yet relax. There was the major issue of their future together to be declared. Contracts had been signed and the apartment had been sold fully furnished. Personal items only would be transported to the U.K. It was a mere eight weeks before Margaret believed she would be travelling with both of her children to begin a new life in Nottingham.

Chapter 34

In the comfort of Ben's bed, Sally lay on her side, her vagina caressing his slowly relaxing penis. Their lovemaking had been intense and their hot fluids mingled in her depths. She looked at the diamond on her finger.

"Ben," began Sally. "Let's not delay things any longer. Mum has a private class tomorrow evening. I have written her a letter and, if you agree, it will be waiting for her when she gets home. I prefer to face the music when she has had a chance to take things in. Are you happy for me to do that? You do want to marry me, don't you?"

Ben wanted nothing more than for Sally to be his wife.

"More than anything," he replied. "But we should face the music together."

They showered together, washing each other's genitals, and gently kissing throughout. They dressed and Sally produced her letter for Ben's approval.

Dear Mum,

I hope you are sitting down to read this letter. I'll come straight to the point. I will not be moving to Nottingham. I thought it best that you know the facts before facing you. Ben and I are deeply in love and yes, we have been lovers for some time. I know that the sex side of life won't shock you – it was only recently that you asked if I should be using the pill. What will be a problem to you, is the age difference between us. Mum, the important thing is that I cannot imagine two people being more in love. I'm sorry that we have had to deceive you all of this time, but I know that you would have done everything possible to come between us. I will continue with

my career, but you must know that regardless, Ben and I will be together,
and when the time comes, we will be married.

Despite not coming to terms with my father's death, I know that in
your heart, you have always liked and admired Ben. You will now accuse
him of using family contact as a means of getting to me. The truth is the
complete opposite. At first, Ben resisted the offer of my *love, but eventually*
was forced to admit that he loves me too.

Mum, he's a wonderful man and makes me so happy. There are some
problems that can't always be easily shared with parents. He has always
been there for the problems best shared with a friend. I can't imagine a life
without my mother, but nor can I imagine a life without Ben. Please don't
make me choose. Please accept that the age difference is unimportant.

A move to Nottingham has brought things to a head. I can see that
it will be a good thing for the family, but it will have to be a move without
me. I will be staying in Spain with Ben. Our decisions have been made —
nothing will stop us being together.

It will be difficult for you, but please try to accept our love. Please try to
be happy for me. I love you, Mum... if you love me, please try to understand.
Sally

"Your letter says it all," said Ben, kissing her lips gently. "Sally, this is
probably the biggest step you will ever take... are you sure?"

She stopped him with a kiss to his lips.

"I have never been more sure of anything in my life," she whispered.

The following night, the lovers held hands in a café bar nearby,
before their confrontation with her mother. Sally was relieved and
excited that her love could finally be declared, but also nervous of the
response from the mother that she had always protected from hurt. It
was around 10.00 pm when Sally turned the latchkey.

"What is all this nonsense?" fumed Margaret, as they entered the
living room. "In two months' time, we will be returning to Nottingham
and *you*, young lady, will be on that plane."

Sally hadn't expected such a hostile reaction, but stayed composed.

"Mum, I am not a minor. You must not talk to me as though I were
a child. You cannot decide my future."

"And *you*, Ben," her mother interrupted. "I was wrong about you. I should never have trusted you. For God's sake, she's a child and you're twice her age."

Ben interrupted and spoke quietly.

"Yes, I am eighteen years older than Sally, but she's not a child. She's more mature than many thirty year olds. I have never hurt her and nor would I ever. I will only ever love her. I would walk out of her life now, if I thought it best for her."

"Mum," interjected Sally. "If I had never met Ben, I would perhaps in time have married a younger man. At thirty years of age, I could have ended up a divorced woman with a couple of kids. If I *then* met Ben, he would be forty-eight. The age difference would then be less of a problem for you."

"But you have no experience of life," her mother spat.

"That's not true," Sally protested.

"What's all the noise about?" asked Michael, as he entered the affray.

"Go for a walk, Michael," his mother instructed.

"No, Michael, sit down. You're not a child either," insisted Sally.

Despite Sally's best intentions, the confrontation was becoming more aggressive. Margaret took up the fight again.

"And what's this insult about Ben being there for you when you have a problem? Whatever the problem, you turn to your parents for support. If your father were alive, he would be ashamed of you," she hissed.

Ben watched the anger build in Sally's face at the very mention of her father and was nervous about the direction in which the confrontation could go. He nevertheless did nothing to defuse the situation.

"Mother," began Sally. "I was fourteen when I was raped by Cliff. You were there for me and I was grateful for that, even though it ended up destroying Jenny's marriage. But Ben was there for me when I was being stalked by a lecturer. He punished him without destroying other people's lives."

"That's the first I've heard of this," said her mother, more calmly. "Had your father been alive—"

Sally stopped her. A second mention of her father was too much and she completely lost it.

"My father?! My father?!" she screamed. "My father would be ashamed of me?! My father would have punished a pervert?! Don't you dare compare Ben with my father. You were there for me when I was raped by Cliff, but where were you, a year earlier, when your precious husband was fucking his thirteen-year-old daughter?! And where were you last year when his filthy brother came near to raping me in the back of his car?! I'll tell you where you were. You were licking the arse of his mother. It was Ben that was there to comfort me and to punish my disgusting uncle. Yes, Mother! My uncle's broken hand was no accident. Ben smashed the filthy fingers that had been in my knickers. I wish he had been around to punish my father!"

She had, at last, totally unburdened herself of the trauma that had been endured for five years, but immediately regretted the state of paralysed shock that her mother fell into. Tears flooded down Sally's cheeks. Margaret sat pole axed, motionless, and her face drawn and deathly white. Michael sat in shock, weeping silently.

"You've made it all up," Margaret murmured, though not believing that her daughter would lie about such things.

She wanted it to be a nightmare from which she would wake, but realised otherwise. The room fell silent during a long pause. Sally sobbed into Ben's chest and her fury melted into compassion for her mother.

"This wasn't supposed to happen, Mum… I'm sorry that you had to find out this way."

Despite the gravity of Sally's revelations, Margaret could find no words of solace for her daughter. She was consumed by the suffering of her own betrayal.

"Go… both of you, just go," said her mother quietly.

They left without another word, but Sally paused at the car door.

"Oh Ben," wept Sally. "I wanted Mum's blessing for us, but now I've completely messed things up."

Ben took her in his arms to comfort her.

"Don't worry… in the long term it's best that your mum faces the truth and you don't have to say the words. I know that you don't want to leave your mother in that state… Off you go, I'll call you tomorrow."

Sally wanted to drive away with her man, but was thankful that Ben understood that her place that night was with her mother and brother.

Sally entered the apartment to find her family sitting as she had left them. Her mother sat motionless though trembling. Michael sat in disbelief, crying softly, with head bowed. She placed a hand on her brother's shoulder.

"Michael, I was wrong to let you hear these things… I'm sorry."

Her mother emerged briefly from her zombie-like trance.

"You must have led your father on," she quivered.

Sally couldn't believe her mother's words.

"Mother! How could you say such an evil thing!"

"For Christ's sake, Mum!" shouted Michael. "She's been through enough!"

Sally's tears flooded, she howled in distress, and rushed to her bedroom in disbelief. Ben stood in the car park and heard Sally's anguish from below, but thought better of returning to the family. He drove home but didn't sleep.

Michael went to his sister's bedroom later that night.

"I'm gutted for you, Sal… I'm sorry, I had no idea."

They wept and cuddled each other for comfort.

*

The next morning, an emotionally drained Sally looked in on her brother. He sat on his bed, with head in hands, deeply disturbed by all that had happened the previous night. They talked for a while and Sally reassured him before going to her mother.

"Don't worry, Michael, I'll sort everything out," she comforted.

Margaret sat rigidly, not having moved from her position eight hours earlier. She was haggard, looked ten years older, and was in a world of disbelief and self-pity. The emotionally battered woman hadn't grasped the gravity of the criminal betrayal that her daughter had suffered.

"You must get some rest, Mum," urged Sally. "I'll go to the pharmacy and get something to help you sleep."

Sally was troubled and continued.

"Mum, I know that you are hurting badly, but there's something I must say to you… What happened with my uncle is history. He's been punished, so forget it. Any phone calls to the Spanish family could finish aunt Rocio's marriage. She doesn't deserve that and I don't want to be part of that happening. More importantly, it could result in a serious backlash for Ben. I'm sorry that I have to say this, but if you cause problems for Ben, I will walk out of your life and never make contact with you again."

There was barely a response. Sally wondered if her mother was on the verge of nervous collapse.

After a visit to the pharmacy, it was late morning when Sally picked up the call.

"I'm outside in the car," said Ben.

"Give me ten minutes," replied Sally. "I'm just settling Mum into bed."

Michael willingly offered to keep an eye on their mother whilst they met.

"I can't stay for long, Ben," Sally apologised. "Mum is in a terrible state – I'm afraid to leave her. I can't call the doctor, what would I tell him? – That she's close to suicidal because I've told her that her husband was a child-abuser?"

"Has she spoken any words of sympathy for what *you've* been through?" asked Ben.

"No, but it's early days – she's in a trance," sighed Sally. "Mum said that children should turn to their parents in times of crisis. I'm hoping that when she can forgive me, she will ring Grandma and pour her heart out. Oh Ben, I've messed things up. This is the day when we should be living together and celebrating… instead, I've made everyone miserable."

"Don't blame yourself," urged Ben. "Longer term, it's best that everything is out in the open."

"But I *am* to blame," wept Sally. "I should have left her in mourning for her husband. She was happy in that state. Now I've shattered her memories!"

"Then I *too* am to blame," insisted Ben, "because you came to my defence. Sally, please don't worry. It will all work out in the end."

"It wasn't supposed to be like this," sobbed Sally. "We should be together today, feeding the cats."

Ben embraced her throughout several minutes of crying.

"Forgive me, Ben – I have to stay with Mum until she can cope… until she can come to terms with the truth. I can't walk away and leave the responsibility with Michael."

"I understand," assured Ben.

*

His understanding nature was stretched as the weeks dragged on. There was little improvement in Margaret's state of physical or emotional health. Her appetite diminished, she suffered huge weight loss, she was unable to work, and would spend hours staring blankly into space. As her condition worsened the doctor *was* summoned and antidepressant medication was prescribed without disclosing the full causal details. Her self-imposed immobility put extra and unfair household pressures on Sally, though Michael stepped up to the plate and became a considerate assistant to his sister. Overnight, Sally became a carer – on continual duty, without which her mother could not even be trusted to use her medication. Ben kept abreast of the family's financial situation and subsidised their existence, where he felt he could do so without Margaret's knowledge. He took on the responsibility of twice-weekly supermarket shopping. Food was unloaded in the foyer of the apartment block, avoiding any contact with Margaret, for fear of inflaming an already delicate situation. The family "walked on eggshells", protective of Margaret´s emotional frailty; they lived on a day-by-day basis, in an atmosphere of depression, and barely communicating. The Crew were being robbed of their hard-earned break from study. In past months Ben had been the source of so much fun and humour for the family, but now the apartment was joyless. On occasions, Michael stayed with his mother, giving Sally and Ben the opportunity to meet. As time went on, their lovemaking seemed more clinical. The love was there, but Sally's intense commitment appeared to wane. Sally spoke less of her love for Ben and more of her concern for mother and brother.

When queried by Ben, she gave assurances that her apparent detachment was down only to family loyalty. Ben decided that he had no right to question loyalty. No reassurances could prevent the evening attacks of panic that Ben began to suffer – that unbearable feeling of fear, without being sure of quite *what* to fear. He feared for their future happiness, without defined grounds for his distress.

The week of the family's departure approached and Sally became more and more distanced, submersed in an ocean of stress and sadness. Ben couldn't summon the courage to ask if Sally wanted to end their commitment. He was terrified of hearing the wrong answer. He off-loaded that responsibility onto Sally, praying that he was imagining the worst.

During the evening before the family departure, they lay together in Ben's bed. Sally spoke of her sadness.

"I'm sorry, my darling, that everything became so complicated. I must travel with Mum, but I'll get Grandma to sort out my mother and everything will be O.K. Let's not talk now... let's make love."

The gentle expression of closeness enjoyed during their sexual union left neither in doubt about the depth of their love. Ben felt totally confident that they would eventually be as one. Sally wept at the thought of their parting. Ben endured the same sadness, but was Sally more than sad? She seemed to be suffering emotional turmoil.

Ben had never doubted that Sally loved him, but felt the onset of a panic attack as she waved briefly and disappeared into the apartment block. Her mother ignored her daughter's unhappiness, but Michael embraced her and spoke words that she wished were possible.

"You should be staying here in Spain... with Ben."

Chapter 35

Margaret refused point-blank to have Ben be part of their departure and the family would travel by taxi to the airport. Even if unable to speak, Ben couldn't fight off the overwhelming desire to see Sally before she left. She perhaps expected it and, as the taxi pulled up, she spotted him across the road from the Departures building. Margaret glared, as her children ran to say a final farewell. Michael embraced him with a warm hug.

"Promise that we won't lose touch," urged Michael.

"A solemn promise," replied Ben.

Michael turned and spoke to his sister.

"Why don't you stay, Sally? You're going to cry yourself to death in Nottingham."

"I must get Mum sorted out," she replied.

Michael shrugged and left the couple in privacy.

"I was going to post it from the U.K.," said Sally, handing Ben a small parcel. "Promise that you won't open it before you get home."

"Another present?" smiled Ben.

"Oh Ben, I *do* love you... I'm sorry for all the mess," Sally murmured.

Her lip trembled and tears welled in her eyes. She kissed his cheek and their lips met briefly. She could control her distress no longer. The tears flooded, she turned, and ran, disappearing into the airport building. Ben wanted to run after her and beg her to stay, but held back, holding on to her final words. "I *do* love you."

He drove off, accepting that he had no option but to ride out Sally's loyalty to family. It was a part of Sally that he admired greatly, but in reality, he wanted to shake sense into a self-indulgent Margaret. His greatest discomfort came from the absence of a reunion timescale.

At home, Ben succumbed to the insistent demands of hungry cats before settling to open the gift from Sally. His heart sank and his gut knotted, as his disbelieving eyes looked at the contents of the box – a lock of Sally's hair and her engagement ring sat on a folded letter. His hands trembled uncontrollably as he unfolded the paper. In an instant he was consumed with dread.

My darling Ben,

This is the most difficult letter I will ever write.

Something terrible has happened. At the time, I lost control and perhaps even thought it best that my mother should know about the bad things that had happened in my life. I was angry at her reaction to our love, but it was foolish and selfish of me to destroy her and Michael's image of husband and father.

I should have kept going that night when Mum told us to leave. Had I done that, I would not be writing this letter. I should never have returned to the apartment—

Mother was upset, Michael was upset, I was upset.

She didn't mean to hurt me, but some terrible things were said. Things that made me feel utterly worthless – perhaps I am.

Michael came to my bedroom that night; we wept together and cuddled in bed for comfort. We cried and escaped into sleep.

I considered not telling you the whole story, but I owe you so much. I certainly owe you the truth, even though it will hurt.

During the night Michael had a sexual dream. The next morning I had semen around Tinkerbell and my bottom. I found him sitting on his bed with head in hands. He was so upset. He thought not, but couldn't guarantee that he hadn't been inside me. I was exhausted that night and remember nothing of it, but perhaps in my sleep I thought it was you. Had you and I kept going that night, it would have been.

Incest seems to haunt me, but please don't think badly of Michael. He is young and his body is racing with hormones – it was an accident. Unlike others, he came to comfort me, not to abuse me.

Of course, to be absolutely safe, I went to a helpful pharmacist for the morning-after pill. Had that been the end of the problem, I would probably have saved you from the hurt of knowing the facts. Now I feel that I have no choice.

Ben, forgive me for hurting you, but you must know the worst. I am one of the unlucky few. The pill didn't do its job and after two missed periods, I find I am now pregnant. I thought of secretly having the pregnancy terminated and saying nothing to you, but decided that I couldn't do that. After all that you have done for me, I cannot bring myself to sneak around deceiving you.

It's horrible to destroy a life – but it must be done and I will have the pregnancy terminated in the U.K. Michael doesn't know that I am pregnant and it must be kept that way.

I have hurt you and my family so badly. I look back now and see that my love for you turned me into a selfish person – I must now spend time trying to undo the harm that I have caused my mother and my brother.

It has been even more selfish of me to involve you in all of my problems. If only I could undo the harm I have caused for you. Forgive me.

Even though nothing was deliberate or sinister, I feel so ashamed of myself and, now, so ashamed of my body.

No matter what, you have always been there for me, but this is one problem that I cannot ask you to share. With feeling so much guilt, you now know why my love for you has been strained in recent weeks.

I feel so guilty and worthless – please forgive that I couldn't confess these things face to face. Ben, you always made me feel so special, but I seem to be a magnet that attracts unhappiness. I am so lucky that I have loved and been loved so deeply, but I want you to move on – you deserve better. I dreamt of being your wife and it breaks my heart to return such a beautiful engagement ring – but it's for the best.

You are such a kind person and my heart bleeds for the hurt you must feel reading this letter. I know that you will want to contact me, but you shouldn't. We must both move on. We must all move on.

I once promised that I would never break your heart and now I've done exactly that. I'm so sorry – you can probably never forgive me for that and I pray that your heart will mend.

Ben, I'm not really a bad person —think of me sometimes with kindness.

Ever yours,
Sally

Ben's tears fell onto the paper as he read.

"Oh Sally," he wept. "Surely you know that I would never desert you... whatever the problem."

He read the letter again and was thrown into a state of panic. The family would now be through check-in and security control. There was little he could do until later that day.

It was vital that he and Sally should speak, but in the meantime he must check on availability of flights. He booked car hire and a flight arriving in Nottingham late afternoon of the following day. He had no knowledge of the grandparents' address, but he did have the telephone number. He booked two nights at a city centre hotel. This was no time to be searching for inexpensive motels.

Sat at his computer, his spinning mind wandered and he browsed the internet to research on the morning-after pill. He found it to be true that the pill fails to work in only a very small percentage of cases. There was one other scenario, he read, in which failure was inevitable.

"Surely not... could it be?" he murmured to himself.

He must know before going to Nottingham. Ben reached urgently for his business pages directory and made the most urgent call of his life. He packed a small suitcase in readiness and arranged for his cat-minder. Telephone calls to the grandparents' home were frustratingly engaged throughout the evening. It became late and Ben decided that it would be best left until the following day.

Calls to both Sally's and Michael's mobiles came back with the same message – "Service Terminated".

Chapter 36

Ben almost fell as he rushed through the heavy glass doors of the clinic. He registered with reception and collected the clear plastic bottle labelled with his name.

He looked at his watch and urged, "It's *so* important. I must have the result within the hour!"

The receptionist was taken aback by the urgency since his arrival and made a call to a doctor after Ben had been ushered to a masturbation suite.

His bloodstream raced with adrenaline; sex was the last thing on his mind and his penis refused to rise to the occasion. Strategically provided soft porn magazines did nothing to assist.

Ben calmed himself. He sat in a chair, closed his eyes, and pictured Sally, her legs straddled, encouraging penetration. His thoughts had the desired effect. His hand worked furiously and as fluid squirted from his penis he struggled to direct his large plum of a helmet to the rather narrow mouth of the bottle.

He wiped some of his juice from the side of the bottle and was hopeful that the quantity, stuck like glue to the inside, would be sufficient.

"I didn't get all of it in the container," Ben apologised to the receptionist. As he approached the desk, she had glanced at the swelling in his pants.

"That looks fine," she replied with a smile.

Ben dismissed any thought of innuendo. He was directed into the office of a female doctor.

"The results are normally through in five to seven days," she began.

Ben interrupted with urgency, relating a tale of unnecessary termination of pregnancy, unless he could fly to the U.K. later that day, with confirmation of his fertility.

"I don't care what it takes," pleaded Ben. "Taxis, helicopters, police escort, bribery."

He had rattled off the drama at such a pace that it left the woman slightly confused, but she accepted the immediacy of the situation and called the receptionist to her office, bearing his sample of testicular fluid. Using pipette, a small amount of semen was deposited onto a glass slide and placed beneath the lens of a nearby microscope. The doctor took a brief look down the eyepiece.

"Call a taxi," the receptionist was instructed.

The doctor returned to her desk and made a call.

Ben had difficulty in following the Spanish telephone conversation that followed, but was relieved when told that, for a fee, the sample would be assessed on immediate arrival at the laboratory.

"Thank you so much," sighed Ben. "In the meantime, how are things looking down *your* microscope?"

"I'm afraid I can't discuss that with you. My opinion must be verified by official confirmation – one way or the other."

She continued.

"I was a little confused with your story. Do you want to be fertile or infertile?"

"Fertile!" exclaimed Ben.

He explained that he had undergone vasectomy reversal operations some years before; surgery that had been only temporarily successful. He avoided going into fine detail, but needed to urgently know if he was "firing live bullets".

Ben listened intently as the doctor confirmed that, on occasions, the repaired tubes re-open to allow passage of sperm. He pressed her to give an unofficial appraisal of his fertility, but her face gave nothing away as Ben was asked to wait in the reception area. He paid the fees for the service and paced anxiously.

An hour passed and Ben waited outside, willing taxis to turn into the drive. Another half-hour passed, but still nothing. He returned to reception.

"Couldn't you ring them?" he urged.

She smiled and complied.

"The taxi is on its way, it will be about half an hour," she comforted.

"Couldn't they give you the result over the phone?" Ben urged again.

"I'm sorry, sir – it doesn't happen that way."

Ben paced throughout an anxious half-hour before following the taxi driver to the reception desk.

"Be patient," smiled the receptionist.

Ben gave the driver a handsome tip and fidgeted nervously. A few minutes passed before he was called to the doctor's office.

She smiled and spoke in broken English.

"I have good news for you. Eighty per cent normal sperm count and the little rascals are swimming around like… in English, I think you call them excited tadpoles."

My God, he thought. *I could have made Sally pregnant any number of times.*

She handed the typed report to an astonished and relieved Ben.

"I have a plane to catch," gasped Ben.

He got to his feet, took the doctor's face in his hands, and kissed her cheeks fiercely.

"Thank you, thank you, thank you," he said quietly and rushed from her office.

The receptionist's face received the same attention from a beaming Ben. He rushed to his car, leaving them both wide-eyed and speechless.

Road works, heavy traffic, and the parking up of his car conspired to make him late for check-in at the airport. He'd had plenty of experience of un-cooperative airline staff. He prayed that today would be the exception. Ben panted for breath as he arrived at the desk.

"Sorry, sir, check-in has closed," came the rather self-satisfied voice.

Ben spotted that she wore a wedding ring.

Unless this woman is completely heartless, he thought, *I will be on that aeroplane.*

"Please, you must help me. Do you have children?" he urged.

"Yes. Why do you ask?" she responded curtly.

Ben produced the laboratory report from his pocket and continued.

"It's a long story and there's no time to explain, but please believe me. Unless I can be on that plane, there's the possibility that a pregnancy could be tragically and needlessly terminated."

She looked briefly at the report and, without any understanding of the drama, picked up the phone, and made two calls. Ben sighed relief as she attached a label to his suitcase.

"It might be useful if you could suddenly develop a limp." She winked, as the immobility vehicle arrived.

"Thank you," he mouthed, as he clambered aboard.

"You're welcome," she said with a warm smile.

Not all airline staff are monsters, he thought.

Chapter 37

Grandma plumped up Granddad's pillows and settled him down for more rest. Now home from hospital, he was in good spirits, but very tired and in need of tender love and affection. Both would be in abundant supply now that the whole family was under the same roof. The arrival of his daughter and grandchildren was a huge joy to him.

Michael was busying himself, organising his personal possessions into his new bedroom. Sally had gone off to attend to urgent matters. Margaret had spent the afternoon chatting with her mother and father, but had volunteered to do some last-minute grocery shopping. The grandmother sat in her sitting room, pondering on the family reunion. It had been warm, but not the excited occasion that she had expected and hoped for.

The long faces of her grandchildren could be explained as short-term distress, having parted from their Spanish friends. But things were different with Margaret. Her daughter had lost weight, looked unwell, and seemed nervously depressed. She sensed that all was not well.

The telephone rang in the hallway.

"Hello, it's Ben, is that Margaret's mother?"

"Yes, hello Ben, please call me Amelia. Margaret has told me all about you. She's not here at the moment, shall I get her to call you when she returns?" offered the grandmother.

"It's actually Sally I need to talk to."

"She's not here either, I believe she went for a walk," interrupted Amelia.

"Please ask Sally to contact me when she returns," urged Ben. "Amelia, it's very urgent. It's actually a matter of life or death."

She was unsettled, but chose not to press Ben on the urgency of his tone. She wrote the hotel name, telephone number, and room number on a pad.

"I'll give her your message, Ben."

A key turned in the lock of the front door as Amelia replaced the receiver. Sally's bowed head tried in vain to hide her tear-stained cheeks.

"Come on, precious... tell me all about it," whispered her grandma.

They sat side by side on the sofa and tears welled in Sally's eyes.

"Oh Grandma... I'm so unhappy. I want to die!"

The tears flooded and Sally howled as her head fell into her grandma's lap.

"Tell me in your own time, darling," she comforted. "Have a good cry."

It was several minutes before words came from Sally.

"Has Mum ever telephoned you from Spain and said anything about family problems?" she asked.

"Problems? No, nothing – I don't know what you mean. She told me about the good news of her lottery win, but nothing about problems. But I'm a wise old lady, nothing will shock me. You can tell all."

Her grandma's ability to withstand shock was about to be tested to the point of destruction. Sally hesitated to open up to her loving grandmother, but she needed the comfort of a bosom that her mother had failed to provide. Through bouts of weeping and sobbing, Sally related the tragic side of her life-story – from the moment her father first abused her... The continued abuse... Being raped by Cliff... How she and Michael had met Ben and enjoyed so much his youthful company... How their mother viewed affection towards Ben as an insult to their father's memory... How she and Ben had fallen in love and become lovers... Tragedy rearing its head again with the attempted rape by her uncle... How Ben had punished him... and a stalker... Her mother's terrible reaction when she and Ben told her of their love. Her mother's physical decline and state of mental depression now that she knew the worst... The terrible shock of it all for Michael... And for Sally, the most heartbreaking of all, her decision to return the beautiful engagement ring that she and Ben had chosen together.

Her grandma's body trembled as she stroked Sally's head, but she listened in silence. The loving grandmother wept as Sally poured out every emotion of sadness and hurt within her. In defence of Michael, she couldn't confess the details of her pregnancy.

Her grandma struggled her words through weeping.

"Oh my child... My precious child... So much hurt, for one so young."

Sally looked into her grandmother's face and pleaded absolution through her tear-filled eyes.

"Oh Grandma, I know that Ben is much older than I am, but it shouldn't have mattered. He is such a wonderful man, he is young at heart, but clever, and always there to comfort and protect me – just as my *father* should have been. When we were at the beach, he even saved two young children from drowning. He is so kind and so brave – he wants to look after me. We love each other so much. I was only *really* happy when we were together... and now I've spoilt the best thing I ever had."

Sally howled distress and grief into her grandmother's shoulder. They held each other close until tears no longer prevented words.

"Right, Sally," said her grandma firmly. "Wash your face and go pack an overnight bag. I will call a taxi."

Sally looked at her quizzically. Her grandma whispered as though divulging a state secret.

"I've had a telephone call... Ben is in Nottingham. He's waiting for you."

The loving elderly lady smiled and, when the penny dropped, Sally screeched ecstatic delight. She climbed the stairs two at a time and her bag was packed in minutes. Sally cuddled her grandma in the hallway as they waited for the taxi.

"What's going on ?" demanded Michael as he descended the stairway.

"Ben's come for me!" Sally beamed.

"Give him a high-five from me," Michael said smiling.

"What about Mum?" a concerned Sally asked her grandmother.

"Leave your mother to me," she was assured. "Michael, when your mum comes home, we will need some privacy."

"I understand." He smiled and kissed her cheek.

"Thank you, Grandma… you've made me so happy," whispered Sally.

Amelia pushed her to the doorway.

"Your taxi is here. I'm exhausted, now please, go and be happy somewhere else."

They laughed as Sally skipped down the drive. It was the first time her grandmother had heard laughter since the family's arrival.

The wise old lady wondered how she would handle the next part of her role.

*

"Margaret," shouted Amelia. "Leave the shopping in the hallway — we need to talk."

Noticing that her mother had been crying, Margaret joined her on the sofa.

"What's wrong? Where are the children?"

"Michael is in his bedroom and Sally is where she belongs… she is with Ben."

Amelia cut short the anger building in her daughter.

"Listen to me, Margaret!… We do our best as mothers, but we often make mistakes. You have failed Sally, just as I have failed you. Sally has told me everything."

"She had no right," fumed Margaret.

"She had every right!" her mother said sharply. "Since the tender age of thirteen, for five years, the child has protected you from the truth. Can you imagine what she has been through? At the expense of her own teenage years, she couldn't bring herself to destroy *your* deluded emotions. I have failed you in the same way. You probably felt shame and couldn't come to *me* for comfort when you learned what sort of a man you had married. I don't know where I failed, but I owe you an apology, just as you owe gratitude and apologies to Sally. She has had years of misery, but then something wonderful happened for her. She found a friend and protector in Ben, and they fell in love… deeply in

282

love. He hasn't judged *her* or her past… they simply adore each other."

"Ben is too old for her," Margaret interrupted.

"Margaret, wake up!" her mother continued. "It has nothing to do with age – it's about feelings. I know that you and I love each other, but we need to repair the bridge between us. I know that *you* love your daughter and it's urgent that even bigger bridges are repaired between you and Sally. You must learn to accept and to hate what your husband was, but please, my love, it's so important… more important than anything, you must, first, wake up to the sacrifices that your daughter made for you. She loves you so much… I understand now why you have all been so unhappy. I can't imagine the hurt that *you* must be suffering. But please, do nothing to interfere with *Sally's* happiness… She and Ben deserve it. My God, how they deserve it!"

Tears rolled down Margaret's cheeks and she sobbed.

"I adored Miguel… I thought he loved *me*. Was I to blame? At first, I refused to believe it. I just can't come to terms with what he did."

"You will, my love, you will… I will help you," her mother said quietly.

For the second time that evening, Amelia held a distraught, sobbing child in her arms.

Chapter 38

Her heart raced as Sally knocked nervously on the door of room 304. It opened and they fell into each other's arms. Ben gasped relief. Sally couldn't stop babbling apologies, explanations, and her love for Ben. He wiped the tears from her face and placed a finger on her lips.

They kissed passionately and then gently. They pressed their bodies so close, they could have become one.

"Come and sit down, precious, we need to talk," said Ben.

They sat side by side on the bed. Ben replaced the engagement ring on the finger of her left hand and Sally wept her inexhaustible supply of happiness tears.

"I love you so much, Ben," she said quietly. "But I've spoilt things, haven't I? Truly, it was an accident; don't hate Michael. I've arranged an interview at the clinic tomorrow. It must be done as quickly as possible."

Her womb still carried a child and her words gave Ben the relief he craved. In reality, a termination was never going to happen with such urgency, but Ben hadn't been prepared to take the slightest risk.

"Whenever you've had a problem, have I ever not been there for you?" asked Ben.

"Never," apologised Sally. "You've always been there."

"Listen to me closely," Ben began. "You must cancel tomorrow's interview. On *rare* occasions, the morning-after pill doesn't work... The pill *never* works if the woman is already pregnant."

Without any understanding of Ben's words, Sally watched as Ben reached for the laboratory report and placed it in her hand. It meant nothing to her. Ben explained his research and his frantic movements that morning and throughout the day.

"I'm fertile," he announced proudly.

Sally absorbed the information. There was a long pause before she spoke.

"Tell me that I'm not dreaming… tell me that the baby inside me is *your* baby."

"*Our* baby," said Ben nodding. "Yes my love... *Our* baby."

They embraced and rolled around the bed kissing and laughing.

"Oh Ben," Sally wept. "Is it possible to die of happiness?"

"I don't think so," laughed Ben. "But you could die of dehydration if you don't stop crying. Come on, let's celebrate and we must make plans."

Sally's face paled.

"Oh my God… I almost killed our baby."

Ben reassured her.

"You didn't. That's all that matters."

During his flight from Spain Ben had taken into account the timings and statistics. He had been forced to accept the slimmest of possibilities that he may not in fact be the father of the child within Sally's womb. They would need to have her pregnancy closely monitored. At some time in the near future he would need to discuss the issue with Sally; but this was no time to say anything that would shatter her euphoria. For now at least Ben was a part of happiness beyond belief; happiness that had been a long time coming.

Sally talked to herself and squealed little sounds of delight as they freshened up.

"A private table for two," Ben requested, as they entered the hotel restaurant.

They held hands across the table as they ate and planned their future. Ben stroked the stone of her engagement ring.

"Ben," Sally began. "I don't want a fancy, show-off wedding – just a simple civil ceremony, as quickly as possible. I like the sound of Sally Styles." She smiled.

"Sally, I replaced the ring on your *left* hand for several reasons. Firstly, we must never be parted again. Secondly, we are not continentals. Thirdly, but only if you agree," explained Ben. "I've given things a lot of thought. You must return to Spain with me, but I think that I should sell up and we should come back to live in the U.K. We will marry as soon as possible. With your grandma's help, your mother will accept things eventually and it would be a shame if our child, or *children*, miss out on the love of a grandmother and great-grandparents. You should transfer the money in your account to a university fund for Michael. Finally, I'm too young to retire – I should take the reins of my…" He paused. "Sorry, *our* business interests again."

"You really *have* been thinking." Sally smiled.

"The plan probably needs some fine-tuning, but what do you think?" Ben asked.

"Perfect," she beamed and kissed his hand.

"Let's eat up and get to the hotel internet," suggested Ben. "I must book your flight and while I do that, you ring Michael. Tell him that should he fancy a day out tomorrow, I've found a bowling alley."

Sally marvelled at how considerate her man could be.

"He will love that. He's very lonely and miserable at the moment."

The loving couple walked in the night-time air before going early to their room. Their minds had calmed and they now floated in a sea of contentment. It had been a day of trauma and intense emotion. They were totally drained. They lay slightly apart in their bed looking into each other's eyes.

"The words don't exist to tell you how much I love you," whispered Ben.

"If you can't tell me, then show me," Sally whispered back.

Ben knelt beside her and kissed her body from tip to toe. His erection grew quickly as his lips sucked at her nipples.

"Come inside me," she said quietly.

Sally parted her legs and guided Ben's penis past her labia into the cavity beyond. She thrust her hips upwards to achieve instant, full penetration.

They gasped as they fell over the edge, into the abyss.

"Pour love onto our baby," Sally murmured.

She sighed gently as her vagina clung to the sliding erection within her.

"Pour your love, Ben," she urged. "Pour your love."

The fertile fluid raced up from his testicles and settled in a pool, deep within the warmth of her body.

"Oh my darling Ben... my darling baby... *our* darling baby," she sighed.

Ben moved onto his side and Sally held herself close.

"I don't want to come, but stay inside me," she whispered.

Sally had no need of an orgasm that night. She needed only the intense delirium that love in its purest form can provide. Ben kissed her brow; they stayed fused as one and fell into a deep sleep.

*

As they slept, on the other side of the city, Amelia looked fondly across the double bed at her recuperating husband. She took his hand in hers and prayed that Sally and Ben would enjoy the same devotion that had blessed *her* marriage. She switched off her bedside light and lay in the darkness. Amelia smiled thoughts of the tender love that she and her husband had enjoyed over the years. She was certain that her granddaughter would enjoy the same tenderness that night.

*

It felt that they were a honeymoon couple as Sally and Ben enjoyed breakfast together. They had slept late, showered, donned fresh clothing, and now, feeding healthy appetites, felt ready to face anything that the world could throw at them. Not normally a morning person, Ben was a different animal. He was in love, revelled in every moment with Sally, and had everything to live for. Sally was the bright-eyed, gorgeous woman that Ben had first met in Spain. She was like a butterfly – flitting and floating with enthusiasm and joy.

Ben made a couple of calls from reception before they set off.

"Who did you ring?" Sally asked.

"Surprise for Michael," said Ben winking.

Ben had also arranged a second surprise.

*

Sally thought it best that, for now, Ben should wait in the car whilst Sally entered the lion's den. Her granddad was in his bed and the rest of the family were half-watching television in the sitting room. Sally approached the sofa and sat beside her mother. She took her mother's hand in hers. Her grandma muted the television.

"Mum, I now know exactly where my life is going. I'm so happy, please be happy for me. Ben and I are so in love. I'm sorry that we had to deceive you when we were in Spain, but you can understand why we had to be so secretive. We are flying back to Spain tomorrow, but we'll move back to live in the U.K. soon – to get married and to be near my family."

Despite her time with her mother, Margaret was still struggling to come to terms with everything. Her body trembled and she sat expressionless as Sally related their plans for the future. Sally said nothing of her pregnancy. Her grandma sat in silence and watched developments. Sally looked across for support. Amelia's slight hand gesture indicated "Be patient".

Her mother finally spoke.

"He's brought nothing but trouble into the family."

"What a shame you didn't marry someone like him," blurted Michael.

"Don't go there please, Michael," said his grandma, stopping him dead.

"Mum," pleaded Sally. "You're wrong. For Michael and me, he has brought nothing but fun. For you, he brought nothing but friendship and I'm the luckiest of all – for me he brought nothing but comfort, support, and above all he brought me his love."

Tears welled and sparkled in the blue-grey of Sally's beautiful eyes.

"Mum, please be happy for me," she pleaded.

"Look at you!" her mother spat. "A silly romantic girl swayed by an expensive diamond on your finger. Money isn't everything, you know."

"Oh Mother, don't you understand?" Sally wept. "I would want to be with Ben if he were penniless. I don't know what this ring cost. Knowing Ben's generosity, it probably is expensive, but I would be happy with a ring from a Christmas cracker."

Margaret sat unrelenting.

"Mum, you say that money isn't everything, but that depends on how you use it. Ben will be angry that I have broken my promise of secrecy, but you should know something... *There was no lottery win.* He managed to get you to accept help without it being a gift. He knew that there was financial pressure and he did it to help *you* and the family... He had it planned *before* we became lovers.¨

¨But I saw a photograph of the ticket,¨ protested her mother.

¨No, Mum... you saw a photograph of *a* ticket,¨ corrected Sally.

She explained how Ben had achieved the deception for a totally honourable reason. Her grandma and Michael shook their heads slowly in disbelief. Margaret bowed her head in quizzical thought. Sally had hoped for a more generous understanding from her mother. She pulled away and stood sobbing. Michael joined her and hugged comfort with his distressed sister. He too wept tears of emotion. The matriarchal grandma finally intervened.

¨Enough!¨ she demanded with authority.

The severity in her voice stunned everyone into silence.

¨Margaret, do you remember yesterday's daughter? – A miserable child, with the world on her shoulders. The same girl walked in here today, a *woman*, bursting with happiness. Happiness like that is priceless. Have you forgotten our talk yesterday? Sally has had to bear many crosses. I will not stand by and watch her carry yours as well. For God's sake, Margaret, at last, in her young troubled life, she has everything to live for. Her joy is missing only one thing. She loves both you and Ben with all her heart. Oh Margaret, after all that she has sacrificed for you. It's not much to ask... hold her tight and give her your blessing!¨

Sally looked pleadingly to her mother. Margaret realised the extent of her selfishness and they rushed to each other's arms. Amelia rose from her armchair and joined them in a communal embrace. The three women wept shamelessly as they hugged.

¨Oh shit,¨ murmured Michael, wiping tears from his cheeks.

*

Ben sat in the car, restless and concerned, during the lengthy proceedings inside Amelia's home.

The door opened and Michael walked down the drive, followed by his grandma. Ben jumped from the car and held out his hand to introduce himself. Amelia pushed it to one side and took him in her arms.

She held him close, reached up, and spoke quietly in his ear.

"Bless you… bless you both."

She leant back and placed a comforting hand on his cheek.

"Don't worry, everything's fine. We are going to have a girly afternoon. You boys go off and have fun."

"Thank you, Amelia," said Ben.

Sally rushed from the house and hugged Ben.

"Pull out your disco dress and silver shoes for later," he said.

"Where are we going?" asked Sally excitedly.

"Surprise!" said a smiling Ben.

"That's enough!" urged Michael. "Come on, Ben, bowling alley!"

"Oooh, better than that," teased Ben. "Go-carting!"

"Brilliant!" yelled the lad.

They exchanged a high-five, jumped in the car, and drove off. Amelia observed their friendship.

"Michael will miss him," she said to Sally.

"Only until we come home or until he has a steady girlfriend," her grandma was assured.

The women waved from the kerbside.

"You didn't tell me that Ben is also very handsome," remarked her grandma.

"He's very, *everything* good," replied Sally wistfully. "And Grandma… when we make love…"

Sally rolled her eyes. Her grandma offered advice with a wink and a smile.

"Always with love… but like there's no tomorrow."

They linked arms and giggled as they returned to the house.

Chapter 39

Ben craved the presence of his woman, but found himself boyishly enjoying the challenge of fending off Michael's determination to end the life of his brother-in-law to be.

"They're not fucking dodgem cars!" Ben yelled, as the lad made every effort to force him off the track.

His words couldn't be heard through a crash helmet and over the roar of two stroke engines. Michael would have ignored the pleas anyway. Being heavier than Michael, Ben's cart was slower, but that wasn't accepted as reasonable explanation for the lad winning every race. Ben dutifully conceded that the boy was a more talented and more ferocious driver. As more paying customers joined the track, it did in fact become apparent that Michael possessed a fearless talent with the machine. A talent that destroyed all opposition that came his way.

Despite his skill, he was cautioned between each session on the brutality of his driving and warned that he would be banned from the track. The next session, he would drive cautiously. The following session, his natural aggression would take over, followed by another caution. So it went on. After two hours, six sessions, and three cautions later, Ben spoke.

"Well done, Michael, you've proved your point; you're the best driver in the county. Let's get a coke."

*

Back at the house, the ladies sat together and talked affectionately. Margaret begged Sally's forgiveness for not being the mother that she

291

could confide in. Sally reassured her that it should be forgotten history and that her blessing made up for the past.

"Perhaps things are meant to be," she said. "Without my father and a move to Spain, I wouldn't have met Ben."

Sally continued her silence on the development within her womb. *One step at a time*, she thought. Her grandma lightened the mood.

"Why don't we go upstairs and have tea and biscuits with Granddad?"

Granddad was blissfully unaware of the dramas that had played out in the rooms below. His wife would put him in the picture when he was fully recovered. Sally held his hand and chatted enthusiastically about everything and nothing.

*

Between sucks through a straw, Michael revealed his new ambition to be a professional racing driver.

"First things first," mocked Ben. "You need a driving licence."

Ben wondered if the eventual declaration and the timing of Sally's pregnancy would be disturbing news for him. Would the boy one day question the issue of paternity? Ben decided that there should be closure and timed his words until they were walking to the car.

"Michael, my friend, you must tell no one… I am going to tell you a secret. Sally and I are going to be parents. Relax, Michael, your sister was already pregnant when you had your little accident. I know all about it and how it came to happen. Don't worry; I know you wouldn't hurt Sally. I completely understand and there are no hard feelings."

Michael's head was bowed in embarrassment and guilt.

Ben placed his hand on the boy's shoulder to confirm friendship with his final words on the issue.

"It's history… we need never talk about the matter again, but in future, stick to wanking, will you?!"

They laughed together and man-hugged warmly.

"You're a great guy, Ben. Thanks. You'll be a great father and I'll settle for a great brother-in-law… Wow, I'm going to be an uncle!"

"And my best man!" added Ben.

Tears welled in their eyes.

"Come on, let's go," laughed Ben. "I'm fed up with *you*. I need to be with your sister!"

Ben sounded the horn as he pulled up outside the house.

"Will you say hello to Ben?" Sally asked her mother.

"Not today, darling," she apologised. "I look an absolute mess and it's all been a bit too much for me. I'll speak with him tomorrow, when you come to say goodbye."

Michael helped Sally down the drive with a large suitcase that had been packed for her return to Spain.

"A great day, Ben – thanks, see you tomorrow," said Michael.

Ben took him to one side and handed him a sealed envelope.

"Driving lessons – we'll look at some wheels when you've passed your test. But it won't be a Ferrari!"

They man-hugged, but Michael was speechless. Sally looked on in adoration of her man's boundless generosity.

The couple drove off to their hotel.

"You too must have driving lessons when we come back to Nottingham."

"Not until after the birth of our baby," said Sally smiling.

During the journey, Ben explained how he had achieved closure with Michael.

"He's a relaxed boy now," he said with a wink.

"Thank you, Ben, you've thought of everything again. I woke up in a sweat last night. If you hadn't rushed from Spain I would have…"

He placed his hand on Sally's tummy.

"You didn't, that's all that matters. Michael is sworn to secrecy… When will you tell your mother?"

"Hmmm… I'm not sure yet. Where are we going tonight?" asked Sally, changing the subject.

"The opera!" announced Ben.

"Ben, I don't like opera," said Sally frowning.

"Sally, you only *think* you don't like opera. We'll leave during the interval if you are bored."

Ben himself was not an aficionado. His taste in music was broad and included some opera, especially the more popular operatic works by the likes of Puccini.

A visiting company were performing Mascagni's *Cavalleria Rusticana* and Ben had managed to book tickets at the hotel reception. He was confident that the "Easter Hymn" would bring tears to Sally's eyes.

The porter took Sally's suitcase to their room, whilst they enjoyed a light snack in the bistro bar. Time moved on and they found themselves rushing to prepare for their night out. Ben hadn't travelled equipped with black tie, but over the years, opera nights had become much less formal. He showered and dressed as smartly as his wardrobe would allow. In contrast, Sally appeared from the bathroom as a vision of unbelievable beauty. He wouldn't have believed the beauty had he not seen her in the same dress the night of the student disco. He remembered the dress slipping from her body that night. It would slip again later.

The air was full of chatter as they arrived in the opera house foyer. They lodged Sally's topcoat in the cloakroom, revealing the full beauty of her flawless skin. She clung to Ben's arm and seemed unaware of the dozens of male eyes that her presence demanded. Dozens of female eyes looked on in envy. Excitement built as they took their seats. Sally was caught up in the eager expectation.

She caught her breath at her first experience of a live orchestra striking up the overture. As tenors, sopranos, and chorus gave it their all, she became transfixed by the performance. The storyline was secondary to the music and live drama. She sat with one hand on her pregnant tummy. Soon into Act 1 the "Easter Hymn" began. Ben leant across and whispered in her ear; ¨The 'Easter Hymn'... our baby is due around Easter.¨

Her eyes widened, she smiled, and returned her full attention to the stage. Along with the whole auditorium, she instinctively rose to her feet to applaud in the dying moments of the crescendo – and yes, it did bring tears to her eyes. Ben enjoyed what he saw of the performance, but much of his time was spent surreptitiously watching the pleasure in Sally's face. He held the hand that wasn't fixed in a protective role on her belly.

"That was wonderful, Ben. I was wrong, I *do* like opera," enthused Sally, as they walked to a coffee bar. "And when the big fat lady and the chorus sang the 'Easter Hymn', I thought I would explode."

Ben cuddled her and laughed at her impromptu critique of Mascagni's composition skills.

"Can we do *lots* of different things when we come back to Britain?" she begged.

"We'll do everything you want – top artist concerts, all the London shows. We'll take your mum and grandparents – and of course, Disney World when the little one is older."

"Oh stop it. I'm going to cry!" Sally pleaded.

They paused and sat on a public bench during their walk back to the hotel. Ben looked to the crystal clear heavens above them and spoke. "Look at that sky, Sally. The trillions of stars and the millions of light years that separate us... And that´s just in the part of the universe that we can see... It´s strange that in the big equation we are all so unimportant."

Sally rested her head on Ben´s arm. "Except to each other," she said quietly.

"Except to each other," repeated Ben.

It was a tired and contented couple that entered room 304 that night. They flopped side by side on the bed, looking at the ceiling. A few minutes passed before Sally spoke.

"Darling, my lovely grandma offered some advice today."

Ben turned his head to look at her.

"Always with love… but like there's no tomorrow."

"What a wise lady your grandma is," said Ben with a smile.

He got to his feet and stripped naked before his eager partner. Sally watched his penis grow at just the very thought of being inside her.

Ben removed her shoes, took her by the hands, and pulled her to her feet. Their faces were close, but they didn't kiss. He released the bow tied at the nape of her neck. His hand moved to her back and fully unzipped her dress. Ben's trembling hands peeled the dress from her shoulders and it fell to the floor, revealing her perfect breasts. Sally stepped out of it and stood in tiny white panties. She took the growing erection in both hands and mimicked the action of her vagina caressing its length. In seconds, it expanded to full extension and girth.

"It's very big. It won't hurt our baby, will it?" she asked.

"No, precious, our baby is tucked away, safely out of reach." He smiled.

Sally knelt and kissed from helmet to base. Her delicate hands cupped his testicles. She stopped and spoke.

"Darling, I know some women do it, but do you mind if I don't put him in my mouth; you know who once forced—"

Poor Sally was still fighting demons. Ben pulled her to her feet and kissed her lips with such tenderness. He spoke gently.

"Why would I want to put something so ugly into a mouth so beautiful?" he questioned with a smile.

"Big Ben isn't ugly," she insisted. "It's just that—"

Ben silenced her continuance with a flurry of kisses over her mouth, her neck, and across her shoulders. He took her buttocks in his hands and pulled her close and upwards. His knees bent and he moved his open mouth from breast to breast. The tongue moved furiously over her firm rounded flesh. Sally moaned as nipples swelled and hardened to the size of small grapes. He suckled like a newborn child.

"Oh Ben, I'm so happy," she sighed.

He laid her on the bed and removed her knickers in a single swift motion.

He took each foot in turn and sucked her pedicured toes. With long strokes of his tongue, he licked between them. Sally murmured the enjoyment of a new sensation. Ben recalled the pleasure that "Zak" had provided years earlier. Sally uttered quiet noises of content, as Ben gazed longingly at the curvature of her buttocks meeting with the swelling of her mound. His kisses travelled the length of her slender legs. Her legs parted to receive the touch of his lips on her inner thighs. Her murmurs became louder as she anticipated the thrust of tongue inside vagina. It was a thrust that didn't happen. Ben's strong arms lifted and turned her onto all fours. Sally looked down past her belly to find his head beneath her loins. His tongue licked slowly at her swollen vulva. He took her by the hips and lifted her mound away from his face. A feverishly waggling tongue was made available.

With desire in his eyes, he invited her to take up the challenge.

"This is a busy buzzing bee. You must try to catch it in your body."

Ben teasingly moved his head from side to side, as Sally's hips urgently sought to trap and guide the source of pleasure to swollen flesh. She ensnared the "insect", it settled onto her clitoris, and Ben teased no more. Now contained, it seemed to struggle furiously to escape the confines of her vagina. There was no escape. Her parted swollen labia settled lightly around Ben's lips. Sally remained motionless, allowing the buzzing bee to do its work.

"Ben... this feels strange, but wonderful," murmured Sally. "It feels as though I'm going to come into fresh air."

Ben's tongue was too busy to reply. She was taken by surprise at the sudden surge of tingling. The tingling rapidly built to fire and she gasped and yelped through a climax. A different climax, not quite like anything she had enjoyed before. Sally gyrated her mound a little, to grasp at the dying moments of pleasure.

"Oh my love," she gasped.

Ben raised her hips again to look at the wondrous sight of labia, gorged with blood and drenched with saliva and love juice. He slipped from beneath and knelt behind her. His eyes took in the beauty of her curves. Her long hair had fallen from her shoulders to rest on the pillow, revealing a slender neck that demanded his kisses. Her back was arched downwards before sweeping up to silky hard buttocks. Her labia remained slightly open at the crotch of parted legs. His erection was close to vertical. He was desperate to be inside her, but resisted.

"Rest for a little while," he said quietly.

Whilst libidos settled, for several minutes he kissed her neck, her back, and buttocks. His thumbs stretched wide her entrance. He looked at the soft, pink fleshy tube, leading to the womb that nurtured their developing child.

His helmet slid into the wet warmth beyond her vaginal lips. The labia imploded a little with his first thrust, only to flower again on slight withdrawal. The tight-fitting tube seemed to suck him inwards. Her body wanted to consume the meal so willingly offered.

Ben became light-headed as a single slide put his helmet into full penetration. The love of his life gasped and then groaned dizziness, as her cavity accepted the enormity of the muscle within her.

Ben tried to imagine how it must feel for her, as his fingers circled the wet flesh that clung tightly around his base. Her moans told him of the pleasure she was enjoying. He took her suspended breasts into his hands and massaged them gently. His open palms rubbed circular strokes of tenderness onto the erect nipples, before taking them between fingers and thumbs.

"My love... there is no tomorrow," Sally murmured.

He began a long process of developing another fire in her clitoris.

Sally reached to roll his testicles in her hand. Slow movement from helmet to base had Ben's desire at begging point. The animal inside Sally demanded instant ejaculation, but Ben allowed his mind to wander, avoiding anything other than a simultaneous climax. Her vagina gorged on the hard flesh sliding along its length.

Ben laid her flat on her belly. Sally closed her legs and grabbed the erection in a vice-like grip. Ben moved his body a little forward and thrust hard downwards, sliding on lubricated labia, into her cavity of desire. The pressure on her clitoris was intense. Her orgasm built quickly, her buttocks moved up and down, in rhythm with his thrusting. Flesh slapped against flesh. They moaned animal satisfaction.

"I'm coming, Ben," she gasped.

Ben was ready. Without a thought of privacy, Sally screamed through her fiery climax. Ben grunted loudly like a bull in pain, as his virile semen squirted into the far depths of her vagina. Her sheath provided orgasmic contractions that sucked the fluids from his erection.

They gasped for breath as they rested, to settle mind and body.

"Ooh... fuck," Sally panted.

"It certainly was!" gasped Ben.

They rolled to their sides and cuddled. They lay fused for some time, satiated and deliriously content.

"Will you wash me, darling?" asked Sally.

Ben took her to the bidet and washed her intimately, just as he had done after their very first sexual union.

He washed himself and the happy couple curled together in bed, whispered their love, and slept.

Chapter 40

Ben was first in the shower the following morning.

"I'm not coming in there with you, I don't trust you!" Sally laughed.

"You over-estimate my stamina," Ben said, laughing back. "But if you're adamant, I'll get dressed, pay up at reception, and find us a good table for breakfast."

At the desk, a couple in their sixties were settling their bill.

"Good morning, we are in room 302," the lady said with a knowing smile.

"Sorry," said Ben smiling. "Did we keep you awake?"

"Not at all," she said with a grin. "Do you and your wife give lessons?"

Her husband interrupted.

"If you looked like *his* wife, I wouldn't need lessons!"

Ben didn't perceive the quip as smutty and smiled graciously.

The lady gave her husband a playful punch. Ben whispered in her ear as they left.

"Always with love… but like there's no tomorrow."

*

Sally kissed Ben as she joined him at the breakfast table.

"Last night was fabulous," beamed Sally.

"Oh, you mean the opera," teased Ben.

"That too," said Sally smiling. "So much love. And when we're married, will we still have the quick naughty ones?"

"Of course," he assured her. "In fact, I've been planning rehearsals.

Later today, the first one will be thirty-five thousand feet above the Bay of Biscay. Tomorrow, we'll stage a performance in the bedroom department of Ikea. We'll find some satin sheets."

"You're crazy," she laughed. "But I like the sound of Bay of Biscay."

They laughed their way through breakfast, absorbed in their love for each other. Ben was relieved that Margaret now had an open and loving relationship with her daughter. He didn't know if her generosity would extend to him.

*

Amelia lifted the atmosphere as she warmly invited Ben into her home. Margaret stood as he entered the sitting room. He walked straight to her and took her hands in his.

"I would never knowingly hurt any of your family," he said quietly.

There was a pause whilst she looked into his eyes.

"I know, Ben," she said. "Take care of my daughter."

"With my life," said Ben.

She placed her head on his chest and hugged him gently.

Sally joined them and tears welled as she embraced her mother.

An hour was spent with Sally enthusing over her very first night at the opera. Her grandma talked her through other operas that she knew her granddaughter would enjoy. Michael made it clear that, in return, he would expect Ben to take him to a rock concert. The time came for au revoirs.

They were stood in the hallway when her grandma produced a wedding ring from her pocket and placed it in Sally's hand.

"Your granddad and I have had many years of happiness."

She turned to Ben, removed her own wedding ring, and pressed it into his palm.

"Have them melted together for two new rings. Continue the same devotion."

"No, Grandma, we couldn't," protested Sally.

Ben joined Sally with adamant refusals.

"It would make an old lady very happy," her grandma insisted. "And when my time comes, precious, I want you to have my eternity ring. It will be perfect with your engagement ring."

Her grandma took Sally's hand and stroked her thumb across the diamond of her solitaire.

Endless tearful hugs and kisses followed, before the couple were allowed to walk down the drive to the car. Sally fastened her harness and Ben fired up the engine. Sally stopped him.

"Hold on, Ben – in for a penny, in for a pound."

She ran back up the driveway. She hugged and kissed her mother.

"Ooh Mum, I almost forgot to tell you. There's another reason why I'm so happy… you're going to be a grandmother!"

Ben smiled as he watched from the car.

Amelia hugged and kissed Sally, Sally hugged and kissed Michael, and Margaret stood with brow in hand, slowly shaking her head from side to side. A laughing Sally waved an imaginary football rattle as she got back into the car.

Amelia placed an arm around her daughter's shoulder and led her inside.

"Come on, Margaret," she chuckled. "I think you need a stiff drink!"

Sally rested her head on Ben's shoulder as they drove to the airport. They were safe in the knowledge that the future family reunion would be a happy occasion. In the wider world and until Sally was older, they would face prejudice, bigotry, and perhaps even hostile disapproval. They cared not. They finally had each other.